MICHAEL
RIDPATH
THE WANDERER

CORVUS

First published in 2018 by Corvus, an imprint of Atlantic Books Ltd.
This edition published in 2019.

Map credit © 2018, Jeff Edwards

9 8 7 6 5 4 3 2 1

A CIP catalogue record for this book is available from the British Library.

Paperback ISBN: 978 1 78239 875 2
E-book ISBN: 978 1 78239 874 5

Corvus
An imprint of Atlantic Books Ltd
Ormond House
26-27 Boswell Street London
WC1N 3JZ

www.corvus-books.co.uk

Printed and bound by CPI Group (UK) Ltd, Croydon CR0 4YY

for Barbara

The Icelanders are the most intelligent race on earth, because they discovered America and never told anyone.

Oscar Wilde

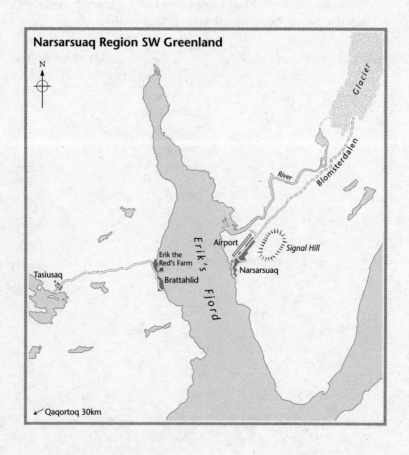

Narsarsuaq Region SW Greenland

N

Glacier

River

Blomsterdalen

Erik's Fjord

Airport

Signal Hill

Erik the
Red's Farm
×
Brattahlid

Narsarsuaq

Tasiusaq

Qaqortoq 30km

PROLOGUE

Italy, 1979

'SO, JOHN. DO you still think the Vinland Map is for real?'

Emilio's dark blue eyes glinted with amusement as he laid the trap for Nancy's husband to lumber into. They were only on their third bottle of wine, dinner was still bubbling in the kitchen, and the sun had not yet set behind the village perched on its hill just above the house. It was still a little early in the evening for Emilio to bait John.

The three of them had polished off two bottles at lunch, and Nancy had felt an incipient hangover when they had sat down on Emilio's terrace, but his fine red wine, the produce of the tiny vineyard lazing beneath them, had soon sorted that out. John and she never drank that much back home. She was rather enjoying it.

'I'm darned sure it's real, Emilio,' said John. 'You Italians have got to face the facts: the Norsemen discovered America, not Columbus. All the evidence points that way. The Viking settlement at L'Anse aux Meadows in Newfoundland. The sagas. You know all that; you've just got to accept it.'

'Vinland' was the name the Norse explorers had given to the land they found to the south-west of Greenland, *vínber* being the Norse word for the grapes they had found there. The Vinland Map had turned up in Geneva in 1957, and had been bought by an American book dealer called Larry, an old friend of John's. It showed the island of Greenland, and next to it, a similar sized island labelled Vinland. What had shocked the world, especially

1

the historians of Columbus's discovery of America, was that the map was supposed to have been drawn by an Italian cartographer in 1440, a full fifty years before Columbus's journey across the Atlantic.

The map had been bought by the millionaire Paul Mellon, who had donated it to the library at Yale. Since then the argument had raged, both in the academic world and among the fraternity of rare-book dealers, such as Emilio, and collectors, such as John.

'I know a few Vikings got lost a thousand years ago and washed up in Canada,' said Emilio. 'I'm not prejudiced against the map. I just know a fake when I see it.'

'But you haven't seen it!' said John. 'I have, and I can tell you it's genuine. And we both know Larry. He's a stand-up guy, I know he believes it's real.' John was leaning forward, his voice rising an octave, his hands chopping the air with frustration. But Nancy knew he was enjoying himself; he liked a good argument with Emilio.

Emilio sat back, his broad mouth twitching up in a half-smile. Everything about Emilio was broad: his brow, his cheekbones, his chin, his chest. He was short, compact, powerful. Nothing like Nancy's tall, stooped husband with his narrow shoulders and domed skull. John was beginning to act a little old, a little weak. Despite his greying hair, Emilio looked younger than his forty-nine years.

Nancy sipped her wine. She loved her husband very much; she always would.

But she was desperately attracted to Emilio.

She had known him for twenty years, ever since she had met him on the first of at least a dozen trips to Europe with John to seek out new items for John's collection of sixteenth- and seventeenth-century books. Emilio had taken them both out to dinner in Geneva, and a business relationship had soon turned into genuine friendship. During the following two decades Emilio's wife, never much present, had disappeared from the scene. She had retreated to Turin, where her parents lived, leaving Emilio to his books, his fabulous manor house in the hills of Tuscany,

2

and his women. A son and a daughter shuttled between the two of them during university vacations.

Visiting Emilio had become the high point of the European trip for Nancy.

And also for John. John liked Emilio too.

'What about the ink?' said Emilio. 'I don't think the map is a fake because I'm Italian. I think it's a fake because it was drawn with modern ink!'

John shook his head, gulping his wine in frustration. It was true: science appeared to be on Emilio's side. Yale had sent the map for chemical analysis and the results had suggested that although the vellum was five hundred years old, the ink must have been manufactured after 1920 because it contained traces of anatase, a titanium compound only added to ink after that date. It was a conclusion John was just not prepared to accept.

'OK, there is anatase in the ink, but I was talking to a guy from the Bibliothèque nationale who said that anatase occurs naturally in some parts of Europe and there are dozens of authentic manuscripts from the fifteenth century with anatase in the ink. Larry says Yale is going to get the map re-examined by another lab.'

Nancy's attention drifted from the detailed discussion of the chemistry of inks, modern and medieval. She sat back, sipped her wine, and let the soft evening sun caress her face. The poplars above them rustled, and a breath of wind propelled a distinctive piquant scent to her nostrils. Capers. From the purple-flowering caper bushes growing out of Emilio's garden wall.

She watched the dark shadow thrown by the mountains ten miles away creep towards the house over the valley of speckled green in front of them. The lane, sweeping down from the house past the vineyard and a small field of sunflowers to the unseen stream at the valley's bottom, made a pleasing arc through the countryside. The composition was perfect, as though the land-scape had been put together by an artist, rather than random geological mutations moulded by a hundred generations of land-owners and peasants. Emilio's ancestors had been drinking their wine and admiring this view for centuries, probably as far back as the time when the Vinland Map was drawn.

Supposedly drawn.

'So what do you think, Nancy?' said Emilio. 'You're the one who really knows the Vikings.'

She was. Nancy Fishburn was a professor of history at a small college in Pennsylvania, where she specialized in the Viking age. She had read many times the two Vinland sagas – *The Saga of the Greenlanders* and *The Saga of Erik the Red* – that described the exploration of North America, and she had taught her students about the discovery of the Viking settlement at L'Anse aux Meadows in 1960. She had just finished writing a book on Gudrid the Wanderer, Erik the Red's daughter-in-law, an extraordinary woman who had been born in Iceland, got married in Greenland, had a son in Vinland and then returned to Iceland, before going on a pilgrimage to Rome.

'Scientists can change their minds. But in fifteenth-century Iceland, the discovery of Vinland was well known. And there were plenty of Europeans who fished and traded with the Icelanders then, especially the English; they would have brought that knowledge back to the mainland. A curious Italian cartographer could easily have heard of it.'

'You think so?' said Emilio, raising his eyebrows.

'Of course,' said Nancy. 'You know Columbus visited Iceland in 1477 on an English merchant ship? He mentioned it in a later letter to Ferdinand and Isabella.' The vast trove of old books about Columbus was one of Emilio's specialities. 'He would have heard about America then for sure. So why couldn't another Italian nearly forty years earlier?'

'Which would mean Columbus really didn't discover America,' said John with a note of triumph. 'He knew about it already!'

'Absurd!' said Emilio. 'You are not making any sense. And your glass is empty.'

They drank another two bottles of wine, gently arguing into the night.

Then they went to bed.

Together.

Nancy paced up and down in the small kitchen and checked the clock above the stove yet again. Ten of five. She had calculated that JoÝ should be back from the island's little airport at a quarter of.

She smiled to herself. The excitement was pathetic for someone who was nearly fifty. The smile widened. But it was fun. She hadn't felt like this since, oh, since she was dating John.

A car slowed outside on the little street. She looked out of the kitchen window and saw the neighbours' Oldsmobile pull into the driveway of the cottage opposite. She spotted a wilting rose in her front yard. She grabbed the pruning shears, grateful for the opportunity to do something and to watch the road.

The front yard was looking good: a riot of peonies, zinnias, larkspur and hollyhocks penned in by the white picket fence, and the wonderful yellow rose that draped itself over their grey shingle cottage. They had owned the little house in Siasconset – or 'Sconset as it was known locally – for fifteen years now, and they both loved it. The garden was Nancy's particular joy, and she planned the blooms for July and August, the only time they could reliably spend on Nantucket. They would be shutting up the house on Saturday and heading back to Pennsylvania just in time for the fall semester.

The kids were already gone. Katie was staying with her cousins on the Cape, and they had just dropped Jonny off at Amherst a few days early for his sophomore year. Which meant it was just the two of them in the house.

And Emilio.

Nancy grinned again as she reached over to snip off the head of a browning blossom.

Because that time two months before in Tuscany had been the most mind-blowing night of sex Nancy could remember. And she was pretty sure that John felt the same way.

They hadn't talked about it since, not even that morning. They didn't need to: it was a wicked secret, shared, more exciting because unspoken.

Emilio said he was bringing something very special for them. Something he had found in Rome. Nancy had no idea what it was, but she was intrigued, as was John.

She looked up at the sound of a car approaching down the street. It was their station wagon, with John at the wheel and Emilio next to him. She straightened and pushed a lock of her fair hair out of her eye. Emilio bounded out of the car, grinning as he held out his arms. They hugged. He was a couple of inches shorter than her, but his arms felt powerful behind her back.

There followed a bustle of chatter and of carrying things into the house. John fixed some daiquiris and soon they were outside in the back yard, around the wooden table under the maple.

'Your garden is as beautiful as ever, Nancy,' said Emilio.

Nancy could feel herself blushing at the compliment. 'Round here it has to be,' she said. 'Sconset's cottage gardens were famous, and you couldn't let the neighbours down.

'Well?' said John. 'Can we see it?'

'All right.' Emilio went back inside and emerged with a battered briefcase, which he put on the table. He reached into the case and extracted a pair of white cotton gloves, which he slipped on his hands. Then he pulled out a folder, inside which, wrapped in tissue, were three sheets of paper. Old, brown paper, covered in tiny writing.

'What does it say?' said John. 'Let me take a look. Is it in Italian?'

'Not quite.'

John bent over the manuscript. He had taught himself Italian and had become familiar with its linguistic development over the centuries.

'Hah!' he said. 'It's addressed to Bertomê. I can guess who it's from. Let me see.'

Emilio smiled and showed him the third page. 'I knew it!' said John. 'Christoffa! It's from Christopher Columbus to his younger brother Bartholomew!'

'That's right,' said Emilio.

John peered at the text. 'I can't really understand it. It's not Italian, is it?'

'No it's Genoese, which is the dialect the Columbus brothers spoke to each other, although they rarely wrote in it. Here. I've translated it into English. That way, Nancy can understand it too.'

Emilio whipped out some crisp white typewritten sheets of paper, and laid them on the table. Nancy picked them up and began to read, with John looking over her shoulder.

'That's amazing,' John said.

Nancy read the three pages, fascinated. She wasn't a Columbine scholar, but it all sounded plausible to her. 'Wait,' she said. 'Those navigational instructions. That island. It's Nantucket!'

Emilio grinned. 'I thought you'd like that.'

PART ONE

Iceland, 2017

CHAPTER 1

EYGLÓ GAZED OVER the valley to the rank of mountains on the other side, a wall of bulging hard grey rock, flexing its muscles in scraps of August sunshine. The valley was broad, flattened by a series of volcanic floods caused by eruptions under the glacier a hundred kilometres to the south. A river, narrow at this spot, threaded its way through sand and meadows where multicoloured horses grazed, dozens of them. A raindrop fell on her nose. She ignored it. She immersed herself in the view. The place. She took a long slow breath. She smiled.

She spoke.

'This is the view Gudrid saw a thousand years ago. I am standing at Glaumbaer, in northern Iceland, the farm to which Gudrid came with her husband Thorfinn Karlsefni after so many years away from Iceland.'

Eygló turned and walked towards the back of a tiny church, clad in corrugated metal, squatting behind a row of turf-covered farmhouses.

'Of course, she had married Thorfinn in Greenland. And they brought back to Iceland with them their little son Snorri, the first European to be born in North America.'

Eygló turned to face left as she walked and talked. She was speaking English, in which she was fluent, but with soft esses and a clear Icelandic trill that English speakers seemed to love.

More raindrops on her nose. And on the far side of the church a large black cloud was rolling towards her from the west. She resisted the urge to gabble her way through the rest of her story before it burst upon her.

'Gudrid had travelled thousands of miles, farmed a new island – Greenland – explored a new continent – America – suffered shipwreck and attacks from Skraelings – what we now call Native Americans. It was here in Glaumbaer that Gudrid the Wanderer hoped to come to rest, to settle down with her small family.'

Eygló stopped. She was now in front of the church, next to a bronze sculpture of Gudrid standing in a ship with her infant Snorri on her shoulder. The drops were falling harder; Eygló resisted the temptation to wipe one from her eyebrow. She cocked her head to one side.

'But Gudrid's travels were not yet over. She had one more journey to take. A pilgrimage to Rome.'

The drops became a torrent. Eygló couldn't help hunching her shoulders, as the cold water flattened her spiky blonde hair.

'Cut!'

Eygló smiled with relief as Suzy, her English producer, waved them towards the church door.

'Let's get under cover!'

Eygló, Suzy, Tom the cameraman and Ajay the sound guy all ran to the shelter of the doorway, where a tall man was talking to a young woman with short dark hair, streaked with yellow. The woman hurried away as they approached.

'Can we use those takes?' Eygló asked.

'What do you think, Tom?' said Suzy. She hunched over Tom's camera, examining the digital images they had just captured.

Eygló stood next to the tall man, who was staring out at the turf farmhouses beside the churchyard: an eighteenth-century reincarnation of that Viking Glaumbaer farm, and now a folk museum.

'"It was here Gudrid the Wanderer hoped to come to rest,"' he said, sarcasm lacing his words. 'You have no idea what Gudrid hoped. For all you know, she wished she was back in Greenland shagging Erik the Red.'

11

'You mean I should have said: "Gudrid stood here and dropped an earring, thereby spawning a hundred pages of bullshit in an archaeological journal ten centuries later"?'

'Ouch.'

Einar Thorsteinsson had been patronizing Eygló ever since she had first come across him when he was a graduate student and she an undergraduate at the University of Iceland. He was now a senior lecturer in archaeology at the university. Very tall, with longish blonde hair and a neatly trimmed beard, he was irredeemably pleased with himself. Eygló had to admit he had some right to be. He was a magician of the past: he could conjure a story out of the most obscure elements – physical elements. Ancient sites of dirt and tiny lumps of material spoke to him. The sagas less so.

And he could be *so* arrogant.

Gudrid and her son were getting very wet. Eygló liked the statue. Although it was consciously modern in an ancient place like this, it was lithe and elegant, evoking Gudrid as the young adventurous woman she was then, rather than the thousand-year-old Viking she had become today.

'You know Gudrid was a real person, Einar. And the sagas tell us enough to know what kind of person she was.'

'You're just guessing,' said Einar. 'It's make-believe.'

Suzy joined them. They had been speaking Icelandic and the Englishwoman hadn't understood them.

'The rain has screwed us,' Suzy said. 'We've still got to do a wide with Eygló against the mountains in the background, that's really important. We'll try again early tomorrow morning – we're going to have to shoot the whole lot again so we get the light consistent. According to my weather app it's fine until about midday, and this valley would look beautiful in morning sunlight. Do you think it will rain tomorrow, Einar?'

Einar didn't answer. Meteorology was beneath him.

'You can never be sure the forecast will be correct in Iceland,' said Eygló. 'But it's always worth a try.'

'OK, we come back tomorrow morning.'

They walked back to the Land Cruiser that Suzy had hired. 'Who was that you were talking to?' Eygló asked Einar.

'Who?'

'The woman at the church door.'

'I don't know. Some tourist asking me whether it was open. Foreign.'

'Are you seeing her later? Showing her the Glaumbaer night-life?'

'Oh, Eygló, you do so misunderstand me,' Einar said. 'That kind of thing is long in my past.'

'Of course it is, Einar.'

Einar's womanizing was legendary; in fact, Eygló had witnessed it at first hand. He had been married for something like twelve years, but that hadn't stopped him. Eygló hadn't seen quite as much of him in recent times, but she doubted Einar would ever change.

A familiar scent tugged at her nostrils, sneaking its way through the fug of damp clothing. It was aftershave, a subtle perfume she remembered Einar bought in Paris. She remembered the night, or morning rather, when she had asked him about it, lying in his bare arms.

But that was a long time ago. And much best forgotten.

Suzy had booked them into one of Iceland's oldest hotels in the small town of Saudárkrókur, just a few kilometres north of Glaumbaer. Eygló smiled when she saw she had been given the *Gudrídur Thorbjarnardóttir* room, Gudrid's room, and she took a quick picture of the wooden door with her phone to tweet. It was the best room in the hotel.

She gazed out of the window towards the harbour, crowded with small fishing boats and a couple of trawlers, out to the fjord behind. She could just see the big rectangular block of rock that was the island of Drangey, moored a few kilometres offshore like a massive supertanker from a bygone age.

She flopped on the bed, pulled out her phone and called her son, who was excited by Liverpool's rumoured purchase of a new attacking midfielder from Arsenal and wanted to tell her all about it. It was coming up to the end of the transfer window for the new football season, one of Bjarki's favourite times of year, and Eygló just liked to hear the enthusiasm in his voice. He was staying with his cousins for a few days – yet another few days. Eygló thanked God she had a patient and helpful sister.

After they had finished, Eygló checked out the Arsenal player on her phone – it was important to be properly prepared for future conversations with her son – and then caught up on Twitter and Facebook. Since the success of *Viking Queens* in America earlier that year, Eygló's social media presence had exploded. Sometimes it was a chore, but actually she enjoyed the attention. And Suzy was keen for her to develop her fan base as widely as possible before *The Wanderer* was broadcast the following year.

She put down the phone and looked around her room. Old wooden furniture, old wooden beams. Elegant, cosy, expensive.

She grinned. This was her life now. She didn't know how long it was going to last, but she was going to enjoy it.

Because, mostly, her life had been crap. Eygló was an optimistic person, famous among her friends for her ability to put a sunny spin on the numerous bad things that seemed to happen to her. There had been a succession of bad men, including Hermann, her husband for two years. She loved history and felt she had real empathy for those Viking men and especially women who had lived in Iceland a thousand years before, but she wasn't brilliant at writing about them, at least in the dry, rigorous style that was expected of historians. She wasn't a total disaster – in fact she was just good enough to cling on to the academic world by her finger-tips, first at the University of Iceland and then at York University in England, from where she had eventually been let go as a junior lecturer three years before. It was Einar who had hired her there, but once he left to return to Iceland, she had lost her protector.

The only undeniably good thing that had happened to her was Bjarki, who was now eleven, innocent and enthusiastic, and whose life was definitely not crap.

But in 2012 she had been put forward by her boss at York to be a talking head for a couple of minutes in a documentary on the history of Yorkshire produced by Suzy Henshaw. Eygló had spoken about the Vikings in York and had captivated Suzy, and later the BBC audience.

Two years later, Suzy had tracked Eygló down in Iceland, where she was working as a temporary high school history teacher, to front a new series called *Viking Queens* about the Norse women who had followed their men across Northern Europe.

It had been a massive success, not just for the BBC in the UK, but in Germany, Australia, Norway, Japan, America, and now, at last, Iceland. Moorhen Productions, Suzy's company, had done well, both financially and in terms of reputation.

Now, Suzy had asked Eygló to present a documentary series about Gudrid the Wanderer, who had emerged as the most popular of the Viking queens with the television audience. They had spent the previous two weeks filming in Nantucket and Newfoundland, and now they were in Iceland, covering Gudrid's childhood and her later years.

Eygló had suggested getting Einar involved: Eygló did the presenting, and Einar added the archaeological expertise. Einar looked good on camera, but his delivery was a little aloof, a cool expert rather than a passionate enthusiast.

Whereas Eygló brought Gudrid to life.

Eygló, Suzy and Einar had agreed to meet for dinner at eight-thirty in a restaurant in a blue building on Adalgata, the old main street lined with brightly coloured houses and shops, some dating back to the late nineteenth century. A pair of ravens swooped around the restaurant, croaking what sounded like an aggressive warning, before perching on the roof of the old store opposite. They unsettled Eygló: it was highly unusual for ravens to be seen in town in the summer. Her grandmother would have said it augured a hard winter, or something worse. Gudrid would no doubt have agreed.

Einar noticed Eygló's disquiet and guessed the reason for it. 'Oh, Eygló,' he said. 'They are only birds. Everyone pays far too much attention to ravens.'

Eygló considered arguing with him, but actually she found his cynicism comforting. Einar believed he was in total control of his world; maybe she could learn something from him.

As usual Tom the cameraman didn't join them. He had gone off to find himself a more comfortable dive where the food would be cheaper and the beer more in evidence. He and Suzy had worked together for years, and Suzy had told Eygló and Einar not to take it personally. Tom was a loner, a former nature cameraman who just liked to be by himself. Or perhaps with a puffin.

Tom's surliness was difficult for Ajay, the shy young sound man. He was only twenty-one, a film-school student at a university in London doing a summer internship with Moorhen Productions. Tom was good at teaching Ajay his trade, but left the poor guy to fend for himself when not working. Eygló felt sorry for him, and had invited him to join her and the others, but Ajay had refused. Eygló hadn't pushed it.

'I looked through today's rushes with Tom,' said Suzy. 'We definitely must try again tomorrow.'

'Will you need me to do my bit again?' asked Einar.

'Absolutely.'

'So it's Snaefellsnes tomorrow night and we fly to Greenland on Friday?' It was Monday; they had three days left filming in Iceland.

'That's the plan,' said Suzy. Gudrid had been brought up on the Snaefellsnes peninsula in West Iceland, and then had sailed to Greenland, following the outlawed Erik the Red. They would be filming at Brattahlíd, Erik the Red's farm on the south-west corner of the island, and a couple of other places in Greenland in which Gudrid had spent some time. Eygló had only visited Greenland once before, and she was eager to return.

Then there was the trip to Italy to look forward to. After a few years in Glaumbaer, Gudrid had taken herself off on a pilgrimage to Rome. Which meant Eygló had to go there too, with Suzy and Tom, of course, but not Einar. Roman archaeology was not his thing. Eygló had never been to Italy; she wondered what kind of hotel she would be put up in there.

The restaurant was full of tourists – everywhere was in Iceland in the summer – and they had to wait to order. When the waitress finally arrived, Suzy asked for a bottle of Pinot Grigio with their food. Going on previous experience, that would be the first of two or three. Einar ordered foal, probably just to wind Suzy up, but the Englishwoman didn't seem to notice.

'Oh, I just got an email,' she said. 'Good news. Marco Beccari is going to join us on Snaefellsnes.'

'Well done!' said Eygló. Even Einar nodded his approval.

Marco Beccari was one of the few truly world-famous historians. An Italian, he had written an influential and highly readable book reassessing the late Renaissance and its effect on the New World. He was now a professor at Princeton, and his presence on their TV programme would give it credibility.

Because *The Wanderer* wasn't just a rehash of well-known facts about Gudrid. It contained a theory, and evidence, that would cause the world to rethink what it believed about the discovery of America.

Without Professor Beccari, the theory would be just another wild hypothesis. With him, the academic world would have to sit up and take notice. And the television audience would too.

Suzy left the restaurant a little early, complaining of an incipient migraine she wanted to nip in the bud. Eygló and Einar followed later, and Eygló went up to her room. There wasn't much else to do in Saudárkrókur, and they were waking up at six the following morning to head back to Glaumbaer.

Eygló checked her phone, and saw that her earlier tweets had somehow roused the ire of Hailey from Oakland who was convinced that all Vikings were rapists and was shocked that Eygló wouldn't accept that their 'queens' were in fact victims. Eygló entered the fray with gusto, thumbs flying over her phone's screen.

She paused to draw her curtains, and as she did so, she noticed a figure hurrying away from the hotel towards the church square. Einar. What's he up to? she wondered. But she was just glad he hadn't knocked on her door. Maybe he had changed after all.

*

Suzy's app proved correct: the weather was beautiful the next day. They arrived at Glaumbaer at seven, a couple of hours before the museum opened. The sun was well above the horizon, having set for only a few hours at this time of year. The air was crisp after the previous night's rain, and there was a smell of cow manure coming from the twenty-first-century farm over the road.

Suzy decided to start where they had finished the day before, and Eygló repeated her words as she trod through the damp grass of the churchyard, following her own shadow in the sunshine. All around her birds sang and squabbled. She tried not to think of Einar's cynicism as she spoke; Gudrid was real to her, so real Eygló felt she knew her.

She turned to face Tom, and as she did so she thought she caught something in her peripheral vision, by the back of the church. But she prided herself on her professionalism and the lack of retakes she required, and so she kept talking.

'Cut,' said Suzy as Eygló finished her last sentence. 'How does that look, Tom?'

As Suzy and Tom examined his camera, Eygló turned to focus on the object she had seen. It was a pair of legs, clad in jeans, stretching out from behind the church.

She walked towards the legs, anxiety building. Could someone have picked this spot to bed down for the night? A tourist who was lost or drunk or both?

Or was it something else? Something worse.

It was.

A small, simple apse of corrugated metal stuck out from the back of the church, and behind it a young woman lay splayed on the grass, face inches from the corner made by the apse and the wall, the back of her head a bloody mess.

Eygló screamed.

CHAPTER 2

MAGNUS CURSED, SWERVED and hit the horn as a black BMW X5 roared past him through the fog. After five years away, he was back in the land of elves and idiot drivers.

He was on that famous stretch of road through a patch of lava on the way to Álftanes that had been diverted around a couple of rocks inhabited by the local hidden people, so as not to disturb them. Álftanes was a small town on a headland just outside Reykjavík, and Magnus had been called out to a report of an assault on a householder who had surprised a burglar. It was not the most serious of crimes, but then there were not that many serious crimes in Reykjavík. In fact, in the month he had been back, Magnus had investigated precisely none.

He approached a large brown wooden house – large by Icelandic standards anyway – that stood on a small point apart from its more modern one-storey concrete neighbours, facing out into grey folds of fog and sea. The flashing lights of two police cars and an ambulance pierced the mist. As Magnus pulled up behind one of the police cars, two paramedics climbed into the ambulance and it drove off.

Magnus didn't recognize the uniformed police constable at the door to the house. He introduced himself. She appeared to have heard of him – it seemed that every police officer in Iceland had, despite Magnus's recent absence from the country.

'The victim is Tryggvi Thór Gröndal,' she said. 'Seventy-one. He was hit on the head and knocked unconscious. He's a

stubborn bastard. Refused to go to hospital *and* he declines to press charges.'

'Why?'

I don't know,' said the constable with frustration. 'Claims the attack was nothing. See if you can get him to change his mind.'

She led Magnus into the house and through to a large living room with a wide picture window looking out on to the fog. On the sofa in front of the window sat an old man, his head swathed in a bandage. In an armchair opposite, a bald uniformed police officer whom Magnus thought he had met before was taking notes. A red-haired woman in her thirties hovered behind the old man. She didn't look happy.

The old man glanced up at Magnus as he entered, deep brown eyes under thick black eyebrows. His face was lined, but despite the wound and his age, he didn't seem frail at all. He seemed strong. And determined.

A stubborn bastard.

With a bruise forming on his cheek, Magnus noticed.

'Ah, a detective! I'm sorry, you have wasted your trip. No crime to solve here.' He had a deep, rich voice that commanded attention.

Magnus ignored him and smiled politely. 'Inspector Magnús Ragnarsson, of Reykjavík CID. Your name is Tryggvi Thór?'

The man grunted.

The bald constable stood up, and Magnus took his place opposite the victim.

'I know you will have told my colleagues what happened, but would you mind repeating it for me?'

'No need,' said the man. His expression was firm and defiant, but Magnus thought he detected a hint of amusement in the old man's eyes.

The woman sighed. She had brown eyes, freckles and a wide mouth with thick lips, the corners of which were pointing down. No amusement there. Her nose ended in a little hook, just like the man on the sofa. She was wearing a white top, a green jacket, smart trousers and subtle silver jewellery. Business clothes. She looked good, Magnus thought. She also looked grumpy.

'I need to go to work,' she said to Magnus. 'Can I leave him to you?'

'Just a moment,' said Magnus. 'Are you Tryggvi Thór's daughter?' He was guessing, given her age and resemblance.

'Yes, my name is Sóley. I dropped by to see Dad this morning on my way in from the airport – I flew in from Brussels this morning. I discovered him on the floor just there.' She pointed to a spot near the desk. There were dark specks on the rug. Blood. 'He was barely conscious, so I called the ambulance. And you lot.'

There was a surprising tinge of contempt in the woman's voice as she uttered these last words. Surprising, because in Magnus's experience the police were usually treated with respect in Iceland, especially by the professional classes.

'Was the door unlocked?'

'It's always unlocked.'

Magnus nodded. 'Did you see anyone leaving the house? Or watching it?'

'No.'

'How about a car?'

'No, I don't think so. I don't know. I wasn't looking, I can't remember. I may have passed a car on the road on the way here; it is a road, after all.' She pursed her lips. 'I don't know why you bother asking me these questions. Dad doesn't want you to investigate whoever attacked him, and even if he did, you wouldn't do anything.'

Magnus frowned. 'Why do you say that, Sóley?'

Sóley just shook her head. 'Can I go now? I really will be late for a meeting.'

'Can I have your contact details?' Magnus said. 'A card, perhaps?' Sóley looked like the sort of woman who would have a card.

Sure enough, she did. Magnus studied it. She worked in the Foreign Ministry, with an impressive title.

'Thank you. We will contact you later, if necessary.'

The woman stooped towards her father as if to kiss him, seemed to think better of it, and left the house.

'Hah!' said Tryggvi Thór. 'That's all you will get out of her.'

Magnus ignored the old man. He stood up and wandered around the living room, examining the windows, the desk in the corner, the photo frames on the shelves, the floor. He paused at the desk. A couple of empty plastic folders lay among a mess of papers.

Magnus never could resist a challenge. There was something going on here and he was going to find out what.

He told the two constables to leave him alone with Tryggvi Thór, and after he had seen them out to their patrol car, returned to the sofa and stared at the man. Who stared back. A full minute passed.

'What did he take?' Magnus asked eventually.

'He didn't take anything.'

'How do you know? Have you checked?'

The old man didn't answer.

'Can you check now?'

'Maybe later.'

'You should check your desk. He took something from your desk. It's a mess; the rest of the house is very tidy – you're a tidy person. The question is: Did the intruder take valuables? Or papers? Something he could sell? Or information?'

Magnus held those deep brown eyes. Intelligent eyes. He could feel that the old man was restraining the urge to speak to him. Magnus waited.

'You are not a bad detective,' Tryggvi Thór said at last. 'But I don't have to answer these questions. I said I don't want you to press charges.'

'Why doesn't your daughter like the police?'

More staring. Then a grunt. 'Would you like some coffee?'

'Thank you.'

The old man stood up and moved through to the kitchen. He gasped and touched his head. Magnus ignored the urge to offer to help. If the old man was that stubborn he could make the coffee on his own.

Magnus waited on the living-room sofa. Outside, the fog

22

was lifting to reveal a calm sea of slate grey and the gritty black Reykjanes peninsula stretching away to the west. The perfect cone of the small Keilir mountain thrust upwards through the remnants of the mist. A lovely view. A lovely house, in fact.

Tryggvi Thór returned with two mugs of coffee and some cakes. The perfect host.

'You must be the Kani Cop?'

Magnus nodded. It was a nickname he had picked up amongst his colleagues on his last stint in Iceland. *Kani* was slang for American. 'How have you heard of me?'

'I have friends in the police. I thought you had left Iceland?'

'I did. I went back to my old job as a homicide detective in the States.'

'Where was that?'

Magnus hesitated before answering. Wasn't he supposed to be the one asking the questions? But, strangely, he was enjoying talking to this man. And maybe he would get something in return.

'Boston. I was born in Reykjavík but was brought up in America from the age of twelve. I came back to Iceland in 2009. Left three years later.'

'But you couldn't stay away?'

'It's not that simple.'

'It never is,' said the old man. 'How long have you been back?'

'Five weeks. I get thrown out of my hotel room tomorrow.'

'Have you got anywhere to go?'

'I think so. It's been a nightmare trying to find somewhere. Things have changed since I was last here: the whole city seems to have been taken over by Airbnb and there is nothing left for anyone else. I think I've found a room in Breidholt – I'm waiting to hear.'

They sipped their coffee in silence for a moment.

'You know I can insist that we investigate this attack,' said Magnus. 'Whoever did this is a threat to other people. Your neighbours. I can get in a forensic team to examine your house. Make sure everything is covered in a nice layer of fingerprint dust.'

'No you couldn't,' said Tryggvi Thór.

'Why not?'

'Because without my cooperation you would never make the case. The prosecutor wouldn't take it on. Your boss wouldn't allow you to waste the time. And the money.'

There was something in that. Magnus's boss, Detective Superintendent Thelma, prided herself on her efficient use of the department's limited budget.

Magnus examined the man opposite him. He knew a lot about the internal workings of the Metropolitan Police. 'So when did you retire from the police department, Tryggvi Thór?'

The old man grunted. 'Nineteen ninety-six. Over twenty years ago. Like you, I left Iceland.'

'Africa?' All living rooms in Iceland were heavily populated with family photographs, and Tryggvi Thór's was no exception. Magnus had spotted several pictures of Tryggvi Thór in a much hotter climate, in many of which he was accompanied by a black woman with a mischievous smile, maybe twenty years younger than him.

'Uganda. I only came back last year.'

'With your wife?'

'No. Charity died. Cancer. She was fifty-two. That's why I returned. We had run a school together, but when she died, I gave it up. My mother also died last year and left this house empty. It was where I grew up; I decided I'd rather live in it than sell it.'

'I'm sorry about your wife,' said Magnus. 'And your mother too.' He drained his coffee. 'Are you sure you won't cooperate? I wasn't kidding. This guy, whoever he was, might try again with one of your neighbours.'

'I think the neighbours are safe,' said Tryggvi Thór.

'Why do you say that?'

Tryggvi Thór said nothing.

'This wasn't a random attack, was it?' Magnus said. 'Someone came here who you knew. You let them in, they beat you up and then they took something. And you know why. But you're not telling me. Perhaps you're scared? I'd be surprised. Perhaps you're hiding something that you don't want coming to light? More likely. Something illegal?'

The old man was looking at him steadily.

'Something illegal?' Magnus repeated the question. He was looking for a tiny nod. Or a shake of the head.

The old man didn't move a muscle.

'All right,' Magnus said. 'I can't waste any more of my time here.' He got to his feet and fished out a card. 'But if you change your mind, or ...' He hesitated. '... if you think you are about to get another visit, give me a call.'

Tryggvi Thór took the card and hauled himself out of his chair, wincing as he did so. He saw Magnus to the front door.

'You know,' he said as Magnus stepped outside. 'You can always stay here, if you like. There is just me in the house, and there's plenty of room.'

Magnus turned in surprise. Tryggvi Thór raised his eyebrows. He meant it.

Odd.

'No, that's OK, thanks,' Magnus said. 'As I told you, I think I've lined up somewhere in Breidholt.'

'Well, if you prefer there to here, that's your choice.' And the old man shut the door.

CHAPTER 3

THE FOG HAD lifted as Magnus drove along the narrow isthmus between Álftanes and Reykjavík. To his left stood the large farmstead of Bessastadir, the official residence of the president of Iceland, a collection of white buildings and a church alone in a meadow. Behind that, across a narrow body of water, rose the jumble of white and grey buildings that was the capital, crowned by the smooth grey concrete missile of the Hallgrímskirkja spire on top of its little hill. Mount Esja, behind the city, was still shrouded in cloud. The desolate black lava flow of the Reykjanes peninsula stretched away to the right. On both sides of the road, the sea glistened and glimmered in the newly liberated sunshine.

Iceland looked washed, clean and pristine. For a moment, Magnus felt his spirits rise. Maybe he had made the correct decision to return after all.

He had been brought over to Iceland from Boston's Homicide Unit at the request of the National Police Commissioner in 2009 to help the Reykjavík Metropolitan Police deal with the big-city international crime that the Commissioner feared was going to become more prevalent in the capital. As America's only Icelandic-speaking homicide detective, he was uniquely qualified for the job. And Magnus had done as he had been asked, breaking a number of difficult cases. The secondment was meant to have been for a two-year period, but Magnus had got an extension to three years. Then things had fallen apart with his girlfriend, Ingileif, and Magnus had returned to Boston.

There, life had been tougher than he had expected. Ever since he had first arrived in America as a child, Magnus had never been sure whether he was Icelandic or American. The three-year stint in Iceland hadn't helped that: he had just become more confused.

But the real problem was Magnus's father.

It was Magnus's father, a professor of mathematics, who had brought Magnus and his little brother Ollie over to America when his mother died. And it was Magnus's father who had propelled Magnus into the police department.

Because, when Magnus was twenty, his father had been murdered in the small town of Duxbury just south of Boston. The police had failed to find the killer and, after years of trying, so had Magnus. Which was why he had joined the Boston Police Department and become a homicide detective. He was very good at his job: it was as if every murder was his father's murder.

Then, in Iceland, he had finally figured out how his father had died and the people who had been responsible. One way or another they had been brought to justice.

In many ways, many important ways, this had brought relief. Relief from the anger, the disequilibrium, the feeling that life was not quite right, that had gnawed at Magnus since he was twenty. But it had also dampened his obsession for the job, tramping the streets of South Boston from one murder to the next. He was still a good detective, but he had lost his edge. If a case was too difficult, if he had worked through all the angles and still not made a breakthrough, he would let it go. Move on. He would never have done that in the past, before he had resolved his father's murder.

Without his all-consuming desire to solve every crime that came his way, the downsides of the job became more apparent. The long hours, the endless paperwork, the human misery.

And, without Ingileif, without the enthusiasm to find another Ingileif, he was lonely.

When the National Police Commissioner called him one morning, asking Magnus to return to Iceland on a permanent basis, Magnus politely refused.

Then he called again. And a third time.

27

The third time was the day after Magnus had visited his little brother Ollie, who only had four more months to go at the Massachusetts correctional facility at Norfolk and was eager to right what he considered to be past wrongs as soon as he got out.

Those past wrongs involved Magnus, at least as far as Ollie was concerned.

So the third time the Commissioner called, Magnus said yes.

Things had changed in Iceland. When he had left, the country was still struggling with the damage caused by the financial crash of 2008 that had almost bankrupted it. Now the economy was booming, fuelled by an unprecedented influx of tourists and Icelanders' ability to look to the future with optimism. Much of this optimism had led to more borrowing, more expensive SUVs bought with other people's money, more speculative buildings going up. So maybe things hadn't changed after all.

Magnus returned to his old department within CID with the rank of detective inspector. Baldur, the previous head of the Violent Crimes Unit, had been promoted to head up Traffic, and had been replaced by Detective Superintendent Thelma Reynisdóttir. Magnus's old colleague Vigdís was still there, still a detective constable, but Árni had got married, been promoted to detective sergeant and moved north to Akureyri. Magnus didn't know whether Vigdís's failure to be promoted was because she was black or because she was a woman. He did know it was not because she wasn't good enough.

He wondered what she would make of Tryggvi Thór. Magnus was sure he was hiding something. He knew who had attacked him, and he knew why.

Normally when someone didn't want to press charges after they were assaulted it was because there was some kind of criminal activity lurking in the background which they didn't want to be uncovered. Drugs, usually, possibly people trafficking, something involving organized crime or gangs. A turf war, an unpaid debt, a contractual dispute.

Magnus would be very surprised if Tryggvi Thór was involved in organized crime. But that was the most logical explanation.

Although Magnus knew that it was traditional Icelandic hospitality to give wandering strangers a bed, he still thought it odd that Tryggvi Thór had offered him a room in his house. Despite Tryggvi Thór's refusal to cooperate, there had certainly been a connection between them, a mutual respect, but they had only met each other once. On the other hand, Magnus had only met the shopkeeper in Breidholt who was offering to rent out his room once. Breidholt was a dreary suburb to the south-east of the centre. Bits of it were pleasant, but not the bit where Magnus would be living.

Perhaps Tryggvi Thór wanted Magnus to help him. Or protect him from another attack.

It was a nice house. Magnus liked Álftanes. And he was intrigued by Tryggvi Thór.

He regretted not taking the task of apartment-hunting a bit more seriously. The hotel he was staying at, which had been paid for by the Metropolitan Police for a month, was adamant about throwing him out the next day. So Breidholt beckoned.

His phone rang. He checked the caller: Thelma, his boss. He answered: 'Magnús.'

'Where are you?'

'Kópavogur, on my way back to headquarters.'

'Well, come and see me as soon as you get in. A tourist has been murdered in the north and Akureyri need some help.'

'All right. Where?'

'Glaumbaer.'

CHAPTER 4

MAGNUS TURNED OFF the Ring Road, which circumnavigated the island of Iceland, at Varmahlíd and headed north towards Saudárkrókur. Within a few minutes he arrived at Glaumbaer. It was just after five o'clock. He had considered flying to Akureyri and driving from there, but it was quicker to get on the road right away.

As expected, there was a jumble of police vehicles parked in front of the church and in the folk museum car park next door, and a number of black-uniformed officers were milling about. He recognized the Forensics Unit's van from Reykjavík, and an ambulance was waiting, doors open, ready to cart the body off to the morgue in the capital. Standing by itself, surrounded by police tape, was a small blue Hyundai.

A familiar figure strode towards him.

'Árni!' Magnus smiled. Árni hadn't changed much. He was still tall and drippy with a puppy-dog grin, but his black floppy hair had now been cut short. Magnus embraced him. 'Or should I say Sergeant Árni? I'm pleased you are on the case.'

'Inspector Ólafur is leading the investigation into a series of rapes at knifepoint in Akureyri. That's why he asked for help from Reykjavík. He knew you and I had worked together, so here I am.'

Árni grinned. Magnus wondered whether Árni's detection skills had improved over the last five years. Maybe they had; somehow Magnus suspected that they hadn't. But he would be good to have around.

Magnus surveyed the scene. The church was of the traditional twentieth-century Icelandic design: off-white metal walls, red metal roof, stubby white tower and a red spire. It was set thirty yards or so back from the main road, a flagpole and a sculpture of a woman in a boat standing just in front of it. The front porch faced the road, and behind the building a slope led down to the Héradsvötn valley. Crime-scene tape fluttered around the churchyard, which was enclosed by low turf walls and a white wooden gate. A line of old farmhouses backed on to one of these walls, each with a steeply sloping turf-covered roof coming down almost to the ground: the folk museum. Magnus remembered visiting the museum with his father on one of the occasional trips to Iceland they made together from America when he was a boy.

Glaumbaer wasn't really a village as such, but there were a number of farms and houses scattered around within sight of the church and the museum. It was a magnificent setting, looking out over the meadows of the glacial river valley to the mountains on the eastern side.

'You haven't moved the body yet?' Magnus asked.

'No. We were waiting for the Forensics Unit to arrive. And you, of course. It's back there, behind the church.'

'Good. Before I see it, tell me about the victim.'

'Carlotta Mondini. Italian. Occupation listed on her passport as student, although she is twenty-six. Almost certainly a tourist. Arrived in Iceland last Thursday. Stayed in Reykjavík for three days and then hired that car from the City Airport and drove up here.' Árni nodded towards the blue Hyundai festooned with crime-scene tape. 'She checked into a hotel in Blönduós yesterday afternoon, dumped her stuff and drove on to Glaumbaer.' Blönduós was a small town about sixty kilometres to the west; Magnus had passed through it on his way from Reykjavík.

'Was she travelling alone?'

'Looks like it. At least that's what the hotels in Reykjavík and Blönduós said.'

'Anything about her background in Italy?'

31

'Not yet. We have been in touch with the police in Milan, who will contact her family. We haven't heard back from them.'

'Who discovered the body?'

'You'll like this,' said Árni with a grin. 'A TV crew. They were filming here early this morning, and they stumbled across it.'

'And why would I like that?' said Magnus.

'They're filming a documentary about Gudrid. You know, the Viking woman who went to Greenland?'

'It's not the people who did *Viking Queens*, is it? Eygló, isn't that her name?'

'It is indeed. In fact it was Eygló herself who discovered the body.'

Árni was right; Magnus was intrigued. He had made sure to watch every episode of the series, which had been broadcast on PBS in America. He had fallen for the presenter, Eygló. There was something bewitching about her evocation of the Norse world a thousand years ago, and her programmes had made him homesick for Iceland.

'That's right. Gudrid lived here, didn't she?' Magnus said, remembering *The Saga of Erik the Red*, one of his favourites. 'Gudrid the Wanderer. After she came back from Greenland.'

'That's what they tell me.'

'An amazing woman,' Magnus went on. 'That sculpture must be her and her son Snorri; he was the first European to be born in America.'

'She may well be amazing, Magnús,' said Árni. 'But she is pretty low on our list of suspects right now.'

Magnus laughed. 'OK, OK. Back to the present. Who is on your list of suspects?'

'No one concrete, as yet,' said Árni, looking sheepish. 'A local child says she saw a man getting into a car parked a couple of hundred metres away. But no detailed description. Apart from that, nothing suspicious.'

'Time of death?'

'The police doctor who examined the body this morning placed the time of death at somewhere between seven-thirty p.m. and one a.m. last night. There was some rigor mortis in the jaw, the body was cool and post-mortem lividity was fixed, suggesting the body had been dead at least eight hours. The TV crew were filming here until seven-thirty last night, so that's the window.'

'OK. Show me the body.'

They donned forensics overalls and signed a crime-scene log, and then Árni led Magnus around the side of the church.

Carlotta Mondini was lying face down a couple of feet from the back wall of the building. The back of her head was smashed into a tangle of blood, brain matter and dark blonde-streaked hair. She was wearing a light blue North Face rain jacket over a grey and black lopi sweater and jeans. Lopi sweaters were a traditional Icelandic design; Carlotta must have bought hers during her few days in Reykjavík.

Edda, head of the Forensics Unit, greeted Magnus. 'You took your time,' she said.

'I don't know how you guys got here so fast,' said Magnus. The Forensics Unit prided themselves on their speed to a crime scene, with some justification. Three of them were busying themselves around the body, taking photographs and sketching the surrounding ground. 'You can't have been here long?'

'Fifteen minutes,' said Edda.

'Any sign of sexual activity?'

'Doesn't look like it at first sight,' said Edda. 'Her clothing hasn't been disturbed, except by us and the district medical officer. No immediate sign of a struggle but we will check for skin under the fingernails.'

'Had the body been moved after death?'

'From the lividity, I'd say it hasn't been moved far. But it could have been dragged here straight after death, of course. We're checking the whole churchyard, but the overnight rain won't have helped.'

'Cause of death the obvious?'

'Blunt instrument wielded with some force.'

'It's interesting it's a blunt instrument,' Árni said. 'The local farmer who looks after the churchyard told us that a pickaxe is missing. He was digging a grave here yesterday and he thinks he left it out overnight. Probably next to the spade.'

Árni pointed to a spade lying on the ground next to the back wall of the church. Magnus scanned the churchyard – there was a pile of freshly dug earth in one corner.

'It definitely wasn't a pickaxe,' said Edda. 'Or at least not the pick itself. I suppose it could have been the pickaxe head.'

'Or the handle?' said Magnus.

'But why not use the pick?' said Árni. 'It would be more effective.'

Magnus considered the question. 'And messier. Maybe our murderer was squeamish? He didn't want to split the skull completely.'

'Or maybe it wasn't the pickaxe after all,' said Edda.

'Any other evidence?' Magnus asked her.

'Too early to say; we're just getting started,' said Edda, waving towards her colleagues.

'I'll let you get on with it,' said Magnus. He turned to Árni. 'No one saw Carlotta here last night?'

Carlotta. The victim now had a name and he was using it. She was already more than just a body. Over the coming hours and days she would develop into an ever more complete personality. And Magnus would find who had killed her.

He was pleased to feel that familiar desire for justice stirring within him, a feeling that had been in abeyance in recent years on the streets of Boston.

'Yes, someone did. Einar Thorsteinsson, an archaeologist working with the TV crew. He was standing at the door to the church when she approached him, asking him if the church was open. He didn't see where she went; his attention was taken up with the other crew members.'

'And that was at seven-thirty last night?'

'About then, yes.'

'And what time did the child see the man getting into the car?'

'Much later. Just before ten. She was cycling back from a friend's house just down the road. She had to be home by ten.'

34

'A bit late,' said Magnus.

'It's summer,' said Árni. He was right; in late August it still didn't get dark until after nine, and kids played outside late into the evening.

'Carlotta can't have hung around here for all that time,' said Magnus. 'Someone else would have seen her. She must have gone away and returned for some reason.'

'Or she was killed earlier and the man the kid saw at ten o'clock had nothing to do with it,' said Árni.

'Any chance this could be linked to the rapes you guys are investigating in Akureyri?' Magnus asked.

'Unlikely. That guy carries a knife. And you heard Edda say there was no sign of sexual assault.'

'Still, it's possible,' said Magnus. 'OK. Let's talk to some people.'

CHAPTER 5

IT WAS SEVEN o'clock by the time Magnus followed Árni's vehicle from Glaumbaer to the nearest police station at Saudárkrókur. The nine-year-old girl lived in a farm opposite the museum. She had said the man she saw was wearing a coat and a baseball cap. She couldn't remember what colour the cap was. Or the coat. The man was really old, like her dad, who was thirty-two. His car was silver and not a 4 × 4. She couldn't remember seeing Carlotta's little blue rental car.

Her parents hadn't noticed anything at all that evening; they had been watching TV.

The curator of the folk museum, a woman of about forty who lived in Saudárkrókur, remembered Carlotta hanging around the museum after it had closed. Carlotta was watching the filming from a distance, and her car was parked alone in the museum car park, not outside the church where it had been left overnight. That suggested that Carlotta had indeed left Glaumbaer after talking to Einar, and returned later. The curator left the museum soon after the TV crew, at about seven-thirty, but at that point she hadn't noticed whether the car was still in the car park. She returned to work at eight-fifteen the next morning, after the body had been discovered by Eygló.

A couple of neighbouring farms lay within a few hundred metres of the folk museum, but none of their inhabitants had seen anything. Once again, by ten o'clock it was almost dark; at seven-thirty Carlotta and her killer would have been in plain daylight and much more noticeable.

There was no sign of a murder weapon, either the pickaxe or any other likely blunt instrument. Or Carlotta's phone.

That last was a problem. These days phones, especially smartphones, provided a wealth of information for investigators: not just records of phone calls made, but emails, Internet browsing history, Facebook pages, everything.

It was highly unlikely that a twenty-six-year-old student had travelled to Iceland without her phone. So the murderer had taken it, which was a clever thing to do.

The drive to Saudárkrókur took about twenty minutes. It was still daylight, but the sun was slinking slowly down towards the mountains to the west, casting the broad valley of the Héradsvötn river in a soft yellow glow. The drive gave Magnus some time to consider what they knew so far. Which was very little. Their chief suspect was a man with a hat driving a silver car.

Unless he was the Akureyri rapist. Akureyri was about an hour away from Glaumbaer. Árni was right, it was unlikely, but it was an avenue they should pursue.

The first forty-eight hours of any murder investigation were key. They had not got very far in the first twenty-four. They needed to find out more about Carlotta Mondini.

Saudárkrókur appeared before him at the head of a fjord, a string of buildings hugging the shore and leading to a harbour. Out to sea, near the mouth of the fjord, the island of Drangey lurked, a platform raised several hundred feet above the water, its cliffs shimmering yellow in the sun.

The police station was in the church square in the centre of town. Magnus parked next to Árni's car, and followed him into the building, which was buzzing with policemen in and out of uniform. Árni introduced Magnus to a detective from Akureyri named Björn, whom Magnus remembered working with many years before on an earlier case, and a couple of local constables.

'And this is Chief Superintendent Jón Kári.'

Magnus turned to see a tall man with thick fair hair and ruddy cheeks approaching him, hand outstretched. 'Welcome to Saudárkrókur,' he said with a reserved smile.

Although his uniform bore the insignia of chief superintendent, Jón Kári was younger than Magnus, probably not more than thirty-five. Iceland was a sparsely populated country outside Reykjavík, and the rural regional chief superintendents could be in charge of a large geographical area that contained a population of only a few thousand and a dozen policemen. In Magnus's experience, they could be defensive towards officers from the capital, especially Magnus, the Kani Cop.

But Jón Kári was friendly and helpful, even offering Magnus the use of his own office, which Magnus declined, preferring to be out in the squad room with the officers working on the case.

'Any news from Italy?' Magnus asked him.

'Björn has something.'

'I have,' the detective said, consulting his notes. 'Sergeant Massimo Tacchini called about an hour ago. He has contacted Carlotta's parents. They are planning to come to Iceland as soon as they can. Tomorrow if possible.'

'What did he say about Carlotta?'

'She was studying for a PhD at a university in Italy. Padua. Sergeant Tacchini said you could call him tomorrow morning. He gave me Carlotta's phone number.'

'That's something. Get on to the phone companies. See if you can put together a call history while she was in Iceland. And locations.'

'I'll do that.'

'Was there nothing else?'

'It was difficult. I don't speak Italian.'

'Doesn't he speak English?'

Björn reddened. 'He does. Mine isn't so good.'

'Have you got his number? I'll call him now.'

'He said he was going home. But he will be in tomorrow morning. Here is the number.' Björn handed Magnus a Post-it.

'OK,' said Magnus. 'Jón Kári. We'll have a case meeting at eight tomorrow morning. In the meantime, I'm going to talk to the TV documentary crew. They were the last people to see Carlotta alive.'

CHAPTER 6

THEY WERE STAYING in the Hótel Tindastóll just a little way down the old main street. Magnus gathered the five of them in the cosy basement dining room, which was otherwise empty, since it was only used for breakfast or as a bar for residents. He recognized Eygló, with her spiky blonde hair and big blue eyes, from the television, although she was shorter than he expected. Next to her at one of the tables lounged a tall man with longish fair hair and a nice growth of stubble: Einar, the archaeologist. Suzy Henshaw was the English producer; her dark eyes stared at Magnus with something close to hostility from a thin, lined face under black curls. Next to her sat a young thin British-Asian guy with big, startled eyes, Ajay Jassal, the sound man, trying to make himself look as small as possible. Lastly, the cameraman, a tough-looking man of about the same age as Suzy, brooded at his own table a little away from the others, nursing a beer. He too was English and his name was Tom Loudon. He was the only one who was drinking.

The atmosphere was tense, a mixture of anxiety, shock and gloom, except for Suzy who looked irritated. Ajay seemed on the verge of tears. The typical response from a group of ordinary people who had been confronted by a murder.

'Thank you for seeing me,' said Magnus in English, taking a seat next to them. 'I know you spoke with my colleagues this morning and have given written statements, but I'd like to go over what you said again.'

'All right,' said Suzy Henshaw in a tone that suggested that she thought it was only just all right.

'Einar, you were the one who spoke to Carlotta, right?'

39

'That's right,' said Einar.

'What exactly did she say?'

'I'm not sure. Something like "Do you know if this church is open?"'

'I see. And what did you say?'

'"Yes, it is." I mean, it obviously was. We were standing right there in the open doorway.'

'And what did she say?'

'I don't know. "Thanks", I guess.'

'Then what happened?'

'She looked into the church.'

'Did she actually go in?'

'No.'

'Then what did she do?'

Einar visibly fought to control his impatience. 'I don't know. She left. I was watching Eygló and the others. Trying to hear what Eygló was saying.'

'I saw her leave,' said Eygló.

'Which way did she go?'

'To the churchyard gate. And then back towards the museum.'

'I see.' This was mighty thin, Magnus thought. 'Einar, did she seem agitated to you?'

Einar thought a moment. 'No.'

'Are you sure?'

Einar took a breath as if biting back a comment. 'No, I'm not sure. The truth is I was ignoring her. I was concentrating on the filming, as I told you.' Einar's disdain for a tourist asking stupid questions was entirely believable.

'Did any of you see her anywhere else yesterday?'

Magnus looked around the five people. Silence.

'Had any of you seen her before anywhere?'

Shaking of five heads. But Eygló, Eygló seemed thoughtful.

'Are you sure?' Magnus looked directly at her.

She met his gaze, and shook her head again. 'No. I'm sure.'

'And you didn't see her speaking with anyone else apart from Einar?'

More shaking of heads.

'All right,' said Magnus. 'Thank you very much.'

'Is that it?' said Suzy Henshaw. 'We waited here all day just for that?'

'Yes, thank you. I appreciate your cooperation,' said Magnus. 'It is a murder inquiry. I'd be grateful if you could let me know anything that occurs to you, however minor it may seem. We don't have much to go on at this point.'

'But you have no objection if we go to Snaefellsnes tomorrow?' said Suzy.

Magnus shook his head. 'We have your cell-phone numbers if we need you.' Suzy was right: talking to them again had been pointless. They had nothing more to say. Except for Eygló, maybe.

Magnus handed each of them one of his cards. Maybe Eygló would call him back with something. You never knew.

'So you're going to Snaefellsnes?' he said to her. 'Gudrid's farm at Laugarbrekka?'

'You are very well informed,' said Eygló. 'There and Ólafsvík.'

'Ólafsvík? What happened there?'

'You will have to watch the programme to find out,' said Einar.

'She's a fascinating woman, Gudrid,' Magnus said. 'Have you filmed at L'Anse aux Meadows yet?'

'We have,' said Eygló. 'And Nantucket. We are flying to Greenland later this week.'

'Nantucket?' said Magnus. 'Do you think they got as far south as Nantucket?'

'They may have done,' said Einar. 'We have found some evidence to suggest so.'

As a boy, Magnus had devoured the sagas, and, unsurprisingly for an Icelander in America, the two Vinland sagas had been among his favourites.

The Vikings often stopped at a place called 'Leif's Booths' somewhere on the North American coast, possibly the modern L'Anse aux Meadows. Gudrid and her husband Thorfinn had ventured a long way south from there to somewhere they named Hóp. There had been much speculation as to where that might

41

be. Possible locations that Magnus had read about included the St Lawrence River, Nova Scotia, Rhode Island and even New York Harbour. But he hadn't heard that Nantucket was a candidate.

'What evidence?'

'As I said, you will have to watch the programme.'

'I'll be sure to do that,' said Magnus. 'So you think Hóp is in Nantucket?'

'It could well be,' said Einar.

'And that's where Gudrid and Thorfinn spent a couple of summers,' said Eygló.

'That's fascinating. What about Rome? Gudrid went to Rome, didn't she?'

'We're going in two weeks' time,' said Suzy. 'After Greenland.'

A thought occurred to Magnus. 'And you are sure none of you know anything about Carlotta?'

Silence.

Later that evening, as Eygló made her way up the steep wooden stairs to the *Gudrídur Thorbjarnardóttir* room, she felt herself shaking again. She had held it together pretty well in front of the others, and had resisted the temptation to have a drink. Her brain, her whole body, was still trying to process the shock of discovering the dead woman. She hoped she would be able to get to sleep that night without the image of the poor girl's crushed skull haunting her, but she knew there was little chance of that.

She briefly closed her eyes and instantly she was back in the churchyard in Glaumbaer staring down at the bloody mess at her feet.

She was stuck with it, probably forever.

She thought about the big red-haired detective with the perfect American accent and the detailed knowledge of the sagas. She could see he had guessed that there was something she wasn't sure about, something she wasn't telling him.

And he was right.

CHAPTER 7

THE SAUDÁRKRÓKUR POLICE had booked Magnus a room at a small guesthouse that was cheaper than the Hótel Tindastóll, unsurprisingly. Magnus woke up at 6 a.m. and after a quick breakfast rang Milan from his hotel room.

Sergeant Tacchini was friendly and seemed helpful, but he didn't really have much information about Carlotta. She lived in a smart suburb of Milan with her wealthy parents; her father owned a textile business. She had spent the last eight years at university in Padua, where she was studying for a PhD. She had gone to Iceland for a brief holiday by herself.

According to her parents and her sister, she had a few friends still in Milan but most of them were in Padua. No enemies. Two casual boyfriends in the last couple of years, neither one serious, neither break-up acrimonious.

No criminal record. No debts – her family was well off and Tacchini had the impression her father would look after Carlotta if she got into financial trouble, or any other kind of trouble for that matter. Her parents insisted that Carlotta had never done drugs, but her sister said she had gone through a phase of smoking marijuana when she was younger. Definitely no serious drug habit. No links to organized crime, either.

No help at all, frankly.

But Tacchini did have two bits of useful information. The first was that Carlotta's parents were catching a flight to Reykjavík via London early that morning. And the other was the subject that Carlotta was studying at the University of Padua.

Archaeology.

Magnus called Vigdís in Reykjavík and asked her to meet the Mondinis' flight at Keflavík International Airport, which was about fifty kilometres west of the capital. He would have liked Vigdís to escort them on a plane up to Akureyri, but she pointed out that the Mondinis had come to see their daughter, or what was left of her, and Carlotta was now in the morgue in Reykjavík. Vigdís couldn't interview them, her English wasn't good enough, so Magnus would have to rely on another detective, or maybe even Thelma. Or drive back down to Reykjavík himself.

There were about a dozen officers crammed into the squad room at the eight o'clock meeting, including Jón Kári, Árni, Björn, two other detectives from Akureyri, the local assistant prosecutor and a handful of uniforms. And Edda, who was staying at another guesthouse in Sauðárkrókur. Not much for a murder investigation, although Magnus had had many successes in Boston with fewer resources.

This one stumped him, though. So far.

Edda reported the results of the forensics team's investigation. While they had filled plenty of evidence bags from the churchyard, there was nothing that indicated an obvious link to a murderer. The overnight rain had made it impossible to tell if Carlotta had been killed somewhere else in the churchyard and dragged behind the church. A preliminary investigation of the victim's vehicle had found nothing of interest, but they were transporting it down to Reykjavík that morning to go over it more thoroughly. Carlotta's car keys were in the pocket of her jeans, but so near the top that they were almost falling out; it was possible the murderer had used them to open her car and then returned them. The keys were clean of fingerprints – even Carlotta's – but it could just be the fabric of the jeans pocket that had rubbed them off. They had checked the spot where the little girl said she saw the man getting into a silver vehicle, a farm track two hundred metres away from the church, and found a faint tyre print that had barely survived the rain. No footprints.

There was little if no new information from any of the other officers, and no obvious places to look. But Magnus wasn't daunted – yet. It was a question of turning over as many stones as possible, and seeing what crawled out from underneath one of them. Something would.

The most important question was whether the killer knew Carlotta. If he, or she, did indeed know her, then Magnus and his team needed to find out more about the victim. Whether she knew anyone in Iceland. Whether she had enemies in Italy. If she had secrets. What those secrets might be.

There was a lot of discussion about her phone and any possible laptop or tablet. Two constables had searched her luggage, which was still in her hotel room in Blönduós – no electronic devices, and there had been none in her car either. Either Carlotta hadn't brought them to Iceland, or the murderer had taken them out of her vehicle.

Björn had got the three Icelandic phone networks working on call records. But the team needed to get into Carlotta's email, which was registered with the University of Padua. To do that they needed the cooperation of the Italian authorities, and a warrant – probably several warrants in triplicate issued in Iceland and Italy. The Italians were not necessarily unwilling, but they had a reputation of being slow and a bit chaotic. Interpol would have to be involved, and prosecutors and judges. There was a well-worn procedure in place for Facebook and the other social media sites, but those too would take time. Jón Kári promised to get on to it.

It was frustrating: who Carlotta had contacted in the last few days would be key.

Then there were her parents. They might be able to help – if the Icelandic police could get more out of them than Sergeant Tacchini had been able to do.

The team needed to piece together what Carlotta had been doing in Iceland. Find out if anyone had seen her between when she left Glaumbaer at seven-thirty and when she had returned later that evening. Where had she gone? The press were all over the story, and Jón Kári could take advantage of that by appealing for information about Carlotta's movements over the previous week. Someone would remember her.

They should also check any Italian tourists staying in the area around Glaumbaer at Varmahlíd, Saudárkrókur, Blönduós and maybe even Akureyri.

Stamps in Carlotta's passport offered up only one trip outside the EU in the last couple of years – a brief visit to the United States via Boston the previous October. Not much help at this stage.

If the killer didn't know Carlotta, then they had to hope forensic evidence would provide some link to a known criminal. Or a local, perhaps? A visitor at the museum that day? They would struggle, unless they discovered a link with the Akureyri rapist; although nothing had been found yet, that was worth pursuing.

They were keeping all avenues open, but at this stage Magnus's instinct, which he shared with the officers in the meeting, was that the killer was known to Carlotta.

He came to a decision. As the meeting broke up he pulled Jón Kári and Árni to one side and told them to coordinate the investigation from Saudárkrókur, while he went down south.

He really needed to get to know Carlotta better and the only way of doing that was speaking to her parents himself.

Magnus enjoyed the long drive down to Reykjavík. He had hoped that it would give him a chance to think over the case, to get some perspective, to work out a new line of attack, but every time he came back to the same thing: find out more about Carlotta.

It was a beautiful morning. The empty road, the mountains, the glimpses of white glacier and grey fjord, the busy rivers running through heathland and lava field, the sheer desolation, even the gusts of wind that buffeted the car, lifted his spirits. Here, in the wilds, he felt like an Icelander; he felt that this was the place he was supposed to be. And now he had a proper case to get his teeth into, he felt he was doing what he was supposed to be doing.

But it hadn't always felt like that in his first month back. Reykjavík was a small town compared to Boston, there was no way around that. And once again he felt like a foreigner. It had been good to see Árni again, and Vigdís had been pleased to see him. But most of the others, even some of those whom he had got to know quite well during his previous stint in the country, seemed to treat him with a certain reserve.

They weren't exactly unfriendly, but they weren't friendly either. Icelanders had so many ties that bound them together: their families, which were vast thanks to the propensity of many of the older generation to have up to nine children; people they knew from school, or from college or university; people from their neighbourhood or the place in the countryside where their grandparents had come from; people they knew from their choir, or the band they used to be in, or the theatre they performed in or the football team they played for, or the host of part-time activities that all Icelanders took part in.

Magnus fit into none of these networks, or virtually none.

He was a foreigner. An Icelandic-speaking Kani Cop.

He had expected this, had been determined not to let it bother him, but it did.

And he still missed Ingileif. It was she who had made Iceland fun, exciting, sexy.

They had managed nearly three years together, but the inevitable had happened and she had drifted off with an airline pilot. Magnus knew she was attracted to him, she might even have loved him, but Ingileif couldn't stay with just one person for ever. Or even for three years.

She had always explained to Magnus that that was the Icelandic way, but he knew it was just an excuse she used. Certainly Icelanders had a more relaxed view of marriage and fidelity than Americans, but there were plenty of them who could sustain a relationship for more than a few years – for life, even. Just not Ingileif.

A week after returning to Reykjavík, Magnus had heard that she had married someone, a wealthy businessman, one of her interior-design clients. Apparently they had a son.

So much for the airline pilot. Maybe she had finally found someone she could be committed to for the rest of her life. Somehow Magnus doubted it. She would find someone else. Perhaps she already had.

Magnus knew that someone else could be him. He hadn't forgotten her, and he was sure that she hadn't forgotten him. If and when they did meet the spark would be rekindled. The fact she was now married would only make it more exciting for her, as would his return to Reykjavík. It would be hard for either of them to resist.

The poor bastard who was her husband would suffer. As would her son. And, inevitably, Magnus.

So he was keeping well clear of her.

His phone rang. It was the hotel in Reykjavík he had been staying at for the last month. He hadn't given up his room for his quick jaunt up to the north.

'When will you be checking out this morning?'

Magnus recognized the manager's voice.

Damn! He had forgotten the previous night was supposed to be his last one.

'Ah, yes, I'm sorry. I've been called to investigate a murder. I haven't had time to arrange something else. Can I stay another three nights?'

'No, Magnús, that is not possible. The hotel is fully booked tonight. And we already gave you an extra week.'

Magnus argued, but lost. It was lucky he hadn't stayed up in Saudárkrókur. He pulled over to the side of the road and dialled the shopkeeper in Breidholt.

'I am sorry, Magnús, I have let the room to someone else. I had not heard from you for several days and she was desperate.'

'But we agreed! I told you I would need the room from the twenty-third.'

'She has already moved in. There is nothing I can do.'

Magnus hung up and stared out of the window of the car at a black-faced sheep, who stared back. He had pulled over at the edge of an old lava field, folds of grey and black stone, nibbled at by green and yellow mosses and lichens. No sign of human habitation as far as the eye could see. Just a couple of sheep.

What now? He didn't have time for this. Finding another hotel room at short notice in peak tourist season would be a pain; it might even be impossible. It would certainly take time, time he didn't have. Could he sleep on someone's floor? Vigdís? He knew she had an apartment in Hafnarfjördur, a few kilometres on the other side of Reykjavík. That might be awkward – there had been a time many years ago when he and Vigdís had overstepped professional boundaries.

Tryggvi Thór.

Why not?

Because Magnus didn't know him. Because there was definitely something fishy about the assault the previous day. Because the nature of that attack suggested he might even be connected to organized crime.

So what? He was a former cop. He had offered. It was a very nice house with a great view of the sea. And it might be interesting.

Magnus called him. 'Tryggvi Thór? You know you said yesterday I could stay with you for a few days? Did you mean that?'

'Certainly,' said the old man, his gruff voice tinged with enthusiasm.

'I'd like to take you up on it.'

'By all means. When would you be coming?'

'Tonight.'

CHAPTER 8

MAGNUS STOPPED OFF at the hotel to pick up his stuff and then went straight to police headquarters on Hverfisgata. The Mondinis were waiting for him in one of the fancier conference rooms in the National Police Commissioner's Office, just around the corner. Detective Constable Róbert had met them at the airport with Vigdís: his English was much better than hers. They had been taken straight to the Commissioner, who had spent half an hour with them to assure them the police were doing everything they could to find the killer. It was a nice touch: murders were uncommon in Iceland, and the murder of a tourist even more so.

Magnus took Vigdís into the interview with him. Vigdís's black skin, which she had inherited from an unknown US serviceman at the NATO base at Keflavík, prompted many Icelanders to assume she was foreign, or at any rate not properly Icelandic, and they frequently tried to speak to her in English. Vigdís was stubborn, and determined that she was as Icelandic as the next blonde-haired blue-eyed pasty-face, and so she refused to converse with anyone in English. Which was sometimes frustrating in police investigations. But over time Magnus had realized that although she didn't speak the language, she did understand it. He valued her opinion on the Mondinis, and he wanted to get her involved in the investigation.

Signor Mondini was a bald man with lively blue eyes and acne-ravaged cheeks. His wife was slightly taller than him, with shoulder-length dark hair and her daughter's long straight nose.

She was heavily made-up, but she couldn't hide the redness around her eyes. They were both wearing jeans, expensive jeans, and well-cut designer jackets.

Wealthy, comfortable, totally devastated.

Magnus's heart went out to them. However many grief-stricken parents he met – or husbands or wives or girlfriends or boyfriends – it always did. Having lost his own father to murder, he understood what it felt like and how important it was to bring the killer to justice. It wasn't really to provide vengeance, or retribution, and it would never bring the victim back to his or her family. But they needed to know that justice had been done.

When he had finally solved his own father's murder, and justice had been done, some of his determination to find other victims' murderers had diminished. But now, watching these two people who had lost a daughter, he felt it come back. It was strange how the empathy which seemed to have left him in Boston was returning. He wasn't sure why.

Magnus introduced himself in English. 'I have just come from Glaumbaer where your daughter was killed,' he said. 'First off, do you have any questions about what happened to Carlotta?'

They did, and Magnus answered them carefully, very aware as he did so how little progress the investigation had achieved to date. Signor Mondini took the dominant role in asking the questions, but his wife's English was better. Magnus explained that the Mondinis couldn't see Carlotta until the autopsy had been performed, but that should happen later that afternoon.

'Now, I have some questions for you,' he said. 'Tell me about your daughter.'

'She was beautiful,' said Signor Mondini. 'And I don't just mean physically. She had a beautiful soul. And she was very intelligent.'

'She had so many friends,' said her mother. 'Everybody loved her, all her friends. They all knew they could turn to her when they were in trouble.'

Magnus let them talk, talk through the generalities of what a wonderful daughter Carlotta had been, and then talk about her childhood, her school, her teachers, her school friends, her university career, her love of history and archaeology. Naturally she had had boyfriends, decent men; what man would not be interested in Carlotta? She had had a glittering career in academia ahead of her, if she wanted it, although really there were many fields in which she could have excelled.

Through all this tears fell, from both the mother and the father.

They loved to talk about her, and Magnus was finally building up a picture of a kind, clever girl, who could be stubborn and liked to get her own way.

'Presumably Carlotta had a computer?' Magnus asked.

'Of course,' said her father. 'An HP laptop.'

'Do you know if she took it with her to Iceland?'

'She was certain to have. She took it with her everywhere. Why?'

'We haven't found it,' Magnus said. 'Nor her phone.' The murderer must have taken her laptop too. Presumably from her car. The detailed forensic analysis of the car hadn't come back yet: maybe it would show something.

'Why do you think Carlotta picked Iceland for a vacation?' he asked.

'Oh, she loved Iceland,' said Signora Mondini. 'She was always talking about it.'

'Had she been before?'

'No, never,' said her mother. 'But she had always wanted to go. She had been to Sweden. Norway with us. Even Greenland.'

'So she liked Nordic countries?'

'Oh, yes. And of course that was her speciality. The Vikings. Viking archaeology. She loved all that ever since we took her to the Viking Ship Museum in Oslo when she was twelve.'

'She much preferred the Vikings to the Romans,' said her father. He smiled. 'She was like that. She liked to take the opposite point of view to everyone else. Including me.' He took a deep breath, fighting back the tears.

'Ah.' Stupidly, Magnus had assumed that an Italian archaeology student would be interested in Italian archaeology. 'Had she ever been on a dig in Iceland?'

'No, I don't think so.'

'No,' said Signora Mondini with more conviction. 'Not Iceland.'

'Where, then?' said Magnus.

'Sweden. And Greenland. Six years ago, when she was an undergraduate. She loved it.'

'I see,' said Magnus. 'And do you know where this dig was in Greenland?'

'It was where that famous Viking came from. The one that they say discovered America.'

'Leif Erikson?' said Magnus. Gudrid's brother-in-law and Erik the Red's son.

'Yes. That's the name.'

Magnus felt excitement building. Here was the lead he had been waiting for. Could it be a coincidence that a TV crew at the murder scene were planning to travel to a place where the murder victim had worked several years before?

Actually, it could. Maybe the same thing that had brought Eygló and her colleagues to Glaumbaer had brought Carlotta: an interest in Gudrid.

'Did Carlotta have any friends in Iceland?'

'Not that we know of,' said Signor Mondini.

'What about that man she met in Greenland?' said Signora Mondini to her husband. 'The director of the site. Do you remember him? He was from York University in England, but I'm sure he was an Icelander.'

Her husband shook his head.

'Yes, you do. She used to talk about him sometimes. She thought he was a very clever man. Inspiring.'

'What was his name?' said Magnus.

'I can't remember,' said Signora Mondini. 'Wait a moment. Erik? Enrik?'

Magnus waited. He would prefer it if she could come up with the name herself. In the end he helped her.

'Was it Einar? Dr Einar Thorsteinsson?'

CHAPTER 9

'**N**OT MUCH PROGRESS on the Italian tourist case, I see?'
Detective Superintendent Thelma was examining her computer screen, which was no doubt filled with reports from Saudárkrókur. Magnus had been called into her office as soon as he had finished with the Mondinis.

'I need hardly tell you that this is a high-profile case and will remain so until it's solved. Tourists don't come to Iceland to be murdered; there are plenty of places they can go in the United States for that.'

Thelma had recently started wearing reading glasses, and she was working on her stare over the rims. She was doing a good job.

She had a reputation for being tough – any woman rising as high as she had in the ranks of the Metropolitan Police would have to be – but she was also smart. She had taken over from Magnus's old boss, Baldur, following a reorganization while Magnus was in Boston, and had been in the job for three years. She was in her early forties – not much older than Magnus – with short blonde hair and a square jaw. She walked with a barely perceptible limp on the false leg she had acquired when she was a junior police officer after a car chase on Saebraut that went wrong.

Unlike her predecessor, Thelma appreciated Magnus's experience and didn't seem threatened by him. Magnus wasn't sure whether this was because she was impressed with his talent, or because she thought it wise to support the Commissioner's pet ideas. Probably the latter.

Magnus ignored the crack about the States. It was more accurate than many he had received over the years. 'Actually, we might have had a breakthrough. I've just been speaking to the victim's parents, and it turns out there is a connection between Carlotta and one of the TV crew who were filming at Glaumbaer. Einar Thorsteinsson.'

'Connection?'

'The mother says they were friends. After Carlotta went on an archaeological dig in Greenland supervised by Einar in 2011.'

'Just friends?'

'We'll see,' said Magnus. 'I'm going up to Ólafsvík to interview him this afternoon. I'm taking Vigdís.'

Thelma raised her eyebrows. 'Who have you left in charge of the investigation in Saudárkrókur?'

'Árni Holm.'

More raised eyebrows, this time with some justification. Magnus knew that the senior investigating officer was supposed to stay at the physical heart of the investigation.

'Jón Kári will help him – he knows what he is doing. I feel it's more likely that Carlotta was killed by someone known to her. If that's the case, then we need to track down everyone Carlotta knew who is in Iceland. And she knew Einar.'

'You *feel*?'

Fair question. 'I'm not ruling out that she was killed by a stranger. In fact, that's what most of the team are working on now.'

Magnus waited as Thelma examined him. Then she nodded. 'Keep me informed. I'll need answers when the Commissioner asks me about progress.'

'I will.'

Magnus got up to leave the office. He hesitated at the door. 'Thelma?'

'Yes?'

'Did you ever know a cop called Tryggvi Thór? Tryggvi Thór Gröndal?'

Thelma looked up at Magnus, thought for a moment and shook her head. 'Must have been before my time. Why?'

'Nothing,' said Magnus.

On his way back to his desk, he wondered at Thelma's answer. She must have been in the police department for almost twenty years. So it was odd that she had immediately assumed that Tryggvi Thór was before her time, unless she knew something about him already, like his age or the fact that he was retired.

Was it odd? Or was it a natural assumption? Magnus wasn't sure.

An email from Sergeant Tacchini in Milan was waiting for him. A friend of Carlotta's, Federico Trapanese, had been in touch. Federico had been discussing something to do with Iceland with Carlotta; Tacchini wasn't sure of the significance, but Federico was willing to speak to Magnus on Skype. Tacchini had left Federico's email address.

Magnus sent Federico a quick message, and within a couple of minutes he was in an interview room with the image of an anxious Italian student staring at him from a computer screen. Federico Trapanese was a thin young man with curly hair and startled brown eyes. Fortunately, his English was excellent.

'I understand you were a friend of Carlotta Mondini?' Magnus said.

'Not a friend, really. More a friend of a friend,' Federico replied.

'So how do you know her?'

'I met her last year,' Federico said. 'I had been in Rome doing some research for my dissertation.'

'What happened?'

'I stumbled across something there, in Rome. Something extraordinary. Something I found hard to believe ...'

CHAPTER 10

FEDERICO'S PULSE QUICKENED as he passed along the avenue behind the enormous bulk of St Peter's Basilica to the entrance of the Vatican Secret Archives and showed his card to the Swiss Guards in their absurd yellow-and-blue-striped uniforms. Like most historians, he loved libraries, especially old ones: the smell, the silence, the atmosphere of reverence for ancient learning and the ghosts of past scholars. The exclusivity of this one and the fact it was guarded by big men in pyjamas added to its allure. He collected the volume waiting for him at the distribution desk in the Index Room and went through to the Reading Room, where he was pleased to see that the desk he had occupied the day before was vacant.

In fact, there were only three other scholars in the room, which made a wonderful change from the crowds of tourists in Rome that week after Easter, 2016.

The desk was a beautiful mahogany construction, and it stood next to one of the tall windows that overlooked the Cortile della Biblioteca, a tiny courtyard in the middle of the Vatican complex. Federico plugged his laptop into a discreet socket and carefully opened the book in front of him.

The Vatican Secret Archives weren't strictly secret, although access was very much restricted. The 'Secret' in the title really meant private: the library housed centuries of private papers and books from popes through the ages, but access was granted to a limited number of carefully vetted scholars.

Of whom Federico was now one. He was spending a week in Rome researching Italian missionaries to China in the seventeenth century, and his supervisor back at the University of Bologna had secured him access to the library to seek out reports sent by these priests back to the Pope in Rome. They were all in the form of handwritten letters, but the volume in front of him was the printed memoir of a seventeenth-century Italian ship's captain who had sailed to China and the New World. On one of his voyages, the captain had transported two of the missionaries Federico was studying.

The book had been printed in 1658, and it looked as if scarcely anyone had read it since then. Wearing white cotton gloves, Federico leafed through and found the relevant voyage. He spent a couple of hours or so deciphering the narrative and typing up notes. Then he gave himself a break and grabbed a shot of coffee from the little kiosk in the courtyard below his window. When he returned to his desk, he idly leafed through the rest of the book.

Four pages from the back, pressed so flat that it was easy to miss, he came across three sheets of paper covered in brown writing. Old paper. Ancient paper.

Curious, he carefully extracted the sheets and laid them out on his desk. He glanced around him: the reading room was almost empty.

He examined the letter, for that was clearly what it was.

What he read startled him. The text was written in a Genoese dialect, with which he was only slightly familiar. He rushed back to the Index Room and the librarians directed him upstairs to the Sisto V room, where he found a Genoese dictionary.

He spent the rest of the afternoon painstakingly translating the letter into modern Italian. Then he transcribed the original on to his laptop. And then, when he was sure no one was looking, he took surreptitious photographs of it with his phone.

Finally, when he had done all of that, he took the book and the letter to the distribution desk to tell them what he had found.

A week later, back in Bologna, Federico was having a quick cup of coffee with an old friend of his, Guido, a fellow graduate student in history. They were sitting outside a little café in an alley just off the Piazza Scaravilli, which was perfectly placed to give its customers a choice of morning spring sunshine or shade. They had chosen the sun.

'So how was Rome, Federico? Were the secret archives all they are cracked up to be?'

'Yeah, I'd say so. And I found something; something pretty incredible.'

'In the library?'

'Stuffed in the back of the memoirs of a ship's captain. It was a letter from Christopher Columbus to his younger brother Bartholomew in Lisbon. Written in Galway in 1477. Can you believe it?'

'Jesus!' Guido, usually unflappable, sat upright. 'What the hell was that doing there?'

'It contained notes made by Christopher Columbus about his visit to Iceland on an English ship from Bristol. It describes a failed attempt they made to get to Greenland. And then, while Columbus was in Iceland, a priest told him about the sagas which described the Viking exploration of North America. Columbus wrote it all down, including detailed navigational instructions from Greenland to some place called Hóp, which is somewhere on the Atlantic coast of what the Icelanders called Vinland. That's America. I suppose someone way in the past must have thought it was relevant to my seventeenth-century ship captain's travels and stuffed the letter in his memoirs.'

'You're right, that *is* incredible! Where is Galway? Scotland?'

'Ireland. It seems Columbus stopped there on his way back from Iceland.'

'So what did you do with the letter?'

'I handed it in to the library staff. But I made a copy and took some pictures. Here.'

Federico fiddled with his phone and showed a picture to his friend.

Guido whistled. 'Cool! Is it real, do you think?'

Federico smiled ruefully. 'The Vatican don't think so, but they said they would get it analysed and let me know. I spoke to my supervisor here about it and he said that there is no chance it's authentic. Apparently there is a reference to a visit to Iceland in 1477 in Columbus's letters, but it's all vague. And by that time the Icelanders would have forgotten all about America, if in fact the Vikings ever did get there. He says that the Icelanders and the Norwegians are desperate to prove that the Vikings discovered America before Columbus, and one of them will have faked it. There are a lot of Columbus forgeries.'

'But the Vikings did discover America, didn't they?' Guido said.

'It all depends what you call "discover",' said Federico.

Guido frowned. 'But if that letter *is* real, it would mean that Columbus knew all about America before he went there.'

'Er, yes,' said Federico.

'That would be awkward.'

'It certainly would.'

'Is that why the Vatican say it's a forgery?'

Federico shrugged.

Guido raised his eyebrows. 'So what are you going to do?'

'There's not much I can do. It's up to others to decide if the letter is authentic. I'm sure if it is they will let me know. And I know nothing about the Vikings myself. My supervisor was pretty firm that I should ignore it.'

'That's a shame,' said Guido.

'That's right. I mean, it's not every day you discover something like this, is it? If they can prove it's a fake, fair enough. But until then, someone should do some checking.'

Guido finished his coffee and glanced at his watch. 'Look, I've got to go. But there's a girl I know from home in Milan who is studying archaeology at Padua. She's a real expert on the Vikings. And she's nice; I'm sure she'd be helpful. Why don't you get in touch with her?'

'OK. Thanks, Guido, I might just do that.'

'Look her up on Facebook and tell her I said you contact her. Her full name is Carlotta Mondini.'

Carlotta responded enthusiastically to Federico's approach, and three days later she took the train from Padua to Bologna and met him at the same café. Federico was immediately taken with her: slender body, long dark hair, quick, intelligent eyes. It was hard not be flattered by her eagerness to meet him.

He had printed off the images he had taken of the letter, and had polished up his translation of the Genoese with the help of a friend. She took the copy of the letter from him eagerly, and then scanned the translation.

'This is amazing!' she said. 'If this is true and Columbus knew about America all along ...'

'I know,' said Federico. '*If* it's true.'

'Have they analysed the paper?'

'The Vatican are working on it.'

'But you said they have determined it's a forgery?'

'That's their initial opinion. And my supervisor agrees with them.'

'And why is that?'

'They just think it is implausible that the Icelanders could have known about America at that time. Even if some of them did travel there four hundred years before, they were just a peasant society, very poor and illiterate, and they would have forgotten it by then. That's assuming Columbus was even able to communicate with them about it.'

Carlotta burst out laughing.

Federico couldn't help smiling in response, but he also coloured with embarrassment. 'What is it?'

'That's so typical! Nobody in this country takes the Vikings seriously.'

'What do you mean?'

'There are two sagas which describe the discovery of Vinland, as the Norse called America. Some of the most beautiful copies of those sagas come from the fifteenth century, which is when Columbus visited Iceland. Literacy was as high in Iceland as anywhere else in Europe at the time. So yes, the locals would certainly have known about the discovery of Vinland. And their priests would have been able to speak to Columbus in Latin.'

'So you think Columbus did hear about Vinland?'

Carlotta paused. 'Thinking about it, if he did visit Iceland, it's hard to see how he couldn't have done. What's fascinating is the navigational descriptions in this letter about where the Vikings went in Vinland. I reread the two sagas yesterday, and this is more detailed.'

'So you think the letter could be real?'

'It could,' said Carlotta. 'Obviously if they find the paper is modern, then that would rule it out, but to discount it just because they think the Icelanders would have forgotten about Vinland in 1477 is plain wrong.'

'Oh,' said Federico.

'Aren't you excited?' Carlotta asked.

'Oh, yes. Yes, of course.'

'Let me guess,' said Carlotta. 'Your supervisor doesn't want you to get involved?'

Federico nodded.

'Well, thank you for showing it to me anyway,' Carlotta said. She pointed to the images of the letter. 'Can I take these with me?'

'Sure,' said Federico. 'I'd like you to. I think someone should take this seriously. Just keep my name out of it if you can.'

'Did you see Carlotta again after that?' Magnus asked

'No. That was the only time. But she sent me a couple of emails to let me know how she was getting on.'

'Did she authenticate the letter?'

'She did. It turned out the paper was made in the fifteenth century in Venice. Apparently she got some experts to go to the Vatican and examine it, and they said it was real. The hand-writing looked like Columbus's, although he didn't usually write in Genoese. I was expecting to hear a lot more about it – I was relieved when I hadn't – until I got an email from a British TV company who are doing a documentary on a Viking woman who went to America. They wanted to interview me; I said no.'

'Why?'

'It's clear my supervisor doesn't want to know; the whole

faculty doesn't want to know. It's a sensitive subject. And I have my career to think about.'

'Why is it so sensitive?' Magnus asked.

Federico shifted in his chair. 'For us Italians, Columbus discovering America is a big deal. He might have been working for the Spanish government, but we view him as one of ours: he is one of the greatest Italians. I mean, we know he was actually looking for a route to China, and he probably didn't realize he had discovered a new continent, but it was a great achievement. We are all proud of him from the time when we are little kids and we first hear about him at school.'

Federico was becoming animated. His body was moving, as were his hands.

'If it turns out he actually knew about America all along from the Icelanders, it would be ...' He grimaced. 'It would be a betrayal of all we knew. It would be a disaster.'

'But aren't professional historians supposed to be seeking out the truth?'

'Oh, yes,' said Federico. 'Yes, certainly. And the Vatican has experts; the faculty here are experts. I am sure they are correct when they say it is a fake.'

Magnus was silent.

'Look. The only reason I came to you was because Guido told me the poor woman has been murdered,' said Federico. 'I don't want to start a battle with my own faculty.'

'I understand,' said Magnus. 'Thank you for getting in touch with us.'

As Federico's image faded from the screen, Magnus wondered whether Einar knew about Federico's discovery. He must do. The whole TV crew must do.

Magnus needed to get to Ólafsvík.

CHAPTER 11

IT WAS TWO and a half hours from Reykjavík to Ólafsvík, and Magnus was glad that Vigdís was willing to do the driving. They retraced Magnus's route of that morning north to Borgarnes, and then they took the dramatic road along the west coast through lava fields and beneath glowering mountains towards Snaefellsnes. On a clear day, Magnus could see the snow-topped peak of Snaefellsjökull floating above Faxaflói Bay from his window in police headquarters in Reykjavík. But that afternoon, the mountains that formed the spine of the peninsula were covered in thick grey cloud.

Magnus filled Vigdís in on the details of the case as they drove, and spoke to Árni on his phone for updates from Saudárkrókur. The only information of any note was that a couple of French tourists had seen a lone young woman with short, streaked blonde hair standing next to a small blue car parked in a lay-by a few kilometres east of town, looking out at the island of Drangey. They had pulled up next to her to share the view. They reckoned the time was between eight and eight-thirty on Monday evening.

If that was Carlotta, it suggested she had driven north from Glaumbaer after her visit there. It sounded as if she was killing time, rather than rushing to meet someone or to do something.

'What did Thelma say when you told her you were bringing me with you?' asked Vigdís.

'Nothing,' said Magnus.

'Nothing? Are you sure? She didn't suggest taking Róbert instead?'

'Well, she raised her eyebrows.'

'I thought so!' Vigdís's lips pursed in frustration.

'That's all she did, Vigdís. It doesn't mean anything.'

'Of course it does. She's undermining your confidence in me.'

Magnus snorted. 'That's dumb, Vigdís, and you know it. What is your problem with her, anyway? She's got to be an improvement on Baldur.' Baldur hadn't liked either of them, basically for who they were. Magnus was a smart-arsed American and Baldur had no idea how anyone could think a black woman could possibly be a detective in Iceland. As far as he was concerned, both of them had been foisted on him by a commissioner who had been swayed by the glamour of foreign ideas. But Baldur was gone now, to sap the spirits of the Traffic Department. Thelma was much more modern in her outlook. She had even spent two years doing a masters in criminology somewhere in the States.

'At least with Baldur you knew who you were dealing with. I can handle reactionary Icelandic males. But Thelma is different.'

'What do you mean? Do you think she has a problem with your colour?'

'No.'

They drove on in silence for a couple of kilometres. The lonely crater of Eldborg emerged from the moisture-filled gloom ahead of them, a ring of rock rising a hundred metres above the rough field of mossy lava.

'Is she the reason why you haven't been promoted?'

'Yes,' Vigdís said. 'No doubt about it.'

'Why?' asked Magnus. 'Did you screw up somehow?'

'Oh, thanks for the vote of confidence, Magnús.'

'Hey, Vigdís, I've seen you break the rules many times. I would never doubt your competence, but I would doubt your ability to do what you are told. Just like I'd doubt myself.'

'Fair enough,' said Vigdís. 'But actually without you around these last few years, I have been remarkably obedient. No, she just doesn't like me.'

'Why not?'

'It took me a while to figure it out. She is one of the two or three successful women in the police. And she had to fight hard to get there, especially when she lost her leg. She was twenty-six then, she could have been invalided out, but she insisted on staying on, and – to their credit – they let her. She's ambitious, she's tough as nails and she's successful. She used to be my role model.'

'Used to be? What's wrong with her?'

'Most women get intimidated or angry when they are the only female in the room, but Thelma likes it. She can handle the men, but she's scared of the women. Since she became head of the department, we haven't taken on a single woman. They've all been men. And it makes me sick.'

'Are you sure?'

'Oh, I'm quite sure. She knows I know. And she knows I don't like it.'

'You're just imagining it, Vigdís. She really doesn't seem like the jealous type to me.'

'You watch her,' said Vigdís. 'Next time you're in a meeting with her and some other men and a woman – me, for instance – you watch her. You'll see what I mean.'

Magnus shook his head.

Vigdís smiled wryly. 'But you'll be OK. At least if I never get promoted you'll still have me to drive you around.'

They headed west and the clouds lifted, shredding on the spine of the mountain range, letting columns of yellow sunshine streak through. They climbed the pass between the south side of the Snaefellsnes peninsula and the north. As they crested the ridge a familiar view spread out before them: the southern shore of Breidafjördur, or Broad Fjord, with its multitude of islands and the West Fjords in the distance.

Two farms clung to the shoreline, separated by a mile of tumbling frozen lava: the Berserkjahraun or Berserkers' Lava Field, named after the two Swedish warriors who had lain buried there for a thousand years.

It was at the farm on the left, Bjarnarhöfn, that Magnus and his little brother Ollie had spent four miserable years of their childhood being looked after by their grandparents. It was at this farm that the key to the murder of Magnus's father in Massachusetts had lain. And it was at Bjarnarhöfn, seven years before, that Magnus had found the body of his own grandfather, who had caused him and his whole family so much pain over the years.

Vigdís glanced at him as she guided the car down towards the plain by the shore. 'Have you been back here?'

'No. Or at least, not since I left Iceland last time. The place is now farmed by my uncle and his wife. I suppose I should go and see them. It's difficult.'

Bjarnarhöfn was the location where Magnus's whole family had been blown apart, collateral damage everywhere. He had done his bit to pick up the pieces immediately afterwards, but he hadn't even told them he was back in Iceland.

'I remember them,' said Vigdís. 'Do you want to stop there now for half an hour?'

'No. We had better get on to Ólafsvík.'

They both knew they could spare half an hour, but Vigdís didn't argue.

They reached the main road running along the coast and turned left, west towards Ólafsvík. Bjarnarhöfn was only a couple of kilometres away, over the heaving and swirling lava field that Magnus remembered so well.

'Is Ollie out of jail?' Vigdís asked.

'Soon. October. He made parole: good behaviour, amazingly enough.'

'Have you seen him?'

'Yeah.'

'Sounds like it didn't go well?'

'No. He blames me for putting him inside.'

'What does he expect? You had to testify. You couldn't lie.'

'I think he thinks I should have done.'

Ollie had been in Iceland when their grandfather had been murdered. But he had been imprisoned in the States for the peripheral role he had played in that other murder nearly twenty years earlier, of their father. The district attorney had called

Magnus as a witness. As a police officer, he couldn't very well refuse to testify, nor could he not tell the truth. And, actually, Ollie deserved to face trial for what he had done. But Ollie didn't see it that way. He thought his big brother, who had stood by him all his life, had finally turned against him.

Part of Magnus agreed with him. But once Ollie was out on the streets he would want to take his revenge on Magnus, in ways petty and not so petty. Ollie had always been an expert in manipulating his elder brother's desire to protect him. Magnus had had enough; now he was in Iceland Ollie would just have to face Boston on his own.

The car sped on and Bjarnarhöfn disappeared behind its mountain.

Forty kilometres further on, they rounded Búland Head, a dramatic bulge of rock pushing out into Breidafjördur, and the small town of Ólafsvík appeared before them: a cluster of houses, a harbour, some fish-factory sheds and a hypermodern church nestled against a steep slope of rock, moss and water.

Magnus called Suzy and told her that he was on his way back to Reykjavík from Saudárkrókur and just wanted to confirm a couple of small points. She said they were filming outside the Pakkhúsid in the middle of town.

CHAPTER 12

THE PAKKHÚSID WAS the only really old building in Ólafsvík: a brown wooden warehouse dating from the mid nineteenth century. As Vigdís and Magnus got out of the car, a distinct smell of fish enveloped them. Ólafsvík was still very much a working fishing port, and a good number of small boats bobbed and clanked in the harbour.

Suzy and Tom were standing next to a camera on a tripod, which was pointing towards the old wooden building. Ajay was holding a boom mic which stretched out towards Eygló and a balding middle-aged man, who was wearing a snazzy pink hooped scarf jauntily tied. The local constabulary were attending the scene to preserve order from the crowds, which consisted of two eight-year-old girls, one with a purple bike and one with a pink one. Magnus recognized the policeman by his magnificent black moustache, Páll, the constable from the neighbouring town of Grundarfjördur.

Páll saw Magnus and Vigdís and started to approach them with a grin, before a look from Magnus stopped him. He returned to keep an eye on the crowd of watchers, which had doubled in size since a couple more schoolgirls had arrived on bikes.

'You've come a long way out of your way,' said Suzy.

'I know, but it's a nice drive,' said Magnus. 'Where's Einar?'

'He's gone off for a wander. He said he would be back in ten minutes, but that was half an hour ago.'

'Shall we go and look for him?' said Vigdís in Icelandic.

'He doesn't know we are here?' Magnus asked Suzy. He had spoken to her only ten minutes before.

'No. No one does. I didn't want to interrupt things. Hopefully this will be the last take of the day. He went to look at the church. I'm sure he'll be back soon. Do you mind if we just get this done?'

It was more of an order than a request. Magnus glanced up at the white church, which was set a little above the town. It was an extraordinary combination of white and grey planes and triangles, graceful in its way. He couldn't see Einar.

'We'll wait,' said Magnus. 'Do you mind if we watch?'

He sauntered over to Constable Páll and his little group of schoolgirls and greeted him.

'I'm going to be questioning a man named Einar Thorsteinsson in a few minutes. Tall guy, late thirties, scrappy beard. We will probably take him to the police station.'

'All right,' said Páll. 'I'll come with you.'

'Thanks. And watch the guy we question. It would be a stupid thing to do, but he might try to make a run for it.'

Magnus returned to Suzy.

'Roll, Tom,' she said. 'Whenever you're ready, Eygló!'

In front of the old warehouse, Eygló took some deep breaths. She spotted Magnus and Vigdís and a look of alarm passed over her face, but only for a second. A few more deep breaths until she was composed again. She smiled.

'This is the old warehouse in Ólafsvík where merchants came from Denmark and elsewhere to store their goods and to pay their customs duty. The warehouse is only a hundred and fifty years old, but merchants have been coming to Ólafsvík for much longer than that. In fact, Ólafsvík was the first town in Iceland to be chartered as a port by the Danish Crown – until 1944 Iceland was a colony of Denmark.'

Magnus wasn't wearing headphones and so he could only just hear what Eygló was saying fifty feet away. But there was something about her voice that thrilled him. Vigdís was listening too.

'Back in the fifteenth century, traders came here from all over Europe, but especially from England. And for centuries before that, Ólafsvík had been one of the main ports for the Greenland trade.' Eygló paused. 'Greenland was an important source of ivory from walrus tusks, and – even more lucratively, and more secretly – of a product which was prized all over Europe.'

Another pause for effect. Eygló cocked her head, tightened her lips, raised the corners of her mouth slightly, preparing her viewers for a surprise.

'Unicorn horn. The long straight single tusk of the narwhal was imported to Iceland from Greenland, whereupon it became magically transformed into the horn of the unicorn, and was sold on to the courts of Europe for a fortune. So the people of Ólafsvík knew Greenland and its Norse settlers well.'

Eygló turned to the middle-aged man. 'This is Professor Marco Beccari of Princeton University, the author of *Thought, Light and New Worlds*, which has revolutionized historians' views on the exploration and conquest of the Americas. So, Professor Beccari, did Columbus discover Iceland?'

The professor grinned and raised his eyebrows, as if surprised by the question. He paused for thought. 'I suppose you could say in a way he did. At least for the Italians and perhaps the Spanish and Portuguese. He visited here in 1477 on an English ship from Bristol, and in a later letter to King Ferdinand and Queen Isabella of Spain he is at pains to describe the country as if he was introducing it to people who had never heard of it. He didn't call it Iceland, but "Thile" after the mythical land of Thule. He seems to have spent several months here; in fact, there is a legend that an Italian nobleman stayed at Ingjaldshóll for the winter, not far from Ólafsvík. The Italians did not know very much about the far north. Neither Italian nor Portuguese ships were permitted to make port in Iceland, which could have been the reason for Columbus's voyage on an English vessel. He writes about exploring the seas to the north of Iceland.'

'Did he find any evidence of a route to America?' Eygló asked. She was looking deeply at the professor, hanging on to his every word. He had a powerful physique and a powerful voice: he spoke clearly and with authority, an authority which seemed to grow under Eygló's gaze. His accent betrayed only a trace of Italian, mixed with British and American tones.

'He may well have done. In his letter he says little about what he learned in Iceland, but he does mention a man and a woman from China of extraordinary appearance washing ashore in Galway in Ireland on two tree trunks. These were presumably two Inuit from Greenland or Northern Canada in a kayak.'

'But we have no evidence that Columbus learned anything of the sagas of Erik the Red and the Greenlanders while he was in Ólafsvík?'

'We didn't, until very recently,' said Beccari. 'But it turns out that the letter to Ferdinand and Isabella was not the only one he wrote about his voyage to Iceland.'

'Cut!' said Suzy. 'That was perfect, Marco. How's the sound, Ajay?'

Ajay gave the thumbs up.

'Is that in the can, Tom?'

Tom nodded.

'OK. Let's do the reverses before we wrap for the day.'

Magnus was fascinated by what Eygló and the professor had said. After his conversation with Federico Trapanese, he was pretty sure what letter the professor was referring to.

His thoughts were interrupted by Vigdís. 'There he is!'

Magnus turned to see the tall figure of Einar striding towards them. He glanced at Páll and nodded. Páll slipped away from the girls, who were still staring at the little show in front of them.

Einar was about thirty yards away before he saw Magnus and Vigdís. He stopped, bowed his head and turned around. Right into the burly, uniformed figure of Páll.

Magnus and Vigdís hurried over.

'Einar. I'd like you to accompany us to the police station. We have some questions we need to ask you.'

Ólafsvík police station was manned by only one officer, Constable Ívar, with the occasional help of Constable Páll. It boasted a tiny interview room and two cells. Einar lounged back in his small wooden chair in the interview room, affecting a casual diffidence. But he was tense.

And so he should be.

Magnus and Vigdís were seated on the other side of the table.

'Tell us about Carlotta, Einar,' Magnus began.

Einar said nothing.

'Tell us how you met her.'

Nothing.

'Greenland?'

Magnus and Vigdís waited. They knew how to wait.

Eventually Einar nodded; he knew they knew. 'All right,' he said. 'I first met her in 2011 on a dig I was supervising. In south-west Greenland. She was an undergraduate student from Padua ...'

CHAPTER 13

EINAR STRODE FROM the little blue schoolhouse they were using as the site lab towards the dig. The damp grass gleamed in the sunshine, a carpet of deep green speckled with yellow and purple flowers. This part of Greenland, the south-western tip, was definitely green, which is why Erik the Red had picked the spot to settle.

It was a perfect place for a landless outlaw from Iceland to claim as his own. Erik's Fjord wound thirty kilometres from Brattahlíd, or Qassiarsuk as it was now known, down to the sea, past formidable mountains which sheltered the farm from westerly gales. But at this point the slopes were gentle, and covered in a thick matting of grass, plenty for the sheep to eat. Erik had nabbed the best site; his companions had built their own farms at various points along this and neighbouring fjords, creating what became known as the 'Eastern Settlement', even though it was on the west coast of Greenland. The 'Western Settlement' was a couple of hundred kilometres further north-west along the coast.

Erik built his farm a hundred metres in from the fjord's edge, just above a brook for fresh water. The scene could have been Iceland or even Scotland, except for a dozen or so serene icebergs drifting up towards the fjord's head from the foot of a glacier just around the corner, twisted sculptures of white and blue. Maybe they were formed from Viking snow that had fallen on Greenland a thousand years before in Erik's time. Possible, although more likely the ice was much older.

Brattahlíd had been a substantial farm, consisting of a long house, various barns and byres, and a tiny little church that had been built by Erik's Christian wife, according to his saga. The site had been excavated in 1932 and again partially in 2005. Unsurprisingly, the 1932 excavation had been an unsubtle affair with trenches and shovels, disrupting the 'contexts' as archaeologists call the layers of soil representing different periods of inhabitation. Brattahlíd had been inhabited from the first settlement of Greenland in about AD 985 until the fourteenth century.

The 2005 excavation had been much more careful, but less extensive, and now Einar was supervising a dig to develop it further. The permafrost in southern Greenland, which had until recently kept Viking artefacts perfectly preserved, was beginning to melt, turning into oxygen-filled slush. Archaeologists had to get a move on if important evidence, especially organic remains, was not to be lost forever.

So far, after five weeks' work, they had turned up very little new. Plenty of bones and beetles and pollen for analysis back in the UK, but, unless they were lucky, not enough yet to justify coming back next year. Einar knew he shouldn't get too downhearted until he had analysed the results himself. He was building a reputation as an expert on the effects of climate change in the Middle Ages on diet, based on studies of what remained of the crops, animals and food, and of medieval excrement. Einar was an expert in Viking shit.

There had been a mini warm period, around the year 1000, when it had been possible to grow grain in Greenland. This had been followed by a cold period from about 1250. Greenland was right at the margin of cultivatable land, sustaining greater or smaller human populations depending on the climate. And in the twenty-first-century climate change was fashionable.

Einar would find some data in there to back up his theory that the warm period was more conducive to agriculture and human habitation in Greenland than people realized. He was good at that, digging around in the data crap to find little jewels of wisdom.

But the treasure hunter within him would have loved to have found a real jewel among all that dirt.

The dig itself was a haphazard rectangle of bare earth, picketed with string and posts, in which a dozen or so people were squatting and scraping. His deputy had returned to York the week before, but there were two competent PhD students from his department and one from Aarhus in Denmark, and a number of undergraduate volunteers from all over the world, all keen, all digging away, all happy to spend their summer vacation in a damp hole in Greenland.

'Einar! I think I've found something!'

It was one of the younger, more inexperienced students, a young Italian woman named Carlotta. She was standing up and waving to him. Despite himself, even after so many years, Einar felt his heart beat slightly faster with the excitement of an unknown discovery.

'What is it?'

'A shell.'

The excitement faded. There were plenty of shells at Brattahlíd – shellfish were a big part of the Norsemen's diet, although oddly fish were not. That was something Einar needed to explain.

'It has a hole in it.'

'Let me take a look.'

It was indeed a shell. A clam. It was half-buried in a wall of one of the previous trench excavations from 1932. It was a light grey, small and round, and there was a perfect hole in the middle of it.

'And look! There might be another one here.'

Sure enough, a tiny sliver of white shell peeked out from the earth.

This was worth taking seriously. Over the next few hours, the archaeologists took photographs and made drawings of the area, before Einar himself slowly and delicately brushed away the soil.

There wasn't just one clamshell, they found six, all with holes. A necklace. Einar had never seen a Viking shell necklace before.

Neither had he seen that kind of clamshell, at least not in the digs around Iceland and Greenland, where the *Arctica islandica* was common. This was something else.

'I know what that is,' said one of the volunteers. He was a genial, tubby American named Craig, from a university in Michigan. A bright kid, Einar had grudgingly recognized. 'It's a hard clam.'

'Are you sure?'

'Sure I'm sure. I go clamming every summer with my aunt on Cape Cod.' He peered at the shells. 'And you know what these might be?'

Einar was irritated. He was the one who was supposed to ask those kinds of questions. But he was also curious. 'What?'

'Wampum. I took a class on Native American archaeology last semester. It's totally wampum.'

The student who had made the find, Carlotta, wasn't classically beautiful, in fact her face was uneven – angles rather than curves, and her nose was too long, but she had eyes that flashed intelligence and enthusiasm for life, and a lithe body, slim, constantly moving. She was easily the most attractive student on the dig, and Einar could tell that he had had her under his spell from the moment he had introduced them all to the site. Out in the field, he could make a site come to life, and that was exactly what any aspiring archaeologist wanted: to live in the past, to feel that they were physically immersed in a world that was centuries old, rather than simply squatting in a ditch in the rain without Wi-Fi.

He had known right away he would sleep with Carlotta. The only question was when.

And the answer was the night after she had discovered the wampum.

Wampum was the name given to intricate strings of beads made of clam- and whelk shells, which were used by Native Americans in what became New England as gifts and a sign of status, and, after the colonists arrived, as currency. But Einar soon discovered that the wampum Carlotta had found was of the most basic kind, consisting only of grey clamshells. It turned out to be the kind used on the island of Nantucket, fifteen miles off the coast of Cape Cod.

Such a find, in the house of Erik the Red, the father of two of the chief explorers of Vinland, Leif and Thorvald Erikson, and father-in-law of another one, Gudrid, was hugely exciting. And worth celebrating.

CHAPTER 14

'WHAT ABOUT LATER?' asked Magnus. 'Did you sleep with Carlotta after Greenland?'

The question of why Einar hadn't told him all this before could wait. First he wanted to get as much out of him as possible.

Einar nodded. 'I suppose you could call it an affair, but it was more like an occasional relationship. Every now and then we would meet up. I was at York University in England then and she was in Padua. Sometimes we would meet in York, sometimes France. We went to Amsterdam once, and Zurich. Venice. Never Iceland.'

'I see,' said Magnus. 'And how long did this affair continue? Or was it still going on when she died?'

Einar's cool crumbled. He closed his eyes and breathed in. When he opened them again, they were moist. 'It ...'

He stopped. Took a breath. Opened his mouth. Closed it again. Swallowed. 'I can't believe she's dead,' he said.

Magnus and Vigdís waited for Einar to regain his composure.

'No. It only lasted a year. My wife was diagnosed with breast cancer. It turned out she knew about Carlotta. She told me to stop and I stopped.'

'Completely? You didn't sleep with her at all after that?'

'No. I mean ...' Einar winced and closed his eyes again, as if ashamed to admit the truth. 'Yes. Once. In Paris last year. But just the once.'

'Was Carlotta happy with that? With "just the once"?'

'Not really,' Einar said. 'But I had promised my wife.'

'Yeah, right,' said Vigdís. Vigdís had a negative view of men's honesty when it came to women, born of harsh experience.

'I'm telling the truth,' Einar said. 'But please don't tell Rósa about the Paris thing. She doesn't know and I don't want her to find out.'

'You should have thought about that before you slept with Carlotta again,' said Vigdís. Magnus was happy to let her needle Einar.

'I know I should!' said Einar, slamming his palm on the table. The sudden outburst took the two detectives by surprise. 'Look, I'm sorry. I know I should have told you all this before. I know I made a mistake, but I am going to rectify that now.'

'You certainly should have told us straight away,' said Magnus. 'Why didn't you?'

'I panicked,' Einar said. 'I didn't want Rósa to find out I had been seeing Carlotta. And I thought you might suspect me of killing her.'

'Indeed we might,' said Vigdís.

'Indeed we do,' said Magnus. 'What was Carlotta doing in Iceland?'

'She came to see me,' said Einar.

'So she could sleep with you?' said Vigdís.

'No!' Einar glared at Vigdís. The needling was working. He fought to control himself. 'No. She came across something in Italy last year: a letter about Columbus and his visit to Iceland. She approached me about it in Paris when I was presenting a paper at the Sorbonne – that was the one and only night we slept together again. We've been corresponding about it since then, but a couple of weeks ago she said she wanted to talk to me about a new development face-to-face.'

'Did you meet in Reykjavík?'

'No. I was determined to avoid seeing her in the flesh.' Einar winced at his own choice of words. 'I said we should discuss it over the phone, but she insisted on meeting up. In the end I relented, but I said definitely not Reykjavík. She could come up to Sauðárkrókur where we were filming.'

'But she saw you in Glaumbaer?'

'Yes. That wasn't part of the plan. She just wanted to …'

'To what?' said Magnus.

'Tease me. Tempt me. I don't know.'

'So then what happened?'

'I told her to go away so that the others wouldn't suspect anything. We were supposed to meet in Saudárkrókur at nine-thirty that evening. She said she would have to make it ten-thirty.'

'Did she say why?'

'No.'

'And you didn't ask?'

'Not at that point. I wanted her to leave me alone. We were standing in front of the church and I knew the others would see us and ask about her, and in fact Eygló did.'

'So none of them knew who she was?'

'No.' Einar shook his head. 'Carlotta and I had agreed to keep her name out of it. The others knew about the Columbus letter, of course, but they didn't know about Carlotta's involvement. Or that she had been a member of the dig in Greenland.'

'I spoke to the guy who found the Columbus letter this morning.'

'Federico Trapanese? Is he here in Iceland?'

'No, he's in Italy; I spoke to him on Skype. Is that the new evidence Professor Beccari was talking about?'

'Yes. It proves that Columbus was told about the Vinland sagas, and it includes sailing directions to a Viking settlement in America.'

'Which one?' said Magnus.

'We think it's Nantucket.'

'Nantucket? Isn't that where you said the wampum you found came from?'

'Precisely.'

'No wonder Carlotta was excited by the letter.'

'Yes. Not only did it show that Columbus knew about America before he discovered it, but also that Gudrid made it as far as Nantucket.'

'So that's why you think Hóp is in Nantucket?'

'That's right,' said Einar.

Magnus remembered the US immigration entry stamp the police had found in Carlotta's passport. Boston. Boston was the nearest international airport to Nantucket.

'Did you go there yourself? Last October?'

'Yes,' said Einar, clearly puzzled at how Magnus knew.

'With Carlotta?'

Einar nodded. 'Yes, with Carlotta. But we didn't sleep together that time, I promise.'

'What *did* you do?'

'It was Carlotta's suggestion. We wanted to see where the Vikings might have settled on Nantucket. We found an old woman there, a historian who happened to have written a book about Gudrid the Wanderer. She knew the lagoon mentioned in the Columbus letter. We are featuring it, and her, in the documentary.' Einar's anxiety deepened. 'I never told Rósa Carlotta came with me. Or Eygló or the others.'

'You wanted to keep it a secret?' said Vigdís.

'Yes. In case my wife got the wrong idea.'

Vigdís looked at him pityingly.

'Back to Monday night,' said Magnus. 'What happened at ten-thirty?'

'We were supposed to meet outside the church in the church square in Saudárkrókur. I got there a little early, maybe ten-twenty-five. Carlotta didn't show. I waited until after eleven, and then went back to the hotel. I texted her to ask where she was, but there was no reply.' Einar swallowed. 'And then, the next morning, I saw her dead behind the church at Glaumbaer. I panicked. I'm ashamed to say my first thought was I didn't want my wife to find out that I had been seeing her.'

'Why not?' said Vigdís.

'In case she thought we were sleeping together.'

'Which would have been a reasonable assumption.'

Einar shrugged. 'Yeah. That's my point.'

'That's really not a good reason for not telling us about your relationship with her,' said Magnus.

81

'In fact, it's a really bad reason,' said Vigdís.

'Yes. I know that. I've been kicking myself all day. I can't believe she's really dead. Even though I saw her body lying there, I couldn't believe it was her.' He blew air out of his cheeks. 'I'm glad I've got the chance to clear things up now.'

'Yeah, right,' said Vigdís again.

'Except things are not really clear, are they?' said Magnus.

'What do you mean?' said Einar.

'Did you kill Carlotta?'

'No!' said Einar. 'Of course not! I've told you, I ...' He hesitated. 'I didn't exactly love her. But I was very close to her. Why would I want to kill her?'

Magnus raised his eyebrows. It was a good question, and one perhaps Einar could answer.

Einar was having none of it. 'Tell me. Why?'

'Take me through what you did the night Carlotta died. You left Glaumbaer at seven-thirty?'

'That's right,' said Einar. 'I had brought my own car and Eygló came with me, with the other two following in their rented Land Cruiser. We drove straight to the Hótel Tindastóll in Saudárkrókur and checked in.'

'Then what did you do?'

'Checked emails for half an hour or so, and went out to a restaurant in town with Eygló and Suzy. Suzy left a little early – she had a headache. I'd say Eygló and I got back to the hotel at maybe nine-forty, nine forty-five. Then at ten-twenty I left to go and meet Carlotta.'

'Did anyone see you?' said Einar.

'I don't know. Maybe the woman at reception, if she was there. The police station is right opposite the church, but I expect that was shut at that time of night.'

'And then what did you do when Carlotta didn't show?'

'Went back to the hotel. And I *think* I said goodnight to the woman at reception, but I can't be sure. I got up early the next morning and met the others in the dining room for a quick breakfast before heading off to Glaumbaer.'

'What colour is your car?' Vigdís asked.

'It's black. A black Toyota RAV4.'

Not the car the local girl had seen the strange man getting into the night Carlotta was killed.

CHAPTER 15

THE OTHERS WERE waiting at their hotel just around the corner from the police station. Einar was stuck in a cell for the time being; Magnus had a few hours before he had to decide whether to formally arrest him.

Eygló was first. Her blue eyes were wide with curiosity.

'Let me ask you again what I asked you in Saudárkrókur,' Magnus began. 'Did you know Carlotta Mondini?'

'No,' said Eygló. 'I had never seen her before.' Those big eyes were all innocence. Magnus felt himself being convinced.

'When I asked you that question in Saudárkrókur, I got the idea that you were hiding something from me.'

Eygló shrugged. Less innocent.

'You see, we now know that Einar knew Carlotta. He knew her very well. She had been a student of his on the dig in Greenland. They had had an affair.'

Eygló's wide eyes widened further. Then she shook her head. 'Oh, Einar.'

'You look surprised?'

'Do I? I don't know why. Einar has an active interest in women. Always has had.' She reddened slightly. 'Me included, a long time ago. He says he's over all that now, but then this woman shows up.'

'Do *you* think he's over it?'

'I don't know,' said Eygló. 'It doesn't look like it. Were they still having an affair when she died?'

'He says not.'

84

Magnus knew she was hiding something. But what?

'Have you ever been to Greenland, Eygló?' Vigdís asked.

Eygló sat motionless.

'Well?'

Eygló blinked.

'Yes. Once.'

'When?'

A pause. 'Several years ago.'

'In 2011?'

Another pause. Then Eygló nodded.

'You went on that dig led by Einar, didn't you?'

Eygló nodded.

'Do you still say you didn't know Carlotta?' Magnus asked.

Eygló glanced at both of them. Then she exhaled. 'All right. I did know Carlotta, but not very well and I hadn't seen her for years. When I found the body, I didn't recognize her at first because she has changed her hairstyle: it used to be long and dark, and now it's short with blonde streaks. I was on that dig in Greenland with her and Einar, but I left a few days before they discovered the wampum. My son had come down with chickenpox back in Iceland.' Eygló winced. 'But then I recognized her name when the police were interviewing me.'

'Why didn't you tell me that when I asked you in Saudárkrókur?'

'I don't know,' said Eygló. 'I didn't want to get Einar into trouble.'

'That's not good enough!' said Magnus. 'This is a murder investigation. We need to get *someone* into trouble. A lot of trouble.'

'I didn't mean that kind of trouble. I mean with his wife. Rósa. She can be very jealous.'

'How do you know Rósa can be very jealous?' Vigdís asked. Magnus could tell she had spotted something. She was clearly better at reading Eygló than he was.

Eygló's cheeks reddened. 'When I was a student at the university, I slept with Einar. And then again when we were both at York University in England. Einar had got me the job there. Einar thought Rósa didn't care, but she did. She told me.'

'Told you what?' said Vigdís.

'To stay away from him.' Eygló shook her head. 'And boy, she meant it. She was pissed off; I mean really pissed off.'

'Sounds fair enough,' said Vigdís.

'Yes. It was. I'm not proud of what I did. I guess I believed Einar when he said his wife knew and didn't care.'

'Did you tell him she had warned you?'

'She asked me not to. By that stage I was so ashamed I just did what she asked.'

'And do you have a sexual relationship with Einar now?' Vigdís asked.

'No way. Not since then. Our relationship is purely professional. We have helped each other over the years. He introduced me to Suzy when she was doing a documentary about York. And I suggested him as an expert for *The Wanderer* documentary series – I knew the wampum find would fit in nicely. He plays it cool, but he loves being on TV.'

Magnus examined Eygló. She looked uncomfortable, as she should; she had been caught lying to the police. Magnus couldn't be sure whether she was telling the truth now. People were always lying to Magnus, but oddly, in Eygló's case, he felt disappointed.

He checked Einar's account of his whereabouts with Eygló. She confirmed that they had driven back to Saudárkrókur together, and that they had both had dinner with Suzy in a restaurant. She also stated she had seen him leaving the hotel later in the evening, and walking along Adalgata towards the church.

So Eygló and Einar's stories matched. No surprise there.

Once Eygló had been escorted from the interview room, Magnus turned to Vigdís. 'That was a great question about Greenland.'

'You seemed to think Eygló was lying about Carlotta. I was just trying to work out how she might have met her.'

'She did lie to us,' said Magnus. 'That's never a good sign.'

'She was covering for Einar. The question is why?'

'Maybe she really did want to protect Einar from his wife finding out about Carlotta?'

'Maybe. Maybe there's another reason.'

'You mean she thinks Einar killed Carlotta?' said Magnus.

'Or she knows he did.'

'And Einar conveniently omitted to tell us that Eygló had been with him and Carlotta in Greenland.'

'There is quite a lot Einar has omitted to tell us.'

'Let's see what the others have to say,' said Magnus. 'I can just about see why Eygló might cover for Einar, but not the others. But first give Árni a call and get him to ask the hotel staff if they saw Einar late that night.'

Vigdís was just finishing her call with Árni when Páll interrupted them. 'Professor Beccari wants to talk to you.'

'Tell him to wait,' said Magnus. 'It's Suzy Henshaw next. We need her to confirm Einar's movements.'

'The professor is quite agitated,' said Páll. 'He has only just found out the name of the victim. He says he knew her.'

Magnus glanced at Vigdís. 'Another one.'

CHAPTER 16

CONSTABLE PÁLL WAS correct: Professor Beccari was indeed agitated. His smooth forehead was glistening, and he started talking as soon as he was shown into the interview room, his hands moving as fast as his lips, his jaunty pink scarf waggling in time with his gestures.

'Suzy said you were enquiring about a murder of a tourist in the north of Iceland, but I had no idea who it was who had been killed,' he explained to Magnus and Vigdís. 'It was only when Einar came out of the interview with you that he told me it was Carlotta. Why he didn't tell me before, I don't know. I cannot believe it. Why would anyone kill her? Was it a rape? I didn't think that kind of thing went on in Iceland? It's appalling news. Appalling.'

'Sit down, professor,' Magnus said. 'And let's take this slowly. I take it you knew Carlotta?'

'Yes. Yes, of course.' The Italian tinge to his American accent had become stronger in his distress. The professor lowered himself into a chair next to the desk at which Magnus was sitting and with an effort composed himself. His hands briefly came to rest on his lap.

'And how did you know her?'

'She contacted me at Princeton a few months ago. Just sent me an email. I get approached by amateur historians all the time, and occasionally by graduate students who should know better. Usually I ignore them, but her message caught my interest for some reason, and I responded. And I'm glad I did.'

'Why was that?'

'Have you heard of Columbus's letter to his brother about his voyage to Iceland? They are featuring it heavily in their television series.'

'Yes,' said Magnus.

'Well, it was that. A friend of hers had stumbled across it in the Vatican Secret Archives. The Vatican said it was a fake, and I assumed it was too. But Carlotta's argument was persuasive – that in fact the Icelanders knew all about Greenland and America, and if Columbus had indeed visited Iceland he would have known about it too. So the next time I was in Rome, I took a look at the original. The Vatican was reluctant to let me see it, but I have a certain standing on these subjects in Italy.' The professor coughed in feigned modesty. 'In the world, actually.'

Now he was talking about himself, Beccari seemed less agitated. More self-confident. His hands were almost still.

'I looked at the letter and the scientific analysis, and, well, I wasn't sure.'

'You thought it was genuine?'

'I thought it might be. You have to be careful when you have a reputation such as mine; it is easy to make a fool of yourself. You remember the Hitler Diaries?'

Magnus shook his head.

'In the 1980s, *Stern*, the German magazine, claimed that they had discovered Hitler's war diaries. Professor Trevor-Roper of Oxford University said they were genuine. He was wrong and his reputation never recovered; it destroyed his life. I have just taken over as Hildreth Professor of History at Princeton. I don't want to follow in poor old Trevor-Roper's footsteps. That would be a catastrophe.' The professor's eyes were wide with horror at the prospect of the demolition of his reputation.

'Did you ever meet Carlotta?'

'Yes. The day after I examined the letter in the Secret Archives she met me in Rome. She said that the BBC was doing a documentary on a Viking woman who had been to America, and was planning to use the Columbus letter. Would I vouch for its authenticity?'

'When exactly was this?' Magnus asked.

'Sometime in April this year.' Beccari pulled out his phone to check his diary. 'The twenty-fifth of April.'

Magnus jotted the date down. 'And how did you reply to Carlotta?'

'I said no, of course. I have my reputation to protect.'

'How did Carlotta take that?'

'She was unhappy. She didn't give up, she asked me to think about it. She understood about my reputation, but she was very persuasive. She said most of the truly ground-breaking discoveries in history were initially rejected by the academic establishment.'

Beccari cleared his throat. 'I'm not sure she is entirely right about that, but I did see her point. She also hinted that I was scared of the other academics. I knew she was trying to provoke me, but once again she had a point.'

'I don't follow.'

'This letter is going to be a big deal once it becomes public. A very big deal. A lot of Italian historians are not going to like it. A lot of Columbus experts.' Beccari grinned. 'They will *hate* to admit that Columbus knew of the existence of America and that it was the Icelanders who told him all about it.'

Magnus could see that although his peers might hate the idea, Professor Beccari was relishing it. 'And so you changed your mind?'

'Eventually, yes, I did. I did some research around the subject, especially on the Norse sources with which I was not familiar, but Carlotta was. And unlike the Hitler Diaries there were no large sums of money at stake here. The more I thought about it, the more I thought it might be genuine. So I agreed to appear on the programme.'

'Carlotta must have been pleased.'

'She was.'

'When did you tell her?'

'A few days ago. She said she wasn't directly involved in the programme herself, so she asked me to contact Dr Thorsteinsson and Suzy Henshaw, the producer, directly. Which I did.'

'How did you contact Carlotta? In person?'

'No. Just by email.'

Magnus thought through what he had just heard. 'So how many times did you actually meet Carlotta?'

'Just the once. In Rome, at my hotel. But she made an impression on me then. She was a bright woman, and very persistent. Do you think the murder has anything to do with this documentary?'

'Did Carlotta say much about Einar Thorsteinsson?' Magnus asked.

'Yes, she did. She described the wampum discovery she and Thorsteinsson had made in Greenland that backed up the implication in the Columbus letter that the Vikings had reached Nantucket. I checked out Thorsteinsson's reputation; he is well respected in his field. And as I mentioned, he and I have been in email contact about this programme. I didn't actually meet him or Eygló Halldórsdóttir or Suzy Henshaw until today.'

'And none of them mentioned the name of the murder victim in Glaumbaer?' Magnus said.

'Not until just now.'

That was consistent with Einar and Eygló keeping their knowledge of Carlotta quiet.

'Are you involved in filming anywhere else?'

'I didn't film with them in America, or in Glaumbaer. I will definitely be involved in Rome next month, although there are still some doubts as to whether we will be able to film actually in the Vatican Secret Archives themselves. And I am planning to go with them to Greenland in a couple of days. It's not strictly necessary, but this whole thing intrigues me, and I would like to see where Erik the Red and his family lived.'

'I wouldn't count on that trip to Greenland going ahead,' said Magnus. 'At least not in the immediate future.'

CHAPTER 17

AFTER THE PROFESSOR left, Magnus and Vigdís summoned Suzy Henshaw. Suzy confirmed what Einar and Eygló had told them. She was surprised to hear that Einar knew Carlotta, but insisted that she had never heard of her herself. She was under the impression that the letter had been discovered by a graduate student named Federico Trapanese, whom they had tried and failed to fix up an interview with in Italy. She confirmed that Einar had had dinner with Eygló and her in Saudárkrókur the evening Carlotta had been killed.

'You left dinner early?' Magnus asked.

'Yes. I felt a migraine coming on. I get them sometimes. I was feeling fine and then my vision started going, I saw zigzags in front of my eyes. I've learned the best thing to do is take a pill and lie down in a darkened room right away. Otherwise it can take me out of action for a whole day. And I couldn't afford that.'

Somehow it didn't surprise Magnus that Suzy had her migraines under control.

'Do you know what time you left the other two?'

Suzy shook her head. 'It was during the main course – I left half my plate. We met at eight-thirty, I think. Maybe nine-fifteen? I don't know.'

Magnus glanced at Vigdís. That meant Einar and Eygló were alone in the restaurant for at least half an hour.

'There won't be any problem with us going to Greenland on Friday, will there?' Suzy asked.

'There might be,' said Magnus. 'Especially Einar.'

'That's not acceptable,' said Suzy, her dark eyes boring into Magnus's. 'Getting on that plane is vital. There are only a couple of flights a week from Iceland to Greenland, and the weather there is suspect. We're nearly into September, and if it starts snowing, we're screwed.'

'Wouldn't the snow look good?' Magnus asked.

'It's *Green*land, for God's sake!' Suzy said. 'That's the whole point. We want to show that Erik the Red found lush farming territory there. We need good weather. And we're scheduled to go to Rome next month – if we miss Greenland now, we won't get there until October, and that will be a disaster.'

'Hey, I'm sorry,' said Magnus. 'But this is a murder investigation. Someone died, someone Einar knew well. It's going to be inconvenient.'

Suzy scowled, but then seemed to take a decision to change tactics. She smiled. 'Look, the BBC is backing this project, as is the Canadian broadcaster, but I run an independent production company. And we are in a difficult situation.' She hesitated. 'Financially.'

'I thought *Viking Queens* was a big success?' Magnus said.

'Yes, it was, and so will *The Wanderer* be *if* you let us film it on schedule. We got involved in a major documentary last year that got pulled at the last minute, and let's just say I really need the cash flow from this one.'

Suzy was clearly an expert at getting things done, and at getting her own way, but Magnus had some sympathy with her. 'I understand, but the needs of the investigation must come first,' he said.

'You know we didn't kill Carlotta,' Suzy said. 'We were all having dinner together in Saudárkrókur. There are witnesses. Let us go to Greenland and then you can talk to us again when we return to Iceland if you have to. And we need Einar. *He* discovered the wampum in Greenland; he has to be in those scenes.'

'Actually, it was Carlotta who discovered the wampum.'

This news seemed to irritate Suzy. 'We can hardly interview her, can we? We *need* Einar.'

'I'll think about it,' said Magnus. 'In the meantime, can we have the film you shot at Glaumbaer and in Nantucket and Newfoundland?'

'Don't you need a warrant for that?'

'I can get one if you like. It's no problem in this country. But I thought you wanted to cooperate?'

'All right,' said Suzy. 'I'll get Tom to give you a copy.'

Suzy departed unhappy, but that was the best she was going to get.

'You'll think about it?' said Vigdís. 'You mean "no", don't you?'

Magnus shrugged.

'I'm not convinced they all have an alibi,' Vigdís went on. She consulted her notebook. 'Suzy left Eygló and Einar alone from nine-fifteen. Maybe Einar left the restaurant then and drove down to Glaumbaer and Eygló is just covering for him. Again.'

'He says he was waiting in the church square at ten-thirty to meet Carlotta. He wouldn't have had time to drive to Glaumbaer, kill Carlotta and return to Saudárkrókur.'

'He had an hour at least.'

Magnus shook his head. 'It would take almost that long just to drive there and back.'

'OK. But who saw him leaving the hotel at ten-thirty? Eygló. Again.'

Vigdís was right. They needed independent verification, more than just Eygló's word.

'Let's have a chat with the cameraman.'

Tom Loudon had little to say, but he had noticed Einar hanging around in the church square when he was on his way back from a bar. He wasn't sure what time that was, just late. Having been assured by Suzy that it was OK, he downloaded the film footage on to a memory stick for Magnus in a format that Magnus could view on a computer.

'So now we have Tom's word that Einar was in the church square as well as Eygló's,' said Magnus.

'He wasn't certain of the time, though,' said Vigdís.

'Let's see what the sound man says.'

Ajay had no alibi for that evening, or not much of one. He had gone out to get a slice of pizza which he had brought back to the hotel, and he had gone up to his room to eat it. He'd spent the evening reading a book, and then gone to sleep at about eleven. He hadn't seen Einar or any of the others all evening.

He said he hadn't known any of the crew before being interviewed in London a month before. He had got the job through his tutor at university who knew Suzy was looking for a good intern. He had found Tom an excellent teacher, but difficult to talk to. He enjoyed the work; it was great experience.

He claimed he had no idea who Carlotta was. He had never visited Italy. He did have a driving licence, however, so in theory he could have driven the rented Land Cruiser back to Saudárkrókur that evening.

Magnus and Vigdís stayed on at the police station: Vigdís wrote up the interviews, and Magnus studied the unedited rushes from Glaumbaer. He went over them three times, but he couldn't spot anything of interest. No sign of Carlotta, or of her car, or of Einar looking furtive or worried.

On the screen, Eygló told a good story. Magnus watched the Newfoundland footage, as much out of curiosity as anything else. Much of it was filmed at L'Anse aux Meadows, a remote site on the north-eastern coast of the island, which wasn't even connected to the outside world by road until the 1960s. Eygló was once again fascinating, supported by Einar and a Canadian archaeologist. There was much speculation about whether L'Anse aux Meadows was actually the Leif's Booths mentioned in the sagas. They visited the possible locations of other places mentioned in the sagas, such as Straumsfjord – 'Stream Bay', Straumsey – 'Stream Island' and Kjalarnes – 'Keel Point'. No mention of Hóp – lagoon. Perhaps they were saving that for the Nantucket episode.

They were ...

Eygló was perched on the gunwale of a heeling sailing boat, a taut tan sail straining behind her. She read from a sheet of paper fluttering in the breeze.

'From Straumsfjord head south along the coast for six days past a cape with strong currents to an island just out of sight of land. On the eastern side of the island, there is a lagoon with sandbars next to the sea which it is only possible to sail into at high tide. There are fields of self-sown wheat and grapevines growing on the hills. The lagoon is teeming with fish.'

She looked up. 'So those are the navigational instructions Christopher Columbus wrote to his brother; the instructions he had been given in Iceland. They are similar to the directions found in the *Saga of Erik the Red*, but more detailed, suggesting they might have come from another version of that saga, now lost.

'We are in Nantucket Sound.' She pointed out to starboard. 'Over there, just out of sight beyond the horizon, is Cape Cod.

'You can see from the chop just here that there are strong currents; this stretch of water has been notorious with sailors since the first fishermen came here from Europe five hundred years ago. Maybe even earlier.

'And over there ...' She turned towards a stretch of low-lying land over her left shoulder. 'Over there is the island of Nantucket.

'According to the sagas, Gudrid and her husband Thorfinn sailed south from their base in Vinland to somewhere called Hóp. For decades historians have speculated where this was, but now we know.'

She paused, cocked her head in that way she had, smiled conspiratorially at the camera and imparted her secret. 'Nantucket.'

Now she was walking up the short garden path of a grey shingle cottage, smothered in a riot of purple, red and yellow flowers.

She paused at the door. 'This is the house of Professor Nancy Fishburn, a long-term resident of Nantucket and the author of a book on Gudrid the Wanderer. Let's see if she can help us identify where Gudrid, her husband and their band of adventurers landed a thousand years ago.' She rapped on the door knocker.

Next Eygló was perched on the edge of a sofa in a cosy sitting room, facing an old woman sitting erect in an armchair, her face criss-crossed with tiny wrinkles, her eyes twinkling with a lively intelligence and wry amusement. The camera lingered on a glass-fronted bookcase of ancient volumes secure behind a metal grille. A scholar's living room; given the bookcase, a wealthy scholar.

Magnus was taken by the old lady immediately, as was Eygló, who displayed her customary fascination with her interview subjects.

'Professor Fishburn, did you ever think that Gudrid could have ventured as far as Nantucket?'

'Scholars have always known that the Vikings may have strayed at least as far south as Cape Cod,' Nancy Fishburn said. 'But there was no evidence until very recently that they ever landed on Nantucket. A few years ago archaeologists discovered wampum from Nantucket at Erik the Red's farmhouse in Greenland, and now there is this letter.'

'It's pretty clear that Columbus is referring to Nantucket,' said Eygló. 'There are no other islands that match this description that are out of sight of land. Given that, where on Nantucket do you think the lagoon of Hóp might be?'

'There are a couple of lagoons on Nantucket,' said Nancy. 'But from this description, the most likely place is Sesachacha Pond. It's just a few miles north of here.'

Then Eygló and Nancy were outside, this time with Einar, standing by some reeds in front of a round expanse of water, about half a mile wide. Although she was leaning on an elegant walking stick, Nancy looked sprightly.

'This would be an ideal spot for the Vikings to settle,' Nancy said. The camera panned to a low hill covered with scrub. 'Up there, the ground rises to give them a view of any approaching attackers. There is also fresh water. There is no self-sown wheat – which was probably wild rice – nor grapevines here today, but there may well have been a thousand years ago when the climate was warmer.

'And over there, behind that sand dune, is the sea.' Here the camera showed a narrow barrier of sand, perhaps ten feet high, bordering the pond to the east. A red and white lighthouse guarded one end of the dune, and a cluster of summer houses the other. 'In the millennium since the Norsemen arrived, the sand and the shore will have been shifted by tides and storms. It is very likely that there could have been access to the sea as described in Christopher Columbus's letter.'

'So this is Hóp?' Eygló asked. 'This is where Gudrid and her husband Thorfinn landed a thousand years ago? Lonely Europeans clinging to the edge of a hostile continent?'

Nancy Fishburn flashed an amused smile. 'Almost certainly, yes.'

'And did they come into contact with the existing inhabitants?'

'They did indeed. Soon after they landed at Hóp the Norsemen were approached by the locals, whom the Norse called "Skraelings". The Skraelings loved the Greenlanders' cloth, and traded it for fur pelts. A friendly relationship had built up between the Europeans and the Native Americans, until one day the Vikings' bull escaped and charged the Skraelings, who fled.

'All was quiet for three weeks, until a large war party reappeared in canoes. Presumably from the sea over there.' Nancy gestured towards the sand dune again. 'They fired arrows at the Greenlanders and then shot a mysterious black object from the catapult, which landed with a terrifying sound. The Greenlanders ran for it.

'Now, Gudrid wasn't the only woman on this expedition. There were several others, including Freydís, Erik the Red's ambitious daughter, who had become a bitter enemy of Thorfinn and Gudrid.

'Freydís was eight months pregnant at this point. She emerged from her tent and yelled at the Viking warriors to stand their ground, but they took no notice. So Freydís picked up a sword from one of the dead Norsemen, turned to face the Skraelings, ripped open her dress and bared her breast. She beat her chest and screamed at them.

'They fled.

'But after that, the Greenlanders decided that the threat from the local Skraelings was too great, and so they abandoned Hóp and headed north back to Keel Point and Leif's Booths.'

*

'Done!' said Vigdís with a final triumphant tap on her keyboard. 'I'm going to the hotel. What about you?'

'Good idea,' said Magnus, closing the video and turning off the computer.

'What shall we do about him?' Vigdís pointed to the cell door, where Einar was languishing.

'Let him go. I'll tell him not to leave town. We can decide what to do with him in the morning.'

'Why not make him sweat it out?' said Vigdís. 'He may have more to say after a night in the cells.'

Magnus shook his head. 'We need to find out more before we lean on him. We'll take him back to the hotel, and get his phone and laptop.'

Constable Ívar looked relieved that he didn't have to spend the night watching over Einar. He had secured a couple of rooms for Vigdís and Magnus at the only hotel in Ólafsvík, which was just a few metres from the police station. It was where the TV crew was staying.

They unlocked Einar. His face remained impassive as Magnus told him he should stay in Ólafsvík the following morning until the police gave him permission to leave town. For a moment Magnus thought Einar was just playing it cool, until he saw Einar's eyes.

They were dull, almost dead.

CHAPTER 18

MAGNUS MET VIGDÍS in the lobby of the hotel the next morning, and they walked the short distance to the police station together.

'Guess who I just saw?' Vigdís said, grinning.

'Who?'

'Einar. Coming out of the room next to mine.'

'And what's so special about that?'

'It's Eygló's room.'

'Huh,' said Magnus. 'That is special.'

The local constables Ívar and Páll were already at the station. Magnus and Vigdís joined them around a speakerphone and they were patched in with Árni, Jón Kári and the other investigators in Saudárkrókur, and with Edda in Reykjavík. It wasn't ideal: it would have been better if Magnus had been there with the rest of the team in the north. He probably should have delegated the interview in Ólafsvík with Einar to another detective.

Who was he kidding? If there was a key interview to be done, then he was going to do it, no matter what the procedures said.

He started off by summarizing his interviews with Einar, Eygló and Professor Beccari the day before. Árni had checked with the receptionist in the Hótel Tindastóll who confirmed that she had seen Einar leave the hotel some time around ten, and return about an hour later. She had gone off duty at midnight, so it was in theory possible that Einar had left the hotel after then, but his alibi up until at least 11 p.m. was solid. She had seen Tom leave the hotel, but she hadn't seen any sign of Eygló or Suzy after they returned from dinner and she couldn't remember seeing Ajay go out for his pizza, nor could she remember Tom's return. She wasn't at the desk the whole time and even when she was, she had taken a number of phone calls; she couldn't be certain of noticing and remembering every movement in and out of the hotel.

The barman and a drinker at the bar in Saudárkrókur remembered Tom's visit that evening, although the pizza place was unsure about Ajay.

The autopsy had been performed on Carlotta the afternoon before. There was nothing surprising about the results. She was in good health; there were no signs of a struggle. Her only injury was a single hard blow to the head with a blunt object. Time of death was probably between 7.30 p.m. and midnight, although it was just possible that she had been killed after that: rigor and body temperature were inaccurate indicators. The body definitely had not been moved far after death, although it could have been dragged behind the church immediately.

So in theory it was just about possible that Einar could have left the hotel in Saudárkrókur after midnight, driven to Glaumbaer, met Carlotta there and killed her. But it was extremely unlikely. Why would Carlotta meet him there in the middle of the night? And there had been that other sighting of the unidentified man at ten o'clock. That tallied with Carlotta rearranging her rendez-vous with Einar from nine-thirty to ten-thirty; perhaps she had another meeting with someone else at Glaumbaer earlier that evening: the man with the silver car.

On the earlier side of the window they now knew that Carlotta had been seen on the shore of the fjord looking at Drangey at eight-thirty, meaning she couldn't have got back to Glaumbaer until at least nine.

Edda made her report. Forensic evidence had turned up nothing. Or rather, it had turned up a lot, but nothing that yet had any significance. There were multiple faint fingerprints on Carlotta's car, which is what you would expect from a rental vehicle. Eliminating them would be a nightmare involving the staff at the rental company and the previous renters, most of whom would be foreign tourists who had probably returned to their own countries.

A number of items had been recovered from Glaumbaer and the churchyard; once again, not surprising for one of the tourist attractions in the area. No signs of blood on the ground in the vicinity.

They had been able to deduce from the faint tyre prints that the tyres on the silver car the girl had seen were Michelin CrossClimate, which could be fitted to a wide range of vehicles. The impressions were good enough to confirm a match with whatever vehicle had been parked there, if they could find it. Magnus would check Einar's Toyota but he was not hopeful.

They had not heard anything new from Italy, either from Sergeant Tacchini or from the University of Padua about Carlotta's email account. This was frustrating. There was no doubt that Carlotta's emails would be illuminating: they would have alerted the police to her relationship with Einar. And although the Icelandic phone companies were cooperative, they hadn't yet been able put together a schedule of calls to and from Carlotta's phone, with locations.

'So, do we arrest Einar?' said Jón Kári.

'I don't think so,' said Magnus. 'We don't have the evidence. And his alibi is good.'

'He did lie to us about Carlotta,' said Vigdís.

'He said he was worried we would suspect him,' Magnus replied. 'And he didn't want his wife to find out he had been seeing her.'

'That doesn't sound good enough to me. A murder inquiry is serious. Most innocent people would have admitted they knew the victim right away.'

'I'm not so sure,' said Magnus. 'His wife sounds the jealous type; if it was going to get him in trouble with her, he might have kept quiet. It would have been the wrong thing to do, but people make bad choices. Plus, we know he was in Saudárkrókur when Carlotta was killed.'

'He could have gone to Glaumbaer later on,' said Árni.

'Highly unlikely,' said Magnus.

'OK. I admit he probably didn't do it,' said Vigdís. 'But he's holding something back from us. And if we lock him up and let him stew for a few days thinking he's on a murder rap, he may decide to tell us.'

This was the classic difference between the way the police in Iceland and the United States worked. The US had much stricter laws about eliciting confessions and their admissibility, and most suspects were told by lawyers to say nothing. Even when you got a confession, the defence lawyers would concentrate on undermining it; a case relying solely on a confession was a weak case indeed. So Magnus was used to building a case without any help from the suspect, sometimes without the suspect even knowing he *was* a suspect. Magnus knew detectives who would even avoid asking the suspect whether he was guilty during the investigation.

Things in Iceland were different. There it was possible to take a suspect, throw him into solitary confinement for a couple of weeks, and then persuade him to confess. So Magnus wasn't surprised that some of his colleagues wanted to lock Einar up, although he was a little surprised that Vigdís was one of them.

But he was in charge of this investigation. 'We let him go,' he said. 'You may well be right that he's still holding out on us, Vigdís, but we need to find out more about him and about Carlotta.'

'OK,' said Vigdís. 'But we can't let him go to Greenland.'

'Let's see how the investigation develops,' said Magnus.

'What about Ajay?' said Árni.

'What about him?'

'He has no good alibi – the pizza place can't remember him. He was supposedly lurking in his room with a book. He seems to have been introduced to the project late in the process; he didn't know any of the others.'

'Doesn't than make him less likely?' said Vigdís.

'He could have been hired by someone,' said Árni.

'To do what?' Magnus asked.

'To kill Carlotta.'

'You mean a hit? Who would have hired him?'

'An enemy of Carlotta's from Italy.'

'He's only twenty-one,' said Vigdís.

'There are plenty of twenty-one-year-old Asians in Britain who want to kill people.'

'So you think a Mafia boss recruited a jihadi to off a twenty-six-year-old student?'

'I don't know,' said Árni. 'I just think we should keep an open mind.'

Magnus knew Árni was appealing to him: he had always encouraged Vigdís and Árni to look for new angles. Árni's stereotyping of Italians and British Asians could hardly have been called open-minded, but on the other hand they shouldn't dismiss the idea that the motive for Carlotta's death might lie in Italy. Magnus did wonder again how it was that Árni had been promoted to detective sergeant and not Vigdís.

'OK. Check whether the anti-terrorist people in Britain know anything about him,' he said.

Magnus doled out tasks for the team for the day. 'Now, get to work everyone.'

Vigdís turned off the speakerphone.

'I really don't think Einar could have got to Glaumbaer and back in time to kill Carlotta,' Magnus said.

'OK,' said Vigdís. 'But Eygló could.'

'What do you mean?'

'She doesn't have an alibi after they got back to the hotel. We know she and Einar are sleeping together.'

'Do we?'

'I just saw him leave her room this morning!'

'They deny it.'

'Of course they do. Just like they denied knowing Carlotta.'

'And why would Eygló kill Carlotta?' Magnus asked.

'Jealousy?' Vigdís said. 'Carlotta is an old girlfriend. Or perhaps Eygló and Einar cooked up the plan together.'

'And how did she get to Glaumbaer?'

'Einar's car. Or maybe she got the keys to the Land Cruiser somehow.'

'What about the man in the silver car?'

'I don't know,' said Vigdís. 'Perhaps he had nothing to do with it.'

Magnus didn't want to think that Eygló had killed Carlotta. He didn't even really want to believe that she had slept with Einar. But a lot of what Vigdís said made sense. It was better than Árni's Ajay theory.

'We should speak to her again,' said Vigdís.

'You've lied to us consistently, haven't you?'

Eygló flinched at Magnus's question. 'I did lie about not knowing Carlotta. I am sorry about that.'

'It wasn't just about Carlotta.'

'Yes, it was.'

'You told us you were not sleeping with Einar.'

'That's right, I did,' said Eygló. She swallowed.

'I saw him leaving your hotel room this morning,' said Vigdís.

'I can explain that ...'

'Oh, yes?' said Magnus. 'You lied to us about knowing Carlotta. You lied to us about your relationship with Einar. Now I have another question for you and you had better not lie this time. Did you kill Carlotta?'

'What?' Eygló raised her eyebrows in surprise. Whether feigned or not, Magnus couldn't tell.

'You heard me. Did you kill Carlotta?'

'No,' said Eygló. 'No! Absolutely not. That's ridiculous. Why would I kill her?'

'Jealousy?' said Vigdís. 'She was a rival.'

'I've told you I do not have a sexual relationship with Einar! Yes, he came to my room last night. Yes, I know I shouldn't have done it, but I let him stay overnight. He was upset about Carlotta and about his interview with you and I comforted him. He needed me, he said. But we didn't have sex; we didn't even kiss.'

'No?'

'Look, I know I can't necessarily convince you about what happened in my room last night. But I didn't kill Carlotta. As far as I'm concerned, she was welcome to Einar.'

'Did you two discuss it?' Vigdís asked. 'Did Einar suggest you kill her for him?'

'No, no, no!' Eygló gritted her teeth and bunched her fists in frustration. 'I know you have to ask questions like that, but that is completely stupid. I did not kill Carlotta. I just didn't.'

Magnus was impressed by Eygló's anger. Just for a moment he felt bad about accusing her, but he swiftly put the thought behind him. Vigdís was absolutely right: they needed to pursue this line of questioning as far as it would go.

'OK. Tell us exactly what you did when you returned to the hotel in Saudárkrókur the night Carlotta was killed.'

Eygló repeated her claim that she had stayed in her room all evening. She said she had been on her phone, on Twitter. She had seen Einar going out. She had read a novel in bed for half an hour, checking Twitter, and had then gone to sleep.

'Do you believe her?' Vigdís asked when they had let her go.

'I don't know,' said Magnus. The truth was he did believe her, but he also recognized his bias. He didn't *want* to think Eygló was responsible for Carlotta's murder. He almost felt that suspecting her was a betrayal of her trust. There was something about her – maybe it was because he had hung on her every word when watching her on TV back in the States. Whatever it was he needed to get a grip. He was being idiotic. Unprofessional. Not something he would admit to Vigdís.

Vigdís turned to the computer on her desk and tapped away. 'Well, it's true she was on Twitter a lot that day. I can't tell exactly what time from her feed now, but it should be possible to check.'

'But she could have tweeted from her phone in a vehicle on the way to or from Glaumbaer?'

'Yes, if she borrowed Einar's car,' Vigdís said. 'And if she did use her phone, we should get location information from the phone companies.'

'That might take them a couple of days.' They were still waiting for the location report for Carlotta's phone. 'Get Árni on to it.'

CHAPTER 19

'WHAT TIME ARE they coming, Grammy?'

Kelly sipped her coffee and watched a group of five Icelandic horses and their riders glide along the sweep of empty beach outside the hotel, their manes flowing in the breeze. She and her grandmother had arrived the night before after a long drive from Reykjavík. The Hótel Búdir stood all alone on the edge of a lava field overlooking the sea – alone apart from a tiny chapel. It was a gorgeous spot.

Her grandmother checked her watch. 'Oh, I think in about fifteen minutes.'

'Are they going to film here?'

'Not precisely here,' said her grandmother. 'At Ólafsvík on the other side of Snaefellsnes, just over those mountains, and I think one or two other places around here. Gudrid was brought up at Laugarbrekka, a farm just beneath the volcano, and it's rumoured Columbus stayed not far from Ólafsvík.'

'I think that's so cool,' said Kelly. 'Imagine him all the way up here.'

'Yes,' said her grandmother absently. She sipped her own coffee. 'Kelly, dear?'

'Yes?'

'Would you mind leaving me alone for an hour or so?'

'I'm happy to see them,' Kelly said. 'In fact, I'd like to.'

'Yes, I know, but this is a private conversation.'

'Private?' Kelly frowned. A week or so after her grandmother had been interviewed in Nantucket by the Anglo-Icelandic film crew, the old lady had announced that she wanted to visit Iceland one last time, and had asked Kelly to accompany her. Kelly had been staying with her in 'Sconset all summer, working in the village store, and was due back at her college in Ohio for her senior year. But she thought she could just about get away with it. Also, she had only been to Europe once before, and Grammy was paying.

It had been difficult to find a hotel room in Reykjavík, but Nancy's travel agent had eventually managed it, and they had arrived in the capital two days earlier. Kelly had loved the little city with its jumble of brightly coloured houses with their tin roofs, and the playful art everywhere you looked. Then Grammy had made a mysterious phone call and announced that they were going up to Snaefellsnes to meet the people who were making the documentary about Gudrid.

And now Grammy wanted to meet them alone. Something was up and Kelly had no idea what.

Grammy nodded. 'Private.'

Kelly opened her mouth to protest. Her grandmother stared her down. They got on very well, and Kelly had loved staying in 'Sconset with her these last two summers, but every now and then Grammy could be quite imperious. This was one of those moments. Argument was pointless.

'Take a walk through the lava field. As I remember it, it's beautiful.'

Ever the dutiful granddaughter, Kelly did as she was told. And it was beautiful, patches of long summer grass shimmering in the golden sunshine. A perfect volcano rose above the lava to the west, crowned by a white topping of snow. Kelly picked her way along a narrow path through a frozen tumult of black lava, between eerie shapes that evoked large hounds, or crows, or trolls' heads. The chapel was surrounded by a graveyard and a little white gate. Unfortunately, the church itself was locked.

She pressed on further into the lava field, through the ruins of a small village, the inhabitants of which were presumably slumbering in the churchyard behind her. The air was fresh, the sky was blue and the sea shushed against the lava a few feet away from the path. Kelly felt her irritation with her grandmother disperse.

Nancy Fishburn had five grandchildren, of whom Kelly was the youngest and, Kelly thought, the favourite. Kelly had lapped up her grandmother's stories about medieval Europe and the Vikings, and she had read Nancy's book about Gudrid the Wanderer when she was fifteen. Inspired by her grandmother, she was now majoring in history, taking every medieval course she could. She had been excited when the TV crew had descended on Nantucket to interview Grammy and also to hear about the Columbus letter and the wampum find in Greenland. She had seen Eygló in *Viking Queens* on TV, and had chatted to her on Nantucket, where the presenter had been really friendly. So Kelly was offended at being excluded now.

After she had been walking for about three-quarters of an hour, she turned around and headed back. When she returned to the hotel, Nancy was still in the bar, staring out at the beach and the wall of mountains that made up the spine of the Snaefellsnes peninsula.

'How did it go?' Kelly asked.

Nancy didn't answer straight away. She sighed. 'OK, I guess. I don't know.'

She didn't look happy. Kelly reached out and squeezed her grandmother's hand. 'Grammy? What's up?'

'I think I've done something very wrong.'

Kelly felt a jolt of horror. How could her grandmother possibly have done something wrong?

'What is it?' Then she remembered Nancy's reticence about her meeting. 'You don't have to tell me if you don't want to.'

Nancy was still staring out at the surf on the beach. Kelly waited.

'No,' she said. 'I think I should tell you.'

'OK.' Kelly waited.

'You know the Columbus letter about the Vikings getting to Nantucket? And the wampum from Nantucket they found in Greenland?'

'Yes.'

'Well.' The old lady swallowed. 'None of it's true.'

'What do you mean?'

'I mean it's all a hoax. The wampum was planted in Greenland. The Columbus letter is a forgery.'

'It can't be! All those experts said it was genuine. How do you know?'

'Because I know who thought up the hoax.'

'And who was that?'

Nancy Fishburn looked her granddaughter right in the eye.

'Me. And your grandfather. And our friend ...'

CHAPTER 20

NANCY STARED AT the letter spread out on the wooden table in her garden in 'Sconset.

'Is it OK out here in the sunshine?' she asked Emilio.

'Sure,' he said, smiling. 'It will be good for it.'

Nancy frowned; Emilio was usually obsessively careful with his wares. 'Can I touch it?'

'Here, use these gloves. We don't want any fingerprints.' His smile broadened.

'It's amazing,' said John.

'Emilio?' Nancy said, suddenly understanding. The sun. The fingerprints. 'Is this a fake? Did *you* do this?'

A twinkle of the eyes was added to the smile.

'Emilio!' Nancy exclaimed.

'It's pretty good, don't you think?' Emilio said. 'When we were talking about the Vinland Map back home, I thought: "I could do that." And so I did. I've seen enough Columbus stuff in my time, real and fake.'

'No!' John said. He bent and peered closely at the writing. 'It's excellent. Is the paper genuine?'

'Yes. It's the spare blank pages of a quire I came across five years ago and kept in case they came in useful. Fifteenth century, probably from Venice.'

'And the ink?'

'Definitely no anatase.' The compound that had cast doubt on the Vinland Map, Nancy remembered.

'Hmm,' John said. 'It looks good to me, but I bet it wouldn't fool the experts.'

'I bet it would,' said Emilio.

John shook his head. 'Something like this, they'd pull out the big guns. International experts, chemical analysis, the works.'

'No problem,' said Emilio. 'You said "I bet". Do you want to bet?'

'What? That no one spots it's a fake?'

Emilio nodded.

'Wait. Are you going to release this out into the world?' Nancy asked.

'How else are we going to know if it will fool the experts?'

'John?' Nancy said, appealing to her husband.

John was smiling. 'A hundred bucks says they'll rumble you.'

'Your Walter Raleigh's *Discovery of Guiana*.'

'What! You've got to be out of your mind. That's one of the most expensive books in my collection.'

'I know,' said Emilio. 'And if my forgery is revealed as a fake you get that English translation of *The Decameron* I was telling you about.'

Nancy glanced at her husband. They all three knew that the Raleigh was worth much more than the *Decameron* translation, but then John was a lot richer than Emilio.

He would never go for it.

But John was fired up. Nancy had seen Emilio seduce John so many times in the past, persuading him to buy treasures for significantly more than they were really worth.

Emilio caught her eye and she felt a thrill of complicity. Emilio knew John would go for it. And he knew she knew he would too.

John sipped from his glass thoughtfully. He turned to his wife. 'What do you think, honey?'

Nancy knew she should tell him not to do it. In fact, it was a really bad idea on so many levels. But part of her wanted Emilio to get away with the Raleigh. She had been seduced too. And that was OK.

She shrugged.

John grinned. 'OK, Emilio. You're on.'

Emilio carefully replaced the forgery in his briefcase, and John refilled the daiquiris.

'How are you going to reveal this to the world?' Nancy asked. 'Are you going to claim you found it?'

'I can't do that,' said Emilio. 'I don't want to sell a forgery, or even recommend it. That would ruin my reputation. And it would be illegal. At some point we will want to reveal it's a fake. So we need to place this somewhere it will be discovered and there will be no connection to us.'

'How are you going to do that?'

'I have an idea.' He explained it to John and Nancy. It was a good one.

More daiquiris.

As they talked, it was clear that John was really taken with the idea of the forgery, even though it would mean he might lose his beloved *Discovery of Guiana*.

'You know what, Emilio? One letter isn't enough. If we are going to make people believe that this is real we need context. Another piece of evidence.'

'What, you want me to forge another document?' said Emilio. 'Isn't one enough for you?'

'Not a document, no. Something else. An artefact, ideally from the Viking period. Nancy, what other evidence would make historians believe that this letter is true?'

'I don't know,' said Nancy. 'I don't like this idea. If people really are dumb enough to believe Emilio's letter, then a whole bunch of historians are going to be wasting a lot of time looking in the wrong direction.'

'What if we promise to reveal it's a fake one year after it's discovered?' Emilio said. 'Any historian who is stupid enough to believe that it's real deserves to lose a few months' work.'

'I don't want to be linked to this,' said Nancy. 'My reputation will be ruined.'

'We'll reveal it anonymously,' said John.

Nancy hesitated. She knew what Emilio and John was suggesting was not just unprofessional, it was wrong. But it was also exciting.

She really didn't want to kill the idea.

'What if we implicated that woman you are always talking about?' said Emilio. 'What's her name? Gudrid. You're always saying she doesn't get enough attention. If we did this right, we could get her the attention she deserves.'

'That's not the kind of attention I meant,' Nancy said.

'All publicity is good publicity,' said John.

Emilio smiled at Nancy, the full broad grin. He reached over and placed his hand on hers. She felt a jolt, almost like an electric shock, that made her want to pull back, but, like an electric shock, she couldn't.

Nancy glanced at her husband. He wanted to do this so badly. And so did she.

'OK,' she said. 'I'll help you.'

They stayed in the back yard late into the night, drinking, eating, talking, planning.

And then they went to bed.

Emilio arranged for the letter to be inserted in the Vatican Secret Archives. The following summer, Nancy and John travelled to Greenland, the remains of an old string of hard-shell clam wampum that they had dug up over by Eel Point in their luggage.

After Gudrid returned from Vinland she had stayed with her father-in-law Erik the Red at Brattahlíd – Gudrid had been married to Erik's son Thorstein before Thorfinn Karlsefni. The site had been excavated in the 1930s, and Nancy knew that the trenches they had dug then were still open.

The difficulty with planting new archaeological material was placing it in the correct 'context', the layer of soil that represented the appropriate era. Finds from Gudrid's time would be in the deepest layer. It would be tricky to insert the wampum shells that deep without disturbing the contexts above, and impossible to ensure that the shells were all placed in the correct context. But during the 1930s excavation, the contexts would have become jumbled up.

So one evening, when there was no one else around, they were able to insert the wampum shells laterally in the side of

114

the trench, so that anyone finding them would think they had been disturbed but not discovered by a previous generation of archaeologists.

Then they waited. And waited. They had assumed that the letter and the wampum would be found within a few months. But the proposed excavation of Brattahlíd scheduled for the following year was cancelled, and the volume in which Emilio had placed the letter was just not taken out of the Vatican Library.

A week after Nancy and John received a letter from Emilio announcing he was intending to move the letter to another book next time he was in Rome, they got some bad news. Emilio had had a heart attack at his home in Tuscany. He was dead.

Six months later, John had a stroke, which crippled him. A year after that another stroke killed him.

By that stage, Nancy regretted the whole thing. Once Emilio and John were gone, the hoax had no point. Nancy just forgot it.

And then in 2011 she read about the discovery of the Nantucket wampum in the paper. She had told herself that if anything was discovered, she would announce to the world that it was a fake. But by that stage she was already over eighty. She told herself she didn't have the energy, but truthfully, she didn't have the courage. She might have written a letter to the archaeologists who discovered the wampum if the consequences had just stayed in Greenland and one or two universities. But the find had caused great excitement in Nantucket among the Historical Association, and if Nancy had admitted John and she had planted it, it would have ruined their reputations. John's reputation in particular; she cared about John's reputation.

When an Icelandic archaeologist and his Italian assistant had tracked her down the year before as a local historian and an expert on Gudrid, she decided to go along with their questions and pretend that the wampum and the letter were real. She missed John, and she missed Emilio. The hoax was their legacy, and she thought she might as well enjoy it for them. By that stage she was in her mid eighties. What the hell, she thought, she was going to die soon anyway.

Then the archaeologist had returned with a film crew in tow and she had agreed to be interviewed. She could almost see Emilio's broad grin as she answered the Icelandic woman's questions at Sesachacha Pond, hear John's familiar chuckle.

But then, after the crew had packed up and left the island for Canada and Leif's Booths, the guilt had set in. Although she had thought the archaeologist arrogant, she had liked Eygló; the hoax, when it was discovered, and it surely would be discovered, would ruin her career. Who knew how many historians would be sent off on wild goose chases?

So Nancy had decided to travel to Iceland to tell them the truth.

CHAPTER 21

OVER VIGDÍS'S OBJECTIONS, Magnus allowed the filming to go ahead on Snaefellsnes, but over Suzy's objections he refused to allow the crew to leave for Greenland without permission from the police. He had persuaded Einar to give up his computer and phone and he and Vigdís had driven back to Reykjavík with them for analysis.

As they were entering police headquarters, Árni called.

'What have you got?'

'Nothing from the phone companies yet,' said Árni. 'But I had an idea.'

Magnus's heart sank a few inches. That was not normally a good sign.

'I checked with the Hótel Tindastóll. They have free Wi-Fi, but you have to log in every time you use it, and their system monitors usage by room and records every time a guest signs in.'

'Really? Did you check Eygló?'

'I did. She logged into the system at eight-oh-two and again at ten-oh-eight. And then once again at eleven-forty-one.'

'So that pretty much means she must have been in her room when she says she was?'

'She didn't have time to drive to Glaumbaer, kill Carlotta and return.'

'What about Einar?'

'Einar logged on at seven-fifty-nine and then again at eleven-twelve.'

'When he came back from the church square. That's consistent with his story too. And the others?'

117

'Suzy, Tom and Ajay all logged on around eight, right after they had checked in. But none of them were on Wi-Fi afterwards.'

'OK, Árni. Good work. Any news on Ajay from Britain?'

'That's going to take a while,' Árni said.

There was something in Árni's voice that Magnus recognized of old. It was the sound of Árni screwing up.

'Árni?'

Árni sighed. 'The British cop promised he would look, but he did point out that Ajay was a Hindu name, if that was any help.'

'So he's unlikely to be a jihadi hitman, then?'

'I suppose not,' said Árni. 'But there is no reason why there shouldn't be a Hindu hitman, is there?'

Magnus decided to put Árni out of his misery, something he should have done earlier. 'Call the guy back and tell him we are withdrawing the inquiry. There is no point in wasting his time. It's just about possible that Carlotta was murdered by a paid killer, but Ajay does not fit that profile and frankly neither does the method. Professional killers don't rely on finding pickaxes lying about.'

'Yes. Sorry.' Árni sounded chastened.

'Good work on the hotel Wi-Fi, though, Árni.'

Magnus had reached his desk as he hung up. 'Did you get that?' he said to Vigdís who had been listening to his half of the conversation.

'I think so. Eygló was logged on to the hotel's Wi-Fi when Carlotta was killed.'

'Looks like it.'

Vigdís made no attempt to hide her disappointment.

There was a note prominently displayed on Magnus's desk telling him to report to Thelma as soon as he arrived. He grabbed a cup of coffee and headed for her office. She was deep in conversation with Snorri, the National Police Commissioner. The conversation stopped abruptly as Magnus appeared.

'I'll come back,' Magnus said.

The Commissioner got up from his chair and gave Magnus a friendly grin. 'No, no, I was just leaving. Go ahead, Magnús.'

Magnus couldn't help wondering what they had been discussing. He hoped it had nothing to do with him.

'Any progress?' Thelma asked when the senior officer had left the room.

'Some,' said Magnus. 'We've established that Einar Thorsteinsson and Carlotta Mondini carried on a relationship several years ago. And she was unofficially helping him research the television documentary they were filming at Glaumbaer.'

'Is there a connection between the documentary and her death?'

'Not sure yet. There are still some leads to chase up.'

'Is Einar a suspect?'

'He has a strong alibi for when Carlotta was killed. But he keeps on hiding things from us. I'm not convinced that he is telling us the whole truth.'

'What about Eygló, the presenter?'

'She has been lying to us too, probably covering for him. But she also has an alibi for the time of death: she was logged on to the hotel Wi-Fi.'

Thelma nodded. 'Because I have had Ingólfur Sveinsson on the phone.' Ingólfur was the Minister of Justice, Magnus knew. 'Margrét, the Minister of Culture, has told him how important this documentary will be for Iceland; they expect it to be shown all over the world. She says it is vital that Einar and Eygló go to Greenland to film it before the weather turns bad.'

Magnus was impressed at how quickly someone had been working. He thought it unlikely it was Einar – he had seemed too distracted. Probably Suzy Henshaw or Eygló or both of them together. That might have explained the Commissioner's presence in Thelma's office.

'But surely if they are suspects in a murder investigation, that must take precedence?'

'That's what I told the minister, and that's what he says he told Margrét Sveinsdóttir. And if you need to keep them in the country, I'll make sure you can – I'll get the Commissioner involved if necessary.'

'But?'

'If it turns out that neither of them is a real suspect, it will be harder to defend the decision not to let him go.'

'I see. Sveinsson? Sveinsdóttir?'

Thelma smiled. 'Yes, the Minister of Justice is the Minister of Culture's younger brother.'

'That figures.' And Magnus had thought Boston's city politics was incestuous.

'Have you ever been to Greenland, Magnús?'

'No.'

'Well, the only direct flights from there are to Reykjavík and Copenhagen, so it will be difficult for Einar to skip town. Maybe you can work something out informally with the Greenlandic and Danish police to keep an eye out for him. We have good contacts.'

'Maybe.'

'So?'

Magnus thought a moment. Einar was always the more likely suspect than Eygló, and he was pretty sure now that Einar hadn't killed Carlotta. Although he wouldn't be surprised if Einar still hadn't told them everything, the man wasn't about to say anything more now. The police would have to search elsewhere for answers.

'All right,' he said. 'We'll let them go to Greenland.'

But as he left Thelma's office, he was not looking forward to telling Vigdís.

CHAPTER 22

'WHAT EXACTLY IS that?' said Professor Beccari, eyeing Eygló's dessert.

'Skyr. It's made from milk – it looks and tastes a bit like yoghurt. Try it. It's good, especially with berries.' Eygló picked up a spare spoon from the place setting next to her, and offered it to the Italian.

He recoiled. 'I've been warned about your Icelandic delicacies. Rotten shark. Rams' testicles.'

'Don't worry. The testicles taste much better when they are mushed up like this and added to the skyr.'

'There are rams' testicles in that?'

Eygló nodded. 'Only a teaspoon or so. Try it. Be brave.'

The challenge to the professor's courage was too much for him to resist, so he took the spoon and tasted the skyr.

'That's actually not too bad. A bit bitter.'

'You can add sugar and cream if you want.'

'It doesn't really have rams' testicles in it?' said Beccari.

Eygló grinned. 'No. Or at least I don't think so.'

'Einar seems distracted,' said Beccari, nodding at an empty plate. Einar and the others had just left the table, leaving Eygló and Beccari, and Ajay by himself a few places away.

They were having an early lunch in the hotel before filming at Ingjaldshóll, a few kilometres away, in the afternoon. The atmosphere had been tense. The crew knew that the police's questioning was focused on Einar, but with the exception of Suzy, who had been encouraging, they had avoided asking him about it.

He had looked miserable. As well he should, thought Eygló. She was still confident that he had nothing to do with Carlotta's death, but she thought he had no one to blame but himself for being implicated. And why had he thought it a good idea to bother her the night before? He had been genuinely distraught and her soft heart had gone out to him. He had insisted he just wanted comfort from her; she had insisted he sleep with his underpants on. But he should never have knocked on her door and she should never have let him in.

But she would have to wait for a good opportunity to talk to him in private. At least the others did not yet realize that she herself was now a suspect.

Damn Einar! It was all his fault.

'Is he a suspect for the murder, do you think?' Beccari asked.

'He shouldn't be, unless the police are complete morons,' said Eygló. 'He was with me and Suzy for most of the evening, and I saw him later on in the street.'

'So Carlotta was killed by a stranger?' Beccari asked.

'I've no idea,' said Eygló. 'I presume so. We don't get many murders here in Iceland, especially not of tourists.' She finished her skyr. 'Don't worry. The police will find whoever it is. They'll have to – no one wants our tourists murdered: they are far too important to our economy.' She was trying hard to sound confident and she thought she was succeeding.

'Can I get you a coffee?'

'That would be nice,' said Eygló.

The professor signalled to the waitress. He was wearing a pale yellow cashmere sweater and his pink scarf even indoors; Eygló was wearing a T-shirt. As so often in the last couple of years, she marvelled at how she was rubbing shoulders with such an august historian, almost as an equal. She was pleased to see that he was lingering. Certain middle-aged men liked her company. She was willing to take advantage of that, especially since none of the others were around.

Besides, she had something she needed to ask him, and she needed to warm him up first.

Start with flattery. 'I read *Thought, Light and New Worlds*,' she said. 'I thought it was absolutely brilliant.' And actually she had. Both read it and admired it. Beccari had achieved the historian's holy grail of putting across ideas that were both original and complex in an entertaining way. The sixteenth century wasn't her period, but there had been so many glowing reviews in the press that she had decided to ask for the book for Christmas two years before. Her mother had given it to her, and she had devoured it.

'I'm glad,' said the professor, with a total lack of surprise or even pleasure at the praise. Eygló found the arrogance a little off-putting, but he probably had earned it more than Einar.

'You know you are a very good TV presenter,' said Beccari. 'You really make the subject come alive. And you have a certain Nordic charm that gives your words a real power.'

Eygló blushed at the compliment. She didn't know whether he was simply returning her flattery, whether he was hitting on her, or whether he believed what he said to be true. She decided to believe the latter.

Professor Beccari was one of the most renowned historians in the world. His words meant something. Her former colleagues back at York or the University of Iceland might think she was a lightweight, but who were they when compared to Professor Marco Beccari?

'Thank you,' she said. 'You must have done loads of television stuff yourself?'

'Not really,' said Beccari. 'I usually avoid it. I used to suffer from that common suspicion among we academics toward popularizing history. Dumbing it down. Distorting the truth to make it entertaining rather than accurate. Slaughtering nuance.'

Eygló winced inwardly. She noted how the 'we academics' excluded her. She wanted to argue, to explain that her enthusiasm for history was perfectly genuine, and there was nothing wrong in sharing it. But she kept her cool.

'*Used* to suffer?' she said. 'You have changed your mind?'

'I think perhaps I have,' said Beccari. 'Sometimes we professional historians forget what drove us to the subject in the first place: the love of the past, the pleasure of imagining what life was like in another century, the vicarious excitement of experiencing a battle or a war or a great international crisis. Or the discovery of Vinland.'

Eygló smiled.

'So I should play my part in encouraging future historians,' Beccari went on. 'As long as I am not misrepresenting the truth, or oversimplifying.'

'I hope you don't think we are oversimplifying?' said Eygló.

'No,' said Beccari. But he hesitated. 'A little perhaps. But I can see it is unavoidable and I need to remind myself of that.'

That was accurate enough, thought Eygló.

'I am looking forward to doing the scenes in Rome,' she said. 'With the Columbus letter. I can't wait until it is right there in front of us. Will I be able to pick it up?'

'Oh, I am sure you will. With gloves, of course.'

'How do you feel when you touch something actually written by Columbus?'

Beccari laughed. 'Oh, I have touched so many things written by all kinds of famous people from the past. You get used to it. But Carlotta Mondini was very perceptive. This particular letter is something special.'

'People have been trying to figure out how far south the Vikings got for years. And now we know the answer.'

'It's much more than that,' said Beccari. 'It will change the whole way we look at Columbus and the discovery of America.' His voice warmed. 'For a couple of decades now, Columbus's position has been precarious. For centuries he has been seen as the man who discovered America. The Founding Fathers venerated him; the United States is full of places called Columbia, including the capital. There is even a country named after him. But he was looking for China. The Norsemen discovered America first, if not the Irish. And when he got to the New World, he was pretty brutal to the people he found there.

'Now, when I ...' Beccari hesitated and glanced at Eygló. 'When we announce to the world that Columbus knew all about America

124

before he got there because the Icelanders told him, I believe it will tip him over the edge.' Beccari chuckled. 'Some people won't like that – my old compatriots back in Italy, for instance.'

This was making Eygló nervous. She was very happy to bring her heroine Gudrid to the attention of the wider world. Trashing one of the most famous men in history was a different matter.

'I had some fruitful conversations with my publishers in New York before I flew out here,' Beccari said, chuckling again. 'Very fruitful. I have an idea for a book that is going to shake Columbine studies to its very core.'

Eygló was struck with a flash of jealousy. She and Suzy had a deal with a small British publisher to produce a slim volume of photographs and text about Gudrid to go with the series. And now this professor was going to make 'very fruitful' amounts of money from their idea!

But then he was the brilliant world-renowned historian and she wasn't.

Their discussion reminded Eygló forcefully of the question she needed to ask him. She wasn't sure how to ask it indirectly; so she asked it straight. 'Could it be a fake?'

Beccari's eyes fixed on her. 'Why do you ask that?' he demanded.

'Oh, I didn't mean to suggest ...'

Beccari grimaced in a complicated Italian expression that seemed to convey doubt and agreement at the same time. 'No, it's a perfectly fair question. I was suspicious at first, naturally, but it *is* genuine, I am quite sure of that. I will stake my reputation on it – I *have* staked my reputation on it.'

And it was quite some reputation. Which was fortunate, because the letter pointed to the authenticity of the wampum; they each supported the other. 'Good,' she said.

'You sound relieved?' said Beccari, a glimmer of suspicion returning to his eyes.

'Oh, no,' said Eygló. 'It's not that at all.'

'Because I am having to take the wampum find on trust,' said Beccari. 'Are you certain about it?'

'Einar is,' said Eygló. 'And he is one of the best archaeologists in Iceland.'

'But you?' Beccari's thick eyebrows were arched under his shining forehead.

'Yes, yes of course I am,' said Eygló. 'But it is comforting to hear an expert like you confirm the letter is real.'

Beccari still looked troubled. 'Well, I hope Einar knows what he is about.'

'Oh, he does, he does. He has total confidence in the wampum. He understands objects – he is not so good with paper. Which is why your opinion is so important to us.

'Ah, here is Suzy,' said Eygló with some relief as she saw the producer approaching them.

'Eygló? Marco?' Suzy said. 'We are leaving in ten minutes.'

Eygló had wanted to check if there was a seed of doubt in Beccari's mind about the Columbus letter. Well, there wasn't. Or there hadn't been – Eygló was a little concerned she had just planted one. Einar would be furious if he found out.

But she hadn't told the professor the complete truth. She had heard something while they were filming in Nantucket that had raised a doubt in her mind, a doubt that would not go away …

CHAPTER 23

EYGLÓ TOOK THE first sip of her margarita. Delicious. She looked out over the beach to the Atlantic, stretching eastwards towards Europe and Iceland. No, not Iceland, that was way to the north. France. Or maybe Spain.

'Cheers!' said Einar, sipping his own drink. 'Oh, that's good. I'd forgotten how delicious these things taste when it's really hot.'

Actually, it was cooler now, but still hotter in Nantucket than it ever got in Iceland. The sun was setting behind them, and Suzy, Tom and Ajay were scurrying around somewhere taking sunset shots, having deposited Eygló and Einar at the bar on the cliffs to wait for them. They were sitting outside, and the bar was full: beachgoers at the end of a long day overlapping with better dressed tourists beginning their evening. A group of students with the confidence of locals were knocking back the cocktails at the table next to them.

It had been a long day's filming. They had started out on a ten-metre sailing boat skimming the waves in Nantucket Sound, before moving on to the village of Siasconset to interview the Gudrid scholar and then on to Sesachacha Pond. Eygló was pleased: she thought she had done rather well. Suzy hadn't used Einar at all; she had got Nancy Fishburn to do his scenes at Sesachacha Pond. But he would have plenty to do when they got to Canada.

'So who was that "young woman" Nancy Fishburn was talking about before we did the interview?' Eygló asked. 'The one who was with you when you came here last year.'

'Oh, no one. Just a postgrad.'

'Anyone I know?'

'No, no. Foreign.' Einar hesitated. 'French.'

'And?'

'And what?'

'And why were you so coy about her? You never mentioned her to me before.'

'It's not what you think,' said Einar.

'Isn't it?'

'No. You know I don't mess around any more.'

Eygló raised her eyebrows.

'It's true! And I didn't want Rósa to find out. I had told her I was going to Nantucket alone. You'll keep this to yourself, won't you?'

'Maybe,' said Eygló, grinning. 'Maybe not. It depends whether you get me another margarita.'

It was just conceivable that Einar was telling the truth about not shagging his postgrad, but frankly Eygló could not be bothered to speculate about his philandering; she had given up on that years ago. Just as long as she wasn't expected to participate.

Einar tried to attract the harassed waitress's attention.

'Eygló?'

She turned to see one of the group of students standing next to her, a short blonde girl with a friendly smile, who looked more like eighteen than the twenty-one she must have been to be served alcohol. 'Aren't you Eygló? The presenter of *Viking Queens*?'

'That's me,' said Eygló. She was gratified. People in Iceland recognized her all the time, naturally, but she had never before been identified when travelling abroad.

'I loved that show,' the girl said. 'It was so cool what those women did back then. I thought in the Middle Ages women were just treated as, like, men's property.'

'They were, mostly,' said Eygló. 'But not necessarily in Scandinavia. I'm glad you liked it. And I'm surprised you recognized me.'

'Well, I knew you were interviewing my grandmother this afternoon. How did that go?'

'That was your grandmother? She was great. She could have been one of the Viking queens herself.'

The girl laughed. 'I'll tell her that. She is great, isn't she? And so smart. She pretends to be dotty, but she isn't.'

'Can I get you guys a drink?' Einar said.

Eygló was surprised at Einar's generosity to random students – most unlike him – until she looked more closely at the group. There were two girls and a boy, and one of the girls was tall and dusky with shoulder-length raven hair and sly dark eyes.

They were a friendly bunch; they all had parents or, in the case of the girl who had recognized Eygló, grandparents who lived or summered on the island, and they were working there for the season in bars and stores. Eygló particularly liked Nancy Fishburn's granddaughter, whose name was Kelly. She was majoring in history at a college in Ohio, and was pleasingly knowledgeable about the Vikings, an enthusiasm she said she had absorbed from her grandmother.

'So do you really think there were Vikings in Nantucket a thousand years ago?' Kelly asked Eygló.

'Sure,' said Eygló. 'We have evidence now – pretty strong evidence – that they were here.'

'The wampum?' said Kelly. 'That was found in Greenland.'

'That's part of it,' said Eygló. Kelly was a little drunk at this stage, but Eygló thought she detected a sceptical edge to her question. She wasn't sure. She knew the English better than the Americans, but she was an Icelander after all; some nuances passed her by. 'You heard about that?'

'Yeah. I remember when it was reported in the *Globe*. The whole family was here then. Grammy was really interested.'

'I'm not surprised.'

'I asked her if she had ever been to the spot where the wampum was discovered, and she told me she had.'

'Really?'

'Yeah. With Pops. Just before he died. They took a vacation to Greenland and went to see Erik the Red's farm. That's where they found the shell beads, right?'

'Yes. It was actually Einar who found them,' said Eygló.

They both looked at Einar, who was regaling Kelly's friends with a story about a trip he had taken to Thailand when he was a student, and the island he had discovered. Eygló had heard it many times before. It seemed to be going down well with his audience; it usually did the first time he told it.

'Grammy gave this weird little smile and said that she knew exactly where the wampum had been found. On the way back to Pittsburgh after the trip, Dad said he was willing to bet Grammy had planted the wampum herself.'

Kelly giggled and Eygló smiled too. It took a second for the implication of what Kelly was saying to sink in. Was she serious? Because if she was ...

'Why did your dad think that?'

'Hi, everyone!' It was Suzy.

'Hey. What are you drinking?' Einar asked her.

'I'm driving. And we had better get going. I made a dinner reservation for eight back in town and we're going to be late.'

'She's the boss,' said Einar to his new friends, grinning. 'I guess we have to go. It's been great talking to you.' This to the girl with the sly eyes, which were now focused very much on Einar.

Eygló wanted an answer to her last question, but in the jostling of their departure she didn't get one. She exchanged waves and smiles with Kelly as Suzy bustled them off to their rented van, where Tom and Ajay were waiting.

They were staying in Nantucket town a few miles away, and Suzy had booked a table at a restaurant there. It was dark now.

Buoyed by the margaritas, and the attention, Einar was very chatty. Eygló was listening to him with half an ear and less than half her brain. She was thinking about what Kelly had said.

Was she joking? Could the sweet old lady Eygló had interviewed that afternoon really have planted the wampum in Greenland? Was she really that sweet? 'Shrewd' might be a better description.

The immediate problem was should Eygló tell the others? And if so, which others? It would be a disaster all round if the wampum had been planted.

Perhaps she should discuss it with Einar before mentioning it to Suzy? But Einar, she knew, would tell her to stay quiet.

Should she wait? Think about what to do? But once she did that, then she would have created a secret, an awkward secret.

Do the honest, straightforward thing. Tell everyone right away, and let them decide what to do. Because if Nancy Fishburn *had* planted the wampum, the sooner they knew it, the better.

She waited for Einar to pause for breath and interrupted. 'That girl Kelly told me something very interesting in the bar ...'

They took the ferry off the island the following afternoon, to Hyannis on the mainland. The plan was to drive from there north to Canada to film other locations that Gudrid had probably visited.

Eygló leaned over the railing at the stern, watching the ship's wake thread its way through the harbour crowded with fishing boats and sleek motor cruisers. The picture-postcard town of Nantucket, with its tall whaling-captain's houses and its white spires, receded at five knots. She thought of the Icelandic equivalents, fishing villages like Grindavík or Ólafsvík, pretty in their own way, but lacking the reek of wealth that emanated from Nantucket and had done so for centuries. In the nineteenth century this had been generated by whale oil harvested from all over the world's oceans; now it came from money skimmed from the global financial markets by the prosperous men in baseball caps and red shorts holed up in those magnificent houses picketing the shoreline.

'That was a good start, Eygló,' said Suzy. 'Let's hope the weather is as sunny in Nova Scotia and Newfoundland.'

'Have you checked the forecast?' Eygló asked.

'Tom has. There's a storm coming through there now, but it might have cleared by the time we film. But we could be OK, even if it hasn't. A bit of grey moodiness would contrast nicely with the sunshine here. Show how tough the journey must have been for Gudrid and the others.'

'Have you thought any more about what Nancy Fishburn's granddaughter told me?' Eygló wanted to make the most of

Einar's absence to discuss it. In the car the previous evening, and at dinner, he had been adamant that Kelly was wrong, and it seemed that Suzy had been happy to believe him.

'Yes, I have. I know Einar's view, but we have to check it out. So I drove out to Siasconset this morning and tracked down Kelly – she is working in the village store.'

'What did she say?'

'She was mortified. She said she hadn't meant you to take her seriously, she was a bit drunk. She said you had got the wrong end of the stick; her father was kidding. He does that all the time. She pleaded with me not to ask her grandmother about it directly; I think Kelly is a little scared of her.'

'Probably justified,' said Eygló. 'I can see how a retired university professor would not want people to think she had planted archaeological evidence.'

'So can I.'

'So you are sure she didn't plant it?'

'I'm sure Kelly doesn't really think she did,' said Suzy.

It wasn't quite the same thing, but Eygló let it go. It was good enough.

They were now passing the spit of sand that marked the edge of the outer harbour and were in open water. The ferry felt much more stable than the sailing boat of the day before.

'I'm glad you told us, though, Eygló. The only thing worse than cancelling the project because it all turned out to be a massive hoax would be not cancelling it and getting caught. That would be a real disaster.'

Eygló smiled. 'Cancelling would be bad,' she said. Her TV presenting career was taking off. The last thing she wanted was for it to crash. Then her life would be crap again.

'Yes,' said Suzy. She sighed. 'I really need *The Wanderer* to work.'

'*Viking Queens* worked, didn't it?'

'Yes. Brilliantly. And we made a lot of money. But we over-extended ourselves on another project, about women and the Crusades. It was big: the BBC were backing it, and a major

US network. It was expensive: actors, CGI, travel all over the Mediterranean. Then *A Cross in the East* came out on a cable network in the US and flopped big time. The US network pulled out and the woman who had commissioned it at the BBC quit to join Netflix. The BBC paid us, but it wasn't nearly enough to cover all our costs, and the programme never aired.'

Eygló winced.

'I had broken the golden rule of television production: don't commit money you don't have. We had ploughed in the profits from *Viking Queens* and then some on the basis it would be an international hit.' She glanced at Eygló and saw her worry. 'We'll be OK. You've probably noticed we're doing *The Wanderer* on a shoestring.'

They seemed to be staying in nice hotels and flying all over the North Atlantic, but it was true there were fewer people involved on location than there had been on *Viking Queens*. Then there had been an assistant producer and a professional sound man rather than a student, and usually a couple of local fixers wherever they went, and lots more equipment. It was a tighter crew this time, which actually made things easier, at least as far as Eygló was concerned.

'The BBC are definitely behind this, as are the Canadian network, and once we've made it I'm sure I can get the History Channel interested in the States. As long as we get this in the can by the beginning of October, we will be fine.'

No wonder Suzy seemed a little tense, Eygló thought. But she was competent and Eygló had witnessed how she got things done, how she overcame every obstacle.

They would be fine. *The Wanderer* would be finished by the beginning of October.

CHAPTER 24

EYGLÓ, SUZY, BECCARI, Tom and Ajay left Einar in Ólafsvík as they drove the ten kilometres further along Snaefellsnes to the isolated church of Ingjaldshóll. The site of the church dated back to settlement times, when a Viking named Ingjaldur chose that hill on which to build his farm. The current incarnation of the church dated from the beginning of the twentieth century, and it was supposedly the first concrete church in Iceland.

It was a lonely spot. Inside was a modern mural of Christopher Columbus, who local legend insisted had spent the winter of 1477 there. It was somewhere to film, a visual backdrop from which to expound the more compelling evidence from Christopher's letter to his younger brother Bartholomew. This, Professor Beccari did with some skill and enthusiasm. When the programme was broadcast, there would be a swift cut to the letter itself in the Vatican. In reality it would be three weeks before they were in Rome, filming the letter itself in the Vatican Secret Archives.

Eygló had come to accept that there was a certain amount of hanging around whenever filming was involved, and she killed ten minutes by walking down the little road from the church. She was still badly shaken by her interview that morning. On the one hand, what should she expect if she withheld information from the police? They were only doing their jobs, and it was hardly surprising if they were not impressed with her lies about knowing Carlotta. Similarly, she couldn't really expect them to believe the truth, which was that nothing had happened between her and

Einar the night before. How could he have been so stupid as to let the black detective see him leaving her room? How could she be so stupid as to let him stay the night?

But while she had been prepared for the possibility that there might be consequences for covering for Einar, it had never occurred to her that they would suspect *her* of killing Carlotta. That really was ridiculous. She would have expected more from Magnus. She had thought he had an air of calm competence about him; that was obviously incorrect. Another man misjudged.

A spasm of panic clutched at her chest. Common sense told her that the police would soon recognize their error. But they did make mistakes. There were miscarriages of justice, innocent people sent to jail.

Get a grip. Focus on the documentary. Trust the police to find who really had killed poor Carlotta. Pray it wasn't Einar.

She turned and climbed back up the hill. Tom and Ajay were packing up their equipment.

She wandered over to them. The weather wasn't bad for filming: small clouds scudded across the pale blue sky, propelled by a firm breeze from the west. From the spot Tom had chosen, the white church with its classic red roof stood tall and strong on its knoll, while behind it the dormant Snaefellsjökull volcano slumbered under its blanket of ancient ice, glistening in the sunshine. The perfect backdrop: a classic Icelandic landscape at its most beautiful.

'Hi, Tom,' said Eygló.

'Hi,' said Tom. Eygló wasn't expecting more. Tom never said very much of anything, but he was an expert in the companionable silence. Once you knew it wasn't just you he avoided conversation with, then you didn't take his silence personally.

He was small, with a full, light brown beard, and thick hairy legs – he habitually wore baggy shorts, no matter what the weather. He was in his mid forties, Eygló guessed, and she thought he came from the north of England; his accent sounded familiar from her time in York. He was tough and resourceful and seemed more comfortable outdoors than in. More than once she was surprised to hear him speaking English rather than Icelandic – he could easily have been an Icelander.

'Can I carry anything?' she asked.

'That's OK,' he said, slinging a heavy camera bag over one shoulder and the tripod over the other. It was incredible how much Tom could carry while still walking rapidly. Ajay struggled along behind with his smaller load.

They set off together towards Suzy's rented Land Cruiser in the church car park.

'Greenland tomorrow, with any luck,' Eygló said. 'If the police let us go. Suzy has tried pulling strings at the Ministry of Culture.'

'Suzy will fix it,' said Tom. 'She always does.'

'Have you ever been? To Greenland?'

'Only to the north. I used to do mostly nature stuff. I did a documentary on walruses once, about ten years ago. No green in sight. Unlike where we are going.'

Eygló was surprised by Tom's relative chattiness, and thought she would make the most of it. 'Did you see any polar bears?'

'Just one. In the distance. I got a reasonable shot of it.'

'Why did you switch from nature?'

'I was "between jobs", had been for some time, and I needed the money. So I did some work for Suzy: a short documentary about monks in Ireland. I enjoyed it; I've always liked history. And Suzy and me work well together.'

'You certainly do.'

For half a minute it seemed as if Tom had run out of things to say, but then he spoke.

'Ajay heard you talking to that professor. At lunch.'

'Oh really?' Ajay must have pretty good hearing, Eygló thought. He had been sitting a few metres away, but then the room had been empty. And he was a sound guy after all.

'You need to be careful,' Tom said.

'What do you mean?'

'About talking down this project. About scaring the professor. We are committed now, all of us. Even if the wampum is a fake, or the Columbus letter, it's too late to do anything about it now.'

136

'But if they are fakes, we have to be honest about it.'

'Oh no we don't,' said Tom. His voice was firm.

'But we have our reputations to think about. Our integrity.'

Tom stopped and looked straight at Eygló. 'You are not listening to me. We don't think about that. We make this film. And then we broadcast it.'

Suddenly his voice had an undertone of threat to it, which took Eygló aback. She had been expecting problems from Professor Beccari or Suzy, but not from Tom.

'Are you worried about losing your job?' she said. 'Can't you just get something else? Go back to nature programmes?'

'It's not me, it's Suzy. She watches my back; I watch hers.'

'She told me that she had overextended herself,' said Eygló. 'That she had to make this programme by the end of October.'

'She might not have said that her house is in danger of being repossessed. And that her little jerk of a husband is threatening to leave her if that happens. And take the kids with him.'

'No, she didn't say that.' In fact Eygló hadn't appreciated what Suzy was telling her: that the failure of The Wanderer would be more than just a professional setback, it would be disaster. Under the circumstances, Suzy was behaving with admirable calmness. For a moment Eygló wondered whether a husband who ran off with the kids when the going got tough was a husband worth keeping, but she knew lots of women who did their best to hang on to bad men. Eygló, at least, had been able to cut them loose, whenever she lumbered herself with one.

'I'll be careful,' she said. 'But if I discover that the wampum was planted by that old lady, I will have to say something.'

'No you won't.' Tom's blue eyes were staring hard at Eygló. 'That's my point, you won't.'

Eygló felt the anger rise up inside her. 'Or what?'

'Look what happened to Carlotta.'

'What!' The anger mixed with a sudden dash of fear. 'Did I hear you right?'

'I think so,' said Tom.

'Are you saying Carlotta was killed because she was about to expose the Columbus letter?'

'Or the wampum.'

'How do you know that?' Eygló asked.

'It's obvious, isn't it?'

Was it? Eygló thought. Not necessarily. How could Tom be so sure?

'Was it you? Was it you who killed Carlotta?'

Tom turned on his heel and strode off rapidly towards Suzy and Beccari who were standing beside the car.

'Tom!' Eygló called after him.

But Tom didn't answer.

CHAPTER 25

MAGNUS WAS QUITE correct: Vigdís was not happy about letting Einar and Eygló go to Greenland. Magnus was grateful it was only a short drive from police headquarters to Borgartún, where Einar's wife Rósa was a partner in a small law firm, but it was long enough for Vigdís to give him her opinion.

Borgartún was Reykjavík's answer to Wall Street, a long straight road that ran along the bay. It had flourished in the noughties, when glossy bank headquarters had bloomed, along with lesser but equally glossy buildings housing accountants, lawyers and the other services ancillary to the great credit boom that afflicted Iceland then. During Magnus's last stint in Reykjavík after the crash of 2008, the heart had been ripped out of the area, as the banks were renamed and *For Rent* signs sprouted everywhere. But now it looked prosperous again.

Magnus and Vigdís pulled into a car park outside a small sleek building of soft brown stone and black glass. Rósa's firm was on the first floor. One of those dark-haired Icelandic beauties with clear skin and clear blue eyes smiled from behind a desk and greeted them. Magnus introduced himself and Vigdís, and said they wanted to see Rósa on a personal matter. Unfazed, the receptionist showed them into a small conference room with a view across Borgartún to one of the banks that had risen from the ashes and was flexing its rediscovered financial muscles.

Magnus looked down at the Range Rovers and the BMWs cruising the street below. 'Are we going to go through all this again, Vigdís? Surely we must have learned something?'

'I'm not sure we have,' said Vigdís. 'I bet all those cars were paid for on credit. I still haven't got over the last mess: my mortgage is just as big as it always was.'

Magnus didn't have a mortgage. He didn't even own a bed. He still hadn't moved his stuff into Tryggvi Thór's place. He had yet to find a property ladder, let alone step on its first rung. What had he done with his life? Ten years before he had been living in the Back Bay of Boston with a successful lawyer who worked in an office much like this. And now? Not a lot of progress had been made.

After ten minutes or so, the door opened and a woman with short blonde hair entered. She was big – at least six feet tall – with the broad shoulders and triangular body shape of a swimmer. Her jaw was square and her eyes blue. She wore a blue business suit and modern gold earrings of a design that Magnus recognized. They came from Ingileif's gallery, and she had often worn a similar pair herself.

She shook Magnus and Vigdís's hands. 'I'm sorry you had to wait a little. It might have been better if you had made an appointment.' She exuded competence and confidence.

'It's not that kind of visit,' said Magnus.

Rósa sat opposite them at the table, pad of paper and slim fountain pen at the ready. 'What kind of visit is it?'

'We are investigating a murder.'

'Oh, really. Whose?'

'Don't you know?'

Rósa hesitated, but only for a moment. 'Carlotta Mondini?'

'That's correct.'

Rósa's eyes held Magnus's. They were sharp, ready to assess difficult questions.

'Have you ever met Carlotta Mondini?' Magnus began.

'We were never introduced,' Rósa said drily.

'We have interviewed Einar a few times,' Magnus said. 'Has he mentioned it?'

'I haven't seen him since it happened,' said Rósa.

'But you must have spoken to him on the phone?'

'Yes. Once. I saw the murder on the news and I called him. We agreed to discuss it tonight when he gets home from Snaefellsnes. Carlotta Mondini has always been a sore subject between us. But of course I am sorry the poor woman is dead. No one deserves that. Have you any idea who did it?'

'So you knew about his affair with Carlotta?' Magnus asked.

'Yes. Or at least the original affair. I found out five years ago when Einar was at York and I had just started up the firm here.'

Rósa's little blue suitcase rumbled over the cobbles of Swinegate. She was moving fast, anxious to get to Einar's flat, which was only a hundred metres away. He wouldn't be expecting her and she hadn't warned him she was early. She had got through Heathrow in record time and managed to catch an earlier train from King's Cross to York than she expected.

For three days the anxiety had been crushing her. Fortunately there was plenty of work to keep her occupied back in Reykjavík, but once she was on the plane to London her impatience had risen. She needed Einar. She grinned to herself.

She needed Einar now!

She rounded the corner into a narrow alley of half-timbered buildings and rang a bell next to a small boutique selling shoes that was always empty.

Her heart thudded as she waited for the door to be open. She smiled. She and Einar had been married nearly twelve years, and been together much longer than that, and her heart still thudded. She knew his did also.

She heard the sound of his feet clattering down the wooden stairs inside, running, and there was a thud as he took the final three in one leap. The door opened and there he was! Tall, those blue eyes dancing at the sight of her.

'Rósa!'

His flat was tiny and on the first floor. He flipped her suitcase into the building and left it at the bottom of the stairs. He dragged her up the staircase, laughing, through the open door to his flat and kissed her hard and deep.

'I wasn't expecting you this early,' he said.

'Really?' Rósa laughed. 'It looks like you're pleased to see me.'

'I am *so* pleased to see you!' he said. He lifted her up as if she were a feather. Einar was tall, but Rósa was almost as tall as him. She was also strong and a little heavy: Einar was the only man she had ever met who could carry her so effortlessly.

He took her through to the sitting room and threw her down on the kilim they had bought together from a man in the bazaar in Erzurum. They were good at this by now: within seconds her jeans were down to her thighs, as were her knickers, and he was inside her, moving up and down with a vigour that was both familiar and a revelation.

It only took a minute or two, yet already his back was sweaty.

He kissed her slowly, gently.

She smiled up at him. And then, unbidden, a tear leaked out of one eye. She sniffed and wiped it.

The glow in Einar's smile switched to concern. 'Rósa? Rósa? What's wrong? I didn't hurt you, did I?'

'Oh, no, no, my darling, no.' She leaned up to kiss him. 'I have just been a bit emotional recently. It's *so* good to see you.'

'Come to bed.'

She stood up, and he gently removed first her clothes and then his. She led him into his bedroom, and within a couple of moments she was snuggled up under his arm, smelling the sweet sweat of sex.

The tears had stopped.

'What is it?' Einar said. 'Tell me.'

She wanted to tell him, she knew she must, but not just then, not at that moment. She wanted to stay in his arms for ever; she wanted time to stop on that Friday afternoon in October 2012.

The future scared the hell out of her.

'You almost missed me,' Einar said, stroking Rósa's hair. 'I was just about to go out and get some champagne. I won't be a minute.'

'Oh, stay here a bit longer.'

'Come on, Rósa. That's what Friday afternoons are for, isn't it? Screwing and drinking.'

Rósa could see Einar was determined. 'OK,' she nodded. The wine shop was only a few minutes' walk away. She didn't need the champagne, but she knew Einar liked the decadence of it. 'Be quick.'

Hurriedly he pulled on some clothes and left the flat.

Rósa lay naked on the bed staring up at the ceiling. Trying not to think.

Einar's phone chirped on the bedside table a few centimetres from Rósa's head. She twisted to glance at it. What she saw made her gasp in horror.

I need to fuck you. Now!

She twisted rapidly away from the phone. No. No. NO!

Oh God. Could she unsee what she had just seen? She had to. Oh, Einar, why? Why? WHY?

She lay there, her chest heaving, trying through concentrating on her breathing to ignore what she had seen. She knew Einar used to do that kind of thing. She had hoped he had stopped, but of course he hadn't.

Who was she? Don't answer that question. Don't *ask* that question.

Who was she?

She rolled over and grabbed Einar's phone. The short text had disappeared. Before she had time to stop herself, Rósa's fingers had flown over the screen and tapped in Einar's code: 1104, the year Hekla erupted, a key date for Icelandic archaeologists, since Norse remains either lay below or above the layer of ash deposited all over the country by the volcano in that year. She knew Einar didn't suspect she knew the code, but it had only taken her five tries a couple of years before to guess it.

There was a whole stream of texts back and forth going back months, all from a woman called Carlotta.

At first Rósa assumed she was an undergraduate at York, but as Rósa scrolled through the texts, she realized who Carlotta was.

She tossed the phone on the bedside table, hunched her knees up to her chest and wept.

'Ta dah!' Einar thrust open the door waving a bottle of cava in front of him. 'Rósa? Rósa, what's wrong?'

He sat next to her and put his arm around her naked shoulders. For a tiny moment Rósa wanted to lean into his familiar body, but then a rush of anger overcame her and she wriggled free.

Fear mixed with concern in Einar's eyes. He knew he had been caught. 'Rósa?'

'Who is Carlotta?'

'Carlotta?'

'Yes, Carlotta.'

'Er. There was a Carlotta on the dig in Greenland. An Italian girl. Actually, she was the one who found the wampum. Is that who you mean?'

'Yes, it is.'

'Oh.'

'How long have you been sleeping with her?'

'I haven't been sleeping with her.'

'Don't lie to me, Einar. Not now.'

'She and I did have a night together maybe. Just after she found the wampum. But that was over a year ago. And I'm really sorry.'

Rósa didn't say anything. She couldn't say anything.

'It was a mistake. You know I've done that every now and then. But I've stopped now, I promise.'

The anger dried up Rósa's tears.

Einar put his hand on Rósa's shoulder. This time she didn't brush it off.

'Rósa? Have some champagne.'

'How was Venice?'

'Venice?'

'Yes. You went to Venice last weekend. With Carlotta.'

'Er …'

'When I called you last weekend and you said you were marking essays, you were in Venice with another woman. A woman who you had been seeing for over a year.'

'Actually, I *was* marking essays.'

'Einar!' Rósa screamed. She shook off his hand and walked over to the window, staring out at the couple of pedestrians in the street below.

She knew Einar slept with other women. He always had. At first she had hoped that he would stop once they were going out, and then once they were married, but he hadn't. She pretended not to notice. She knew he loved her more than any of the others, she never doubted it for one minute. There had been one who had been serious – Eygló – and although Rósa hadn't confronted Einar, she had confronted the other woman, who had backed off in shame.

But with that exception she was pretty certain none had ever lasted for more than a night or two.

Maybe she was wrong. Maybe Einar had a whole string of steady girlfriends all over the world; maybe she was just one of many.

'Damn you, Einar! Not now. Why now?'

'Hey, look, Rósa, I'm so sorry.'

'I want you to get rid of her,' Rósa said.

'Yes of course,' Einar said in his conciliatory voice. 'Of course I will.'

'No, I mean it!'

'And I mean it,' Einar said. But he didn't. She knew that. He knew that.

She turned to face him. 'Einar, the reason I was crying earlier. Before I found out about Carlotta ...'

'Yes?'

'I have breast cancer.'

Einar's jaw loosened. He looked at Rósa with a mixture of horror and compassion. And love. Deep love. She could see it.

'When did you find out? Why didn't you tell me?'

'Three days ago. And I'm telling you now.'

Einar sat, his eyes never leaving Rósa, his face a battlefield of emotions.

'Einar, I'm going to ask you again. I want you to stop sleeping with Carlotta. And any other woman after her. Will you promise me that?

145

He closed his eyes. He looked up to the ceiling, then back at Rósa. His lower jaw wobbled. Rósa realized he was on the verge of tears himself. Rósa had never seen Einar cry.

'Yes,' he said, his voice so quiet she could barely hear it. 'Yes. I promise you, Rósa. I will not sleep with Carlotta again. Nor with any other woman.' He swallowed. 'Ever.'

Rósa looked at Magnus and Vigdís. 'And I thought he kept that promise. Did he?'

Magnus didn't answer.

'Carlotta was here in Iceland, wasn't she? She was found dead at Glaumbaer where Einar had been filming that day. It was on the TV news. I'm no fool.'

That was for sure. 'So you think he had restarted the affair?' Magnus asked.

'Had he? You know; I don't.' She was still cool, but her blue eyes were piercing. There was anger there.

'We don't know for sure,' said Magnus. He did know that Einar had a very awkward evening with his wife ahead of him.

'Do you think my husband killed her?' Rósa asked.

'Why would he do that?' said Magnus.

'I have no idea,' said Rósa. 'And furthermore I find it impossible to think of my husband as a killer. An occasional scumbag, perhaps, but that's different.' Her eyes hardened. 'Don't play games with me, Inspector. I know you have a job to do, but I have a marriage to protect. Tell me what you need to know and I will endeavour to answer. But don't try to trick me into incriminating my husband.'

'I won't play games,' said Magnus. 'But I do need to know how much you knew about Carlotta, and about your husband's relationship with her. Has Einar told you anything about a letter that was discovered in the Vatican archives last year, written by Christopher Columbus to his brother? Does he discuss his work with you?'

'Oh, yes, he does. I've always been very interested in what he's doing. In fact that's how we met; we were students together. I loved archaeology, and I would have liked to stick with it, but one of us had to earn some real money and so I went to law school. So I know about the letter and the wampum that Carlotta found in Greenland. But I thought the guy who discovered the letter was called Federico. Federico Trapanese, I think?'

'He may have discovered it, but it was Carlotta who told Einar about it. We think that's what she wanted to speak to him about in Saudárkrókur.'

'So you mean they weren't having an affair?'

Magnus shrugged. He really didn't want to mess with this woman's marriage any more than he had to; there was no need to mention Einar's trip to Nantucket with Carlotta. 'As I said, we don't know. Einar denies it.'

'Of course he does.'

Magnus had one more question to ask. 'As a lawyer, I am sure you will understand the reason for my next question. Where were you precisely last Monday night?'

'I was in London seeing a client. I left on Sunday and came back late on Monday night.'

'Can you give us details of your flights and hotel?'

'By all means,' said Rósa. She pulled out her phone, tapped it, scribbled flight numbers and a London hotel name down on her pad and tore off the sheet to give to Magnus.

Rósa hadn't returned to Keflavík Airport until 10.30 p.m. on Monday night. If she had driven directly from Keflavík to Glaumbaer, she wouldn't have arrived there until three or four in the morning.

On their way out, Rósa asked the receptionist to show Magnus and Vigdís the confirmed flight details and check-in confirmations on her computer and to print them out. It would take a day or so to check the London hotel; they would be unable to request the information from the hotel directly but would need to go through the British police. But Magnus was confident that the hotel would confirm that Rósa had stayed the night there.

Rósa hadn't murdered Carlotta.

CHAPTER 26

MAGNUS'S CAR WAS parked next to a low wall facing Borgartún. As he opened the door he saw a blonde woman walking along the pavement, a small boy attached to her left hand.

He stopped.

She looked up.

Her eyes met his. Grey eyes. Sad. Familiar. So familiar.

Ingileif.

'Hi,' said Magnus.

The sadness left the woman's eyes to be replaced by confusion, and then a smile, the warm enthusiastic smile that Magnus knew so well.

'Magnús! I didn't realize you were back in Iceland?'

'You didn't? I've been here a month. I would have thought you would have heard by now.'

Ingileif glanced at Vigdís. 'Are you back with the police?'

'Yes. Permanently this time.'

'Oh.'

Magnus couldn't mistake the lack of enthusiasm in that monosyllable.

Neither could Ingileif. 'Sorry. I mean, great! Boston didn't work out?'

'Not really.' Magnus grinned hesitantly. 'I still can't figure out whether I'm an Icelander or an American.' It was something he and Ingileif had discussed frequently while he was living here the last time.

'You didn't get in touch?'

'No,' said Magnus simply. He wanted to explain that he had been afraid to even see her. That he didn't trust himself or her not to rekindle a relationship that had been so destructive for both of them before.

'Oh,' she said again. It was five years since Magnus had seen her, and she had changed. Her face was more lined, her blonde hair a little longer. And despite her apparent enthusiasm to see him, Magnus sensed an air of weary sadness about her that was new. But the little nick in her left eyebrow that he remembered so well was still there.

'Are you still working in the gallery?'

'Yes. Business is picking up. And I'm doing some interior-design work for people. And there is Ási.'

Magnus looked down at the small red-haired boy who was staring straight back at him with piercing blue eyes.

He squatted down so he was level with the boy, the boy's eyes peering over the low wall between them. 'Hi,' he said. 'My name is Magnús. How old are you?'

'Hello,' said the boy, still staring straight at him. 'I'm four. How old are you?'

Magnus grinned. 'I'm forty-one. And a half.'

He stood up. 'Named after his grandfather? That's good.'

Ási was short for Ásgrímur, the name of Ingileif's father, a doctor who had died on a mountainside many years before – murdered. It was, indirectly, the reason Magnus and Ingileif had met.

'Yeah,' Ingileif said. 'We must be going. We're off to meet Hannes; he works along here.'

'Hannes?'

'My husband.'

'Oh, yes, I'd forgotten.'

Ingileif smiled quickly and pulled her son down the street. The little boy twisted to look at Magnus again, and then, feeling the tug on his arm from his mother, turned away.

Back at the station some progress had been made. They now had the call history and location of every call Carlotta had made while she was in Iceland. There were not many of them. There were only two Icelandic numbers: Einar and the hotel in Blönduós in which she had stayed. There was a US number and texts to and from a couple of Italian numbers, which the Italian police would check out. She had made no calls, even to Einar, on the day of her death; they had all been made from Reykjavík in the few days before.

They also had a more limited analysis of where Eygló's phone had been on the night of Carlotta's murder. It had never left Saudárkrókur after eight o'clock.

Magnus handed over Einar's laptop and phone to Computer Forensics, who would mirror it and return it to him, before analysing it. Forensics had checked the tyre prints of Einar's RAV4, and they didn't correspond with those found on the farm track where the girl on the bike had seen the man get into his car.

Sergeant Tacchini had reported back. He had driven to Padua himself and spoken to a number of Carlotta's friends there, including a former boyfriend. Naturally, they were devastated to hear about her death. A couple of close girlfriends had heard of Einar, but knew little about him except that he was an Icelandic archaeology professor and that Carlotta was very keen on him. They knew about the discovery of the wampum in Greenland, but Carlotta didn't seem to have told anyone about the Columbus letter. Her friends said she had been excited about the trip to Iceland; they put it down to seeing Einar again.

Her supervisor spoke highly of Carlotta. She had always been enthusiastic about the Vikings – she had been the only under-graduate from Padua to go on the dig to Greenland, and the only graduate to go to Sweden. The supervisor had never heard Carlotta speak about Einar Thorsteinsson, and indeed had never heard of him herself.

There was no sign of any enemies in Padua, or of any involve-ment in drugs or any other criminal activity. No one could think why anyone would want to kill their friend.

The university bureaucracy were still waiting for the appro-priate authorizations from a judge to release details of Carlotta's email account, but through her friends Tacchini was able to forward screenshots of Carlotta's posts on her Facebook page going back several years. Vigdís started working through them. Magnus gave Tacchini the two Italian numbers Carlotta had texted, and Tacchini promised to check them out.

Árni called to say that the Akureyri police had had a break-through in the rape case, and had just made an arrest – a thirty-one-year-old hospital porter named Gudni Fridriksson. They would ask the suspect about Carlotta, and his whereabouts on the night Carlotta was murdered.

Vigdís followed up with the British police and the London hotel, who promised to get back to her within twenty-four hours. Icelandair confirmed that Rósa had indeed flown from Keflavík out to Heathrow on Sunday evening.

A man from the Italian Embassy showed up, demanding on behalf of Carlotta's parents to know how the investigation was going. Magnus told him there were still plenty of leads to follow, trying to project a calm confidence he didn't quite feel, but it seemed to satisfy the diplomat.

Árni and his team were busy interviewing tourists, in particular Italian tourists, in the area of Saudárkrókur, but without any success. There were no more leads from locals at Glaumbaer either.

They weren't yet stuck, but they were heading that way.

CHAPTER 27

EYGLÓ GOT BACK to her tiny apartment in Kópavogur just before six, in time to make Bjarki his dinner. Bjarki was playing *Football Manager*; he had ditched *FIFA*, which had been his favourite computer game for years. He said *Football Manager* was more of a challenge, but it seemed less sociable than the other game.

Eygló had given up trying to ration gaming time years ago. Bjarki always seemed to get his homework done one way or another. He was actually doing quite well at school.

'Hi!' she shouted.

'Hi!' he replied, his gaze never leaving the screen. He was a little small for his age, slim and quick, and pretty good at football, which was still what seemed to matter at his age.

'So I hear that Arsenal guy is going to Chelsea?'

'He'll never do that,' Bjarki said. 'He wants to play for Liverpool – at least he'll get a place in the team with us. I just hope we don't overpay like we did for that Egyptian guy from Roma. What we need now is a really good defender.'

Eygló didn't argue; on matters to do with the valuation of soccer players, Bjarki was the undisputed king. It was comforting to know that if he ever screwed up his exams and failed to get to university, at least he could still become the manager of an English Premier League football club.

She thought of asking him how school had been, or his stay with her sister Andrea while she had been away, but there was no point. And she knew from her sister that he had been fine. He would be staying with her other sister, Soffía, for the next ten days while Eygló was in Greenland. That would be fine also: there were two younger cousins who idolized Bjarki, and Soffía thought he was a good influence on them.

Eygló owed her sisters, big time.

She grabbed some sausages out of the fridge and started to make a salad.

She felt safe here, in her apartment with Bjarki, but it wouldn't last. Tomorrow she would be going to Greenland with Suzy, Einar, Professor Beccari, Ajay. And Tom.

Tom's threat had really shaken her. She now saw him in a totally different light. Previously, she had taken his unwillingness to talk as evidence that he was the strong, silent type: loyal, competent, reassuring. Now she feared it was an indicator that he was a weirdo or a sociopath, and that his loyalty to Suzy was more like blind worship than respect.

She had no idea what he really thought or why he did what he did.

And what had he meant when he had reminded her of Carlotta's fate? Did he mean that whatever unknown person had killed Carlotta had done it to prevent questions about the authenticity of the Columbus letter or the wampum? Or did he mean that he knew who had killed Carlotta and why?

Or, and this was the most frightening alternative, had it been he who had murdered the Italian woman? She would soon be travelling to Greenland for ten days with this guy.

Eygló had been asking more questions about the wampum than she had let on to Tom or Beccari. As soon as she had arrived back in Iceland after the Nantucket trip, she had consulted the record of Einar's dig at Brattahlíd in 2011 to see whether there was any indication there that the wampum might have been planted. There wasn't, although the report did state that the shells had been found in a disturbed context adjacent to the 1932 trench.

As Eygló thought more about it, she realized that in normal circumstances it would be extremely difficult to plant the wampum

153

clamshells convincingly. But if the contexts had become jumbled at the edge of the old excavation trench, then the wampum shells could have been planted at any depth without raising suspicions. However, just because the shells could have been planted, didn't mean they had been.

Eygló and Einar had had a tense conversation on the way back to Reykjavík from Ólafsvík in Einar's car. Einar told her that Professor Beccari had grilled him about the wampum, but Einar was confident he had put up a robust defence. Eygló believed him; Einar really knew his stuff when it came to Norse archaeology, and his arrogant self-assurance could only have helped.

But when Einar had wondered aloud why Beccari had suddenly become suspicious, Eygló had foolishly repeated her lunchtime conversation with the professor. As she had expected at the time, Einar was furious. In his mind, there was no doubt at all that the evidence that Gudrid had reached Nantucket was genuine. Nancy Fishburn's granddaughter was joking, she had said she was joking and Eygló should have left it at that.

The only thing that worried him was the fear that Eygló would undermine other people's confidence in that fact – in particular Beccari's.

Eygló was chastened. Maybe Einar was right. Eygló had done the correct thing in passing on Kelly's comment about Nancy Fishburn, but Suzy had checked it out, as had Eygló herself, and no evidence had come to light that the Nantucket theory was false. Perhaps she should just keep her mouth shut.

But what about Carlotta's death? Tom's threat had had its effect. Although she was unsure how seriously to take it, it scared her. She had no intention of dying for the sake of archaeological truth. From the stove she could see the back of Bjarki's blond head on the sofa in the living area. She was his only parent. Sure, her two sisters would look after him somehow if anything happened to her, but the thought of what her death would do to him, and of how she would miss him growing up, filled her with dread.

She knew she should go to the police: tell them about Tom's threat and about Kelly's suspicions of the wampum in Greenland.

Then Inspector Magnús could figure out what to do with the information.

But her initial trust in the big policeman had been blown. OK, she could see why he had been upset that she had lied to him about knowing Carlotta, and she could certainly see why he was suspicious of Einar. But to accuse *her* of killing Carlotta was just absurd. If he had any brains he should realize that she couldn't possibly have done that.

She wasn't going to go to the police. It would blow up *The Wanderer* project, destroy all their reputations and Suzy's house and marriage, and she would be calling Tom's bluff. If it *was* a bluff; she really didn't want to find out whether it was or not.

'Dinner's ready!'

She watched Bjarki as he squeezed ketchup on to his sausages and marvelled again at how much love she felt for a normal boy doing normal things. Especially that evening with everything else that was going on. She hoped that somehow his life would be less complicated than hers. Fewer mistakes. No drugs. No destructive relationships. No psycho Englishmen threatening to kill him.

What would he become? she wondered. Whom would he marry? Would he marry? What about his own kids?

She had no idea, and she rather liked it that way. It was still possible to feel optimistic about a future that had not yet been set in stone.

'Mum?'

'Yes.'

'Did you see that murder in the north on telly?'

'Yes, I did.'

'It was at Glaumbaer. Wasn't that where you were filming?'

'Yes, it was.' Eygló had not been intending to tell Bjarki about the murder, but at that moment she desperately wanted to be honest with him. 'In fact, it was me that discovered the body. In the churchyard.'

'Really?' Bjarki looked up at her, his eyes widened with excitement. Then they clouded. 'Was there blood and everything?'

'Yes.' Eygló said. 'It was quite unpleasant.'

'Oh.' She watched as her son processed the information. 'Did the police come? Detectives and people?'

'Yes, there were lots of police and I spent a long time talking to them, answering their questions.'

'Have they found who did it?'

'No, they haven't found the murderer yet.' She wanted to reassure him, to tell him that the murderer couldn't possibly have anything to do with her, that she was safe, that he was safe. But she couldn't do it: she couldn't bring herself to lie to him, even if it was obviously in his best interests. She had lied enough: she wasn't going to lie any more to the person she loved most in the world.

'Oh.' Bjarki stuck his head down and worked on his sausages and chips. As Eygló munched her salad, she could tell he was thinking, but she had no idea what he was thinking. Was he intrigued? Was he scared? She regretted telling him, but she knew she would have regretted keeping the whole thing from him even more.

They finished their dinner in silence. She was still sitting at the table as he got up and put his plate in the dishwasher. As he passed her on his way back to his computer game, Bjarki hesitated and let his hand rest on hers, just for a moment.

Eygló blinked and a single tear ran down her cheek. Bjarki didn't see it; he was back at his game.

CHAPTER 28

MAGNUS LEFT THE station at six-thirty. His stuff, which he had picked up the previous day from the hotel in Reykjavík, was still in the back of the car. He called Tryggvi Thór to warn him he was coming, and drove out to Álftanes.

'Ah! It's the homeless policeman,' Tryggvi Thór said as he answered the door without a smile. The only sign of his injury was a crease a couple of inches long creeping through his thick steel-grey hair.

'That's sadly true,' said Magnus. 'Thank you for helping me out. Sorry I never made it here last night, I had to go up to Ólafsvík at short notice.'

Tryggvi Thór grunted. 'Follow me.' He led Magnus up the stairs to a small room with a view over the sea. 'This is yours,' he said. 'There's a bathroom next door. Bring your stuff up.'

He left Magnus alone in the room. Magnus did as he was told, making a couple of trips to the car to carry up his meagre possessions.

The room was cosy and decorated in an old-fashioned Icelandic style. The walls were splattered with small paintings of Mount Hekla and fishing boats, framed embroidered aphorisms and black-and-white photographs of men in suits and women in traditional Icelandic dress. The furniture was old and dark and a forest of little wooden and ceramic ornaments covered every surface. Amongst them, two jaunty Icelandic flags waved at him. A bookcase held a few rows of ancient hardbacks and some yellowing paperbacks. At least there was a decent-sized bed. Magnus recalled that Tryggvi Thór had recently inherited the house from his mother. Clearly he had not touched this room since then.

It was a far cry from the black, white and glass minimalist style beloved of modern Icelanders, including Ingileif. But Magnus rather liked it. It felt like a warm, safe Icelandic nest.

He spent a few minutes unpacking his stuff and putting it away. His encounter with Ingileif had shaken him. It wasn't just the surprise of seeing her; he had known that was inevitable at some point. She seemed to have lost her warmth and exuberance. Perhaps it was marriage and motherhood or maybe she was just having a bad day. But her face looked worn by more than just one bad day.

He wondered what she thought of him: he too had aged, of course.

He needed to think through the Carlotta case. But first he really ought to go downstairs and spend a couple of minutes being sociable to his host. Although he knew it was the kind of thing Icelanders did, he was still grateful to Tryggvi Thór for getting him out of a hole.

Tryggvi Thór was outside, sitting in one of two wooden Adirondack chairs, staring out over the sea. The sun had escaped the clouds and was simmering the sea in ruffles of yellow and grey. It was cool in the light breeze and thin sunshine, but that didn't seem to bother Tryggvi Thór.

'May I join you?' Magnus asked.

'If you like.'

Magnus slumped into the other chair, and let his eyes rest on the sea, and the bleak blackness of the rugged Reykjanes peninsula stretching out towards the Atlantic. The cone of Mount Keilir thrust up from the lavascape, a segment of geometric order in a jagged wilderness.

Tryggvi Thór said nothing. Magnus let the sun stroke his face and the sound of the seabirds and the occasional car lull him.

'Coffee?' Tryggvi Thór said eventually.

'Yes, thank you,' said Magnus.

'Or a beer?'

'You bet. I'd kill for a beer.'

Tryggvi Thór disappeared inside and returned a minute later with two bottles of Gull.

'Cheers.' Magnus took a sip. It had been a long day: the beer tasted very good.

'Are you working on the Italian tourist case?' Tryggvi Thór asked.

'Yeah. I'm the senior investigating officer.'

'How's it going?'

'We are making some progress. But not enough. In fact, I'd say we are almost stuck.'

They sat staring at the sea for a couple more minutes. Magnus was beginning to feel more relaxed than he had for a long time.

'Do you want to tell me about it?' said Tryggvi Thór.

Actually Magnus did. But: 'I can't. You know – it's confidential.'

'Of course.'

'Were you a detective? When you were in the police.'

'Yes,' said Tryggvi Thór.

Magnus's brain was beginning to clear. Talking about a case with a civilian was unprofessional. And in Iceland where everyone was connected to everyone else it was a particularly bad idea. Yet.

'There are three ways we can go,' he said. 'Either we can treat this as the killing of a lone female tourist by a stranger. That happens in other countries, but frankly not very often here. Or she was murdered by someone she knew in Iceland. It turns out she was having an affair with an Icelandic archaeologist who supervised the dig she was working on in Greenland. The man was a womanizer and his wife was unhappy about the affair and got him to finish it.'

'Those both sound plausible. What's the third?'

'Carlotta and this archaeologist – his name is Einar – were caught up in a couple of discoveries related to Gudrid the Wanderer and the Vikings' exploration of America.'

'OK.'

'Now, from what I understand, when they make these finds public, there is likely to be a big fuss. One of them suggests Columbus knew about America and how to get there all along, and that will be a big deal. I don't have evidence that there is anything fishy about these finds, but I can't help wondering if there might be. I've always had an interest in the sagas and Norse history and I know my colleague will say I'm just getting distracted. But it's worth bearing in mind.'

'And who is your colleague?'

'Vigdís Audardóttir. Do you know her?'

'The black girl?'

'Yeah.'

'She was after my time. But I have heard of her. Who would have thought of a black detective in Iceland? And a female one too. Is she any good?'

'She is very good.' Magnus knew he sounded defensive, but he was used to working with plenty of black detectives in Boston, while – for all their ostensible liberalism when compared to American society – many Icelanders were still not comfortable dealing with black people.

'Good,' said Tryggvi Thór. 'I sometimes wonder how my daughter would find life if she was working here in Iceland.'

'I thought she was working in the Foreign Ministry?'

'Not Sóley. Greta, Charity's daughter. She's at medical school in Kampala. She also is black.'

'Does she speak Icelandic?'

'Not really. I hope she will learn some day. She's been here a couple of times during vacation from medical school. It's great for me to see her, but she doesn't like the cold. I miss her.' He paused. 'And I miss her mother.'

Magnus didn't say anything.

'So what about the affair between the Italian tourist and the archaeologist?' Tryggvi Thór asked.

Magnus told him. All about Einar and Carlotta, and about Rósa and Eygló, and about the wampum and the Columbus letter. Tryggvi Thór listened mostly in silence, although he did ask one or two questions. As Magnus spoke, the case arranged itself in his mind.

'What is the motive?'

'That's the question; that's what I need to find out. The most obvious motive is something to do with Einar and Carlotta's affair. Maybe Einar and Carlotta had a fight about it. Maybe she threatened to leave him, or she didn't accept that he was leaving her. Or maybe Rósa was jealous and wanted to get rid of her husband's lover. The trouble is, both Einar and Rósa have alibis.'

'So you think there might be some motive related to the TV documentary? What?'

'I don't know. But there is something odd going on with these discoveries and the documentary. It just doesn't *feel* right. Too many secrets. Too much serendipity.'

'Coincidences happen in real life,' Tryggvi Thór said.

'That's true. But it's odd that these two finds should suddenly point to Nantucket. The wampum they found in Greenland is credible. And I suppose the Columbus letter just might be. But both of them together?'

'Doesn't the fact that the two finds point to the same thing make them more likely to be authentic? They can't both be fakes, can they?'

'I suppose not ...' said Magnus.

The sun was sliding downwards and to the right. A touch of pink glimmered at the base of a small cloud, but it would still be hours until the sun actually disappeared below the horizon. Sunset in Iceland was a drawn-out affair.

'I have a question for you,' said Tryggvi Thór. 'I asked you earlier about motive. If they *were* both fakes, would that give anyone a motive to kill Carlotta? If Carlotta was threatening to expose them somehow?'

'Possibly,' said Magnus. 'It would turn the TV documentary into a disaster. Eygló would look like a fool. As would Einar. And Suzy Henshaw, the producer. But we have no evidence that Carlotta was threatening anybody.'

'You mean you don't have any evidence yet,' said Tryggvi Thór.

'So you think there might be something in the archaeology after all?'

Tryggvi Thór snorted. '*I* don't know. That's for you to decide. Want another beer?'

Magnus grinned as Tryggvi Thór went back inside. He was nowhere near cracking the case. Talking it through with Tryggvi Thór, he realized that the most likely motive for the murder was something to do with a love triangle gone wrong in a way he hadn't yet figured out. But the archaeological angle was worth pursuing; if the wampum and the Columbus letter were fake, that might change things.

Or not.

Tryggvi Thór had just returned with the beers when a woman's voice shouted a greeting from within the house.

'That's Sóley,' Tryggvi Thór said. 'She will claim she was just passing, but she's checking on me. No one "just passes" Álftanes. Out here!' he shouted.

Sóley emerged from the back door of the house, but her smile disappeared when she saw Magnus, who had got to his feet. 'What's he doing here?'

'Meet my new lodger, Magnús,' Tryggvi Thór said with a note of triumph. 'You said it would be good if someone was living here with me.'

'But he's a policeman!'

'He is. Just like I was.'

'I hope you're charging him rent?'

'So do I.' He turned to Magnus. 'We need to discuss the rent.'

'That's fine with me,' Magnus said.

Sóley's cheeks were pink as she looked at the two men. She really didn't like policemen. 'Why don't you have your own home?' she said. 'Has your wife thrown you out?'

'I don't have a wife,' said Magnus calmly.

'Then why do you want to stay with my father all of a sudden? And why are you letting him, Dad?'

'Magnús has just arrived in Iceland from America,' Tryggvi

162

Thór said. 'It's true he worked here before for a few years, but only since, what, 2007?'

'Two thousand and nine,' said Magnus.

'And you think that makes a difference?' Sóley said.

'Yes, I do, actually,' said Tryggvi Thór, who was still in his seat.

'What is it I don't know?' said Magnus, wondering why it should matter so much to both of them that he knew nothing about the Metropolitan Police before 2009.

'Don't you know it?' Sóley spat back.

There was silence as they both looked at him. He didn't know what the hell they were talking about. 'No. Will you tell me?'

'If you're such an ace detective, you should be able to work it out for yourself,' said Sóley.

'I could use a little help,' said Magnus.

'Let's just say that it's obvious that the attack on Tuesday wasn't random. It was a warning.'

'Sóley!' Tryggvi Thór barked.

'Dad, how can you keep it quiet from the police when the police are obviously involved?'

'She is letting her imagination run away with her,' said Tryggvi Thór.

'Oh, Dad!' Sóley's face was still flushed and the anger still suffused her words, but her eyes were moist with tears. 'Why couldn't you just stay in Africa?'

'This is my home, Sóley.'

'Yes, but ... Can't you be more careful, for God's sake?'

'I'll be all right.'

'No you won't!' The tears were flowing now. 'I'm going. And you ...' She faced Magnus. 'Mr Policeman. Just make sure my father doesn't get hurt.'

With that, she was gone.

Tryggvi Thór blew air through his cheeks. 'Before you ask, Magnús, I'm not going to tell you anything. Nothing, do you understand?'

'Wait a moment,' said Magnus. 'There's something going on

here, and I need to know what it is.'

'No you don't. You really don't. And if you want to stay here, then no questions. It's really that simple.'

Magnus shrugged. 'OK. But I'm holding out for just one more. Do you have another beer?'

CHAPTER 29

MAGNUS GOT INTO work early the next morning to find an email from Computer Forensics with early extracts from Einar's laptop, in particular email traffic with Carlotta. The amount of data on personal devices had increased exponentially in recent years to a point where it would take humans months to read it all, so extracting relevant information had become an art involving keywords and algorithms. Email correspondence with Carlotta was an obvious place to start.

Magnus skimmed it. The tone on Einar's part was business-like, whereas Carlotta's was much lighter, with flashes of wit and hints of flirtation. The subject matter was almost entirely the Columbus letter and the efforts of Carlotta and Einar to authenticate it. Carlotta repeated her discussions with Federico Trapanese and the Vatican, and her successful attempt to get Professor Beccari involved.

Carlotta had twice suggested meeting up to discuss things in Reykjavík or London or Paris, both times being gently rebuffed by Einar, who said it wasn't necessary. The second suggestion had been made only a month before, and after Einar's rejection of the idea, Carlotta had said she would come to Iceland anyway and would call him.

Magnus cross-referenced Einar's call records and saw that Carlotta had indeed done so on the same day that she had sent the email, speaking to him for thirteen minutes.

Einar addressed Carlotta 'Hi Carlotta' and signed off 'Cheers'. Carlotta greeted Einar with 'Hey' and signed off 'Love'. Although they were both fluent in English, it was a second language for both of them, so Magnus was wary of reading too much into that. It was clear that there was no steamy relationship being conducted between the two of them, although there were hints that Carlotta might have wanted one.

All of which corroborated what Einar had said.

Although Einar used text repeatedly with lots of his contacts, there was no texting between him and Carlotta. Probably because that was how Rósa had discovered their relationship back in 2012.

The computer guys were unlikely to be in yet – they had clearly been working late, so Magnus sent them an email thanking them for what they had got so far, and asking them to search for correspondence between Einar and his wife, especially any messages mentioning Carlotta. Those could be interesting.

'How was your night on Álftanes, Magnús?' Magnus looked up to see Vigdís dropping her bag behind her desk.

'Good. It's a nice place. Great view of the sea.'

'Has the old guy kicked you out yet?'

'Actually, he seems to like me. Unlike his daughter.'

'Coffee?'

'Yes, please.'

Vigdís returned a couple of minutes later with two steaming cups and handed one to Magnus. 'So?'

'So what?'

'So what did you think of your son? That was the first time you met him, right?'

Magnus stared at Vigdís.

'Oh, Magnús! Don't tell me you didn't realize?'

'What? You mean Ingileif's kid? Ási? Why do you think he's my son?'

'Because he looks just like you, dummy. Same red hair. Same blue eyes. Same bruiser's jaw. I can't believe you didn't get that! That's why Ingileif was so hesitant.'

Magnus shook his head. 'He can't be my son. She would have told me.'

'Would she?'

Magnus knew Vigdís disapproved of the way Ingileif had treated him. And indeed their break-up had been caused by Ingileif sleeping with somebody else. Magnus tried to recall dates. It was probably four months between the last time he had slept with Ingileif and the date he left Iceland. He hadn't said goodbye to her in person. She could have been pregnant and he would never have known. And that was five years ago: Ási was four.

Magnus knew Ingileif well, or at least had known her then. And although Ingileif should have told him about a son, she might not have done.

He recalled Ási's steady gaze.

He smiled. 'To answer your question, Vigdís, I liked him.'

'That's good. Now, it's time to call Saudárkrókur.'

There was a lot to talk about. The Akureyri police had presented Gudni Fridriksson, their rape suspect, with fibre evidence linking him to one of the rapes, and he had confessed, not only to that crime, but to three others as well, including one that had not been reported. But he was adamant that he hadn't killed Carlotta.

He lived alone, but he had been seen returning to his flat by a neighbour early on the evening of Carlotta's death, and he had called for a pizza at nine, which had been delivered at nine-thirty. In theory the alibi wasn't 100 per cent cast iron, and it was possible that a suspect would admit to rapes but not to murder, but the investigating detectives were confident Gudni wasn't hiding knowledge of Carlotta's death.

Sergeant Tacchini had confirmed that the Italian texts were innocent messages to Carlotta's friends in Padua about things she had seen in Reykjavík. The US number Carlotta had phoned from Iceland turned out to be Professor Beccari, which made sense since Carlotta and Einar were trying to persuade him to endorse the Columbus letter on the TV documentary. Still nothing from the University of Padua about Carlotta's email account, and Vigdís hadn't found much of interest in her Facebook posts. She wasn't very active: no posts at all from her last trip to Iceland, and no sign of Einar on her page. In fact, her posts were all in Italian. Vigdís had had to laboriously paste everything into Google Translate to get a rough idea of what Carlotta was talking about. The police in London had confirmed with Rósa's hotel that she had actually stayed there.

Magnus distributed more tasks for the coming day, giving Vigdís the job of reviewing whatever data the forensics guys came up with from Einar's computer. The documentary crew were due to fly to Greenland late morning, and Magnus decided he would speak to them at the airport before they left, and return Einar's phone and laptop.

Vigdís started a more thorough analysis of what the computer guys had sent through. Magnus sat at his own desk and stared at his screen.

So he was a father? Huh. He liked the idea.

Without really thinking about it, he had always assumed he would become a father, but at some time well in the future and with an as yet unspecified woman. Now it looked like it had already happened. And with Ingileif.

For all her faults, she would be a good mother. And if you were going to bring up a child alone, Iceland was the place to do it.

There were many questions to be answered. Would Ingileif allow him access to Ási? The boy had his own family, his own stepfather in the shape of Hannes. Or perhaps this Hannes guy acted as Ási's dad. Presumably Ási had no idea who his real father was.

There would be problems, but Magnus would find a way to see his son again.

There were a lot of things Magnus could or should be doing. There were the previous day's interview reports from Sauðárkrókur to go through, and he wanted to do some of his own research on the Columbus letter. How likely was it to be real? Were there a lot of Columbus forgeries out there?

But instead he typed 'Tryggvi Thór Gröndal' into the criminal records database. There was just a brief mention that Detective

Sergeant Tryggvi Thór had been charged with corruption in 1996, but that the charges had been dropped. No explanation.

Nineteen ninety-six was before the digitization of all criminal records, so, with a glance at Vigdís scrolling through her own computer screen, Magnus called Records and asked them for the file from their archives. Half an hour later one of the clerks brought it up and dropped it on his desk. It was extremely thin.

'Is this it?'

'That's all we've got,' said the clerk. She didn't hang around to chat.

Magnus opened the file. Just one sheet of paper, from the court, recording that charges had been dropped.

That wasn't right. Even if Tryggvi Thór had only been under arrest for a few days, a few hours, there should be much more paperwork than that. Especially if a policeman was the suspect: a case like that would have lawyers all over it and good record-keeping would become doubly important.

The file had been emptied. By whom? And when?

CHAPTER 30

KELLY EMERGED FROM her hotel and consulted the map she had grabbed from the front desk. The hotel was situated halfway up the hill in the middle of Reykjavík, and she decided to begin with the big concrete church at its top. Nancy had said she was feeling tired and had urged Kelly to go out for a stroll, while she went back to bed for an hour or two. Kelly was supposed to knock on her door at eleven.

Kelly loved Reykjavík. It was small enough to be manageable, large enough to be busy. The view from the top of the hill was amazing: mountains and sea on all sides, and those cute little red, white and blue houses. She liked just looking in the stores; with the exception of the odd tacky tourist joint, they were original and imaginative. And expensive. Kelly had quickly realized the whole of Iceland was expensive, and had decided to let Grammy pay for everything. She had saved some money over the summer in Nantucket, but she would need it over the coming semester at college.

In the end, she decided to splash out on a cup of coffee in a café that looked more Moroccan than Icelandic. She thought about what her grandmother had told her the day before, about the wampum and the Columbus letter being fake, about the whole thing being a hoax. She still couldn't believe her grandmother, normally so proper and so sensible, had done that. Part of her admired the old lady; part of her was shocked. Nancy herself seemed to regret it deeply.

Kelly believed her father really had been joking when he had said that Nancy had planted the wampum in Greenland, but it was his intuition about his mother that had sprung the idea into his mind. Kelly had been mortified back in 'Sconset when she thought she had misled Eygló. Turned out she hadn't misled her after all.

And now Kelly was the bearer of the secret.

Nancy said that she had done her duty now she had told the TV people; it was up to them what they did with the information. It sounded as if they were going to go ahead with the documentary anyway and bury the whole thing. Nancy had said she was happy to go along with what they decided. Part of Kelly fervently agreed; part of her knew it was deeply wrong.

Now she wished her grandmother hadn't told her anything about it. She would just have to place her trust in the old lady and her decision.

She got back to the hotel and knocked on Nancy's door. No reply. She knocked a couple more times and listened. Nothing.

Kelly was worried as she made her way back to her own room down the corridor. She knew she had no reason to be: Nancy was very tired and must be sleeping soundly.

She tried to read a book, all the while wondering how long to leave it until she tried again.

She gave it thirty minutes. Still no reply. She was becoming more worried; she knew she shouldn't be, but she was. She considered asking the hotel to open the door, then rejected the idea. But the worst that could happen was that Nancy would be a little upset with her. Nancy had looked pale – maybe she was ill rather than just exhausted.

So she went downstairs. The manager was totally understanding, and a minute later he had opened the door to Nancy's room.

Nancy was lying on her back, fully clothed, her eyes shut.

'Thank you,' said Kelly to the manager, and she gently touched her grandmother's arm. 'Grammy? Grammy, wake up!'

Nothing.

'Grammy!' The old lady looked very still. No sign of her chest moving at all. 'Grammy!'

'Let me have a look.' The manager hurried over to the bed and felt Nancy's brow. Then he put his ear to her chest. Then he felt for a pulse. He turned to Kelly, his face grave.

'I'm sorry.'

CHAPTER 31

FLIGHTS FROM ICELAND to Greenland departed from the small City Airport in the heart of Reykjavík, rather than the international airport at Keflavík. Magnus decided to take the direct route over the hill at Thingholt, rather than the faster route around it.

He made for the Hallgrímskirkja on the summit and parked outside, right underneath the statue of Leif Erikson staring westwards over the city towards Vinland, his battleaxe by his side. He strolled down Skólavördustígur, the short straight street that ran down from the church towards the centre of the city. There were galleries on either side, and Magnus paused outside one of them to look in the window.

Behind the displays of intricate silver jewellery and stained glass, he could see Ingileif. She was speaking to a well-dressed middle-aged woman, possibly a Danish or German tourist, and showing her some fish-skin bags, subtly patterned in silver, yellow and blue.

His heart lurched. Any man would think Ingileif was attractive. But to Magnus, she was beautiful. Absolutely beautiful.

And she was the mother of his son.

He wasn't sure what to say to her about that, how to acknowledge it, *whether* to acknowledge it. And the careful policeman in him recognized that Vigdís might be wrong; Ási might be someone else's child.

Ásgrímur. Magnus grinned at the name. It would hardly be the coolest name in an American elementary schoolyard, and its diminutive would be even worse. But it wasn't just Ingileif's father's name. He in turn had been named after a Viking ancestor mentioned in the sagas, who had lived on a farm near Mount Hekla and killed a neighbour, his foster-brother Gaukur of Stöng. It was the kind of bloodthirsty detail Magnus would have loved as a boy. Would Ási?

Ingileif would have known how much Magnus would appreciate the name. Maybe that was one of the reasons she had chosen it.

The doorbell rang as the tourist left the shop, her purchase in a shopping bag. Magnus looked through the window into the gallery to see Ingileif staring right back at him.

Their eyes met. It was difficult to read Ingileif's expression. Questioning.

If she was asking a question, Magnus didn't know the answer. He turned on his heel and walked rapidly back up the hill to where he had parked his car, feeling like a bit of a weirdo. Police officers were not supposed to stalk their former girlfriends.

He drove straight to the airport. Eygló, Einar, Suzy, Tom, Ajay and Professor Beccari were all gathered there having checked in. Magnus pulled all but the professor into a police interview room at the terminal.

Suzy was not happy. 'I hope you are not going to make us miss the flight.'

'Don't worry,' said Magnus. 'I'll be quick. I need to return Einar his phone and his laptop.' He took them out of his bag and handed them to Einar. 'Our forensics team has just taken copies, nothing has been interfered with, although both devices have been charged.'

Einar took them without a word. He looked just as drawn as he had in Ólafsvík. Magnus guessed his conversation with Rósa the night before must have been difficult. And it would take him more than a few days to recover from Carlotta's death.

'Once you have finished in Greenland we expect you to return here. That applies to all of you.'

'That's what our tickets say,' said Suzy. 'Return flights.'

174

'I know. But no changes to destination. I have contacted the authorities in Greenland to keep an eye on you. That's especially true of you, Einar. I'm sure we will have more to talk about when you return.'

'OK,' said Einar. 'But won't you have found the murderer by then?'

'I hope so,' said Magnus, trying to give his words a confidence he didn't feel. 'One last question for you all. Do any of you have any doubts about your documentary? I mean the evidence that Gudrid actually went to Nantucket? What do you think, Suzy?'

'What has this got to do with the poor girl's murder?'

'Please answer the question.'

'All right,' said Suzy. 'I did have some doubts when Eygló first told me about Einar's discoveries. But the wampum and the Columbus letter back each other up. We might have had our doubts about each one individually, but the combination is convincing. I'm prepared to go with it.'

'I see. Eygló?'

'I think it stacks up. The sagas tell us that Gudrid and Thorfinn went somewhere on the east coast of America. There is now more evidence for Nantucket than anywhere else.'

'Einar?'

The dullness left Einar's eyes as he looked straight at Magnus. 'Like Suzy, I am persuaded by the two pieces of independent evidence. We have checked them out as thoroughly as we can. I wouldn't risk my academic reputation unless I was sure.'

'What about Carlotta? What did she think?'

'She was the most enthusiastic of all of us,' Einar replied. 'It was she who believed in the Columbus letter when the Vatican wanted to ignore it.' He smiled sadly. 'No, Carlotta was certain that Hóp was in Nantucket.'

'All right, you can go now,' said Magnus. 'But if you think of anything that might cast doubt on any of this, let me know, will you?'

They mumbled their assent, and Magnus let them return to Departures.

He was about to follow them when he noticed a phone lying on the table. He picked it up to take it out to whoever had left it, and then he stopped himself.

He sat down and waited.

After a minute or so, there was a knock at the door. It was Eygló.

'I left my phone,' she said.

'On purpose?'

Eygló nodded.

'What have you got to tell me?'

'I'll tell you as long as you promise not to hold me here. I don't want the others to find out.'

'I can't promise that, if what you tell me is directly related to who killed Carlotta.'

'It isn't. You asked if we had any doubts about the reliability of the evidence that Gudrid went to Nantucket. But, as I said, I'll only tell you if you don't keep me and you let me go back to the others.'

'Are you scared of something?' Eygló certainly looked anxious.

'Look. Do you want me to talk, or do you just want to ask me questions?'

'OK,' said Magnus.

'All right,' said Eygló. 'I'll be quick. It was when we were filming in Nantucket two weeks ago ...'

Magnus listened as Eygló explained quickly and succinctly about meeting Nancy Fishburn's granddaughter and about Kelly's father's suspicion that Nancy had planted the wampum at Brattahlíd herself. Then Eygló explained that when Suzy had checked up on the story, Kelly had claimed her father was joking.

'And you don't believe her?'

'I don't know.'

'Why didn't you tell me this before?'

'I said, no questions. Can I go?'

Magnus considered keeping Eygló back, or indeed keeping the whole lot of them back so they missed their flight. But there would be political consequences. And actually, although what

Eygló had told him was interesting, it didn't amount to proof that the wampum was fake.

'Go on,' he said. 'And thank you.'

She picked up her phone and hurried out of the interview room.

He followed her out into the departures hall, and watched her join the other five through the gate and out on to the tarmac where the plane was waiting to take them to Greenland.

He turned and made his way to the terminal entrance, trying to decide what credence, if any, to place in Eygló's information. All right, Kelly's father's conjecture that his mother had planted the wampum was just speculation, and third-hand speculation at that. But the fact that Nancy had stated that she had once visited Brattahlíd was interesting. Very interesting indeed.

Magnus's brain scarcely registered that he recognized the woman rushing past him with her head down. He turned to see her showing her boarding card to the ground staff at the gate.

Rósa.

He hurried after her, calling her name.

At first she took no notice, but Magnus shouted louder and she was forced to stop and turn to meet him.

'Rósa! Where are you going?'

'Greenland. With my husband. I've taken a few days off work to join him.'

'Why?'

'A holiday. And the last few days have been tough for him. Tough for both of us, actually. But if you'll excuse me, I'm late.'

'No. You'll have to get the next flight.'

'Sir?' The woman at the gate was preparing to intervene, but Magnus flashed his warrant card.

'You have no right to stop me, unless you are arresting me. Are you arresting me?'

'No, I merely want to ask you a few questions.'

'You have let my husband on to the plane – he was in Saudárkrókur at the time of the poor woman's murder. I was in London, as you know. Now, I'm a lawyer. Either you arrest me, or you let me get on that plane.'

Magnus stared at Rósa. She was calm but firm. She knew her ground.

He let her go.

'You were a while,' said Einar to Eygló in English as she joined them airside. 'Did the cop ask you more questions?'

'He tried to, but I wouldn't let him,' said Eygló. Out of her peripheral vision she saw Tom and Ajay a couple of metres away fiddling with some sound equipment, but she could tell from Tom's bearing that he was concentrating on her reply. That was good: she had thought of a little story to explain her absence and she wanted him to hear it. 'It took me a while to find him. He'd taken the phone and he was going to hand it in to the airport lost property. He could have come after us with it! I think he was just being difficult. It's lucky I caught up with him or I would have had to go to Greenland without it.'

'He seems suspicious about the Nantucket theory,' said Einar. Beccari was safely out of earshot.

'It's his job,' said Eygló. 'He's suspicious about everything. It would have helped if you had told him you knew Carlotta at the start.' She knew she was being hypocritical; she too had kept things from the police that she shouldn't have. But her comment had the desired effect of shutting Einar up until they were on the plane.

Suzy, Einar and Eygló were seated next to each other. Suzy had given Eygló the window seat, which was good of her since the approach into Narsarsuaq Airport was supposed to be spectacular. Beccari had booked his ticket later, and seemed happy enough to be seated alone with his tablet. Tom and Ajay sat together several rows back, also by the window, from where Tom planned to get some shots of the approach. It was unlikely they would be able to use the footage in the final documentary, but Suzy was considering chartering a helicopter for aerial shots, and Tom's filming would be useful to decide where to go.

Despite Tom, Eygló felt good to be on the aeroplane, away from Magnus's prying questions. She hadn't slept well the night before. In the early part of the night, she had determined that she would tell the police everything. She had fallen asleep for a couple of hours and had then woken up terrified that she would be killed and that Bjarki would lose his mother. So don't tell the police a thing.

At five-thirty she had got up and made herself some coffee. With wakefulness and the morning her fears had subsided, but only a little. She still didn't know what to do; it was only when she was listening to Inspector Magnus trying to make sense of the case that she had decided to talk to him. If someone, anyone, including Einar, had killed Carlotta, they deserved to be in jail and she shouldn't get in the way of Magnus putting them there.

She felt that she had explained things well enough to Einar to keep Tom happy, and he should be less concerned about her making difficulties once they were all in Greenland. She intended to ask Einar some detailed questions about contexts and the precise location where they had found the wampum shells when they were filming at Brattahlíd, but she would do that in Icelandic with Tom out of earshot.

A flight attendant made an announcement that they were just waiting for one more passenger to board before pushing off the stand. The weather in Greenland was clear, and warm for the country – fifteen degrees. That was good.

'How did it go last night?' Eygló asked Einar in Icelandic. 'With Rósa?'

Einar winced. 'Not very well. I slept in the guest room.'

'Oh.'

'I told her. About you and me two nights ago.'

'You what! What an incredibly stupid thing to do!'

'I had to. I had promised her that I wouldn't hide anything from her. I mean to keep my promises.'

'Yes, but …' Eygló sighed in frustration. 'You did tell her that nothing happened between us?'

'Of course I did.'

'Did she believe you?'

Einar winced again and shook his head. 'I don't think so.'

Jesus! Eygló definitely didn't want Rósa as an enemy. She was almost as scared of her as she was of Tom. At least Tom would now assume that Eygló had kept quiet as he had asked. Whereas Rósa? Rósa would be as jealous as hell.

'Well, I'm glad we are putting a thousand miles between her and me,' Eygló said.

Einar seemed to stiffen.

'Hello, Eygló.' It was a woman's voice, a voice Eygló recognized. She looked up to see the tall figure of Rósa standing in the aisle, bending down towards her with a tight smile on her face. 'Do you mind if I sit next to my husband?'

CHAPTER 32

BACK AT POLICE headquarters, there had been a breakthrough in the north.

An Italian tourist, a twenty-five-year-old man named Dario Anzalone, was travelling around Iceland by himself, and had been staying in a hostel in Dalvík the night of Carlotta's murder. Dalvík was about 120 kilometres from Glaumbaer. Anzalone had returned to the hostel a little after midnight; he had seemed agitated and jumpy. Two of the other guests, a young Dutch couple, had noticed him and wondered what was wrong. They were now in Reykjavík and had just seen an item on the Internet about the murder and the hunt for suspicious Italian tourists, so they had called the police.

Anzalone was now staying in a hostel in Egilsstadir, in the east of the country. He was out of the hostel at that moment, but local police were waiting for him to return there.

'Do you think you should go back to Saudárkrókur?' Vigdís asked.

'It's good news,' said Magnus. 'But I think Árni and Jón Kári can handle it. Can you check with Tacchini whether any of Carlotta's friends in Italy have heard of Anzalone? And see if they are Facebook friends?'

'OK, I'll do that. Did you see our suspects get on the plane to Greenland?'

'Yes, I did,' said Magnus. 'Plus one other. Rósa.'

'Rósa? Didn't you stop her?'

'I couldn't, not without arresting her. She is a lawyer; she knows the rules.'

'What the hell was she doing?'

'She says she needs to spend time with her husband. It's been a difficult few days for them. It's just about plausible.'

'Huh!' said Vigdís. 'Oh, by the way. Thelma wants to see you.'

Magnus met Thelma in the corridor, walking rapidly towards her office with that unique gait of hers. It wasn't exactly a limp, more a flick as she propelled her artificial left leg in front of her right, giving her a slight roll, as if she was on the deck of a ship. She could do it at an impressive speed, and indeed she didn't usually waste much time going from A to B.

She took her place behind her desk. 'How is the Carlotta case going?'

Magnus repeated what Árni had told him about the Italian tourist in Dalvík.

Thelma seemed pleased. 'Are you going back to Saudárkrókur, then?'

'Maybe,' said Magnus. 'I'll see how Árni gets on.'

'And you let Einar and Eygló get on the plane to Greenland?'

'I saw them off at the airport. They are in the air right now.'

'Good,' said Thelma. 'If the Akureyri suspect firms up, we would have looked bad keeping them here.'

'I still think Einar is involved somehow,' said Magnus. 'I'm just not sure how.'

'Keep me informed. And I want a word with you about that guy you mentioned yesterday, Tryggvi Thór.'

'Oh, yes?'

'I asked around. It turns out he was thrown out of the police in 1996 for corruption.'

'I know, I looked at his file. There is very little in it apart from that the charges against him were dropped.'

'Yes, they dropped the charges, but he was as guilty as hell. They didn't want a court case because it would have looked bad. But he was drummed out and it was suggested that he leave the country. I hear he went to Africa.'

'And came back last year.'

'I also hear that he lives in Álftanes, and that you are his new lodger.'

How the hell did she know that?

'He was the old man who was attacked on Tuesday,' Magnus said. 'I met him then and he offered me a place to stay until I am sorted.'

'Haven't you found somewhere yet? You've been here a month.'

'I did, but it fell through.'

'Well, I suggest that you don't stay with a bent cop, especially not Tryggvi Thór. It doesn't look good.'

Magnus raised his eyebrows. Thelma was watching him steadily. She meant it; it was a warning.

Maybe she was right. Cops don't like bent cops; Magnus certainly didn't. He had come across a couple in Boston, had a bad run-in with one of them. The question was: was Tryggvi Thór really a bent cop? It was a question Magnus didn't have the time to answer.

'Did you tell Thelma I was staying with Tryggvi Thór?' Magnus asked Vigdís when he had escaped Thelma's office.

'No.'

'I wonder who did. She's just warned me off him.'

'Bloody typical. Poking her nose into your personal life. What right has she to say who you live with?'

Magnus had forgotten how much Vigdís didn't like Thelma.

'I've been thinking,' said Magnus.

'Novel approach.'

'There is definitely something wrong with the Nantucket theory.'

'Oh, Magnús! Don't tell me. You stayed up late last night reading *The Saga of the Clueless Viking* and discovered Gudrid and Thorfinn actually landed on the South Pole.'

'No, listen, Vigdís. I'm serious.'

'OK,' said Vigdís. 'I'm listening.'

Magnus repeated what Eygló had told him at the airport.

Vigdís was doubtful. 'If Suzy checked it out and the girl said it was a joke, it was probably a joke.'

183

'Yes, but Nancy Fishburn wrote a book about Gudrid. And she just happens to live on Nantucket. And she visited the place in Greenland where the wampum connecting Gudrid to Nantucket was found.'

'If she's a fan of Gudrid, it's not surprising she went to Greenland,' said Vigdís. 'The only coincidence is that she lives in Nantucket herself. And I'm not sure that's *that* big a coincidence.'

'How's this for a coincidence? Carlotta found the wampum. Carlotta was working on the Columbus letter. Carlotta is now dead.'

Vigdís was silent for a moment, thinking. 'Let's say this old lady cooked up a hoax. So what?'

'It would be bad news for the people making the documentary: Einar, Eygló and Suzy. It would be a public humiliation.'

'Maybe. But would that be enough for them to murder someone? I mean, they would have to cancel the documentary. They might lose some money. But bad things like that happen to people all the time and they don't kill for it. None of them seems unbalanced: a bit intense maybe, a bit stressed, but not killers. Plus, they all have alibis for that night, don't they? They were in Saudárkrókur eating dinner together.' Vigdís shook her head. '*I* think it has something to do with Rósa and Einar. It's a classic love triangle gone wrong. Jealous girlfriend, jealous wife, scheming husband.'

'You yourself said they all have alibis. Look, it's a lead,' said Magnus. 'And someone needs to follow it up. I'd like to talk to her.'

'Good luck getting Thelma's approval for you to fly to Nantucket,' said Vigdís. 'That really would be a wild goose chase.'

Vigdís was right. 'I know, I know. But I'll see if I can get a detective there to ask questions.'

Magnus didn't know any police officers in Nantucket himself, but he made some calls to his former colleagues in Boston, and was soon speaking to a detective in the Nantucket PD, who agreed to go out to Siasconset and interview Nancy Fishburn.

That evening, back at Tryggvi Thór's house in Álftanes, Magnus pulled down *The Saga of the Greenlanders* and *The Saga of Erik the Red* from his collection and read them through.

When he came to the descriptions of the mysterious lagoon at Hóp, Magnus recalled the pond in the footage from the TV documentary. Even if it turned out that Gudrid, Thorfinn and their crew had not landed there, there was still some similar lagoon somewhere along the north-east coast of North America that they had visited a thousand years ago. Magnus marvelled at the idea of a handful of Europeans clinging on to the edge of a vast continent in AD 1000.

Gudrid really was an extraordinary woman. To have journeyed so far and seen so much of the world, so long ago. She had travelled from Iceland to America and back again. Magnus had travelled from America to Iceland and back. And now he was trying to put down roots in Iceland for the second time.

Gudrid had been married three times, and had given birth to her own son in a foreign land. Magnus might have a son in Iceland, but then again he might not. It was all probably a result of Vigdís's lively imagination. And even if Ási was Magnus's son, would Ingileif acknowledge the fact? Magnus hoped she would. Part of him hoped too that it might bring them back together; perhaps she still cared for him?

He sighed and closed his book.

He and Ingileif were not good for each other; he knew that now.

CHAPTER 33

TRYGGVI THÓR PULLED out into the centre of the road and overtook four tourist buses in a row ahead. Four! All heading to the Blue Lagoon, and it was still only nine o'clock in the morning. He was on the road to Grindavík from Reykjavík, seeking isolation. On either side stretched the barren black lavascape of the Reykjanes peninsula, scored with treacherous gullies and crevasses where baked stone had cooled and cracked, Ahead, a pillar of steam rose from the power station that fed the artificial lagoon.

One of the reasons he had left Africa, with its teeming life of all kinds, was to rediscover the barren desolation of his home country. With the tourist boom, this was harder to find, especially in high summer when the more intrepid foreigners in their hired cars spread out all over the country in search of lonely corners.

Tryggvi Thór knew a corner that he hoped they had not yet found. He drove past the lagoon and around the outskirts of the fishing village of Grindavík, heading east, past a couple of farms into another lava field. The paved road became unpaved track, running about a kilometre in from the sea. He turned off it and drove down towards the water and a small car park in the midst of volcanic debris, shielded from the west winds by a burly wall of lava that had spilled into the sea millennia ago and frozen hard.

The place was known as Selatangar. And it was empty.

Good.

He slipped on his daypack and followed a footpath through the stones to the east, away from the wall. It was noticeably cooler than it had been that morning, and a sea mist lurked just a hundred metres offshore. As he walked he saw it creep and slide towards him. It reached out and grabbed a pair of eider ducks splashing in the swell, smothering them in its milky clasp. The black beach was cluttered with driftwood, bleached almost white from its long journey through the Atlantic.

In the higgledy-piggledy jumble of rocks, stones and pebbles, it was difficult to spot the first sign of human habitation, a circular pile in which fishermen had lived 150 years before. The place had been a seasonal fishing settlement from the Middle Ages until some time in the nineteenth century, a warren of drystone hovels linked by paths cut through the lava. Rows of boulders stretched out into the sea: primitive breakwaters to protect the open fishing boats as they landed their catch, which would then be hung out to dry for months on wooden racks erected along the shore.

Tryggvi Thór halted and listened to the silence. Except it wasn't quite silent: the wavelets lapped against the beach, a breath of wind rustled through the rocks, and his own blood thudded gently in his ears. The moist sea air massaged his face in a delicate tingle.

It wasn't absolute silence, but it was the loneliness he had sought.

A cormorant appeared as if by magic from beneath the grey water slopping against the pebbles. The mist had ventured ashore now, slinking along the narrow paths between the dwellings.

He wondered what it would have been like inhabiting those harsh stone buildings – cramped, damp, cold, with nothing green in sight – and he marvelled again at the toughness and dogged determination of Icelanders in centuries gone by. Not that they had much of a choice.

Tryggvi Thór's parents had occasionally brought him and his brother here when they were kids back in the fifties, and they would happily spend all afternoon running through this abandoned settlement, playing all kinds of games.

A ripple of movement in the mist attracted his attention. He stared at the swirling moisture. It was nothing. Unless it was

'Tanga-Tómas', the local ghost his father had told him stories about.

This was why he had come back from Africa, places like this.

And to right a wrong. To do his duty.

What did that mean for someone who had spent more than two decades away from his homeland?

It still meant something. Even though Tryggvi Thór had been bewitched by Africa, had fallen in love with one of its women, had produced his own African daughter, he had remained an Icelander. And as he had aged, and especially since Charity had died, that had become more important to him.

No one had ever suggested that Tryggvi Thór was anything but tough, even at seventy-one. Yet the attack on him in his own house had shaken him, as it was supposed to do. It had made him question whether doing what he was planning to do was worth it.

There was corruption all over the world: Tryggvi Thór had witnessed it on a large and small scale in Africa. Yet Iceland should be better than that. Amazingly, for a few years at the beginning of the century Iceland had teetered at the top of the World Corruption Index as the least corrupt country in the world. But Iceland had its own special form of corruption: people who knew each other looking out for each other. During the financial crisis the depth of this corruption had been laid bare for all to see. Elections had been fought and won and then lost on the issue. Although many Icelanders were infuriated with the way those in power helped their friends, they also understood. After all, *they* helped their friends. In an environment as tough as Iceland, you had to, because one day you would need help in return.

Low-level corruption he could have ignored, but in truth there wasn't much of that in Iceland. Tourists didn't get shaken down by armed police as they drove around the country. Icelandic corruption wasn't like that; it operated on a much higher level. And the corruption Tryggvi Thór had come home to confront was at the highest level.

His daughter Sóley was as sickened by the corruption as anyone else; it was where her antipathy to the police had come from. She was rising high in the diplomatic service, high enough to see the networks in action. Sóley had guessed what her father was up to, why he had returned to Iceland, but he hadn't confided in her. Not that he didn't trust her to keep his purpose to herself – he certainly trusted her. It was just that she was always so worried about him. She treated him like an old man, to be fussed over and protected. He might be seventy-one, but he didn't *feel* like an old man.

There was no doubt he was in some danger, though. With Charity gone, he thought that didn't matter, but of course it did. Sóley and her children would miss him if something happened to him. Símon, Tryggvi Thór's son, wouldn't care. They hadn't got on since Fanny, Símon's mother, had divorced Tryggvi Thór right after he was thrown out of the police. Like his mother, Símon had never forgiven him, never believed that Tryggvi Thór wasn't corrupt himself.

Well, screw Símon.

But then there was Greta, at medical school in Kampala. She did matter. Tryggvi Thór missed her so badly. He wanted to live long enough to see her become a doctor and start her own family.

He struck out further along the shore, picking his way through the moss-spattered lava.

He was glad that he had asked the Kani Cop to stay with him. They had a lot in common. It was not just that they were both Icelanders who had spent a long time abroad; it was also that Tryggvi Thór recognized something of himself in Magnus, something of the cop he used to be.

Tryggvi Thór instinctively trusted Magnus, and there were not many police officers he could say that of.

Stones rattled behind him, and he turned.

No one.

He stopped and listened. Nothing

The path had petered out to barely discernible worn patches in otherwise jagged lava, and so he made for the beach. The tide was out and it would be easier to walk along the shore through the black sand.

After a few hundred metres, he decided he had gone far enough, and began to retrace his steps. The mist had overwhelmed the shoreline and it was difficult to see more than a few metres ahead. He could hear the sea, to his left, but he couldn't see it any more. Following the path as it threaded its way through the stone dwellings would take him back to his car, but he checked the compass he always carried with him just to make sure he was going in the right direction.

He passed by one of the circular hovels. He felt rather than heard a rush behind him. He began to turn but then ...

He opened his eyes. He was cold, and his head hurt. Again. His face was pressed hard on to cold stone, a rough edge biting into his cheek.

With an enormous effort he commanded his neck muscles to lift his head a centimetre and his brain exploded in pain. He let his head fall again on the stone.

He could see the gaping entrance to the half-submerged stone dwelling from where his attacker must have pounced. Behind it a deep white cloak of fog smothered everything.

He had to move. No one would come this way, especially not in this weather. So much for his idea of escaping the tourists. There were all kinds of places he could have gone for a walk where a gaggle of Chinese tourists and their guide would have found him. But not here. Not at Selatangar.

He tried again to heave himself to his feet. He tried three times, and finally he was standing, one hand clasping the stone wall of the hovel.

He felt dizzy and he felt nauseous.

He took one step along the path back to the car park.

He took another.

Then he collapsed.

CHAPTER 34

MAGNUS WOKE THAT morning to find an email from the Nantucket detective. He had visited Nancy Fishburn's house in Siasconset, but she was not at home. Her next-door neighbour said she was away on vacation with her granddaughter.

In Iceland.

That was interesting. It looked as if he would have a chance to speak to her himself after all.

He and Vigdís dialled up Saudárkrókur for the morning case meeting. The news from the north was not encouraging. The Italian tourist, Dario Anzalone, was in the police station at Saudárkrókur protesting his innocence and doing it convincingly. He claimed he had been out late that night trying to catch the northern lights – tricky in August – and that he always looked wound up. He was certainly behaving like a wound-up kind of guy. More to the point, he was travelling around Iceland by bus, so he had no independent means of transport to get him all the way from Dalvík to Glaumbaer and back in the late evening. The police had been unable to identify any connection between Carlotta and Anzalone, but they were still working on it.

Magnus told the others about Nancy Fishburn being in Iceland; none of them sounded much interested by the news. Magnus could feel that they didn't think the subject of the documentary had much relevance to Carlotta's death. But they were professionals; they knew every lead had to be followed up. And Magnus was the boss.

Magnus and Vigdís got to work on the hotels. It didn't take long. Within twenty minutes Vigdís had something.

'Good and bad news,' she said.

'You've found Nancy Fishburn?'

'Yes. But she's dead.'

It took Magnus and Vigdís five minutes to get to the hotel. The manager met them in the lobby and took them through to his office, where he explained that the old lady had died in her sleep the day before. He was a neat man in his late thirties, with close-cropped fair hair. He looked competent: concerned, rather than distraught.

'Did the district medical officer see her?' Magnus asked

'Yes. Right away. He pronounced her dead. An ambulance came and took her away. To the morgue presumably.'

'So he didn't spot anything suspicious?'

'No. I saw her myself. She was lying on her bed, fully clothed. She was in her eighties; her granddaughter said she had been feeling ill. Elderly tourists die sometimes. Exactly like this.'

'Didn't it strike you it was odd she was fully clothed?'

The manager shrugged. 'No. She had been dressed when she came down to breakfast with her granddaughter. She was having a lie-down afterwards.'

'Any signs of a struggle? Bruises on her skin? Had the furniture been moved?'

'Not that I noticed.'

'Has the room been cleaned yet?'

'Yes. But no one stayed in it last night. It will be booked for tonight, though.'

Damn. There would still be plenty for forensics to work on, but the most obvious evidence would have been tidied up or taken to the laundry.

'Cancel the booking. The room is now a crime scene.'

'A crime scene! What, you think she was murdered?'

'I think she might have been.'

The manager winced. Magnus could see what he was thinking. Murders might add a frisson of excitement for the guests, but they were not good for business.

Tough.

'Is her granddaughter still here?'

'Yes. I think she's in her room now. Her father is flying in tomorrow to sort things out.'

'Can I speak to her?'

As the manager went to fetch the girl, Magnus instructed Vigdís to get on to headquarters for reinforcements to establish a crime scene, and to the morgue to get the autopsy done as soon as possible. She should warn the forensic pathologist to look for any sign of homicide when he did the autopsy.

'It could be a natural death,' said Vigdís tentatively.

'I know,' said Magnus. 'But we need to work on the assumption that it isn't.'

Magnus met Nancy's granddaughter in the manager's office. Kelly Fishburn looked younger than her twenty-one years, short, blonde, with chubby pale cheeks and red eyes. She seemed briefly comforted by Magnus's familiar American accent, but that only lasted a few moments, once she heard why he wanted to see her.

'You really think Grammy was murdered?'

'We are not certain, but we think so, yes.'

'But why? Like, who would do something like that? Nothing was stolen, was it?'

'We think it may have something to do with the TV documentary being made about Gudrid the Wanderer. Do you know anything about that?'

Magnus could see from Kelly's expression she did know something.

'Kelly?'

'Oh! I know Grammy wouldn't want me to tell anyone.'

'You have to, Kelly. She's dead. We need to find out why.'

'And you really think it might have something to do with her death?'

'An Italian tourist was murdered a few days ago in the north of the country. On the same day and at the same place as the TV crew were filming.'

'Oh my God! I saw that on the *Reykjavík Grapevine*.' The *Reykjavík Grapevine* was an English-language website and newspaper.

'We believe she met your grandmother in Nantucket last year, with an Icelandic archaeologist. So, yes, I do think they might be connected.'

'OK.' Kelly took a deep breath. 'Yes, I do know about that documentary. That's why we came to Iceland: so Grammy could meet with the TV crew.'

She told Magnus what Nancy had said about the wampum in Greenland and the Columbus letter being a hoax, and how Nancy had brought Kelly to Iceland with her to try to straighten things out, although she had told Kelly at the time they were just going for a vacation.

'Do you know who specifically your grandmother was meeting on Thursday morning in Snaefellsnes?'

'No. She didn't say. I did speak with Eygló the presenter myself in Nantucket after she had interviewed Grammy a couple of weeks ago. I told her my dad had thought that maybe Grammy had planted the wampum herself. But I was like, it's a joke; I thought it *was* a joke.'

'Do you know what whoever your grandmother met was planning to do with the information?'

'It sounded like they were going to ignore it.'

'Really?' Magnus's eyebrows shot up. 'And your grandmother was going to let them?'

Kelly squirmed in shame, presumably on the old lady's behalf. 'Yes. She said it was their call. I guess she was relieved it wasn't going to come out.'

'And you? What did you think?'

Kelly hesitated. 'Well, she was wrong, wasn't she? They were all wrong. But it wasn't up to me. She swore me to secrecy.'

'Why did she tell you?'

'She said someone needed to know. Someone young. She didn't actually say it, but I know she didn't want to die without passing the secret on. She was very old – eighty-seven, I think. In some ways I was flattered she told me. But actually I wish I'd never known. And now I've told you.'

'You had to,' said Magnus gently. 'You didn't have any choice.'

Kelly nodded unhappily.

'Did Nancy ever mention Carlotta Mondini?'

'She was the tourist who was murdered?'

Magnus nodded.

'No. I told her what I had seen on the news site at dinner the night we got back here. She said that Glaumbaer was where Gudrid ended up in Iceland, but I didn't really make any connection with the documentary.'

'Did she?'

'I don't know.' Kelly thought for a moment. 'Maybe. She went quiet, come to think of it. And actually, when she told me about the Icelandic archaeologist tracking her down last year, I think she said he had an assistant with him. Was that her? '

'Probably.'

Magnus asked more questions about Kelly's conversation with Eygló in Nantucket, about the timing of Nancy's meeting at the Hótel Búdir in Snaefellsnes, and what she and Nancy had done the morning of Nancy's death. Kelly suggested that it was possible Nancy had been trying to get her out of the way while Nancy met someone; after all, that was what she had done in Snaefellsnes.

The someone who may have killed her.

Kelly had no idea who that someone might be.

Magnus finished with Kelly and emerged from the manager's office into a hotel buzzing with policemen. He went up to Nancy's room, which was already crawling with Edda's people under the bright lights they had set up. There was plenty to do; staff and guests had to be questioned to see if they had seen anything strange or had recognized Einar or any others of the TV crew. Nancy had died a couple of hours before the crew would have checked in at the City Airport for their flight to Greenland.

Magnus spoke to the district medical officer on the phone,

who confirmed he hadn't noticed anything suspicious, but who sounded understandably embarrassed that he had missed something and should have called the police.

Magnus then called the forensic pathologist, Gudjón, directly, asking him to look for signs of asphyxia or needle punctures, which were the two least visible methods of killing. Internal bleeding from a blow or straightforward poisoning might also be hard to spot initially, but would show up clearly in a thorough autopsy. Gudjón said he would set to work within the hour.

It was at times like this Magnus appreciated the Icelanders' willingness to get on with things.

Magnus was still at the hotel when Gudjón called back three hours later.

'Asphyxia,' he said. 'No obvious sign of the cause, but given it's a bedroom, we can assume a pillow over her face.'

It was what Magnus had expected. Smothering with a pillow was the classic MO to murder an old person. They were often not strong enough to resist, and, as in Nancy's case, the result was a dead elderly victim who looked as if she had expired in her sleep.

'Any sign of a struggle?'

'None that I can see. And I've looked pretty closely.'

'Could the body have been moved?'

'You mean: was the victim smothered elsewhere in the room and moved to the bed?'

'That's what I was thinking.' If Nancy met someone in her room, she would have been more likely to be sitting in the chair than on her bed.

'Hard to say. There are no signs of it, but it's possible if it was done gently.'

'OK, thanks, Gudjón.'

'I'll write up my report when I get the toxicology results back. And I'll call you if I find anything else of interest.'

There was no doubt about it. Nancy Fishburn had been murdered.

CHAPTER 35

MAGNUS RETURNED TO headquarters to report to Thelma. The short drive back from the hotel gave him a welcome few minutes of peace to think. There must be a link between Carlotta's death and Nancy Fishburn's. He didn't yet know whether Carlotta had discovered that the whole Nantucket Viking thing was a hoax, or how. But assuming she had, who would suffer enough from her discovery to kill her? And then to kill Nancy Fishburn?

Einar? Eygló? Suzy Henshaw? They would all bear some loss if the project fell through. But enough to kill for?

And which one of them had met Nancy and decided to go ahead with the documentary regardless? Or was it all of them?

Magnus needed to speak to them, but they were all in Greenland.

Vigdís was waiting for him. He could tell she had something.

'What is it?'

'I was thinking about Rósa,' Vigdís said. 'You know I haven't been happy about her and Einar?'

'Yeah, I know.'

'I remembered that the confirmation from Icelandair only explicitly mentioned that Rósa had taken the flight out to London.'

'OK.'

'So yesterday I asked them to check the return flight. They got back to me just now, and it turns out that although Rósa had checked in online the evening before, she didn't show. She wasn't on the plane.'

'Did she get an earlier flight?' Magnus's heartbeat quickened.

'Not with Icelandair, no. But I checked with WOW air and she got a flight first thing on Monday morning from Gatwick Airport with them. It arrived at Keflavík at ten-thirty.'

'Plenty of time to get to Glaumbaer for the evening.'

'Exactly.'

'Check the cameras at Hvalfjördur,' Magnus said. Hvalfjördur was a deep fjord on the Ring Road from Reykjavík to the north. It was a bottleneck, only possible to avoid with a hundred-kilometre detour. There was a tunnel under the fjord, and a camera at the exit, recording every car that drove through.

Einar, Eygló and now Rósa. They were all in Greenland together.

Magnus had to go to Greenland; they couldn't wait for them all to return to Iceland.

Thelma was unhappy about the cost, but she accepted there was no choice, especially when Magnus pointed out that the reason all their suspects were out of the country was that the Ministers of Culture and Justice had leaned on Thelma to let them go.

Getting to Greenland was not easy. The next direct flight from Reykjavík didn't leave for a couple of days, and Magnus couldn't wait that long. So he booked himself on to a flight to Copenhagen that evening, and another from there to Narsarsuaq in Greenland in the morning.

Álftanes was on the way to Keflavík Airport. Magnus grabbed an overnight bag and left a note for Tryggvi Thór, who was out.

He was at the gate, standing in line to board, when his phone rang.

'Vigdís?'

'I'm glad I caught you. We've just heard back on the Hvalfjördur cameras. Rósa's car came through the tunnel at one-seventeen p.m. on Monday afternoon. One occupant. And then it returned heading south at four-thirty-seven a.m. on Tuesday morning.'

'Well done, Vigdís!'

That put Rósa very much in the frame.

'And there is something else.'

'Yes?'

'Tryggvi Thór was found unconscious again. At Selatangar, along the coast from Grindavík. He was lucky, a French tourist stumbled on him in the fog.'

'Was he attacked?'

'We don't know yet; he might well have fallen. It looks as if he had gone for a hike there. Róbert is at the hospital checking it out.'

The queue for boarding was shuffling forward and Magnus was getting very close to the gate.

'Vigdís, can you do me a favour? Check up on Tryggvi Thór yourself. And if he tries to tell you it was an accident, don't believe him.'

'Magnús! I'm in the middle of a murder investigation!'

'Thanks, Vigdís. Got to go.'

Magnus was worried about the old man. Something was going on there, something bad.

He hung up and showed the woman at the gate his boarding pass and passport. There was not much he could do about it now.

PART TWO

Greenland

CHAPTER 36

'**C**UT!'

Eygló stopped talking. She was standing ankle-deep in lush green grass a couple of metres from the neat outline of the walls of a tiny square chapel, built by Gudrid's mother-in-law a thousand years before. Erik the Red's longhouse stood just a short distance down the hill. Eygló was talking to Tom, who was pointing his camera towards her, Ajay's boom mic hovering above him, and Suzy standing just behind the two of them.

It was their first day's filming in Greenland and it was not going well, or at least her scenes weren't. It had been a long, frustrating afternoon for everyone.

Einar was standing a few metres away, next to his wife, Rósa, both glaring at her. Professor Beccari, too, was watching, his face set in a frown of concerned sympathy. Aqqaluk, the Greenlandic fixer Suzy had hired, was off to one side murmuring on his mobile.

'Take ten,' said Suzy to her assembled crew, which really only numbered Tom and Ajay. She approached Eygló, smiling. 'Here, walk with me.'

They waded through the grass, scattered with wildflowers of yellow, blue and delicate pink. At each step a cloud of tiny moths rose a metre into the air and subsided. They were only a hundred metres from the edge of what had been known as Erik's Fjord, on the other side of which spread the airfield at Narsarsuaq, where they had landed the day before.

Erik's longhouse had stood at one end of the straggling village of Qassiarsuk, the modern name for Brattahlíd, a sparse community of farms, green meadows, a school, a church, a hostel and a dock. This was where Erik the Red had built his farm, where Gudrid had lived, and from where Erik's sons Leif, Thorvald and Thorstein, his daughter Freydís, and Gudrid and Thorfinn Karlsefni had all set out on their various voyages to Vinland. It was a key focus of the whole documentary.

And Eygló was screwing it up.

Suzy led Eygló a few metres down the little gully of the stream that ran down to the fjord, so that they were out of sight of the others. 'What's wrong, Eygló?'

'Wasn't that last take good enough?' Eygló said. She had tried really hard to make it better.

'It was OK,' said Suzy. 'But you can do so much better than "OK". Where is the excitement that you do so well? Imagine what it would be like for Erik, an outlaw who had been kicked out of Norway and then Iceland, to arrive at this beautiful green empty place where he could finally settle down without interference? All this free land! And imagine his family setting off on those voyages to Vinland. You can do that, Eygló. You can imagine that. You can imagine that better than anyone else I know, better than Einar, better than Mr Grand Professor Beccari. You know you can do that, don't you?'

Eygló nodded.

'What's the problem? Is it Einar? Is it Rósa?'

'No, no, she's fine.'

'It is Rósa, isn't it?' said Suzy. 'Ever since she joined us, you and Einar have looked miserable. I don't need to know what's going on between the three of you—'

'There's nothing going on between the three of us!' Eygló interrupted sharply.

'All right,' said Suzy. 'But you just stay here for a couple of minutes, and I'll go back and tell Rósa to take herself away. Einar too. What about Beccari?'

'No. No, he's fine,' said Eygló, who had a feeling that the professor was on her side.

'OK, he stays. And then you'll come back, and we will try

again. And this time, you will do it as well as I know you can.' Suzy took Eygló's shoulders and looked into her eyes. 'OK?'

Down here, by the stream, out of sight of the others, Eygló could feel Suzy's confidence in her give her strength. She nodded.

Suzy turned and climbed up the small slope over the lip of the gully.

Eygló stood by the stream and took some deep breaths. The brook babbled loudly and half a dozen wagtails bobbed and darted around her. Somewhere in the distance some twenty-first-century farm machinery rumbled. A gentle scent rose up from the wildflowers, mixing with a touch of twenty-first-century cow manure. It was a rare cloudless day, another reason Suzy was keen to get as many scenes in the can as she could.

Gudrid would have come down to this very stream to fetch water, to wash clothes. Eygló grinned. Perhaps to escape her in-laws.

Eygló could do this. She was ready.

But when she climbed up the slope, Suzy was speaking to a small group of people gathered around an old Land Rover and a pickup truck down by the road.

'Eygló!' Suzy called. 'Over here!'

As Eygló approached the group she could tell they were archaeologists: the clothes, the facial hair, the spectacles, the doughty muddiness of them. The smallest of the group, an Asian-looking woman with long shiny dark hair, smiled when she saw Eygló.

'Hi, Eygló. I don't know if you remember me? Anya? Anya Kleemann.'

'Yes, I do remember you!' said Eygló with a smile. 'You were on the dig with us here back in 2011.' She was a Greenlander of about Eygló's age doing a PhD at Aarhus University in Denmark, as far as Eygló could remember.

'That's right. I heard you were going to be filming here.'

'You look like you've come from your own excavation somewhere?'

'Tasiusaq. It's just a few kilometres over the hill that way.' She pointed northwards. 'In the next fjord. A thirteenth-century farmhouse.' She gave a shy smile. 'It's my first dig as supervisor.'

'Cool.'

'I thought *Viking Queens* was brilliant, by the way,' Anya said.

'Thanks,' said Eygló. 'It was Suzy's idea. She produced it.'

'And now we're doing Gudrid the Wanderer,' said Suzy.

'Great subject,' said Anya. She looked over to the meadow under which lay the ruins of the Brattahlíd longhouse. 'Presumably you are talking about the wampum?'

'Of course,' said Suzy. 'Were you there when it was found?'

'I was,' said Anya. 'But it was an Italian girl who found it. Carlotta, isn't that right, Eygló?'

Eygló nodded. She could tell Anya had spotted the change in her and Suzy's expression. But Eygló didn't want to explain, not in front of Suzy.

Fortunately, Suzy took charge. 'I'm afraid Carlotta died recently. She was murdered. In Iceland.'

'Oh, no!' said Anya. 'That's dreadful. What happened?'

'The police are trying to figure it out,' said Suzy. 'And not doing a very good job of it.'

'My God.' Anya looked stunned. 'I didn't know her well – I only met her on that dig, but I liked her. That's horrible.'

Eygló nodded. It was. It was definitely horrible.

'You know she contacted me a couple of weeks ago? Out of the blue, really. I hadn't heard from her since the dig. It was about the wampum.'

Please shut up, thought Eygló. A few days before she would have been eager to hear what Anya had to say about why Carlotta wanted to talk to her about wampum, but now Eygló just wanted to change the subject.

As did Suzy. 'Would you excuse us, Anya?' she said. 'We are on a tight schedule, and I need my archaeologist back.'

'We should get going,' said Anya. 'Are you staying at the hostel in the village?'

'No. In the hotel over in Narsarsuaq,' said Eygló. 'We're there for a couple of days.'

'Well, maybe we'll come over and have a drink with you one evening?'

'That would be great,' said Eygló.

'Einar Thorsteinsson is with us,' said Suzy.

'I remember Einar,' said Anya. 'I thought he and Carlotta had a thing going?'

Oh Christ, thought Eygló. This just gets worse. 'Einar's wife is here as well,' she said.

Anya got it. 'OK. See you later.' And with that she and her troupe drove off back towards the village.

'Ready?' There was a hint of worry in Suzy's glance; Eygló wasn't sure whether she was afraid that Eygló had been put off her stride, or that Eygló had noticed that Suzy had shut down any conversation about the wampum.

Eygló nodded. 'Let's do it.'

But as she waded through the grass back to the ruins of the chapel, she couldn't help thinking about what Anya had said. Carlotta had wanted to speak to her about the wampum. Eygló assumed that Carlotta had doubts and had communicated them to Anya. The police back in Iceland should be told. But Eygló sure as hell wasn't going to tell them, and she wasn't going to follow her original plan of quizzing Einar about the find either.

She took up her position by the outline of the tiny chapel. She stared down at the grass and the yellow flowers – buttercups, she thought – and took a couple more deep breaths, trying to force herself back to Gudrid and Erik and Thjodhild, Erik's wife who had built the church.

She flinched as Tom approached, waving a light meter near her face. 'You've been a good girl, haven't you?' he said softly. 'No more questions about the wampum being planted?'

'No,' said Eygló. 'No, I promise you.' She was glad Tom hadn't been there to listen to what Anya had told them, but he would no doubt hear it from Suzy, one way or another.

'Excellent,' Tom said. 'Then you've got nothing to worry about.' He winked. 'Just get this take right, eh?'

He returned to his camera.

But his words, which he had meant to be comforting, wrenched Eygló crashing back to the twenty-first century. She thought of

Carlotta, who had spent several months at this very spot and whom she had seen lying lifeless behind the church at Glaumbaer less than a week before. She thought of Rósa and her jealousy of Carlotta and now of Eygló herself. And she thought of Tom, only a few metres away from her.

She was destined to spend the next ten days with Tom and Rósa. There was no escape in Greenland – you couldn't even drive from one settlement to the other.

She was trapped. She was scared. She was so very scared.

The fear, the awfulness of Carlotta's death, overwhelmed her. She burst into tears.

'Cut!' Suzy said, her voice tense with frustration. 'That's all for today. We'll try again tomorrow.'

CHAPTER 37

AQQALUK SAID IT would be an hour before the speedboat arrived to carry them back across the fjord to Narsarsuaq and their hotel, so Eygló wandered away from the others in search of solitude. There was an outcrop of red rocks just behind the village, on which perched a statue of Leif Erikson, and Eygló headed for it. As in Reykjavík, he was depicted staring towards America. Halfway there.

She sat on the grass at his feet and looked out over the water. A parade of small icebergs lay in the channel, drifting slowly up the fjord from where they had calved from the glacier out of sight just around the headland to her right. She had felt isolated in Iceland many times before, but this was a new kind of isolation. Brattahlíd was not connected to anywhere by road, except a couple of farms in the next fjord. She could easily see the dusty runway and buildings of Narsarsuaq on the other side of the water. That had been an American airbase built during the Second World War, and heavily populated with servicemen during the Cold War. Now it was a plain of dust, drab buildings and fuel tanks, surrounded by rocky hillsides and water. Oddly, it served as one of the two international airports into Greenland.

The nearest town was Qaqortoq, thirty kilometres down the fjord towards the sea, and only reachable by boat or helicopter. That place only had five thousand inhabitants.

And just out of sight, behind the rock faces to the north and east, the second largest icecap in the world heaved, pushed and slowly slid, stretching back for thousands of kilometres towards the North Pole.

It may have seemed a place of safety to Erik the Red, but it certainly didn't to Eygló.

She heard the panting of someone climbing up the hill to her left, and she tensed. She hoped it was Einar and not Tom or Rósa, but she was relieved when Professor Beccari's bald head and pink scarf appeared.

'Do you mind if I join you?' he asked.

'No, please do,' said Eygló. 'It's quite a view.'

The professor squatted down beside her. He was wrapped up warmly, even though it was fourteen degrees, hot for Greenland. His pink scarf peeked out of his windcheater.

'You'll be OK tomorrow,' he said.

'I hope so,' said Eygló. 'I feel so unprofessional!'

Beccari grinned. 'It is your unprofessionalism that is your secret. Don't lose it.'

'Thank you,' said Eygló. Although she had always wanted to be taken seriously as a proper academic, she knew Beccari was right.

'It's probably the shock of the murder of that poor woman. You were the one who found the body, weren't you?'

Eygló nodded. 'It was a shock. It still is.'

'Is that why everyone is so miserable?'

'What do you mean?'

'I mean, it's not just you. It's Einar and his wife. What's she doing on this trip? It seemed like he wasn't expecting her to come, and he doesn't seem happy that she's here.'

'I don't think he is,' said Eygló. It was true: Einar looked absolutely miserable.

'I don't know how to put this,' Beccari said, 'and of course it's none of my business, but it seems as if there is the classic tension between a man, his wife and a – how shall I say? – a beautiful female friend.'

'That's me, right?' said Eygló.

Beccari shrugged and waggled his hand in what Eygló assumed was an assenting motion.

Damn right it was none of his business, she thought. It was clear that despite his august status, Professor Beccari was a natural gossip who had spotted sources of tension and wanted to find out more. But at least he was being honest in his curiosity.

'It's not that straightforward,' she said. 'There is nothing going on between me and Einar. There might have been once, many years ago, but not now.'

'Does Rósa understand that?' Beccari asked.

'Not sure,' said Eygló. 'I've seen you talking to her in the last couple of days. What do you think?'

'I don't know. I feel she is sad and she is angry, but I haven't asked her why. She is an intelligent woman. Well read. And she knows her history. I enjoy talking to her.'

Rósa was very intelligent, and could be charming if she wanted to. She was also unlikely to be overawed even by someone with Professor Beccari's ego.

'I wish she would just go back to Iceland,' Eygló said.

Beccari didn't answer.

'It's good to have seen where this wampum was found,' Beccari said. 'Einar was very convincing that it was real.'

'Einar is convincing.'

'But is he right?' Beccari asked. 'You seemed to have had your own doubts earlier?'

'No, not really doubts,' said Eygló. Certainly while she was in Greenland she was not going to question the wampum, or the letter. She was going to remain a true believer and get out of Greenland alive.

Beccari looked at Eygló closely, and then smiled. 'I'm glad to hear it.'

They sat in silence for a minute or two.

'I think I will leave this evening,' he said.

'Don't go.'

Beccari raised his eyebrows in surprise.

'It's good to have you here,' Eygló said. Although it was hard to imagine Professor Beccari actually protecting her, the presence of someone unconnected with the madness of Carlotta and her death was reassuring. With him around, she just felt safer.

'I've seen what I came for: Brattahlíd. And I would like to see a couple of other places in Greenland before I go back to the States. I'll take the helicopter to Qaqortoq this evening and stay there. It sounds interesting.'

Eygló had visited the town once on her previous trip to Brattahlíd. It was picturesque on the surface, a jumble of multi-coloured houses tumbling down three hillsides to the sea, but she had remembered sensing an undercurrent of bored desperation.

'Yeah, it's pretty,' she said. 'But we are heading up to the Western Settlement once we have finished here. You would enjoy that.'

'I don't have time for that, and you must admit your colleagues are not very congenial travel companions at the moment. Good luck with the rest of the filming. I am sure you will be brilliant.' He reached over to pat her hand, and then stood up to leave.

Eygló let him go. There were still twenty minutes till the boat left, and she wanted solitude.

'Eygló?'

She turned in panic as she recognized the voice. It was Rósa. Where the hell had she come from?

Rósa sat down next to her, right next to her so they were almost touching. Rósa was a big woman. Eygló tensed.

'Eygló. We need to talk.'

CHAPTER 38

VIGDÍS MADE HER way to Ward Three of the National Hospital in Reykjavík. She was very familiar with the layout; a police officer was a regular visitor to hospitals one way or another. She asked at the nurse's station which bed was Tryggvi Thór's.

She was busy with all the activity following Nancy Fishburn's murder and she didn't have time for this. Fortunately, the hospital wasn't far from the hotel where Nancy had died, and so she could slip away for half an hour. The crime scene was being processed, witnesses were being interviewed, reports were being written, but Magnus was right: all the answers lay in Greenland.

As she approached his bed, she saw a man she recognized standing next to it. He was in his fifties, tall, with close-cropped brown hair turning to grey and a thin red beard: Jakob Ingibergsson, the famous businessman who had cut quite a dash before the financial crash, and whose companies were still operating.

Tryggvi Thór obviously had friends in high places.

The businessman saw her hovering, and said a swift goodbye to Tryggvi Thór before leaving, ignoring her as he brushed past her.

Tryggvi Thór's head was bandaged and a large rose of purple blood vessels blossomed on his cheek. Sharp brown eyes stared out at her from his ravaged face.

'You're Vigdís, aren't you?' he said before she had a chance to introduce herself. 'Magnús's pal?'

'That's right,' said Vigdís.

'I don't know what you're doing here. I told your colleague it was just an accident.'

'Magnús asked me to check up on you. Can I sit down?' Vigdís indicated the grey plastic chair next to his bed.

'No.'

Vigdís sat on it anyway. It was still warm from the millionaire businessman's arse. Magnus had warned her Tryggvi Thór would be difficult. She was sure she could handle him.

'Róbert told me that you slipped and fell,' she said, taking out her notebook. 'Can you tell me exactly what happened?'

'I slipped and fell.'

Vigdís gave him one of her 'don't bullshit me' looks. She had several. 'You expect me to believe that? Only a few days after you were attacked at home?'

'Yes, I do.' They stared at each other for a couple of moments. 'OK. I don't remember exactly what happened. I think I must have fainted as a result of the head injury earlier this week, and I hit my head as I fell.'

Vigdís had to admit that sounded plausible.

'You have to admit that sounds plausible,' said Tryggvi Thór with a hint of a smile.

'You would have died if that tourist hadn't found you,' said Vigdís.

The shadow of the smile dissolved. 'I know. I was lucky.'

'You might not be as lucky next time.'

Tryggvi Thór didn't respond.

'Magnús is concerned about you.'

'Magnús should mind his own business. Now please leave.'

Vigdís sat there watching him.

A minute passed.

'OK. If you're not going to leave, tell me what it's like being a black Icelander.'

Vigdís rolled her eyes. 'You have got to be kidding! That's none of your business.'

'Neither is my head injury any of yours.'

'It is my business if someone is trying to kill you,' said Vigdís. 'Actually, I don't care too much about that, but I know Magnús does.'

'Is he honest?' Tryggvi Thór asked.

'Of course he's honest! He's a policeman.'

Tryggvi Thór snorted. 'I used to be a policeman. You and I know they are not all honest.'

'Yes, you would know that since you got drummed out of the force for corruption.'

'Well?' said Tryggvi Thór.

Vigdís sighed. 'Yes. Yes, Magnús is honest. Irritatingly, inflexibly honest.'

Tryggvi Thór smiled. 'And you?'

Vigdís refused to respond to his smile, even though she wanted to. She nodded. 'Yes. I'm honest too. Almost as bad as him.'

'Good,' said Tryggvi Thór. 'I think I believe you.'

Vigdís snorted.

'The reason I asked you what it was like being a black Icelander, Vigdís, is that my daughter is black. Very black: about the same shade as you.'

Vigdís knew from the reports on the earlier attack in Álftanes that Tryggvi Thór had returned from twenty years in Africa. She hadn't read of a daughter.

'What's her name?' she asked, in spite of herself.

'Greta.'

'And is she here in Iceland?'

'She visits occasionally, but she is in medical school in Kampala. So. What's it like?'

Vigdís sighed. Despite herself she was intrigued by a half-Icelandic, half-African woman whose father was a cop.

'It's crap, basically. I never met my dad: he was an American serviceman who left my mum before I was born. So I have been brought up entirely an Icelander. I'm just as much an Icelander as you: more, in fact, because I have lived my whole life in this country.'

'OK,' said Tryggvi Thór. 'So why is that crap?'

'People don't treat me like that. Icelandic people. I know we're not supposed to be racist, but many of them can't handle someone who is black and speaks Icelandic as well or better than them. They keep trying to speak to me in English. I don't speak English.'

'That's a shame.'

'And why is that?'

'Because Greta barely speaks any Icelandic. I would like her to be Icelandic. Like you.'

'What does her mother think about that?'

Tryggvi Thór's face sagged. Vigdís knew she had made a mistake. 'She's dead, isn't she?' she said. 'I'm sorry.'

Tryggvi Thór said nothing.

'Next time Greta comes to Iceland, tell her to get in touch with me.' Vigdís left her card on Tryggvi Thór's table. 'We'll communicate by tribal dance.'

CHAPTER 39

THE WHITE GLARE of the Greenland icecap emerged in the distance through Magnus's aeroplane window. There were plenty of questions he needed to ask the TV crew in Greenland. What they knew about the hoax. Which of them had met Nancy Fishburn on Snaefellsnes. What their movements had been the morning Nancy had been killed.

But his first priority had to be Rósa, who was emerging as a prime suspect for Carlotta's murder. The connection between Carlotta's death and Nancy Fishburn's was as yet unclear, but there would be one, and it would probably involve Rósa. Maybe she was covering for Einar? Magnus didn't know.

He pulled out his notebook and jotted down notes for the interview. Rósa was a smart lawyer. Once she figured out she was a serious suspect for Carlotta's murder, she would probably keep shtum. Magnus thought he could just about get away with interviewing her as a witness rather than a suspect, at least initially. It was an important distinction in Icelandic criminal law and one Rósa would be aware of. Magnus needed to tempt her to divulge as much information as possible before she realized that he knew she had lied to the police about her trip to London.

The plane descended over massive icebergs the size of ocean liners, reached the mountainous coastline and picked up the flow of a fat ribbon of glacier that darkened from white to grey and blue as it cracked and wrinkled in a frozen tumult of centuries-old ice the closer it came to the sea. The aircraft banked low around a cliff and into a long thin fjord with a drab plain bisected by a runway on one side and green hills on the other: the green of Brattahlíd, part of a narrow strip of vegetation clinging to the south-west edge of an enormous block of granite and ice.

Because of Greenland's semi-autonomous status with Denmark, there was no immigration control for flights from Copenhagen in the small terminal, but two uniformed police officers, one male and one female, watched the arriving tourists and returning Greenlanders.

Magnus approached them and held out his hand. 'Hi, I'm Magnus Jonson,' he said in English, using the American version of his name. His father's name was Ragnar Jónsson, which meant that in Iceland Magnus was known as Magnús Ragnarsson, but when he had arrived in America at the age of twelve, using his father's last name had proved much easier all round.

'Josepha Paulsen,' said the female officer. 'And this is Constable Jens Frandsen.'

Vigdís had been in touch with Inspector Paulsen, who was the police chief from Qaqortoq, the nearest big town further down the fjord towards the sea. Paulsen was Inuit, with wide, strong cheekbones and a firm mouth that broke into an unexpectedly sweet smile. Frandsen was twenty years younger than her, Danish, with fine blonde hair that was cut so short you could barely see it.

'*Taler du dansk?*' Paulsen asked. It was a fair question. Both Iceland and Greenland had been colonies of the Danish Crown, and until recently Danish had been compulsory in Icelandic schools. But there was also a linguistic dance when Icelanders and Danes met: the Icelanders preferring to speak English rather than be at a disadvantage in the colonial language.

Magnus had no choice. 'I'm sorry. I left Iceland when I was twelve, so I never really learned Danish.'

'That's OK,' Paulsen replied in heavily accented English. 'Your colleague in Reykjavík said that you would prefer to approach Rósa Helgadóttir yourself, so we haven't detained her. They are all filming at Brattahlíd on the other side of the fjord. We can take you there now.'

'Great. Let's go.'

There wasn't much to Narsarsuaq. It was dominated by the airport, outside which ran a long straight road which led to a cluster of large rectangular functional buildings: warehouses, sheds, small apartment blocks. Paulsen and Frandsen led Magnus over the road to a police car parked next to a little green hut bearing the word *Politi*. They sped down the straight road, scattering suitcase-dragging tourists from the Copenhagen flight, to its end at a small harbour of three or four jetties.

They dropped into a marked police speedboat, and soon they were zipping across the fjord, dodging sedate icebergs on their way. Frandsen was driving.

'Can you give me some background on Rósa Helgadóttir?' Paulsen asked.

Magnus described as succinctly as he could Carlotta's murder and the possible relationship of Einar, Rósa and the Italian tourist, and also Vigdís's discovery that Rósa was in the north of Iceland at the time of the crime. He mentioned Nancy Fishburn's murder and the need to establish a connection with Carlotta's death.

Paulsen seemed to pick it all up quickly; her English was good, and she was sharp. 'It looks like you may want to make an arrest,' she said.

'It's possible,' said Magnus. 'I don't know about the paperwork?' Although Denmark and Iceland had very good police links, international arrests were always problematic. The fact that the Icelandic criminal justice system was closely based on the Danish model would help.

'We can hold her for twenty-four hours without charging her,' Paulsen said. 'We would take her to the station in Qaqortoq. Our prosecutor here is efficient; that should give you time to get a request from Reykjavík.'

'How do we get to Qaqortoq?' Magnus asked.

'Helicopter,' said Paulsen. 'Or boat; but that's slow.'

Magnus had seen a number of red helicopters bearing the Air Greenland livery on the tarmac at Narsarsuaq.

The boat pulled up at the dock on the other side of the fjord, where an unoccupied police car was waiting for them. 'We don't have a policeman in Brattahlíd, but we do keep a vehicle here,' Paulsen explained, and she fetched the keys from a man in an unkempt red kiosk by the harbour.

They drove along an undulating road past half a dozen large farms and a church, before they reached a small group of people standing a few metres away from the road.

As Magnus approached, he noticed that there were only five of them: Eygló, Suzy, Tom the cameraman, Ajay the young sound guy and a Greenlander whom he didn't recognize. No Rósa. And no Einar for that matter.

Suzy made no attempt to hide her unhappiness at seeing him. 'What on earth are you doing here?' she said. 'Can't you give us a moment's peace?'

Magnus glanced at the others. Tom looked inscrutable, Ajay and the Greenlander curious, and Eygló scared. That was interesting.

'I'm here to see Rósa to ask her some questions. And actually I will probably have more questions for all of you.'

'How many times is this?' Suzy protested. 'If you weren't so incompetent you would know what questions to ask, and you would only need to ask us once.'

'That's not the way murder investigations work,' said Magnus patiently. 'By their nature, new evidence comes to light, which leads to new lines of inquiry. But to start with, it's Rósa I really need to see. Where is she?'

'She is back at Narsarsuaq. I told her to stay away from our filming, at least today.'

'Why was that?'

'She was distracting the others,' said Suzy, with a quick glance towards Eygló.

Interesting, Magnus thought. Maybe it was Rósa who was scaring Eygló and not him. He saw Tom move a little closer to Eygló and mutter something to her. Just for a second, there was real fear on her face, and then she regained her composure.

More interesting. Clearly, all was not sweetness and light in the documentary team.

'What about Einar? Is he with her?' Magnus asked.

'Probably. We did a couple of takes with him first thing this morning, and then the boat took him back across the fjord.'

Magnus turned to Paulsen, who had been listening. He had plenty of questions for Suzy and her colleagues, but they could wait. Rósa first. 'Looks like it's back to Narsarsuaq.'

There was a guest house and a hotel at Narsarsuaq, and the TV crew were staying in the hotel. It, too, was a rectangular functional building, two storeys high, with a rank of flagpoles standing to attention outside it. Neither Rósa nor Einar were there. The receptionist said that Rósa had left the hotel soon after the others that morning, and that Einar had arrived later, at about ten o'clock, and had asked after her. Then he too had left.

It was now two-forty-five.

As they drove back towards the airport terminal and the police hut, Magnus spotted Einar at a wooden table outside a tourist office hut just next to the airport perimeter, sipping from a plastic cup. Sandwich wrappings testified to lunch.

Einar didn't look especially pleased to see him. 'What are you doing here?' he asked.

'Looking for your wife. Do you know where she is?'

'She's gone for a hike. A place called the Blomsterdalen. It's that way.' Einar pointed north of the airport, where the road became a track before it curved out of sight into low hills. He frowned. 'I don't understand why you have come all this way to speak to her.' He looked worried.

'I'll want to speak to you too,' Magnus said. 'But later.' He turned to Paulsen. 'What's this Blomsterdalen?'

'The valley of flowers,' Paulsen translated into English for Magnus's benefit – unnecessarily, for the Icelandic word was almost the same. 'It's on the route up to the nearest glacier.'

'Can we drive?' Magnus asked.

'We can part of the way,' said Paulsen.

'Let's go then.'

Frandsen drove the police 4 × 4 north past the airport and along the banks of a riverbed, probably half a mile wide, with a narrow stream meandering through it. Magnus recognized the destructive signs of glacial flooding. The road was empty of people until they came to a couple with small backpacks studying a lone stone chimney.

'That's all that remains of a massive American military hospital,' said Paulsen. 'The rest burned down in the 1970s. I'll go and ask them if they have seen her.'

She jumped out of the vehicle and strode over to the couple. She was back in a minute. 'No sign of her.'

The river disappeared to their left as they drove on an increasingly rough track. They crested a small hill, and then there was the Blomsterdalen, a bowl of deep green surrounded by steep cliffs and the riverbed. There were indeed flowers everywhere, blue, purple, yellow, and the bobbing white heads of bog cotton. On the far side of the valley, a couple of miles away, the river emerged from a gorge, and high up, above the wall of rock, Magnus could see the smooth white tip of a glacier, one of the southernmost fingers of Greenland's icecap.

The road petered out to a footpath crossing a ditch, and the three police officers climbed out of the vehicle.

No Rósa. No obvious sign of any human being.

Frandsen grabbed a pair of binoculars, and carefully surveyed the valley.

Silence. Apart from a twitter of a bird and the hungry buzzing of a bee behind them. And the rustle of the grass in the breeze.

'What now?' said Magnus.

'She might have gone up to the glacier. You need to climb that rock over there.' Paulsen pointed to the cliff at the far end of the valley. 'There is a path, but it's difficult. Is she in good shape?'

Magnus remembered Rósa's swimmer's physique. 'Probably.'

'Do you want me to go and see?' said Frandsen. He was young, fit and ready for a rapid hike.

While Paulsen was considering the constable's suggestion, Magnus heard the familiar croak of a raven, followed swiftly by another. Not far away, a couple of hundred yards into the valley, five of them were circling above a clump of dwarf willow trees next to a stream. One of them dived down.

'Over there!' Magnus pointed. 'See anything? By those birds.'

Frandsen swung his binoculars in the direction of the ravens.

'What do you think they are circling over?' Magnus said. He had spent four years of his childhood at the farm at Bjarnarhöfn, long enough to know that ravens behaving like that meant a dead lamb. Or sheep.

Paulsen threw him a worried glance. Greenlanders were hunters; she knew what the ravens meant. 'There are no sheep here.'

Magnus set off at a trot through the grass and bushes, followed by the inspector. It could be any animal. A fox. A very lost sheep. Another bird.

Or it might be Rósa.

He pushed his way through the low willow bushes, yelling and waving his arms to scare the ravens away. They were reluctant to leave their feast.

It was Rósa. And the birds had got to her.

CHAPTER 40

THERE WERE ONLY two police officers to deal with the crime scene: Magnus was out of his jurisdiction. Paulsen left Frandsen to guard the scene and keep the birds off, and she and Magnus sped back to Narsarsuaq in the car, with Paulsen calling Qaqortoq on the radio in urgent Greenlandic for reinforcements.

There was one obvious suspect and Paulsen named him. 'From what you've told me, Einar had a motive to murder his wife if he thought she had killed Carlotta. Revenge.'

'That's true,' said Magnus.

'OK. We'll pick him up now and ask him a few questions. Then I'll need to coordinate the other officers from Qaqortoq when they get here. There should be a police doctor on his way as well.'

'What about forensics?'

'They'll come down from Nuuk.' Nuuk was the capital of Greenland, a few hundred miles up the coast.

Einar was no longer sitting outside the tourist office café. One of the staff said they had seen him go into the small US airbase museum next door. They found him there, staring at large wall-mounted photographs of Bluie West One, as Narsarsuaq airfield was called during the Second World War, teeming with aircraft and servicemen. He was the only visitor in the room.

'Einar!' Paulsen said.

He turned, a spark of irritation disappearing rapidly when he saw the two police officers' expressions.

'I am sorry to tell you we have found your wife. She is dead.'

Shock struck Einar hard in the face.

Paulsen and Magnus waited and watched. The surprise looked genuine, but Magnus had seen surprise faked just as well many times in the past.

'Where?' Einar said.

'In the Blomsterdalen.'

'How? Was it an accident? Or ...'

'She was stabbed,' said Paulsen. 'At least we think she was stabbed.' It looked as if her chest had been slashed, but the ravens had made a mess of the area, and of her face, so it was hard to be certain.

The little colour there was in Einar's face left it, and his mouth opened. He seemed dazed.

'Can you come with us, please, Einar? We have a few questions.'

The police hut was close by. Paulsen sat Einar down on one side of a crowded desk while she took the other, and Magnus took a seat on the side of the little room. For a moment Magnus was worried that she would do the interview in Danish, which Einar probably spoke, but she kept to English for his benefit.

'Did you kill your wife, Einar?'

That was direct, thought Magnus.

'What? You think I killed her?' Einar looked in disbelief at Paulsen and Magnus. 'Fair enough you might think I killed Carlotta, but not Rósa. She's my wife, for God's sake! Why would I kill her?'

'Answer the question, Einar,' Paulsen said. 'Did you kill Rósa?'

'No,' said Einar. 'No, no, *no*!' The last word was shouted.

'All right,' said Paulsen calmly. 'I want you to tell me your precise movements from when you left your colleagues at Brattahlíd this morning until when we saw you this afternoon.'

Einar closed his eyes, took a deep breath, and muttered, 'I can't believe this,' in Icelandic.

'Please speak English, Einar,' said Paulsen. She had a pen and notebook ready. 'What time did you get the boat across the fjord?'

Magnus could see what Paulsen was doing: getting down the details which could be quickly checked by her colleagues when they arrived, before she started asking questions about motive and Einar's relationship with his wife.

Einar's description of his movements that day was incoherent. It looked as if he was having difficulty thinking straight, but of course he might just have been trying to confuse Paulsen – it was impossible to say. He claimed he had started out to follow Rósa to the Blomsterdalen, but had got as far as the site of the old US military hospital and given up and turned around. On his way back he had climbed the steep hill above the airport and sat up there for a while. Then he had descended to the village and stopped in the café for lunch. And that was where Paulsen and Magnus had found him. During this whole period he hadn't looked at his watch, or so he claimed.

'What about your clothes? Have you changed them today?'

Einar was wearing jeans, boots, a T-shirt, a cardigan and a jacket. 'No.'

'Are you quite sure?'

'Of course I'm sure.'

'Let me look,' said Paulsen. 'Stand up.'

He did so, as did she, and she inspected his clothing and his hands, looking for blood or other evidence. Magnus couldn't see anything and neither could she. No doubt the forensics people would examine everything much more thoroughly later.

'Empty your pockets.'

Einar did as he was instructed. A wallet, Danish and Icelandic change, a phone, two scrunched receipts and some keys. No knife.

'Am I under arrest?'

'Not yet,' said Paulsen. 'But I am going to handcuff you and ask you to stay here.'

Paulsen slapped a pair of cuffs on Einar, and then beckoned Magnus to follow her out of the police hut.

'Can you watch him for me? By all means ask him questions if you write his answers down, but probably best to leave off anything he did today until I get back? Is that OK?'

Magnus nodded.

'My police officers will be here soon, and I need to organize things. Oh, and Magnus?' Paulsen looked at Magnus's large frame.

'Yes?'

'If you need to restrain him, do.' She grinned.

'I will,' said Magnus and joined Einar back in the police hut.

They sat in silence. Magnus didn't know whether Einar had killed Rósa. It was certainly a possibility and it was natural for Paulsen to detain him.

Einar glared at Magnus for a few seconds. Then his face cracked, he bowed, put his head in his cuffed hands and sobbed. Magnus watched.

Eventually, the sobbing stopped and Einar sat up. His eyes were red and he wiped his nose with his sleeve. They had been real tears. But Magnus had seen men who had killed their wives and wept afterwards.

'You know Rósa followed Carlotta to Glaumbaer the evening she was murdered?' said Magnus in Icelandic.

Einar's eyes burned through the tears with anger. With hatred, even.

'Did you know that?' said Magnus.

Einar didn't reply.

'I think you did know that.'

Nothing.

'Do *you* think Rósa killed Carlotta?'

Magnus waited. Einar held his eye for a few moments and then looked up at the ceiling. He sighed and squeezed his eyes shut. He was in pain. There was no doubt that if he hadn't killed his wife, this conversation would be painful. But then it might be just as painful if he *had* killed her. The fact he was an emotional mess didn't tell Magnus anything.

He met Magnus's eyes again, the hatred subsiding. 'I really don't know,' he said, shaking his head. 'I'd like to think she didn't, but I just don't know.'

Magnus had only known Einar a week. At the start of that week, his lined face could have been described as rugged. Now it was ravaged. His eyes were red, the sockets blackened as if they had been bruised. The cocky self-assurance had gone. Einar was falling apart.

'Tell me,' Magnus said quietly.

'Tell you what?' said Einar, with an attempt at defiance.

'Tell me about Rósa and Carlotta.'

Einar slumped back in his chair and nodded to himself. 'All right. You know that Carlotta and I had an affair several years back, but then Rósa found out about it and told me to stop? And I did?'

Magnus nodded.

'OK. And, as I told you in Ólafsvík, I had arranged to see Carlotta in Saudárkrókur last week, and Rósa knew nothing about it?'

'Yes.'

'So when I saw Carlotta behind that church with her head cracked open, my first thought, my very first thought, was that Rósa had killed her. I knew how angry Rósa would be if she had discovered we were meeting. Then, well, then I thought I was being paranoid; I mean, Rósa can be an angry woman, but she wouldn't actually *kill* anyone. But I decided to keep quiet about recognizing Carlotta. It wasn't just so that Rósa wouldn't find out that Carlotta and I were meeting; it was also because I thought maybe she *had* killed her. And if it wasn't her, but someone else, then you would find the killer and it wouldn't matter that I knew Carlotta. I thought at the time Eygló hadn't recognized her from Greenland, so ... well ... so I kept quiet.'

'Even though you thought Rósa might be a murderer?'

'If she had killed Carlotta then it was all my fault. Or mostly my fault. She's my wife, goddammit, I wasn't going to shop her to you!'

'OK,' said Magnus. 'Did you talk to her about it?'

'How could I? She called me when she saw the murder on the news. I didn't know how to ask her if she had killed Carlotta, at least on the phone. So I just kept it matter of fact. I was expecting her to ask me all about it, to demand to know what Carlotta was

227

doing in Iceland, but the thing is she didn't.' Einar's expression became even more pained. 'Afterwards I wondered why she didn't.'

'What do you mean?'

'It felt like she had known all along. That Carlotta was in Iceland. That Carlotta was dead. I mean *before* she had heard it on the news. Which implied ...'

'... that she had killed her?'

Einar nodded. 'That's what I thought, although I couldn't admit it to myself, so I just didn't think too hard about it. But I decided to keep quiet about knowing Carlotta in the hope you guys would turn up someone else – that rapist in Akureyri or something.'

Einar swallowed. 'But the thing is, I was devastated when I saw Carlotta's dead body. And if Rósa had killed her ... She shouldn't have done that. I was angry. I was ashamed. I was suspicious. I blamed myself, I blamed her, I blamed Carlotta – she shouldn't even have been in Glaumbaer.'

He gathered himself. 'So, Rósa and I agreed not to talk about it until I got back to Reykjavík.'

'Which wasn't until the night before you came out here?'

'That's right.' Einar breathed deeply. 'The problem was that I spent the night before that in Ólafsvík with Eygló.'

'We know,' said Magnus.

'Yes, your partner saw me, didn't she? Whatever it may look like, we didn't sleep together, or at least we didn't have sex. But after the whole Carlotta thing, I couldn't hide that from Rósa. We had to be completely honest. I had to stop hiding things, so I told her, that evening.'

'And she didn't like it?'

'No. She didn't believe nothing happened. She started a row. It lasted all night. And, eventually, I asked her about Carlotta.'

'What did she say?'

'At first she denied she knew Carlotta was in Iceland before she saw her murder on the news, but by that stage I could tell she was lying. And then she told me the truth. Or I *think* it was the truth; at least I did then. When she was telling it to me.'

228

Magnus waited.

'She knew I was seeing Carlotta. She read my emails, even though I had password-protected them – she guessed the password, and they were on my Gmail account so she could access them any time from her own computer. So she knew Carlotta was coming to Iceland, and where we were meeting in Saudárkrókur. She told me she was furious, and she wanted to catch us. She was going to scare both of us into stopping the affair, or what she assumed was an affair.

'She decided to come back early from her trip to London. She drove up to Blönduós and tailed Carlotta to Glaumbaer. She saw us filming and Carlotta talking to me. Then she followed Carlotta up to the fjord near Drangey and then back to Glaumbaer later. She assumed Carlotta had arranged to meet me there: she wanted to catch us red-handed.'

Magnus was making notes as he listened. 'And Carlotta didn't spot her?' It was difficult to follow people on empty Icelandic roads.

Einar shrugged. 'Never underestimate Rósa,' he said. 'And Carlotta wouldn't have been looking out for her.'

'OK. Then what happened at Glaumbaer?'

'She *says* ...' Einar hesitated. 'She said that she saw Carlotta go into the churchyard. And then after about twenty minutes a man came out to Carlotta's car, took something out and then returned to the churchyard. Rósa waited, but there was no sign of Carlotta, although she did see the man leave the folk museum car park on foot and walk along the road. Rósa waited ten minutes and then sneaked into the churchyard herself. There she saw Carlotta's body.'

'Did she say why she didn't report it?' said Magnus.

'She was going to. And then she thought, just like I did the next morning, that she would be the obvious suspect. So she just left. Drove straight back to Reykjavík.'

Magnus remembered it was possible to get from the churchyard at Glaumbaer to the folk museum round the back of the church away from the road.

'Who was this man? Did she recognize him?'

'No.'

'Was he young or old? Did he look like an Icelander? What did he take out of Carlotta's car?'

'I don't know!' protested Einar. 'I didn't ask anything about him, so she didn't tell me. I wasn't even sure there *was* a man.'

'I can see that,' Magnus acknowledged. But he was pretty sure he knew the answer to his last question: Carlotta's HP laptop.

'So we kind of made peace,' Einar said. 'Or at any rate we fell asleep. But the next morning, we started arguing again. Did we trust each other? I wasn't going to believe that she hadn't killed Carlotta if she wasn't going to accept that I hadn't had sex with Eygló.' Einar sighed. 'It was stupid, but we were both tired. Me especially. I wasn't making a lot of sense.'

'So then she came after you. To Greenland?'

'Yes,' said Einar.

'Why was that? To try to straighten things out?'

'Yes. But not just that. She had something else to tell me.'

'Which was?'

'Her cancer was back. And it was going to kill her. Soon.'

CHAPTER 41

'DID YOU KNOW that the wampum find and the Columbus letter are an elaborate hoax?' Magnus looked steadily at Einar, whose eyes flicked briefly up towards him.

'They are not a hoax. They've been thoroughly checked out.'

'They are a hoax, Einar. A hoax perpetrated by a woman named Nancy Fishburn and her husband and a friend of theirs who was a rare-book dealer. You met her in Nantucket.'

Einar stared at Magnus. 'You are not serious?'

'I am. Her granddaughter told me so.'

'Her granddaughter is lying. Or confused. She was the one who confused Eygló back in Nantucket in a bar. She was drunk.'

'I don't think so. Nancy told her all about it last week, and she told me. Are you surprised?'

The anger in Einar's eyes fizzled out. He took a deep breath and closed his eyes. 'Why should I be surprised? Everything else has fallen apart, why shouldn't that?'

'Did you suspect they were fakes?'

'No,' said Einar.

'Did anyone else?'

Einar hesitated. 'Eygló, maybe. But Professor Beccari authenticated the letter. And the wampum was genuinely from Nantucket, I'm certain of that.'

'Oh yes, it was. But it was planted by Nancy Fishburn herself nearly forty years ago in the open trench at Brattahlíd.'

'Oh, great. I hope you have arrested her!'

'We can't. She was murdered on Friday morning before you all left for Greenland. In a hotel in Reykjavík.'

'Oh God,' said Einar. 'I suppose you suspect me of that as well?'

'When did you last see her?'

'I don't know. Three weeks ago in Nantucket, I suppose. When we were filming at the lagoon Gudrid and Thorfinn landed at.' Einar winced. 'The lagoon we *thought* they had landed at.'

'What did you do Friday morning? Take me through that day up to the point I saw you at the City Airport.'

'You do suspect me! I don't believe it.'

'What time did you wake up?' Magnus asked, notebook at the ready.

Einar claimed he had stayed at home that morning. Suzy had asked him to meet the rest of them for breakfast so they could discuss what they were going to do in Greenland, but after his tense night with Rósa, Einar hadn't bothered to show up. He had stayed at home until it was time to go to the airport. He doubted any of his neighbours would have seen him.

Rósa had gone to work as usual that morning, or she had said she had. Einar had no idea then that Rósa was going to jump on the plane to Greenland with him, and although she hadn't told him this herself, Einar suspected she had booked her ticket at the last minute – probably that morning.

As for the Thursday morning in Snaefellsnes, Einar insisted he hadn't gone to meet Nancy Fishburn – he didn't even know she was in Iceland. Einar reminded Magnus that he had handed over his computer and phone at the police station in Ólafsvík that morning, and after that he had gone straight back to his own hotel. The others had driven off later to film at Ingjaldshóll, but that was well after the meeting with Nancy.

The door of the police hut opened and Paulsen reappeared with a constable, who led Einar away in handcuffs. Magnus followed them outside, where other police officers freshly arrived from Qaqortoq were busying themselves. Two of them jumped into an unmarked pickup truck and sped off up the road towards the Blomsterdalen.

'We've set up an incident room in the school,' Paulsen said. 'There isn't enough room in the hut.'

Magnus watched as the constable inserted Einar into a police vehicle and drove him away.

'Did you ask Einar whether Rósa killed Carlotta?' Paulsen asked.

'He says he doesn't know,' Magnus replied. 'But he suspects she might have. He knew she followed Carlotta to Glaumbaer – that's where the murder took place. I'll write up the interview as soon as I can.'

'Thanks. I'll talk to him myself again soon. Our working assumption must be that he thought Rósa killed Carlotta, and then he killed Rósa in revenge.'

Magnus nodded.

'So we'll need any evidence you have from Iceland that Rósa murdered Carlotta. Can you get on to your people there?'

'Sure. Am I staying at Narsarsuaq tonight?'

'Can we leave that open for now?' said Paulsen. 'I might need you in Qaqortoq for the prosecutor.' Then she gave Magnus that oddly sweet smile she had flashed before. 'Thanks for your help on this, Magnus. I know we were supposed to be helping you.'

'No problem,' said Magnus. 'If we do this right we should both get a result.'

He retrieved his bag from the back of the police vehicle, where it was still stowed, walked the quarter-mile to the hotel and found a quiet corner of the lobby to make some phone calls and write up his interview with Einar on his laptop for Paulsen.

He called Vigdís and told her the news about Rósa. He also explained Paulsen's theory about Rósa killing Carlotta and Einar killing Rósa. Vigdís liked the part about who had murdered Carlotta. Magnus wasn't so sure, but he would keep an open mind; it was certainly the correct priority to pursue. He asked Vigdís to send summaries of the evidence in the Carlotta case to Paulsen in Greenland and to coordinate with Árni and Jón Kári in Saudárkrókur about building a case against Rósa.

Vigdís reported back on the investigation into Nancy's murder: no forensic evidence of any note, and nothing from all the interviews the police had carried out. Now they would have to go back and ask the hotel staff if anyone had seen Rósa that morning. She could have gone to the hotel and murdered Nancy in her room before going on to the airport. But Magnus wasn't clear why Rósa would have done that. To protect her husband from the scandal that his discoveries were a hoax? That didn't sound right.

Gather the evidence and then make sense of it.

'Did you see Tryggvi Thór?' Magnus asked her.

'I did. In hospital. He's a bit of a mess. And he is a miserable old bastard.'

'Do you think he was attacked?'

'For sure. He didn't admit it; he claims he must have fainted and fallen, but he was pretty comprehensively beaten up. Again. His daughter seems to think so too. She is one angry woman. She claims he needs protection.'

'Can we give it to him? Will Thelma sign off on it?'

'This woman says he needs protection *from* the police. It's weird; I mean, she's in the diplomatic service, she should know better. She has clearly lost it.'

'What does Thelma say?'

'Nothing. She hasn't taken any interest. If I were you, I'd find somewhere new to live when you get back here.'

Magnus grunted. He could feel his stubbornness kicking in. He wasn't going to be moved out of a perfectly nice house because its owner had been beaten up twice, even if the owner refused to admit to it. And in Tryggvi Thór he suspected his stubbornness had found a soulmate.

'There's something going on there, Vigdís. Can you ask around? Maybe an old-timer who was in the force when Tryggvi Thór was there?'

'I don't want to feed your paranoia,' said Vigdís. 'But if the police really *are* covering stuff up, we have to be careful who we ask.'

'Maybe a retired policeman?' Magnus paused to think. 'What about Emil?'

Emil was a detective from Akranes whom Vigdís and Magnus had worked with when Magnus was last in Iceland. 'He retired, didn't he? If he's still alive.' Emil's health had not been good.

'Yeah. I can go and see Emil,' said Vigdís. 'I'm pretty sure he worked as a detective in Reykjavík before transferring to Akranes, in which case he might have known Tryggvi Thór well. He probably is still around; I think I would have heard if he had died.'

Magnus called Árni and repeated what he had told Vigdís. Árni and Jón Kári had been working on sightings of Rósa and her car. But it was already a week and people's memories were fading. They had one sighting of Rósa from a resident of one of the farms around Glaumbaer, a young farm labourer who thought he had seen her waiting in a car, but he was hesitant about the time, or even the day. Árni promised he would step up the investigation of that angle.

Magnus wrote up his interview with Einar and then sent it by email to Paulsen. A muffled thudding roar erupted outside, as two red Air Greenland helicopters lined up to land – they seemed to be always buzzing in and out of the airport. Magnus could see the school the police were using as an incident room from the hotel, a shed distinguishable from the others by a swing and a see-saw outside it, and a mural of an elephant and a giraffe surrounded by sunshine and jungle on one of the walls. They looked cold.

A police vehicle and a pickup pulled up outside the building and disgorged the TV crew: Eygló, Suzy, Tom, Ajay and the Greenlander, who must have just returned from Brattahlíd over the water. Two police officers led them inside.

Magnus asked to interview the crew one by one after Paulsen and her colleagues had finished with them. They agreed that Paulsen would speak to them about Rósa, and Magnus about Nancy Fishburn. He was given a classroom to himself for the purpose, the grey breeze-block walls brightened by a collage of posters and kids' pictures.

First up was Suzy Henshaw. Magnus and she perched on two ludicrously small children's chairs with an undersized table between them.

She looked harried, dark smudges underpinned her dark eyes, and the lines in her face had deepened, but she sat upright and defiant on the little plastic chair.

'I'm so sorry hear about Rósa,' she said. 'What's going on?'

'That's what I'm going to find out,' said Magnus. 'With your help.'

'It can't have anything to do with us,' said Suzy. 'But I will answer your questions, obviously.'

'Did you meet Nancy Fishburn on Thursday morning at the Hótel Búdir on Snaefellsnes?' Magnus asked.

Suzy hesitated, examining Magnus before answering. Gauging how much she could say.

'Yes,' she said.

'Why?'

'She wanted to talk about the documentary. About Gudrid. We had interviewed her in Nantucket and she had been very helpful.'

'Did she have anything to tell you?'

'Not really,' said Suzy. 'Nothing important. She had some ideas about Gudrid; she had written a book about her back in the seventies. Nothing that we could use.'

'Did you know she was murdered on Friday? In Reykjavík?'

Suzy's eyes widened. She swallowed. 'No, I didn't know that.'

'And do you still say she had nothing to tell you?'

'No,' said Suzy, swallowing again, the confidence visibly draining from her face.

'So she didn't mention that she had placed the wampum at Brattahlíd? Or that her Italian book-dealer friend had forged the Columbus letter?'

'No.' Suzy drew herself up, but Magnus could tell she was on the verge of cracking.

'Suzy. I know this whole thing is a hoax. The world will know very soon. It's over. It's all over.'

Suzy blinked.

'The secret is out. But this is a murder investigation – three people have died. I don't know why, and you have to help me. So, I ask you again, what did Nancy tell you?'

Suzy's back bowed a little, but then she raised her chin in an attempt to hang on to her defiance. 'You are right. Nancy told me it was all a hoax. That she, her husband and their Italian friend had cooked the whole thing up. I didn't believe it at first, I thought she was just a scatty old lady, but she was very convincing with the details.'

'What did you say to her?'

'I was furious. I asked her why she hadn't said anything when the wampum was found. Why she hadn't told Einar when he tracked her down in Nantucket last year, or why she hadn't admitted it to us when we had asked her about the Columbus letter on camera. I mean, she screwed us well and truly. My house is on the line. My marriage is on the line. I *need* this to work; I need the cash or it's bankruptcy. I told her all that.'

'And what did she say?'

'To be fair to her, she was upset. She understood. I asked her what she was planning to do, and she said she would leave it up to me. She said she was very sorry; it was her duty to tell me what she had done, but it was up to me to decide what to do. She would keep quiet.'

'And you decided to ignore it all, and carry on making the film?'

Suzy nodded. 'Basically, yes. What choice did I have?'

'Didn't you think it would come out eventually?'

'It might have done. But as long as I had been paid I would survive. And maybe I would seem like the innocent victim, as long as Nancy kept quiet. I *am* an innocent victim.'

'"As long as Nancy kept quiet"?' Magnus said. 'She's quiet now.'

'Oh no,' said Suzy, her voice gaining strength. 'I know what you are doing now. You're going to blame me for killing her!'

'Did you?' said Magnus.

'No! No way.'

'Where were you between nine a.m. and eleven on Friday morning?'

Suzy paused. 'That was the morning we flew here, wasn't it? I met up with the others at our hotel. The Centrum in Reykjavík. We met at eight-thirty for breakfast to discuss what we were going to do in Greenland. We talked for about three hours. Then we went back to our rooms and packed, and I got a taxi with

Tom and Ajay to the City Airport. We got there a bit over an hour before the flight left – just after twelve-thirty, I would guess.'

Magnus did some calculations. Kelly had first knocked on Nancy's door at about eleven that morning. The Hótel Centrum was near the Parliament downtown, about a kilometre away from Nancy's hotel in Thingholt. If the others confirmed Suzy's story, then Suzy hadn't killed Nancy. And it did agree with what Einar had told him.

'The hotel staff at the Centrum would remember it,' Suzy said. 'We kind of took over the dining room.'

'What about Einar?'

'Einar wasn't there. I had asked him to come along, but he didn't show up. He sent me a text saying he had things to do. I was pissed off with him and told him so.'

'Had you told anyone else about what Nancy had said about the hoax?'

'No.'

'Einar? Eygló? Professor Beccari?'

'No. None of them. And certainly not Beccari. Eygló had had some suspicions in Nantucket; she had spoken to Nancy Fishburn's granddaughter who had had some doubts about the wampum, but I managed to convince Eygló that they were blown out of proportion.'

'Did you have your own doubts?'

'I was worried, yes. But I couldn't afford to have doubts.'

She turned away from Magnus and stared at a poster on the wall showing a brightly coloured map of Denmark, with a piglet grinning at its centre. Her shoulders slumped.

'That's it,' she said. 'That's the end of Moorhen Productions. It's all over.' She pursed her lips. 'This is going to be a night-mare. I'm going to have to call my husband. I deserve it, though. When Nancy told me it was all a hoax I should have called the whole thing off right then. Then maybe she would still be alive.' She paused. 'Who do you think killed her? And what has Rósa's death got to do with this?'

'I don't know,' said Magnus. 'But I will find out.'

Magnus spoke to Tom next and then Eygló. Tom was surly and uncommunicative, beyond confirming that he, Suzy, Eygló and Ajay had met at the Hótel Centrum the morning Nancy was killed.

Eygló was distraught to hear that Nancy had been killed. 'I really liked her,' she said. 'She was very smart and her book on Gudrid is great. Who did it?'

Everyone had the same question. Magnus didn't have the answer.

Eygló was also devastated to hear that the letter and the wampum were fakes, although – as Magnus knew – she had suspected it.

Last up was Ajay. He had less at stake in the success of *The Wanderer* than the others, but he was overwhelmed by the murders taking place around him. He corroborated the others' story about the Friday morning meeting, but as Magnus dismissed him, he hesitated.

'What is it, Ajay?'

'It's probably nothing,' he said. 'But when we were filming in Iceland, I overheard Tom talking to Eygló. We were carrying our equipment back to the vehicle, and she joined us. It sounded to me like he was threatening her.'

'Threatening her?' said Magnus. 'Threatening her how?'

Ajay repeated what he had heard: Tom warning Eygló that the filming of this documentary was vital to Suzy, and that Eygló should keep her mouth shut. Or else what had happened to Carlotta might happen to her.

'Did Tom ever talk about Rósa?'

'No, I don't think so. In fact, I never saw him speak to her. He isn't very talkative.'

'I've noticed,' said Magnus. 'You didn't think to tell us this before?'

'No,' said Ajay, looking unhappy. 'To tell you the truth, I'm a bit scared of Tom myself. Could he have killed Carlotta?'

CHAPTER 42

Magnus RETURNED TO the hotel and found himself a nice bench on a little deck outside, ordered a beer, and watched the sun set. It was cool, but the sky was still clear, and he was wearing his coat. The brown, dusty runway stretched out in front of him, and behind that the fjord slunk southwards, a thoughtful milky blue. Magnus was fascinated by the stately icebergs lined up in its central channel, drifting oh-so-slowly up towards the head of the fjord. Which seemed to be the wrong direction: maybe they were being pushed somehow by the glacier disgorging them into the neighbouring fjord, or maybe it was the wind or the tide. The bergs were a subtle mix of gleaming, slippery white and translucent blue. One looked like a sculpture of a motorboat, and another was in the shape of a fist with its middle finger raised towards Erik the Red's farm at Brattahlíd on the far shore.

Or maybe it was raised at Magnus, the modern Icelandic interloper.

Magnus didn't feel the euphoria of a case closed. Although Paulsen was doing all the right things, they weren't there yet. Einar looked a broken man: in the space of a week he had lost his lover, his wife and, when the hoax was made public, his career. At this point Magnus couldn't tell if it was grief or remorse that was crushing him, but he suspected that if Einar had killed Rósa, he would soon confess. Maybe Paulsen was coaxing a confession at that very moment.

Magnus frowned. Maybe not.

As for Nancy's murder, it looked as if Einar had no alibi, and it was quite possible Rósa didn't either – Vigdís was checking. It was most likely that one or other of them had killed Nancy, having found out somehow that she was going to blow the whistle on the hoax. If Einar confessed to Rósa's murder, he may well tell the police which of the two of them had killed Nancy.

But there were a lot of loose ends. It didn't quite make sense.

'Hi.' Magnus turned to see Eygló holding a large glass of wine. 'May I join you?'

'Sure.'

She sat down. She looked out over the water towards Brattahlíd. 'Is that iceberg giving us the finger?'

'I was wondering that myself.'

'I wouldn't be surprised. You know, I was really looking forward to coming to Greenland, but I think this will be my last time. This has been a shitty week.'

Eygló looked very small as she sat hunched up in her jacket opposite him, small and pale. And yet there was a toughness there that was absent from Einar.

'Yeah,' said Magnus.

'Of course, it was a worse week for Rósa. You know she told me she was going to die?'

'What!'

'Yes, yesterday. We had done some really bad takes, and Suzy had called it off for the day. I was sitting on the hill overlooking Brattahlíd, talking to Professor Beccari, and then Rósa showed up and sat herself down right next to me. She said she was going to die soon and I could have Einar. She meant cancer – apparently her breast cancer has come back with a vengeance. But maybe she knew someone would kill her.'

'Did she seem afraid?'

'Of the cancer? Or of someone else?'

'Of either,' Magnus said.

'No,' said Eygló. 'No; she was a brave woman. She seemed determined, though. I told her I didn't want Einar, but I don't think she believed me.'

'You told Inspector Paulsen all this, presumably?'

'Oh yes,' said Eygló. 'I'm getting pretty experienced at giving interviews to the police.' She sipped her drink. 'At least this time no one thinks I killed anybody.'

'Ah,' said Magnus. His automatic response was to justify his and Vigdís's suspicions as being an inevitable part of a professional investigation. But he knew it was no fun being a suspect in a murder inquiry. 'Sorry,' he said. 'We got that wrong.'

At least his interview with her in the classroom that afternoon had been short and straightforward.

Eygló nodded, accepting his apology. 'You know, I was afraid myself when Rósa showed up on the plane at Reykjavík.'

'What were you afraid of?' Magnus asked.

'Einar had told me that she knew about us spending the night together in Ólafsvík. What an idiot!'

'You or him?'

'Good question. Both of us. I shouldn't have let him stay. I'm too soft on Einar, I always have been. And he *definitely* shouldn't have told Rósa about it. For someone who is naturally so sneaky he does have these random fits of honesty, especially where she is concerned.'

'And you thought she was jealous?'

'I *knew* she was jealous. The question is what she would do about it. I didn't know whether she had somehow killed Carlotta, or got her killed. Have you figured that one out yet?'

Magnus hesitated before replying. 'I'm not sure.'

'Well, I thought she might do the same to me. And then it was her that wound up being killed. Which makes me feel bad.'

'Why?'

'You know. Thinking bad thoughts about her. I suppose the Greenlandic police think Einar killed her?'

'He was wandering around somewhere in Narsarsuaq when she was murdered, and the rest of you were at Brattahlíd.'

'Do *you* think Einar killed her?'

'It's certainly a possibility worth exploring,' said Magnus. 'And he may well have killed Nancy Fishburn as well.'

'Oh, you're such a policeman!'

'I try,' said Magnus with a smile.

'Well, I know he didn't kill Rósa.'

'Oh yes?'

'He loved her too much.'

'They had had a long and emotional argument. People sometimes lose their heads after those. Especially with people they love. I've seen it many times, sadly.'

'Yes, but not the way Einar loved her. She loved him too.'

'She seemed like a tough woman to me.'

'That's a big part of why he loved her. Einar manipulates women: he manipulated me. But she was different from the others; he never could control her. He would escape her for a bit, but then she would reel him back. Always. She was in charge; her power over him gave him a sense of security that he couldn't get from another woman. Look, if they hadn't loved each other so much, they would have split up years ago.'

Over the years, Magnus had cleared up several murders in Boston where a man had killed his wife. Marital tension, a loss of temper, drink. Mostly the husbands had had a violent past, but not always. Often they loved their wives. But it was true; they weren't really like Einar.

He didn't answer.

'And if he knew she was going to die soon, why murder her anyway?'

'I don't know,' said Magnus. Because he didn't.

Eygló sipped her wine thoughtfully.

'I expect it doesn't matter much now,' she said. 'But there is a Greenlandic archaeologist working at a site in the next fjord west of here, Anya Kleemann. She was on the dig with me and Einar and Carlotta in 2011. She told me that Carlotta had been in touch with her recently asking about the wampum. Very recently, like in the last couple of months or something.'

'Really? Did she say what Carlotta was worried about?'

'No. I changed the subject. Suzy was there and I didn't want to stir things up. But you might want to go talk to her. To Anya.'

243

'I might,' said Magnus. Then a thought struck him. 'Why were you so concerned about stirring things up?'

Eygló was silent for a while. The sun was setting over a mountain to the west, a golden streak glinting off the grey waters of the fjord.

'I was scared. I'm still scared.'

'Why?'

'Isn't it obvious? Carlotta. Then Rósa. Why not me?'

'But if Einar killed Rósa because she killed Carlotta, and we have Einar in custody, then there is nothing to be scared of.'

'Yeah, but I don't believe Einar did kill Rósa. Which means someone else did. The same person who killed Carlotta.'

'OK, I can see how you were scared of Rósa. But she's not a threat any more. So who else is there?'

Eygló glanced at Magnus. She shrugged.

'Tom?' Magnus suggested.

Eygló's eyes widened. 'Tom?' she said, with an attempt at innocence.

Magnus felt a flash of anger. At this point he expected honesty from Eygló.

Eygló seemed to understand. 'Sorry. Yes, Tom. I'm afraid of Tom. How did you know?'

'Ajay overheard him threatening you back in Iceland. Hinting that you might suffer the same fate as Carlotta. And I saw the way you looked at him at Brattahlíd earlier today.'

'It was more than a hint.'

'Do you think he was implying he killed Carlotta?'

'I don't know. I assume so.'

'Could he just have been taking advantage of Carlotta's death to scare you?'

'Yes, I've thought of that; he could. But he's such a creep. I thought his strong-silent-type act was almost cute, but now it weirds me out. I mean, it's all very well being a loyal employee, but that's loyalty bordering on obsession.'

'So what exactly is Tom's relationship with Suzy, do you think?'

'I don't know. They are clearly a good team and she respects him as a cameraman. I doubt they have a sexual relationship, if that's what you mean. But he seems to idolize her. And there's something creepy about him. Who knows what's going on inside his head?' Eygló shuddered. 'Ugh.'

'Was he definitely at Brattahlíd all day today?'

Eygló nodded. 'Yes. We were filming, and he's the guy with the camera, so nothing much happens without him. We had a break for lunch, and he went off by himself like he often does, but that was only half an hour, tops.' She sighed. 'Actually the filming today went pretty well, especially compared to yesterday. I was rubbish yesterday.'

'So we know Tom couldn't possibly have killed Rósa today,' said Magnus. 'On the other hand, Einar could.'

'Einar didn't kill her,' said Eygló. 'And I'm still scared. I don't know what's going on.' She looked at Magnus with something close to pity. 'And I'm not sure you do, either.' She sighed. 'It was too good to be true.'

'What?'

'These documentaries. My new life. You know, I thought I was good at it.'

'You *are* good at it,' said Magnus.

Eygló shook her head. 'I'm just a talking head. A blonde talking head. A short blonde talking head.'

'No. No!' Magnus was surprised at the vehemence of his insistence. 'You really get what it was like to be a Viking a thousand years ago. And you make it seem fascinating; and important. I was glued to *Viking Queens*.'

Eygló smiled. 'Yeah. But you are a bit of a history nerd, aren't you, Inspector Magnús?'

Magnus grinned. 'OK, that's true. But that means I know a bit about it. I'm your target audience. And you hooked me.'

Eygló looked as if she was about to make some barbed comment, but then she smiled shyly. 'Thanks.'

'So don't give it up.'

'I'll have no choice. Suzy will go bankrupt. Everyone will know Einar and I fell for a hoax, and I'll never get any job related to archaeology in Iceland again.'

'Can't you try your luck in Britain?'

'After Brexit? They probably wouldn't let me in. And the States won't be any easier these days.'

'Don't give up, Eygló.'

Eygló sipped her wine. 'At least I'll still have Bjarki. And he will still have Liverpool Football Club.'

'Is Bjarki your son?'

'Yeah. He's eleven. He's a straightforward guy. You can rely on him.'

'Lucky you,' Magnus said.

'Yeah. Do you have children, Magnús?'

'I don't know.'

'You don't know!' Eygló raised her eyebrows. 'Do you know how bad that sounds?'

Magnus grinned sheepishly. 'Doesn't sound good, does it?'

'So what is it? A kid in every port?'

'Not quite. I saw my ex-girlfriend a few days ago. And she had this little boy with her. Ási.'

'And she said he was yours?'

'She hasn't said anything. I didn't ask. I didn't even think about it, but afterwards my partner, Vigdís, said there was a similarity. And the age matches up.'

'Not much of a detective, are you?'

'Er. No,' said Magnus. 'But Vigdís is pretty good.'

'So, are you going to talk to her? Your ex?'

'Do you think I should?'

'Of course you should! You might be a crap detective, but you're a lucky man. Seriously, kids might be inconvenient, but when the world treats you like shit, sometimes that's all you've got.'

'Maybe you're right. But I think you are underestimating my detection skills.'

'I'll rethink that as soon as you finally figure out that Einar didn't kill Rósa.'

A police car drew up in front of the hotel and Paulsen jumped out. 'Hey, Magnus, come on!'

'Where are we going?'

'Qaqortoq. Bring your bag. We are taking Einar into custody there. And I'd like you to talk to the prosecutor in the morning.'

CHAPTER 43

IT WAS A dramatic hop from Narsarsuaq to the town of Qaqortoq. The sun had set, but the three-quarters moon had already risen, bathing the rock, water and icebergs in an eerie grey-blue tinge. The great Greenland icecap ran out of steam a few miles north-east of Narsarsuaq, and from there fingers of fjords stretched twenty miles down to the Atlantic. Water and land became a tangle of grey, black and silver, except that everywhere there were shards of ice glinting in the water, some as big as ships. Magnus was fascinated by them.

Paulsen was sitting next to him on the left side of the helicopter facing outwards. Einar was in cuffs on the central seats at the back, wedged between two police officers. Magnus could feel how keyed up Paulsen was by the excitement of the investigation. Magnus was impressed: she seemed to be doing a good job of organizing resources in difficult circumstances. He had been involved in a number of cases in rural Iceland – Carlotta's murder being a typical example – and they were tricky. Because of the sparseness of the population, and hence the tiny numbers of local police, expertise had to be drafted in from long distances. In Iceland, this often involved much driving; in Greenland it involved helicopters. Lots of them. Thelma would have hated the expense.

But despite Paulsen's efficiency, or perhaps because of it, Magnus was feeling sidelined. That was fair enough when it came to Rósa's murder, but not Carlotta's nor Nancy Fishburn's. It now looked likely that Rósa had murdered Carlotta in Glaumbaer, but that still had to be properly investigated and evidence gathered;

it wasn't good enough for Paulsen to assume it just because she needed to support her own theory about Rósa's death.

There were other possibilities. Tom, perhaps. Or Einar himself.

But Tom and Einar had alibis for the night of Carlotta's murder.

What about Suzy? She had supposedly gone to bed with an incipient migraine that evening. She could have driven out to Glaumbaer; she had the keys to the rental car. And she certainly had a motive for shutting Carlotta up *if* she realized that Carlotta was going to expose the whole documentary as a hoax.

Maybe Suzy. Maybe Suzy and Tom working together?

And then there was Nancy Fishburn's death. That was still a mystery.

Within twenty minutes, the helicopter scooted up and over a looming mountain to reveal a giant cruise ship glimmering in the moonlight. Right next to it, as if anchored, crouched an iceberg, almost as big, its centre hollowed out by some celestial hand. Little yellow lights spilled over the hillside facing the two vessels.

Qaqortoq.

The helicopter lowered itself on to a helipad jutting out from a rock thirty feet above the sea. As soon as the aircraft touched down, Paulsen grinned at him and undid her seatbelt. Magnus grinned back, but he wasn't happy to be this far from the investigation.

He could feel the stubbornness kicking in.

When Eygló got back to her room at the hotel in Narsarsuaq, she flopped on to her bed and closed her eyes, her phone lying impotently beside her. Facebook could wait. She had nothing to tell her followers except she was a loser.

Her life was going to be crap again.

Why had she ever thought it would be anything else? Suzy, *Viking Queens*, *The Wanderer*, all had seemed too good to be true. And that was because they were. How could she or Einar have ever believed in the wampum? And as for Professor Beccari, if he was such a goddamned all-important genius, he should have figured out that the letter from Christopher Columbus to his brother was a forgery.

It was such a shame! Because the story of Gudrid was a great one anyway, and one she would love to have told. They hadn't needed the Nantucket angle. They had been greedy: greedy for fame, greedy for the excitement of discovery, the thrill of the new theory. Treasure hunters who had discovered fool's gold. And all Eygló had really wanted to do was share her love for her heroine with other people. If they had only stuck to that.

Oh, well. She had lived a crap life before. She would live one again.

She was pretty sure Liverpool were in the Champions League that year; maybe they would win it! Eygló smiled. That would make Bjarki happy.

She glanced at the tupilak she had bought him from the hotel gift shop, sitting on her bedside table. It was kind of creepy: a small carving of a Greenlandic monster made from caribou antler. She liked to buy Bjarki little souvenirs from the places she went, and he dutifully lined them up on his bookshelf, but she was having second thoughts about this one. Too creepy.

She threw it in the bin.

She had to speak to him. She just prayed that Rósa's death hadn't made it to the RÚV television news yet, or that if it had, Bjarki hadn't seen it.

He was on his laptop when she called him up on Skype. She recognized his cousin's bookshelf behind his head, lined with thick volumes of Harry Potter in Icelandic.

'Hi, Mum. Did you see that guy didn't go to Chelsea after all? He's coming to Liverpool! What did I tell you?'

'No, I missed that,' said Eygló, smiling broadly. 'That's good, isn't it? I haven't had a chance to watch much news here.'

'You've got keep up, Mum,' said Bjarki. 'We still need a defender, though, probably two, and there's not much time until the transfer window closes. I'm worried we're buying too many midfielders.'

'That could be a problem.'

'I wonder if they ever play *Football Manager*? They would make so much better decisions if they did.'

For a wonderful ten minutes, Eygló was immersed in Bjarki's

world, which was almost entirely one of football. He didn't ask about Greenland once. Ordinarily, Eygló would have been a little put out by her son's lack of interest in her life, but not just then.

There was a knock at her door. 'I have to go, darling,' she said. 'Goodnight. Speak to you tomorrow.'

''Night, Mum.'

She closed Skype and, still smiling, walked across her bedroom and opened the door.

Then, and only then, did she remember she shouldn't have. Because there was Tom.

She tried to shut the door in his face, but he was too quick. Within a couple of seconds he was in her room with the door closed behind him.

She stepped back. Why the hell had she let him in? She should have stopped for a moment to think who would be knocking on her door at ten o'clock at night. Talking to Bjarki had lowered her guard.

'Leave, Tom. I didn't invite you in here.'

Tom was wearing a grey T-shirt and shorts. He wasn't tall, but he was taller than Eygló. And he had muscles – large biceps and rippling hairy forearms. She knew he was strong: she had seen him lugging around prodigious amounts of equipment.

Tom took a step towards her. She took two steps back.

'The cops have discovered it was all a hoax,' he said.

'I know. They told me.'

'How did they know that?"

'Uh. I think the old lady's granddaughter told them.'

'And why do you think that that Icelandic cop Magnus asked her about it?'

Eygló swallowed. 'I don't know.'

'When he interviewed me this afternoon he said he had had reason to suspect the wampum was a fake. Now, why would he think that?'

Eygló opened her mouth to scream, but Tom was quick. She found herself pinned against the wall, with his hand over her mouth. 'No screaming. No screaming, Eygló, or I hurt you.'

Eygló could feel the rough strength of Tom's hand against her face, his fingers on her cheeks. His blue eyes were ablaze with anger. His nostrils flared millimetres away from her face, and she noticed a tiny spot of snot stuck to a hair sticking out where it shouldn't. This close up she could see that Tom had suffered from acne when he was a kid, and he hadn't shaved for a day or two. Droplets of stale beer tickled her nostrils.

'OK, if I let you go, will you keep quiet?'

Eygló didn't answer.

'Well?' He tightened his grip on her mouth.

She was terrified. What would he do to her? She nodded.

He pushed her on to the bed and stood over her.

'You spoke to that American policeman in Iceland, didn't you?' he demanded.

She tried to answer, but she couldn't. He looked furious. What would he do to her?

She had to answer. She nodded again.

'Why?' It wasn't exactly a shout, more of an urgent growl. 'I told you what would happen if you spoke to the cops.'

He had. Oh, God, he had.

Wait a minute. Eygló's brain cleared. What *was* he going to do to her?

She tried to say something.

'What?'

She cleared her throat and tried again. 'You didn't kill Carlotta, did you?'

This threw Tom for a moment. 'I could have done.'

'No you couldn't,' said Eygló, sensing a chink in what she was beginning to realize was Tom's bravado. 'Very few people kill other people. At least not these days.' They had in Viking times, she had to admit, if only to herself. If they were in a saga, she would indeed be dead now. But they were not. They were in a hotel room in the twenty-first century and Tom was a cameraman, not a gangster.

'I warned you,' said Tom. 'I told you that if this series gets pulled, Suzy will go to the wall. I'm not prepared to let that happen.'

'What is it with you and Suzy, Tom?'

Tom's face flushed under his beard. 'What's that supposed to mean? There's nothing between us. I've known Suzy a long time; we just look after each other, that's all.'

'Well, it's happened, Tom,' said Eygló. 'This little town is crawling with cops. If you hurt me, I'll tell them and you'll end up in jail.'

'No you won't.'

'Yes I will.' Eygló held his eyes. She *would* tell them if he touched her. And now she knew and he knew he wasn't going to hurt her.

'Sit down, Tom.' She nodded towards the only chair in the room, tucked under a desk.

Tom hesitated, and then pulled out the chair and sat on it.

'This is going to be really bad for all of us. But the problem isn't that the hoax has been discovered: that was always going to happen. The problem is that we believed it in the first place. That's Einar, that's me, that's Professor Idiot Beccari. And that's Suzy. That's why we're in this mess. Because we all made a mistake. A big mistake.'

'I never believed any of it,' said Tom.

'Then why didn't *you* say anything?' said Eygló. 'Why didn't you tell Suzy what you thought?'

Tom didn't answer, but he reddened.

'You can keep up your silent, brooding jungle-man pretence if you want, but then you have to take responsibility for what happens when you don't speak up. Don't you?'

Tom's blush deepened. He breathed in through those flared nostrils. He was listening.

'Look, I'm really sorry for the mess Suzy is in. I hope she finds a way out of it. But I'm not sorry I tipped off Magnus. It would all be so much worse if this came out when the programmes aired.'

'If you had only—'

'No, Tom,' said Eygló gently. 'No. They would have uncovered it anyway. Or *someone* would have done.'

That was too much for Tom. He glared at Eygló, stood up and left the room, slamming the door behind him.

CHAPTER 44

A POLICE CAR PICKED up Magnus from his hotel just before eight o'clock the following morning, and drove him down the hill to the police station. It was only about a quarter of a mile, and Magnus would rather have walked.

The sunshine of the previous day had gone, and a low cloud was pressing down on the mountaintops above the little town. But despite the gloom, Qaqortoq had a jolly appearance, certainly much jollier than its Icelandic counterparts. Unlike an Icelandic fishing village with its houses of white and grey concrete or metal siding, the houses here were made of a brightly coloured imported wood: mostly red, but also blue and yellow. A harbour was dominated by the shape of the mighty cruise liner and its almost-as-mighty pet iceberg.

The car drove down to a small square with a silent fountain in its centre and an old low wooden building, similar to the Pakkhúsid in Ólafsvík, guarding the corner next to the water. This, it transpired, was the police station.

Magnus had been awake for a while, emailing Árni and Vigdís in Iceland. They had applied for a warrant to search Rósa's home and office and seize any computers she might have there; it should be granted that morning. The circumstantial evidence was strong that Rósa was at Glaumbaer when Carlotta had died, but there was as yet no proof that would stand up in court that she had killed her.

The standard of proof required was lower now, because she was no longer alive to be prosecuted and there were no inquests in Iceland, but the police had to be certain that she had indeed killed Carlotta, not least to be sure that Carlotta's murderer wasn't still at large.

Magnus wasn't yet convinced. It was probable they would turn up the evidence to convince him; it would just require patience, thoroughness and a little imagination.

And he was still wondering about Suzy Henshaw.

As for Nancy Fishburn's murder, the staff at Rósa's law firm confirmed that she had been in the office all morning, until dashing off for the airport – presumably she had stopped at home to pick up a suitcase, but that needed to be checked. Rósa's assistant recalled that Rósa had booked the flight to Greenland that morning, just after she had got into the office, and had announced that she was taking a couple of days off at the beginning of the following week.

So, Rósa hadn't killed Nancy Fishburn. Once again, Einar was looking the best bet for that. The Reykjavík police would interview their neighbours to see if anyone saw Einar leave home that morning early enough to have met Nancy at her hotel.

When Magnus arrived, a meeting was beginning, with Paulsen in charge. Most of the faces around the table were Inuit, with the exception of two Danes, one young, one old. All were in uniform – the police force in Greenland didn't seem to run to detectives in civilian clothes, so Magnus felt out of place in his jeans. The discussion was in Danish, which Magnus found almost impossible to follow, but the grizzled Danish constable sitting next to him helped with the odd translation into English. At least the legal system wasn't too different from Iceland's.

From what Magnus could figure out, Einar hadn't confessed. Nor were his whereabouts clear for a four-hour period in the late morning, when he claimed he had walked part way to the Blomsterdalen. A Danish tourist had seen him about a kilometre north of the airport on the track towards the Blomsterdalen; that tallied with Einar's story. No one had seen him on Signal Hill, the hill above the airport. Another witness, a Dane who lived at an isolated summer cabin on the other side of a small lake from the route to the Blomsterdalen, reported seeing a lone figure on the road jump off it to hide behind a bush when a car drove by. The figure was far too far away to be identified, but the witness thought it was a man and that he wasn't particularly tall. Which Einar was. But then the witness wasn't absolutely sure.

The police needed better than that.

They had already received Rósa's phone records from TELE Greenland, which was impressively quick work, and Magnus asked for a copy of them so he could send them to Reykjavík to be cross-referenced with Carlotta and Einar's records from there.

Three forensics guys from Nuuk were present: they were police officers in uniform with specialist forensics training, but they hadn't had time to do much the evening before. Constable Frandsen had found the murder weapon, a vicious-looking hunting knife of the kind that could be found in every Greenlandic home, tossed into the brush twenty metres from the body.

Paulsen invited Magnus to deliver a brief report in English on the investigation in Iceland of Carlotta's and Nancy's murders, and the possible connection to Rósa's. But as Magnus spoke, he realized the connections didn't quite make sense: something was missing. He was beginning to think it would only be when Paulsen persuaded Einar to confess that they would have the true picture.

Paulsen said something rapidly in Danish – Magnus wasn't quite sure what it was, except that it included the word 'Beccari'. Then she repeated it in English for his benefit. Professor Beccari had called the police first thing that morning to say he had some information to give them about Rósa. Paulsen had asked him to come into the station at nine-thirty and she invited Magnus to join her for the interview.

Paulsen doled out tasks to the assembled officers, most of which centred on finding witnesses to establish a precise timeline for Einar's whereabouts during the day. Then she sent them off to the helicopters and Narsarsuaq.

Paulsen wanted Magnus to join her for a briefing with the

local prosecutor, but first Professor Beccari was waiting to speak to them.

The professor was sitting in the station's interview room, staring out of the window at the fish market by the harbour. A stall was covered in seal flesh and blood. A gory sight.

'I wasn't expecting to see you here,' he said to Magnus. 'So there *must* be a link to Carlotta's murder.'

'We'll see.' Magnus noted that Beccari had already made the link himself. 'But this is Inspector Paulsen's investigation.'

'What have you got to tell us, professor?' Paulsen asked.

'It's about poor Rósa,' Beccari said. 'The moment I heard she had died, I knew I had to get in touch with you.'

'How did you hear?'

'At breakfast at the hotel some guests were talking about a murder at Narsarsuaq. A tourist. So I immediately called Eygló who told me it was Rósa. The poor woman! It was definitely murder?'

Beccari's hands were flashing in much the same agitation as Magnus remembered when he had first interviewed him about Carlotta's death.

'She was stabbed,' said Paulsen.

'Right.' Beccari paused. 'Then I have something to tell you.'

He gathered himself and began his story. 'I joined Rósa and the television crew coming over here to Greenland. I have always wanted to visit this country and it seemed like a great opportunity. But if you've spoken to them you'll know that the atmosphere among the team was really bad. Something to do with Einar and Eygló and Rósa. It was obvious to anyone that they were all upset with each other, and it was becoming really unpleasant. So on Saturday I decided to leave them and explore Greenland by myself for a couple of days. I've been staying here.'

'At the Hotel Qaqortoq?' It was where Magnus was staying; it was probably the only decent hotel in town.

'That's right. Anyway, I ended up talking with Rósa a fair bit, because the rest of them were not speaking to each other. We got on well; she was an intelligent woman, and I like intelligent women. Saturday's filming had been a disaster and Suzy ended it early. I was sitting in the back of the boat with Rósa, returning across the fjord to Narsarsuaq. Until that point she had always seemed cool and in control. But she looked scared.

'I asked her what was wrong. She seemed to think for a few moments and then said that she had something important to tell me. If nothing happened to her, then I should just forget that she had said anything. But if something *did* happen to her then I should tell them that she was sorry for what she had done.'

'"Them"? What did she mean by "them"?' Paulsen asked.

'That's exactly what I asked! But Rósa said if something happened to her I would know whom to tell.' Beccari looked at Magnus and Paulsen with incredulity. 'I thought, how could I possibly know? I asked her what she had done, and of course she wouldn't tell me. She said maybe nothing would happen to her, in which case I should just forget the whole conversation, but she begged me, if something did happen, to do what she had asked me.'

Beccari's blue eyes were popping. 'Well! What was I to do? She seemed deadly serious, and very upset. So I promised. What else could I do?

'The boat arrived at Narsarsuaq and we all got off, and I didn't get a chance to speak to her alone before I left them later that afternoon to catch a helicopter flight here. Except as I was saying goodbye, Rósa whispered: "You will do as I asked, won't you?" And I said yes. And that's the last I saw of her.'

'So that's why you have come to see us now?' Paulsen asked.

'Of course.'

Paulsen glanced at Magnus. They both knew what Rósa was talking about. Magnus raised his eyebrows and Paulsen gave a tiny nod of assent for Magnus to ask a question.

'What do you think she meant?'

'Then or now?' Beccari said.

'Both.'

'When she said it, I had absolutely no idea. But afterwards, as you can imagine, I thought about it quite hard.'

'And what did you think?'

'Well, at first I thought it must have something to do with Einar and Eygló: the little ménage à trois or whatever it is they have going on. Rósa had done something that she needed to apologize to one of them for, but she couldn't face doing it herself. But yesterday I took a trip to Hvalsey – you know, the old Viking church there – and I was just sitting there thinking about it. And it seemed to me that when Rósa said "if something happens" she meant something more permanent. And then I thought about Carlotta's death. And, well, I wondered whether she had had anything to do with it.'

'Which is why you thought I had come here?' said Magnus.

Beccari nodded.

'So who do you think you need to tell that Rósa was sorry?'

'Carlotta's parents, I assume. Don't you think? I mean, once I heard from Eygló that Rósa had been murdered, it all made sense. Or have I got it completely wrong?'

'I think you may have got it right,' said Paulsen.

'Why do you think she told you?' said Magnus.

'If you mean why me, I think it's because I am an outsider and I have a certain authority, if you know what I mean. I guess I'm Italian so I can talk to Carlotta's parents. Although I am not sure that they would find it particularly comforting to hear that their daughter's murderer was sorry.

'And if you mean why did she tell anyone, I have no idea. Guilt, maybe? Your guess is as good as mine. Better, probably.'

Magnus shrugged.

'So you reckon Rósa killed Carlotta?' Beccari asked.

Paulsen nodded. 'It's looking that way.'

Beccari shook his head. 'I would never have believed it. And now she wants me to tell the parents she's sorry.'

'You don't have to do that,' said Magnus.

'I don't know,' said Beccari. 'She seemed so upset when she asked me and I promised. But if she *was* a murderer, then I don't really owe her anything, do I?'

'I'd say not.' A thought occurred to Magnus. 'Before you knew she had been killed, yesterday, when you were at Hvalsey and you had figured out she murdered Carlotta: were you going to tell us?'

'Hah!' Beccari said. 'I was afraid you would ask me that question. I really didn't know what to do. It was just guesswork on my part – I could easily have been wrong. And I had promised her to keep quiet. The truth is, I was going to mull it over. But then when I heard she was dead, my mind was made up.'

'Thank you for coming in,' said Paulsen. 'When are you leaving Greenland?'

'I've a flight booked back to Reykjavík later today, and from Keflavík on to New York tomorrow,' said Beccari. 'Can you let me know how the investigation goes, Inspector?' he said to Magnus. 'Especially when you have decided whether Rósa did kill Carlotta. I will need to figure out what to do about her parents.'

'OK,' said Magnus. As Beccari stood up, Magnus hesitated. 'I do have some bad news about the theory that Gudrid and Co. landed in Nantucket.'

Beccari looked at him sharply. 'Oh yes?'

'Yeah. It's all a hoax. The wampum.' Beccari's face showed a mixture of horror and anger. 'And the Columbus letter.'

'I don't know about the wampum,' he said. 'But I do know the Columbus letter is genuine.'

'I'm sorry,' said Magnus. 'I spoke with an old lady who lived in Nantucket who planted them. Or she planted the wampum; her friend planted the letter in the Vatican. It's a fake.'

'No! Are you sure? I don't believe it! Who is this old lady? How do you know she's telling the truth?'

All thoughts of Rósa and Carlotta had obviously left Professor Beccari's mind as he contemplated the threat to his reputation.

'I'm sure. Look, I can't give you the details because it is related to an ongoing investigation, but I wanted to warn you.'

'I think you are mistaken,' said Professor Beccari, haughtiness having taken over from horror. 'And I warn you that you and this old woman, whoever she is, must be careful about questioning my judgement, unless you are both on very solid ground.'

'All right,' said Magnus, all sympathy for the professor disappearing. 'But I don't think the old lady will care very much about your threats.'

'Why not?'

'Because she was murdered. On Friday morning in Reykjavík.'

Beccari seemed to realize he had gone too far. 'Oh. That's … that's terrible. OK, look, I'm sorry. I'm sure you told me this in good faith. But that letter is authentic – I'm certain of it.'

'Her name was Nancy Fishburn, ' Magnus said. 'Did you know her?'

'No. Wait – did she write a book on Gudrid?'

'Yes, that's her.'

'I glanced at her book in the library. But I have never met her, no.'

Paulsen let Beccari go. 'We'll be in touch.

'Sounds as if Rósa knew what was going to happen to her,' she said once the professor had left.

'I guess so,' said Magnus. 'Unless she was referring to her cancer? Eygló said Rósa told her it was killing her.'

'That doesn't sound right to me,' said Paulsen. 'It sounds to me as if she was expecting something more sudden.'

It sounded like that to Magnus too.

'Einar must have threatened her,' she said. 'Perhaps there was a history of this? Maybe Einar had tried to kill her before. Or beaten her. Does that seem possible to you?'

'Unlikely, from what I've seen of their relationship.'

'I don't know about Iceland, but in this country you can never tell.'

'No, that's true of Iceland. And America.' And pretty much anywhere else, Magnus suspected. You couldn't tell what went on in anyone's marriage, but you did know that there was more abuse than ever came to light. 'But I'd have thought if he did threaten to kill her, it would be over something specific.'

'Like he had just discovered she had murdered Carlotta? Or she had confessed it to him?'

Magnus nodded. 'Maybe.' He thought a moment. 'I wonder if Professor Beccari would ever have mentioned it if Rósa had not been killed?'

'I don't know, but I'm glad he did,' said Paulsen. 'Now, let's get to the prosecutor's office.'

CHAPTER 45

ACK IN ICELAND, Róbert was arranging the warrant to search Rósa's home and office and seize her computers. While Vigdís was waiting, she decided to take the opportunity to drive out to Akranes and see Emil.

He actually lived on a farm twenty kilometres to the east of the town. For a property owned by a retired policeman, Vigdís was surprised at how prosperous it looked: a new barn, dozens of horses grazing in paddocks bordered by smart wooden fences, a yard that was almost gleaming. The farmhouse itself – stained white concrete walls and a red metal roof – was noticeably tattier than its yard.

The door was answered by a tall thin woman of about sixty: Linda, Emil's wife. Despite only having met Vigdís once or twice, she recognized her immediately; people usually did. She greeted her warmly and led her through to a living room, where Emil was sitting in an armchair facing the home meadow, reading that morning's *Morgunbladid*.

'Someone to see you, Emil.'

He looked up, his eyes betraying confusion. Vigdís was shocked at what she saw. The last time she had seen him, he had been a large, very large, man in his late fifties, with a thick moustache and several robust chins. The moustache had gone, and so had much of the fat, leaving loose folds of skin around a haggard face. There was still a tiny little paunch above his jeans, but his legs appeared stick thin. Although he would only be in his sixties, he looked ten years older.

Two walking sticks leaned against the armchair.

'Hi, Emil,' she said, approaching him with a grin and holding out her hand. 'Vigdís.'

The confusion left Emil's eyes and a smile brightened half of his face. One corner of his mouth stubbornly pointed downwards. 'Ah yes,' he said. 'Vigdís! How lovely to see you. Forgive me if I don't get up. Sit yourself down!'

Emil's voice was slurred. Vigdís knew he had had a heart attack, but he had clearly suffered a stroke as well. She couldn't help wondering what effect it had had on his brain. On his memory.

'Can I get you some coffee?' Linda asked.

'Yes, thank you,' she said, sitting on a chair next to Emil. 'What a lovely farm you have here!'

Emil snorted. 'It used to belong to Linda's parents. Unfortunately we have been unable to keep it up, what with only my pension. We sold the farmland and the yard to some people from Reykjavík, but we managed to keep the house.'

That explained the difference between the well-kept yard and the run-down farmhouse.

'How are you doing, Vigdís? Are you still in the Violent Crimes Unit? Or has it been reorganized again?'

Vigdís exchanged some departmental gossip with Emil, who said that the only policeman from Reykjavík whom he saw these days was Snorri – the Commissioner and a friend from his younger days. Emil asked about Magnus, and Vigdís told him he was back in Iceland.

'Are you here on official business?' Emil asked.

'Semi-official,' said Vigdís. 'Do you remember a cop called Tryggvi Thór? Tryggvi Thór Gröndal?'

'I certainly do,' Emil said. 'We worked together when I was at Hverfisgata. A good man. What about him? He went off to Africa, didn't he? Is he back in Iceland?'

'Yes, he is. He was the subject of an assault last week at his house in Álftanes. And then again a few days ago. He was quite badly beaten up.'

'Oh. I'm sorry to hear that. Have you any idea who did it?'

'No. He doesn't want us to pursue it. In fact he claims the second assault was just a fall.'

'I take it I'm not a suspect?' he said with a lopsided grin.

'No,' said Vigdís. 'But we are trying to find out why he left the police force.'

Emil frowned and fiddled with one of the flaps of loose skin hanging around his neck. 'Have you tried looking in his file?'

'Yes. There is virtually nothing in it.'

Emil nodded and then closed his eyes. Vigdís waited. Just as she was beginning to fear that Emil had fallen asleep, his eyelids twitched open.

'Hence your description of your business as "semi-official"?'

'That's right.' Vigdís waited. 'You said Tryggvi Thór was a "good man". That's a strange way to describe a corrupt cop.'

'I never could believe Tryggvi Thór was a corrupt cop.'

'So what happened?'

Linda came in with coffee and some little cakes. She sensed the tension in the room. 'Are you all right, dear?' she said.

'Oh yes, yes,' said Emil.

'Don't tire him out,' Linda said to Vigdís, before retreating to the kitchen.

'It was a long time ago,' Emil said. 'Tryggvi Thór was investigating a suspected case of fraud at an insurance company. He was just in the early stages. He said he had an inside source and he went to meet the guy by the Pearl.' This was a prominent hot-water tower that overlooked the city from a wooded hill. 'The guy gave him the information in a thick envelope bound with a couple of metres of strong packing tape. Tryggvi Thór tried to open it, but couldn't. As he was struggling with it, he was arrested by two policemen.'

'Arrested? Why?'

'They had a tip-off it was a bribe. And sure enough, inside was half a million krónur in cash.'

'That sounds like a set-up to me,' said Vigdís.

'It certainly does,' said Emil. 'That's what Tryggvi Thór said and that's what I think. But of course it depends how you tell the story.'

'It should have been easy to check. Talk to the whistle-blower. Look for evidence of fraud at the company. Didn't anyone do that?'

'Yes. Or they say they did. They say they found some evidence of minor fraud. The perpetrator admitted to it and also claimed he had bribed Tryggvi Thór to keep quiet. He was the guy Tryggvi Thór claimed was the whistle-blower.'

'Oh. Did it go to court?'

'No. It was all hushed up. The insurance company agreed not to press charges. Tryggvi Thór was fired; the fraudster was fired from the insurance company. From what you say, nothing was put in the file.'

'Why was it hushed up?'

'That's a good question,' said Emil.

Vigdís frowned. 'What was his name, this fraudster?'

'I can't remember. I may never have known. I didn't work on the case.' Emil's voice was flagging, his words were now so slurred they were hard to make out.

'Can you remember the name of the insurance company?'

Emil closed his eyes. Was he trying to remember, or was he going to sleep? 'Emil?'

'It was Hekla Fire and Accident,' he said.

Vigdís made a note. 'And who was Tryggvi Thór's boss at that point? Who fired him?'

'It was Thorkell. Thorkell Holm. He must have retired by now.'

He had. Three years previously.

'What was Tryggvi Thór's reaction?'

'He was angry. He tried to fight it, but he didn't get anywhere. In the end it was almost as though he quit in disgust. I saw him afterwards for a drink, and he said he was going to Africa to do some good. He was very angry.'

'And you?'

'It didn't seem right to me. But then I've always liked Thorkell

266

– I couldn't believe he would get rid of Tryggvi Thór unless there was a good reason.'

'And what do you think that reason was?'

'That's another good question,' Emil said. Then he closed his eyes. Within seconds his face had relaxed and his breathing became lighter, more regular. He was fast asleep.

As Vigdís drove back to Reykjavík she pondered what Emil had told her. It certainly sounded like a set-up. But, as Emil himself had admitted, there were two sides to most stories. Vigdís too had liked Thorkell: he had been her ultimate boss, the chief superintendent in charge of CID in the Reykjavík Metropolitan Police. He was also Árni's uncle.

Back at the station, Vigdís looked up Hekla Fire and Accident, a company she could dimly remember hearing of. It took a few minutes, but she eventually found it. It had been bought by a businessman in 1994, and in 1999 had been merged with another, larger insurance company recently acquired by the same man, and changed its name. Tryggvi Thór's sacking would have happened in about 1996.

None of that particularly attracted her attention. But the name of the businessman did.

Jakob Ingibergsson.

The man whom she had seen at Tryggvi Thór's bedside.

CHAPTER 46

AFTER A BUSINESSLIKE meeting at the prosecutor's office in Qaqortoq, where they tackled the bureaucracy of international police cooperation, Magnus and Paulsen took a helicopter back up the fjord to Narsarsuaq. He told her he wanted to speak to the archaeologist who had been on the dig with Carlotta, Einar and Eygló at Brattahlíd in 2011. Paulsen was surprised, but was happy to proceed on the Rósa case without him. As far as she was concerned, unless they found one, or preferably two, witnesses who were certain Einar was somewhere other than the Blomsterdalen when Rósa was murdered, he was going down.

Magnus called Eygló from the airport at Narsarsuaq and asked her if she would help him track down Anya Kleemann. Paulsen found a local to take them across the fjord: a short Greenlander named Noah who didn't speak any English. They picked up Eygló at the hotel and drove down to the harbour. Within a couple of minutes they were speeding across the water in a small motorboat, weaving around the icebergs.

About half a mile downstream, towards the sea, a water jet spouted several feet into the air. A moment later a tail fin flapped and disappeared beneath the surface.

Noah turned to them and grinned. '*Hval*,' he said in Danish. The same as the Icelandic word. Whale.

'Tom came to see me last night,' said Eygló.

'Did he threaten you? If he threatens you I can warn him off. Or get Inspector Paulsen to arrest him.'

Eygló grinned. 'He did threaten me. I was scared at first. But I handled him. He was bluffing.'

Despite all that had happened, she seemed to Magnus to be stronger that morning.

'Where is Einar?' she asked.

'In a police cell in Qaqortoq police station.'

'It doesn't look good for him, does it?'

Magnus shook his head.

'I'm still sure he didn't kill Rósa.'

'That's up to Inspector Paulsen to decide,' said Magnus. As soon as the words were out of his mouth, he wondered why he had passed the buck so easily.

They reached the little harbour at Brattahlíd, and Noah tied up the boat. He told Eygló to wait in Danish. Magnus and Eygló stood next to a wall running along the side of the dock, surrounded by empty pallets, a pile of tyres, some gas canisters and a couple of trailers. The red kiosk was empty, but an old Land Rover was parked a few yards down the track.

It was low tide, and about a hundred yards further along the shore, a berg had become stranded on a patch of brown sand, a giant ice cube sweating in the sun. Two local boys, dressed only in swimming trunks, were trying to push it, but it wouldn't budge. To Magnus's amazement, one of them turned and sprinted into the sea, splashing and laughing. The other joined him with no hesitation. The sea temperature couldn't have been more than a few degrees above freezing; even the craziest of Icelanders, and there were some pretty crazy Icelanders, wouldn't have tried that.

A hairy hiker carrying a massive rucksack trudged into view. He sat down a few feet away, dislodged his load and swigged water from a bottle. The aroma of a week in the wilderness assailed Magnus's nostrils.

'How far is it to Anya's site?' said Magnus.

'About seven or eight kilometres.'

'I hope Noah is coming up with transport.'

They waited a moment, Eygló examining her phone.

'Did Professor Beccari call you this morning?' Magnus asked.

'Yes,' said Eygló. 'He had heard about a murder at Narsarsuaq and was worried it might be one of us. I told him it was.'

'Did he seem surprised when you said it was Rósa?'

'Er . . .' Eygló hesitated. 'I'm not sure. Concerned, yes. Agitated. But actually, it was as if he was expecting it.'

Magnus told her about Beccari's brief conversation with Rósa and Rósa's message for Carlotta's parents, if that was indeed whom it was intended for.

'Wow,' said Eygló.

'It struck me that your conversation with her was similar,' Magnus said. 'When she told you about her cancer.'

'Yes, that's true.'

'Was it definitely cancer she was talking about? Could it be that she thought her life was in danger? That someone was about to murder her?'

Eygló considered the question. 'No, she was definitely talking about cancer. But maybe she was doing the same thing with me: preparing for her death. It was just sooner than she led me to believe.'

She frowned. 'This *really* doesn't look good for Einar, does it? I mean, if Rósa told Professor Beccari something was going to happen to her soon, it implies she thought she was going to be killed. And Einar is the obvious killer.'

Magnus nodded. 'That's what Inspector Paulsen thinks.'

'And you?'

'I think that too,' Magnus admitted.

His phone rang. It was Vigdís describing her interview with Emil, and seeing Jakob Ingibergsson at Tryggvi Thór's bedside: the man who owned the insurance company and who had got Tryggvi Thór thrown out of the police force.

'It stinks, Vigdís.'

'To high heaven.'

'If Tryggvi Thór really was taking a bribe, why cover it up?'

'Because other people were involved?' said Vigdís.

'Possibly. Probably. But who?'

'Thorkell Holm was the guy who sacked Tryggvi Thór.'

'Thorkell is a good guy,' Magnus said. But so too was Tryggvi Thór.

He heard the whine and clank of petrol engine and metal and Noah appeared at the helm of an all-terrain vehicle.

'I've got to go, Vigdís, and you had better get back to investigating Rósa. But thanks for doing that for me.'

As he hung up, Noah motioned for Magnus and Eygló to hop on, and conducted a quick discussion in Danish with Eygló about where exactly they were going. The hiker tried to ask Noah in German-accented English about boats across the fjord, but Noah ignored him.

The ATV seemed to be the vehicle of choice in Brattahlíd – they encountered three as Noah drove along the road that ran the length of the village past the yellow Leif Erikson Hostel, a bright blue school building, a red church with a spire and the remains of Erik the Red's farm. There was no sign of past excavations there now, just low mounds of lush green grass and wildflowers tracing out the lines of ancient walls.

'You know the trench from the nineteen thirties was open until the nineteen nineties?' shouted Eygló above the roar of the ATV. 'Einar tidied up much better after his excavation. So when Nancy Fishburn came here in the early eighties, there would have been tempting earthworks to tamper with.'

Magnus envisaged a younger version of the old lady he had seen in the Nantucket TV footage scrabbling in the earth with her wampum shells while her husband kept watch to make sure no one was coming. An arresting image.

'Maybe I shouldn't say this,' he shouted back. 'But you could put the hoax into your documentary, as well as the real Gudrid. That might be a way of rescuing it.'

'Not a bad idea. I'll suggest it to Suzy.'

Magnus was unsure whether he liked his own suggestion. Suzy should have come clean the moment Nancy had told her about the hoax. But Eygló deserved a break.

Past the site of the real longhouse lay a modern reconstruction, fenced off and covered in a turf roof. Noah turned left up a rough track which climbed the hill above Brattahlíd. Magnus looked over his shoulder at Erik's Fjord and Narsarsuaq airfield

271

on its far side, and then the view disappeared and they were in a wilderness of close-cropped grass and bare rock, dotted with sheep. The track was made of a deep red earth and stone, and Noah seemed to enjoy the jolts as they headed west – Magnus had the impression he was trying to get airborne wherever he could.

They zoomed over the crest of a hill marked with a series of a dozen or so stone cairns and then they were on the other side. In front of them spread a large green bowl containing a couple of farm buildings, and behind it another fjord. Whereas the fjord they had just come from at Brattahlíd had contained ten to twenty stately icebergs drifting alone, this one was chock-full of shards of ice large and small. The green hillsides were scattered with purple, blue and yellow flowers, and farm machinery in various stages of disrepair. They zipped past an ancient Massey Ferguson tractor of rusty grey that looked like it hadn't been moved for fifty years.

Noah slowed and turned to Eygló. He pointed to the far side of the valley, which was an impossibly bright deep green, and there, a hundred feet or so up a hillside, a small group of people clustered around a rectangle of bare earth, next to a large canvas awning. Eygló nodded.

Tasiusaq, the farm that dominated the valley, was a prosperous one, boasting major blue metal barns and an array of white plastic-covered rolls of hay. Noah roared past it, turned on to a lesser track and headed for the dig.

A tall kid with red hair and a wispy beard greeted them in an American accent. Magnus noticed his Brown Bears T-shirt. Eygló asked for Anya, and the kid led them to the group of archaeologists scraping, scratching and peering at the earth.

'Are you still at Brown?' Magnus asked the guy, whose name was Nate.

'Junior year.'

'I was there a couple of decades ago.'

'Cool. You an archaeologist?'

'Um. No. I'm an Icelandic policeman.'

'Cool.' Nate managed to inject so much doubt into that word.

'Yeah. It's true what they say: the world is your oyster with a degree from Brown.'

The slightest pause. Then, as Nate considered the possibility that he might wind up as a policeman in Reykjavík: 'Cool.'

Behind them, the ATV's engine gunned into life, and Magnus turned to see Noah whizzing off down the track towards the farm.

'Is he coming back for us?' he asked Eygló.

Eygló shrugged. 'No idea.'

Anya waved and grinned when she saw Eygló approaching and gave her a hug. 'It's great to see you,' she said in a fluent American accent.

'And you,' said Eygló. 'This is Magnus from the Reykjavík police. He's investigating Carlotta's murder.'

'OK,' said Anya, more serious now.

'Do you mind if I ask you some questions?' Magnus said.

'Sure,' said Anya. 'Let's go over here.'

She led them to a table and chairs underneath the large awning and poured them a cup of coffee from a thermos. There were three tables in all, and the others were covered with archaeological paraphernalia – lots of trays, meshes, bags filled with tiny artefacts, labels, notebooks and a couple of microscopes. Nate took a seat at one of them and attacked what looked like a lump of mud with a toothbrush. Magnus felt a momentary pang that he hadn't become the archaeologist Nate had assumed he was.

At first sight, Anya Kleemann looked like one of the Inuit Magnus was becoming familiar with. She was round – a round face and round body, but her eyes were also round, and blue. Magnus's sketchy knowledge of genetics suggested European blood on both sides. She told Magnus a little of her own background: a childhood in Greenland, university in Denmark, a masters in America and then a PhD at Aarhus. She was an expert on Norse settlements in Greenland – this was her patch.

'How's the excavation going?' Eygló asked Anya.

'Usual story. It looked like we were getting nowhere, when we found something last week. A coin. English. Minted in the reign of Richard III.'

'Richard III? The king they found buried in a car park? I remember him from York. Remind me of his dates?'

'Fourteen eighty-three to eighty-five,' said Anya with a grin.

'Fourteen eighty-three? How the hell did it get there?' Eygló asked.

'Precisely,' said Anya. She explained to Magnus: 'The last written record we have of the Norse settlers in Greenland is a description of a wedding in 1409. We don't know when they died out here, or even if they just upped and left. We do know they were still trading with the English after this time, but this looks like pretty strong evidence there were still Norsemen farming here in the 1480s. Or later.'

Magnus recalled Columbus's trip to Iceland in 1477. And the letter to his younger brother he didn't write describing it. So there were still Norse settlers in Greenland even then.

He asked Anya about the dig at Brattahlíd in 2011. She remembered the discovery of the wampum as one of the most exciting moments of her career. She described how Carlotta had found a couple of shells with holes in them, how Einar had revealed more, and how the American student had identified them as wampum clamshells.

'Did anyone have any doubts about their authenticity?' Magnus asked.

'Not at the time, no,' said Anya. 'But I wondered about them afterward.'

'What did you wonder?'

'Well. You probably know that we were re-excavating an area that had been dug eighty years before. That meant that all the contexts were confused around the trench. They missed stuff: in those days they used shovels; now we use brushes. We found all kinds of things they didn't see. So it's perfectly possible, likely even, that those archaeologists would have missed a wampum shell. But all of them? I checked the reports of the excavation from the nineteen thirties, and there was nothing about finding a shell with a hole drilled into it.'

'Did you mention your doubts to Einar?'

'No.'

'Why not?'

'Einar is a good archaeologist. He has a great reputation. And he is cautious, usually. Cynical, even.'

Magnus could believe that.

'So I didn't want to doubt him.'

'Did he intimidate you?' Magnus asked. 'Threaten you?'

'No, no, nothing like that. And my doubts were just that. It was my opinion, not evidence.'

'What about Carlotta? Did you get to know her well?'

'Pretty well. There weren't many of us on the dig and we were thrust together for weeks on end. It was a pretty good bunch,' Anya said, looking to Eygló for confirmation.

Eygló nodded.

'Usually there is one jerk who annoys the hell out of everyone else, but I don't remember that at Brattahlíd.'

'What was she like, Carlotta?'

'She was good fun. Lively. Smart. Quite frankly, it was good to have an Italian around. You can have too many Danes and Icelanders.' This with a teasing glance at Eygló.

Eygló grinned. 'It's true.'

'Did you notice anything between Carlotta and Einar?'

Anya smiled. 'Oh yes. I think it started after Carlotta made the discovery. They tried to be discreet, but we were all packed together in that school building, and everyone noticed. It was almost like she'd gotten a gold star for finding the treasure.'

'What was their relationship like? Could you tell?'

The smile disappeared. 'It was classic professor–student. She worshipped him and was flattered he was interested in her; he thought she was young and attractive and wanted to get in her pants. And he did.'

Magnus nodded. 'And did you stay in touch with Carlotta?'

'Not really. We were friends on Facebook. I might have seen a couple of updates, but actually I think she usually posted in Italian. Until this summer when she contacted me.'

'How did she contact you? Facebook?'

'No. Email. She must have gotten my address from the university website.'

'And what did she say?'

'She asked me if I had any doubts about the wampum. I told her I was concerned that they hadn't found a single shell in the nineteen thirties and that seemed odd.'

'Did you ask her why she suddenly wanted to know?'

'Yes. I mean, it did seem strange, since she was the one who discovered the shells. She would be the last person who would want to undermine her own discovery.'

Magnus nodded.

'She said that she had found documentary evidence that Thorfinn Karlsefni and Gudrid had travelled to Nantucket. That sounded pretty cool to me. Carlotta said that it sounded cool to her, but she had just discovered something that put the evidence in doubt. And that had gotten her thinking about the wampum.'

'Did she say what this thing was?'

'No. And she wouldn't be specific about the nature of the documentary evidence either, but she did say she suspected who had forged it, whatever "it" was, and who had planted it. I assumed it must be a new copy of a saga or something. She was being coy about it, and I didn't like that – it didn't seem necessary.'

'And all this was by email?'

'Yes.'

Magnus was frustrated. If the Italian police had got their act together, he would have had that information by now, without having to travel to a godforsaken hillside in Greenland to get it.

'Do you know what it was, this documentary evidence?' Anya asked.

Magnus nodded.

'And?'

Magnus thought there was no reason to keep the information from Anya, so he told her about the Columbus letter. And then he told her that the wampum was fake; or that it was real wampum, but that it hadn't arrived there by Viking longship but by modern airliner, and it had been planted at Brattahlíd in 1980.

'My God!' said Anya. 'And that's the story you were doing the documentary about?'

Eygló nodded.

'It would be a great story.'

'If it was true,' Eygló said. 'But it's all a hoax.'

'So you'll have to cancel the TV documentary?'

'No choice,' said Eygló.

'Oh, I'm sorry.' Anya winced in sympathy. Then she turned to Magnus. 'But does all this have anything to do with Carlotta's murder?'

It was a good question. 'I don't think so,' he said, thinking of Rósa and Einar and jealousy.

Anya frowned. 'Hmm,' she said.

They sat in silence for a moment.

'Yes?' said Magnus. 'You didn't tell Einar when you had doubts before. You have doubts now?'

'Oh, I don't know,' said Anya. 'But it *is* similar. It seems like too much of a coincidence. Carlotta discovers that all this stuff is fake and is killed before she has a chance to tell anyone about it? I don't know. It doesn't sound right to me, but you're the policeman.'

She had a point. 'You may have heard a woman was murdered in the Blomsterdalen yesterday? An Icelandic woman.'

'They told us at the hostel this morning,' said Anya. 'I was going to ask, is that related?'

'Yes, we think so. She was Einar's wife.'

'Ah.' Anya frowned. 'Do you think Einar killed her?'

'They do,' said Eygló. 'They've locked him up. But I know they are wrong.'

'Without giving too much away about our investigation, we think Carlotta's death has more to do with her sexual relationship with Einar than with the wampum or this Columbus letter.'

'Oh, I see,' said Anya. Then she looked straight at Magnus. 'It still doesn't add up.'

CHAPTER 47

THERE WAS NO sign of Noah, and although Anya was willing to offer Magnus and Eygló a lift back to Brattahlíd, she couldn't. One of her team had taken the Land Rover to the dock and crossed the fjord to Narsarsuaq to get supplies. She was expected back in an hour or so, and Anya suggested they wait.

Magnus said he would prefer to walk; good exercise, clean air and isolation might clear his head. It needed clearing and he wasn't sure why. He was disappointed when Eygló volunteered to join him, but they strode the first couple of miles in silence. Magnus set a good pace, but Eygló was fit and intrepid. And her legs, although short, moved fast.

The hills were bustling with bees and small birds. A pair of ravens dodged in and out of thermals by a cliff high to their left. The red dirt track crunched underneath. The air bit cool and refreshing into their cheeks.

Magnus's brain emptied.

But then Eygló broke the rhythm. 'You *know* Einar didn't kill Rósa, don't you, Magnús?'

Magnus let his irritation show. 'Can you shut up about that? Figuring out the identity of a perpetrator isn't a question of what you believe. It's a question of evidence.'

'Well, in that case, your evidence is all wrong.'

'Look. Inspector Paulsen is the investigating officer. She is working on the assumption that Rósa killed Carlotta at Glaumbaer and so Einar stabbed Rósa. She has got a team of well-trained police officers gathering evidence. They will find people who saw Einar near the scene of the crime. They will find forensic evidence that puts him there. It probably won't take them that long.'

'No they won't,' said Eygló.

Magnus ignored her.

They passed by a small pond. The pass reminded Magnus a little of the road from one side of Snaefellsnes to the other, just by the family farm at Bjarnarhöfn. Except Greenland was the land of icebergs, not lava.

'Anya knows Einar didn't do it,' Eygló said.

'Anya knows nothing about the case.'

'Anya is a smart woman. She said that it must have something to do with what Carlotta had discovered.'

'That was just her opinion.'

'And you didn't even tell her about Nancy Fishburn's murder. That *must* be linked to the hoax somehow.'

Magnus didn't respond.

'You're not comfortable about this, are you, Magnús? You know something's not right.'

Magnus had had enough. He stopped and turned to face Eygló. But she was grinning at him.

She was right, damn it! Magnus wasn't happy about it. And he didn't know why.

They stood facing each other. 'OK, look,' Eygló said. 'It's going to be at least an hour until we get back to Brattahlíd. Just do me a favour. Assume that Rósa's death had something to do with the hoax and whatever Carlotta had discovered about it. Think it through.'

Magnus's initial reaction was not to do Eygló a favour. But he knew that what really irritated him about Eygló's comments was that some part of him shared her doubts, and he wasn't prepared to admit that either to her or to himself.

Those doubts wouldn't go away until he dealt with them.

'All right,' said Magnus. 'Let's walk.'

'So. What do you think Carlotta had discovered that made her want to contact Anya? It was something she wanted to tell Einar that was worth flying all the way to Iceland for. Something about the letter.'

'OK, let's say she suspected it was a fake,' said Magnus. 'Why would she do that?'

Eygló trudged on. 'She found another expert? Someone who disagreed with Professor Beccari?'

'Who might that be?'

'Another Italian academic?'

'Or someone at the Vatican,' Magnus said. 'Maybe they had a better reason than she originally thought to doubt the letter.'

'You could ask them,' Eygló said.

'We could,' said Magnus. 'But let's say that an expert at the Vatican did have proof that the letter was a fake. I'm really not sure why that would mean she was killed. The proof would come out from this expert anyway, whether Carlotta was alive or dead; nobody gains.'

They walked on. Magnus's brain was working. To some extent, Eygló was correct. Although he had considered Carlotta and the wampum, he hadn't thought much about her involvement with the Columbus letter. All those years ago, a rare-book dealer had forged it and inserted it into the Vatican Secret Archives.

'You know Anya said just now that Carlotta had figured out who had forged it? What exactly did she say, can you remember?'

'Oh, let me think,' said Eygló. 'She said that Carlotta "suspected who had forged it, whatever 'it' was, and who had planted it". I think those were her words.'

'So do I,' said Magnus. '*We* know who forged it: Nancy Fishburn's rare-book dealer friend. I think his name was Emilio. But from what Anya said, Carlotta was implying someone else planted it in the Vatican Secret Archives.'

'Did she imply that?' said Eygló.

'Yeah, I know,' said Magnus. 'It's vague. I'm trying to remember exactly what Kelly told me about who her grandmother had said had planted it, but I can't. I suppose I assumed it was Emilio. But maybe it was an accomplice. Let's assume for a moment that it *was* someone else, how could Carlotta have discovered who?'

They pondered that. 'I have no idea,' said Eygló after a minute. 'What about you?'

'I'm thinking.'

'I'll shut up, then.'

Kelly had said that the book had scarcely been taken out since the hoax was hatched. Maybe the Vatican Secret Archives kept records of who had taken the book out and when. It seemed like the kind of thing an ancient library might do. Or maybe not: lots of people, lots of books, many years. Worth checking, though.

'You've thought of something,' Eygló said.

'I have,' said Magnus.

'Well?'

Magnus told her.

'OK. Let's call them. The Vatican.'

'When we get back to Narsarsuaq.'

'No, now.'

'How would we do that?'

'Look.'

Although they were still out of sight of Brattahlíd and the fjord, Eygló pointed to a couple of towers on a hilltop two miles away, no doubt providing phone coverage to the village. She pulled out her phone. 'See?' she said, showing him the screen. 'Three bars. And 4G.'

She sat on a rock and worked her phone. 'The Vatican Secret Archives, right?'

In less than a minute, she tapped a key triumphantly and put the phone to her ear. 'Yes, good afternoon,' Eygló said in English. 'I have Inspector Magnús Ragnarsson of the Reykjavík police here. He is investigating a murder, and he would like to speak to the head librarian.'

She nodded and then looked up at Magnus. 'There you go.'

So Magnus sat on a rock in the wilderness of Greenland and spoke to the keeper of one of the world's most exclusive libraries in Rome.

Magnus repeated Eygló's introduction. 'I am investigating the murder of Carlotta Mondini in Iceland on August twenty-first. She was an Italian postgraduate student.'

'Oh, yes, I remember her.' The head librarian had a soft Italian accent, but his English was clear and precise. 'She has been murdered? I am very sorry to hear that.'

Magnus's heart beat faster. Eygló had placed herself next to him on the rock and could hear what the librarian was saying. She gave Magnus the thumbs up.

'You say you remember her? Have you seen her recently?'

'Short hair with blonde stripes? A postgraduate? From Padua, I think?'

'That's right,' said Magnus.

'Yes, then I certainly remember her. She came into the library last year. She was asking about a volume of memoirs written by a Genoese sea captain in the seventeenth century. Another student, a friend of hers, had found a letter crammed in the back pages of the book. It purported to be from Christopher Columbus to his brother. My colleagues analysed it: a fake of course, and we told him that. My impression was that this Carlotta Mondini believed that the letter was real. Absurd.'

'So she asked to look at the book herself?'

'No. She just wanted to know who had ordered the book up from the stacks in the past.'

'And were you able to provide her with that information?'

'With difficulty,' said the librarian. 'But we keep comprehensive records here.'

'I don't suppose you wrote the names down somewhere?' said Magnus. 'Or perhaps you could check your records again for me.'

'There were three names,' said the librarian. 'Two of them I would have to look up, but one of them I remember. It is a famous one, at least in our country. Probably all over the world. In fact, he came back to look at the letter earlier this year. He seems to think it is genuine too.'

'And what name is that?' said Magnus. Although now he knew the answer.

'Beccari. Marco Beccari.'

CHAPTER 48

'SEE?' SAID EYGLÓ.

'Professor Beccari,' said Magnus.

'Carlotta discovered he inserted the fake letter.'

'It could be a coincidence.'

'Oh, come on!' said Eygló. 'How likely is that?'

'Very unlikely. But I can find out.' Magnus checked his note-book for Kelly Fishburn's cell number. He dialled it.

She answered.

'Kelly, it's Inspector Ragnarsson. How are you doing?'

'All right, I guess. My dad's here now, which is great.'

'Good. I have a question for you. Did your grandmother say that her friend Emilio placed the Columbus letter in the Vatican Secret Archives himself?'

There was a pause. 'I assume it was him, but I really can't remember. I'm sorry.'

That was disappointing. 'Do you think Emilio or your grand-mother might have known a man named Marco Beccari?' Magnus asked. 'He would have been about twenty, twenty-five at the time.'

'I don't know. Let me ask my dad. He's right here.'

Magnus heard Kelly's voice repeating his question. Then a man's voice appeared on the phone.

'This is John Fishburn, Kelly's father. My mother knew Marco Beccari. So did I, as a matter of fact. I remember him when we were both kids. And of course Emilio knew him.'

Magnus felt foolish. He was missing something. 'Why is that?'

'Because Marco Beccari is Emilio Beccari's son.'

Yep. He had missed that.

But Carlotta hadn't.

Magnus thanked Kelly's father and hung up. He and Eygló looked at each other. 'Did you get that?' Magnus asked her.

'Yeah, I heard it,' said Eygló. 'So Beccari knew all along the letter was a hoax.'

'Because his father had asked him to plant it in the Vatican Secret Archives.'

'That would really screw him if it came out.'

'You mean because of his reputation?'

'Absolutely. It would all be over. There would be a massive scandal; the press would love it. He'd be fired from Princeton, no one else would hire him, no one would publish his books; it would be total humiliation. If the world finds out this is a hoax, it's going to be bad for Einar and me, but it will be so much worse for him. We were duped; he was a perpetrator. And he has much further to fall than we do.'

'He struck me as quite a proud man,' said Magnus.

'Very.'

'He would be totally destroyed.'

The conclusion was obvious, and Eygló voiced it. 'Does that mean Beccari killed Carlotta? To shut her up?'

'It may well do,' said Magnus, thinking it through. 'We know Rósa was at Glaumbaer when Carlotta was killed. Rósa told Einar that she discovered the body, and that just before then she saw a man take something out of Carlotta's car, and later saw him leave via the folk museum. Einar didn't seem to believe she really saw anyone, and we didn't either. But perhaps it was true.'

'That man was Marco Beccari. And he killed Carlotta.'

'Before she had a chance to meet Einar at Saudárkrókur as she had arranged. Do you know whether Beccari was in Iceland then?'

Eygló frowned. 'No. He agreed to take part in the shoot at Ólafsvík at the last minute. Carlotta was killed on Monday, and we met Beccari in Ólafsvík on Wednesday. I've no idea when he flew into Iceland. Could have been before Monday, couldn't it?'

'We can check with the airlines,' said Magnus.

'All right.' Eygló furrowed her brow. 'But if Rósa did see Beccari at Glaumbaer, wouldn't she have recognized him?'

'Hm. Depends whether she had ever seen him before.'

Eygló's eyes opened wide. 'I think she only met him for the first time on the plane to Greenland.'

'And she recognized him then,' Magnus said. 'He figured it out, and killed her.'

'But wouldn't she just have told the police?' Eygló asked. 'Called you in Iceland?'

'Maybe she was intending to,' said Magnus. 'Or maybe she wanted to confront Beccari herself. So she agreed to meet him in the Blomsterdalen.'

'That would be stupid.'

'Depends on what she wanted to say. She was a cool customer.'

'She certainly was,' said Eygló. 'She never gave the impression that she recognized Beccari, but then she would be quite capable of hiding that if she wanted to.'

'And she didn't tell Einar.'

'That's not necessarily surprising.'

'Let me check something,' Magnus said as he pulled up Vigdís's number on his phone, turning away from Eygló.

As he was waiting for her to pick up, a ewe trotted into sight from behind some rocks, a black lamb almost her size close behind her. Both animals stared at him. He stared back. The lamb lost its nerve and darted back and forth, not sure whether to run for it or to stick close to Mom. The ewe ambled away.

Vigdís answered just as her phone was switching to voicemail. 'Hi, Vigdís,' Magnus said without preamble. 'Can you check something for me? Can you find out when Professor Beccari arrived in Iceland last week? He will have rented a car. We need to know the registration, and whether it was caught on camera travelling north through the Hvalfjördur tunnel before Carlotta was murdered.'

Vigdís grasped the implication of Magnus's question immediately. 'Are you serious?'

'I am.'

Silence.

'Vigdís?'

'I was thinking about Rósa's phone records you sent me. There was a US number I recognized from Carlotta's records.'

'Beccari?'

'That's right. Hold on.' Magnus could hear the taps of Vigdís's keyboard as she looked something up on her computer. 'Here it is. Rósa and Beccari spoke for nine minutes at twenty-one-fifty-two Greenland time on the twenty-fifth. That's Saturday night.'

'The evening before Rósa was killed. Beccari would already have left them in Narsarsuaq. He would have been in Qaqortoq.'

'You can get the Greenland telecoms company to check the location.'

'Good idea,' said Magnus. 'Thanks, Vigdís. And let me know as soon as you get anything on the Hvalfjördur tunnel.'

Magnus hung up and relayed his conversation to Eygló.

'So Rósa and Beccari could have been arranging to meet?' Eygló said.

'They could have been. In which case either Beccari never left Narsarsuaq, or, more likely, he got a helicopter back that day just to meet her at the Blomsterdalen.'

'I still think she would have been stupid to meet him somewhere quite so isolated. Rósa wasn't that dumb.'

'We'll see,' said Magnus. 'Air Greenland will have the details if he did fly there and back. Time to call Inspector Paulsen.'

Paulsen didn't answer so Magnus left a message on her voicemail. He and Eygló set off at a brisk pace on the track towards Brattahlíd. They had only been going for ten minutes before Paulsen called back.

'Sorry, Magnus,' she said. 'I was just interviewing a French tourist. He is adamant that he saw Einar on Signal Mountain between twelve-fifteen and twelve-forty-five yesterday afternoon. No doubts about the ID – he had seen Einar with Eygló and Suzy before at breakfast at the hotel. Definitely the same guy. And if Einar was on Signal Mountain at that time, there was no way he could have had time to walk to the Blomsterdalen, murder his wife and get back to Narsarsuaq when we met him at two-fifty. And there was not enough time earlier that morning after he had returned from Brattahlíd. So we've lost our only suspect.'

'Don't worry,' said Magnus. 'I think I've got another one for you.'

CHAPTER 49

PAULSEN AND MAGNUS went straight from the airport at Qaqortoq to the hotel, with a local constable in tow. While Magnus had been making his way over the fjord to Narsarsuaq, Paulsen had checked with Air Greenland. Beccari had indeed made a day trip by helicopter from Qaqortoq to Narsarsuaq the day before, arriving at eight-fifteen and leaving at two. He had had time to meet Rósa in the Blomsterdalen and kill her. He was booked on a flight out from Narsarsuaq to Reykjavík later that afternoon. Paulsen and Magnus could have waited for him to show up at Narsarsuaq, but they had decided to go straight to Qaqortoq and arrest him there.

If Beccari had killed Carlotta and Rósa, he had probably killed Nancy as well, and for the same reason. Once Nancy became aware Marco Beccari was involved with the documentary, she would have realized that he hadn't let on to the others that the letter was a fake. When Kelly had told her about Carlotta's murder, Nancy may well have remembered the Italian girl from Einar's visit in Nantucket. If she was the smart woman that everyone said she was, then she would have figured out that there was a possibility Marco Beccari might have killed Carlotta. And rather than coming to the Icelandic police, she might have contacted Beccari himself. And met him in her hotel, after sending Kelly away.

Beccari had just checked out of the Hotel Qaqortoq, and the hotel shuttle bus had taken him to the airport: Magnus recalled spotting the bus stopped outside the terminal. So he and Paulsen retraced their steps.

The airport was no more than a small terminal building, a couple of sheds containing fire trucks and bowsers and a round concrete apron built on a rocky promontory sticking out into the sea. The Air Greenland clerk at the desk said that Beccari had just checked in, but his helicopter had been delayed for an hour. The woman thought she had seen him stroll out of the building.

Magnus and Paulsen made a quick circuit of the terminal and its toilets, which took them only five minutes, then Paulsen suggested they wait for Beccari to return. She began to make some calls.

Magnus kicked his heels for five minutes, but he was impatient. He left the terminal building and walked up to the road. To the left was the route into town: Beccari probably hadn't gone that way, or they would have spotted him. The road twisted around to the right along the top of some small cliffs above the sea.

Magnus turned right. The road rounded an outcrop of rock and passed beneath a small playground. Two women were sitting on a bench watching three tiny children on a merry-go-round. And a few yards away, sitting on a raised slab of granite staring out to sea, was Professor Beccari.

Magnus climbed a narrow footpath and skirted around the playground behind Beccari. He crept up to him and took a seat right next to him on the granite.

'Hello, professor.'

For a moment Beccari looked startled to see Magnus, but he swiftly recovered his composure.

'Ah, Inspector. How's the investigation going?'

'Pretty good,' said Magnus.

Beccari nodded. 'So you are sure that poor Dr Thorsteinsson is your man?'

'No. Dr Thorsteinsson isn't our man.' Magnus fixed his eyes on Beccari.

'Oh,' said Beccari, unnerved by Magnus's stare. 'Do you have another suspect?'

'Yes.'

'Hm.'

Beccari looked away, down to the water below them. Out in the fjord the giant iceberg Magnus had seen the night before stood immobile in the water. The cruise ship had gone. Further in, just a few yards from the cliffs, an empty motorboat bobbed up and down on its mooring.

'Marco' – Magnus used his first name – 'I know that you planted the Columbus letter in the book in the Vatican. And I know your father Emilio forged it.'

Beccari tensed. He was still staring hard at the sea beneath the cliffs. Magnus let the silence stretch as Beccari considered his response. 'That doesn't mean I killed anybody,' he said eventually.

'We have details of the car you rented at Keflavík Airport when you arrived in the country. We're checking the cameras at the Hvalfjördur tunnel on the Ring Road for the day Carlotta was murdered. We will soon know what time you drove past them. We know you flew to Narsarsuaq yesterday, giving yourself just enough time to get to the Blomsterdalen and kill Rósa. And I am sure we will be able to place you at the hotel in Reykjavík where Nancy Fishburn was smothered with a pillow.

'We've just started. Now we know where to look, the evidence will pile up. Forensics, fingerprints, DNA, witnesses. We will put you at the site of three murders in two countries, no problem.'

Magnus waited while Beccari digested all this. 'Of course you will,' he said eventually. 'I'm amazed that I've gotten this far. I mean, I was so lucky that Rósa and then Einar presented themselves as suspects. If I'd had the chance to plan it properly, you might have found things more difficult.'

Magnus was amazed at the man's ego and confidence in his own intelligence. Naturally the genius historian could have staged the perfect murder if he had had the time to put his extraordinary mind to the problem!

'So you didn't intend to kill Carlotta?'

'No. I mean, at the back of my mind, I thought I might have to. But I hoped to persuade her.'

'Persuade her of what?'

'I don't know how much of this you have figured out yet,' said Beccari. He glanced at Magnus, who gave no response.

'The reason Carlotta got in touch with me in the first place was that she had enquired at the Vatican who had checked out the volume in the past fifty years. There were only three names, and mine was one of them, so she got in touch with me to ask whether I had noticed a letter from Christopher Columbus to his brother. I said I hadn't. Then she told me that a graduate student had found it, but the Vatican authorities suspected that it was a fake.

'Naturally, I told her the Vatican must be correct. I wanted her to drop the whole thing.'

'Presumably you knew your father had faked it?'

'Yes. He told me all about it at the time, and about Nancy and John's plan to plant the wampum in Greenland. I was studying at Pisa, and Papa knew I had been researching in the Vatican Secret Archives and so I could get access. I think that's why he decided it was a good home for the fake. I should have refused him. He thought it was very amusing, and I knew the Fishburns and liked them, but as a professional historian I knew this was wrong. Not just criminally wrong, but morally wrong. It would mislead academics like me, cause them to waste time.'

Beccari sighed. 'But Papa was very persuasive. He was charming and he was persistent. And beyond that, I was always trying to please him. That's why I became a historian in the first place. That's why it has always pained me that he never lived to see me become a professor at Princeton.' Beccari smiled. 'He would have loved that. He loved Americans and American universities, and not just because they were some of his best customers. So I said yes.' For the first time Beccari looked up at Magnus. 'I planted the letter.

'I regretted it immediately, but then I just shoved it out of my mind. Which was really stupid. After Papa died I should have gone right back and extracted the letter; then everything would have been fine. But some part of me denied that I had ever planted it; the whole thing had nothing to do with me.'

Beccari shook his head. 'And then Carlotta's friend found it.'

'I can understand why you told her it was a fake. But why did you change your mind and authenticate it?'

'It became clear that Carlotta wasn't going to take my word that it was a forgery and drop it. She said they had other evidence pointing to Gudrid settling in Nantucket, and that she and some Icelandic friends of hers were going to make a documentary about it. An international documentary. In that case it would be much better if everyone thought the letter was real.

'So I went to Rome and took another look at my father's work. It was extremely well done. So well done that it made me wonder whether he hadn't actually made other forgeries, but that is by the by. I felt that my best bet was to be bold and bluff it out. So I told Carlotta the letter was real and I let her run with it.

'I knew there was a good chance I would get found out in the end, but this seemed to me my best chance of escaping detection. I begged Carlotta not to tell anyone that I had missed the letter myself in 1979 – I said it would be embarrassing – and Carlotta was willing to go along with that. She was just so pleased to have my blessing, she would have done anything I asked.

'So, it all looked good. Until Carlotta called me three weeks ago and said she wanted to speak to me again about the letter. She had doubts and she was going to talk to Einar about them. In fact, she was going to Iceland to see him.

'I knew I was in trouble. I almost confessed then. But the consequences to my career would have been catastrophic. I have my enemies in the academic world, especially at Princeton, and they would have lost no time in plunging in the knife. For someone in my position to have planted a forgery would be a scandal. It would ruin my reputation and the reputation of the university. And ... And my reputation is important to me. I have made a major contribution to the understanding of history, and I have more to do. Quite simply, I am one of the top historians in the world. Without history ... I am nothing. I tried to imagine what would happen to me if I was unmasked as a forger, and I just couldn't. It was too terrible.'

Beccari was searching Magnus's face for understanding.

Magnus could believe he wasn't exaggerating. For someone with an ego like Beccari's, the shame of being unmasked as a forger would be too horrible to contemplate.

'I see,' Magnus said. 'So you agreed to meet Carlotta at Glaumbaer?'

'Yes. At that point I didn't plan to kill her. I just wanted to hear what she had to say and find some way to keep her quiet. I typed up an offer for her to take up a post in the history department at Princeton. It might have come in useful.'

'And what did she have to say?'

'She had just read some interview with me online from a few years back, where I had said that my father was a rare-book dealer. That he was the one who had gotten me interested in history – which was true, of course. Anyway, she remembered from her visit to Nancy Fishburn in Nantucket that Nancy's husband had collected rare books. She had done some googling, and discovered that there used to be a rare-book dealer called Emilio Beccari and she even found the introduction of an obscure pamphlet on antiquarian books where his name was mentioned along with John Fishburn. So she wanted to know if Emilio was my father, and if I could explain the connection. Apparently she had been in touch with an archaeologist in Greenland who had some doubts about the wampum as well.

'I didn't do a good job. I admitted that my father's name was Emilio, but I said I had no idea who his clients were. It was just a coincidence that I had taken out the volume in which the letter was found.'

Beccari shook his head. 'She just didn't believe me. Once she started considering the possibility that the letter was a fake, it was obvious that I must have been the one who planted it. She said she was going to Saudárkrókur that very evening, and that she would tell Einar.

'I pleaded with her. I showed her the letter offering her the job at Princeton. I offered to outright bribe her, give her cash. But none of that worked. It just proved to her that the letter was a fake and that I had planted it.

'She turned and walked away. We were standing at the back of the churchyard, away from the road, out of sight of anyone. I knew once she reached the front of the church and went through the gate, it would all be over. My reputation, my chair at Princeton, my books, my ideas, everything. In those seconds I realized that if I let her tell the world what she knew, I would kill myself. I would *have* to kill myself – I would have no choice. I couldn't face my colleagues, my family, the memory of my father. Myself. I would have to end my life.

'And then I thought: Why? Why should I have to end *my* life? Why not hers?'

Beccari licked his lips and swallowed. 'I had no time to think it through: I had to act. There was a spade and a pickaxe leaning against the back wall of the church. So I grabbed the pickaxe and whacked her over the head – not with the pick itself, I couldn't do that, but with the flat bit. She crumpled.'

He paused, swallowing again, staring at his feet. 'I could tell right away she was dead. Then I started thinking. No one knew we were meeting – Carlotta had told me that. The churchyard was quiet, there was no one around, and although there were some neighbouring farms, they were quiet too. It was late – still daylight, but everyone was at home. I dragged her behind the church. I knew I had to get rid of the pickaxe, and then I had the idea of getting rid of Carlotta's laptop and phone too, so you wouldn't find her emails to me. Her phone was in her pocket, and the laptop was in her car. I threw them into the sea with the pickaxe on the way back to Reykjavík.

'Then I went to meet the TV documentary crew a couple of days later in Ólafsvík as though nothing had happened. And it seemed to work. You never suspected me. It looked like I was going to be lucky.'

One of the little kids from the playground scrambled over to where Magnus and Beccari were sitting. He stopped right in front of them, inches away from a ten-foot drop down to the road. Magnus was alarmed and turned to look at the two women on the bench. They smiled and waved – they didn't care that the kid was about to plunge to his death. Greenlanders clearly had a different sense of personal risk.

Beccari avoided the child's big brown eyes. 'Your mom wants you,' Magnus said in English, pointing to the women. The child may or may not have understood the words, but he turned and ran back to the playground.

'And then Nancy Fishburn showed up in Iceland?'

Beccari nodded. 'The first I heard of it was an email she sent me. She said she had spoken to Suzy and now she wanted to speak to me. Could I meet her at her hotel in Reykjavík?

'So I did. At first, it looked good. She had told Suzy about the hoax, but Suzy had wanted to keep it all a secret, and Nancy had agreed. But it turned out Nancy had just heard about Carlotta's murder. I said that had nothing to do with me. I'm not sure whether or not she believed me, but she said she was going to have to speak to the police and tell them what she knew about me.

'I couldn't let her do that. So I smothered her with a pillow while she was sitting down in a chair in her hotel room. It wasn't hard – she wasn't strong. Then I lifted her on to the bed, and hoped people would think she had died of natural causes.'

'It almost worked,' said Magnus.

'It was a shame – she was a good friend of my father's, but she had to die.'

CHAPTER 50

'S O WHAT ABOUT Rósa?' Magnus asked.

'Ah, Rósa. Apparently she was following Carlotta and saw me in Glaumbaer. I had no idea. She didn't know me then, but she did recognize me when she met me getting on the plane to Greenland. Once again, I had no idea. In fact, she was quite friendly to me.'

'So she didn't say anything about identifying you?'

'No, not then. But the evening I left the crew and came here to Qaqortoq, she called me. She told me she had seen me at Glaumbaer, and she was pretty sure I had killed Carlotta. She had also figured out that the whole thing was probably a hoax: she guessed that I must have been involved somehow – she was a smart woman.

'I told her she was crazy, of course. But then she said she had a deal for me. She said she wouldn't tell anyone she had recognized me if I told her all about the hoax. She realized that if she told the police she had seen me at Glaumbaer, the hoax would come out and it would be really damaging for Einar. She said she only had a few more months to live and all she cared about was him.

'I thought about it, and decided to trust her. So I told her what I knew about the hoax: the Columbus letter and the wampum. I promised I would do my best to keep it quiet, and she said that as long as the hoax remained a secret, she wouldn't tell the police about me.

'Of course, I agreed. But then she said if she or Einar ever became serious suspects for Carlotta's murder, she would have to tell the police she had seen me. And if the hoax did come out she would tell the police too.

'I wasn't happy with that, but I didn't think I had much of a choice.'

Beccari glanced quickly at Magnus and then back at his feet. 'That night, I couldn't sleep. I haven't had a decent night's sleep since Glaumbaer. But the more I thought about it, the less I thought I could trust Rósa. She was a smart lawyer; somehow she had gotten herself in a position where she had a hold over me. She seemed like the kind of woman who was always going to use that pressure. And at that point, she didn't even know that Nancy had died. Once she found that out, she might put two and two together and realize I had killed the old lady as well.

'All kinds of things could go wrong. I just couldn't trust her to keep quiet.

'It was clever of her to wait until I had left Narsarsuaq. With me at a distance, she was safe. If she had told me while we were all together, I could have figured out a way of catching her alone and then dealing with her permanently.

'You know I told you she and I had a conversation on the boat crossing the fjord back to Narsarsuaq?'

'Yes.'

'Well, we didn't talk about her expecting someone to kill her – I just threw that in because Eygló had already told me Einar was a suspect for Rósa's murder, and I wanted to put him further in the frame with you. What we did talk about was her plan to hike to the Blomsterdalen the following day.

'She was going to be alone, miles from anywhere. I got out of bed and checked the Blomsterdalen online. It was a remote valley. I looked at the flight schedules and realized I could get a flight from Qaqortoq to Narsarsuaq first thing, and then fly back here in the afternoon. It was risky, but doing nothing was risky.

'I went to the supermarket as soon as it opened and bought a knife. Then I flew out to Narsarsuaq and hiked to the Blomsterdalen myself to wait for her. And I killed her.'

So Eygló was right: Rósa hadn't been stupid enough to arrange to meet Beccari alone in the valley. 'Was that really necessary?'

'I think so. Besides, she was going to die anyway. I just made it quicker. And once you have killed twice, it's kind of easier to kill again.'

'I've heard that before.'

Beccari sighed. He looked up at Magnus, tears in his eyes. Magnus had the feeling that Beccari was very sorry – sorry for himself.

'So what happens now?' Beccari asked.

'Inspector Paulsen arrests you. You get tried for murder in two countries; we get to fight with the Greenlanders about who goes first. You spend a long time in jail.'

Beccari nodded.

'You know, Marco,' said Magnus. 'It is a shame that your father never knew what you are really like.'

Anger flashed through the tears. Magnus didn't care. Beccari deserved to be locked away for a long, long time. Magnus's only regret was that he would be tried in Greenland or Iceland: he really needed to spend the rest of his life in a US penitentiary.

Magnus stood up, turned away from Beccari towards the airport, and called Paulsen, telling her he had found Beccari by the playground and she should come and arrest him.

He heard the scrabble of falling stones behind him, and saw Beccari slide down the rocks to the road below.

Magnus yelled as Beccari bounded across the road and leaped into the air.

It was only ten or fifteen feet to the sea below. Magnus heard the splash as he followed Beccari down the rocks and over the narrow road.

He could still see the ripples where Beccari had hit the water below him, but no sign of the man himself. Magnus stared at the slow swirl of the sea. Beccari didn't look like much of a swimmer, but perhaps he had struck out under water. The surface broke as the long neck of a cormorant bobbed up. The bird looked around for a couple of seconds and then dived down.

People usually floated, didn't they? Could Beccari have got stuck down there somewhere?

Then, slowly, the hump of Beccari's light brown jacket broke the surface, his pink hooped scarf training behind it. He was face down.

His body was only a few yards from the rocky shore line.

Magnus couldn't understand why Beccari hadn't broken the surface face up.

Magnus was a good swimmer. He knew CPR; he knew mouth-to-mouth. If he got to Beccari quickly, he had a good chance of saving him.

But the water was cold, dangerously cold. He had no idea how long a healthy body could survive in water that cold before hypothermia kicked in, but he thought it must be at least ten minutes. Probably half an hour. Paulsen was on her way and there were helicopters and motorboats galore close by.

Was it worth risking his own life for Beccari? Eight years before, Magnus had watched as a murderer had drowned in the waters of a powerful waterfall. Even though there was nothing he could reasonably have done to save the man once he had fallen in, he had relived the moment with regret: no, with guilt.

He could save Beccari.

He laid his phone on the rock, took off his coat and his shoes, paused for a moment and jumped.

CHAPTER 51

A S HE WAS in mid-air the realization hit Magnus he had no idea how deep the water was. Perhaps Beccari had banged his head on a rock just below the surface. Too late to do anything about that now, except to resolve to bunch his legs as soon as he hit the water to slow his descent.

Impact was like a giant fist smashing against his body, clutching him and squeezing. It wasn't the resistance, it was the cold: cold like nothing he had ever felt before. All the nerves, all the muscles in his body seemed to convulse. He could feel his mouth attempting to open in an involuntary gasp; somehow he managed to keep it closed. His lungs exploded.

He did pull up his legs but he had no idea where he was, or even which way up. He opened his eyes. The sea was green; white bubbles from his splash surrounded him. His lungs demanded air immediately – holding his breath was not an option. He hadn't quite managed to keep his mouth completely closed in the moment after impact; some water had trickled in, stimulating a coughing reflex. A surge of panic over-whelmed him, and a compulsion to flap his arms and legs. But which way?

He told himself to stay still, just for a couple of seconds so that he could tell which way was up. The bubbles cleared, slipping off together. Up. Sand, rock and seaweed appeared in one direction, a lighter shade of green and blue in another. He pushed with his arms to change his attitude so that his head was towards the surface, and kicked and flapped.

Ordinarily, Magnus could hold his breath under water for a minute or more. Now he only had a few seconds. His chest was exploding. His clothes were dragging him down.

He couldn't keep his mouth shut any more. It opened just as he broke the surface, he took two lungs full of air and then he was under again. He resisted the insistent messages from his body to flail wildly and took a couple of deliberate strokes upwards.

Once again, his face broke the surface and he kicked and flapped with arms and legs to keep his face above the surface.

The explosion in his lungs was joined by his heart. His heartbeat galloped, the blood roaring in his ears. Despite his face being above water and free to gasp air, his lungs were telling him that he didn't have enough oxygen. He seemed to be breathing in without having time to breathe out.

Panic was tugging at his heels, pulling him down towards the bottom.

Hyperventilation.

Slow down. Calm down.

He held his breath. Froze his limbs. Let his body sink and his head go underwater just for a couple of seconds before kicking back to the surface.

It worked. He was still gasping, his pulse felt like it had hit two hundred, but a steady flow of oxygen was reaching his lungs.

He looked around him. Beccari was floating face down about ten yards away. The rocky shore was close, but there seemed nowhere to cling on safely. A better bet was the motorboat a little further out to sea. Maybe Magnus would be able to climb on board. If not, he could at least hang on to the mooring line.

He began to take some tentative strokes towards Beccari. After the initial shock, where the cold had felt like a blow, now it was painful. Magnus could see why Beccari had surfaced face down; he must have gasped for air as he had plunged beneath the surface, and filled his lungs with seawater. Magnus had been foolish to jump after him, but now he was in, he would do his best to extricate Beccari.

It was difficult to swim or to make any forward progress at all. He found himself making swift, useless strokes; once again he tried to calm himself, to swim slowly and deliberately.

After what seemed like an age, he reached Beccari. He was exhausted. He reached out to grab Beccari's clothes to try and turn him face up, but his fingers wouldn't grasp him. He got closer, reached out again. Beccari sank underwater. Surfaced. Magnus just couldn't grip; his fingers wouldn't obey instructions from his brain. His body was shutting down, extremities first.

He gave up trying to get a hold of Beccari, and instead pushed Beccari's side upwards, trying to flip him over on to his back.

It took him four attempts, but eventually he succeeded.

Beccari wasn't breathing. He had drowned; it was probably too late to resuscitate him, but Magnus was in the water now, he may as well try. It wasn't far to the motorboat.

Off Duxbury Beach in Massachusetts, Magnus could have grabbed Beccari under the chin and pulled him the distance in less than a minute. But here, in Greenland, with both of them fully clothed, Magnus was making no progress.

Not just that, but his limbs were beginning to ignore messages from his brain. It was only with the greatest of difficulty that he could move his arms and his legs at all. It was bad.

And it was going to get worse.

In another couple of minutes Magnus would lose the ability to keep his own face above water. He had to get to the boat before that.

He let go of Beccari and struck out for the boat. But he was losing strength; not just strength, he was losing control over his body. For the first minute or so he made some progress, but then even that stopped. There was a tiny current which was gently tugging him away from the boat. Once again, in normal circumstances, he could easily have overcome it, but now all he could do was keep his head above water.

He wasn't going to be able to do that for much longer.

He was going to drown.

His left arm went first. It would no longer move, and his right was barely making any upward pressure.

He was going to drown.

His life didn't flash in front of his eyes, but he did think: who would care? His parents were dead. His brother Ollie would be pleased. Vigdís and Árni would be upset, it was true, as would Ingileif.

And then he thought of the little boy with the red hair peering over the wall at him on Borgartún, with those piercing blue eyes.

He sank beneath the surface.

He flailed his remaining failing arm and kicked with both legs. His face met the air and he took a gulp.

And then he sank.

His right arm wasn't working properly now, but he summoned all the strength he could in his legs for one more surge. He broke the surface, another gulp and under again.

A hand grabbed him under the chin and yanked. This time his face broke the surface and stayed out of the water.

'Come on, Magnus, you big bastard, keep swimming!' It was Paulsen's voice. 'You can do it. Help me now.' He could feel her body in the water bumping behind him.

He tried, pushing downwards with his one arm, kicking feebly with his barely responsive legs.

He tried to say something to Paulsen, but all he could do was gasp for air. She was tugging him along towards the moored motorboat. He kicked and paddled, trying to do his bit to keep moving, keep his mouth and nose above the surface, keep alive.

His eardrums were underwater and he heard the urgent buzz of an engine. It became louder and half a minute later a large bright orange shape surged into his peripheral view.

'Grab this,' said Paulsen as she shoved a red and white plastic ring into his arms. He clutched it. It floated.

He floated.

Several strong arms grabbed him and heaved him upwards and over the edge of the boat. He was shivering uncontrollably as someone thrust a blanket over his shoulders.

Paulsen sat next to him. Her uniform was sodden, her long black hair hanging in damp strands down her broad face, but she was barely even shaking. She was a Greenlander: built to dive into near-freezing water and emerge unscathed.

Magnus wasn't.

Paulsen flashed him that unexpected sweet smile. 'Are you OK?'

Magnus tried to answer, but his teeth were chattering so much, he settled for a nod.

He fought to control his jaws. 'Where's Beccari?'

'We'll fish him out next,' said Paulsen.

'Good.'

Paulsen put a hand on Magnus's shaking arm. 'You know, Magnus? He wasn't worth it.'

CHAPTER 52

'SO, INSPECTOR MAGNÚS, who did you think was most likely to have killed Carlotta Mondini when you took on the case?' Eygló looked up at Magnus, her eyes wide, her lips slightly parted as if the words he was about to utter would be the most fascinating she had ever heard. They were standing on the strip of green that ran beside the bay in front of the National Police Commissioner's Office, more photogenic than the police head-quarters, which was a squat office block around the corner by the bus station.

He couldn't help responding with warmth. Suzy had told him not to act like a policeman following best procedure, but rather like an inquisitive sleuth. Magnus understood the difference, and Eygló made it easy. 'I didn't know. You always have to keep an open mind. It could have been a local who had never met her before: there had been a series of rapes in the north of Iceland. Or it might have been someone from her past life in Italy. But a tourist murdered in this way is unheard of in Iceland.'

'Yet the cause of her death turned out to be an Icelandic woman who had been dead for nearly a thousand years.'

Magnus grinned. 'That's not so surprising. There were plenty of murders in Gudrid's day. Iceland was a much less peaceful place.'

'Cut!' shouted Suzy. 'That was great, Magnus.' She glanced at Siggi, the new Icelandic cameraman, who nodded. 'Ajay?'

'It's good,' said the sound man.

'That's a wrap, then. Glaumbaer tomorrow!'

305

Suzy had come up with ingenious ways of interweaving the hoax and its discovery, as well as the murders of Carlotta and Nancy, into the existing documentary. The BBC had loved it when she had pitched it over the phone. The Greenland takes would have to stay as they were, but a few new scenes involving Magnus in Reykjavík and Glaumbaer should set the scene for the murder investigation. The National Police Commissioner had been more than happy to release Magnus for the job. The Ministry of Tourism was keen that Carlotta's death should be seen as something other than the random murder of an unlucky tourist who was in the wrong place at the wrong time. Carlotta's parents had given their blessing too, and had even returned to Iceland to be interviewed.

Kelly had agreed to talk about her grandmother; in fact she had been eager to. Nancy Fishburn was emerging as a heroine of the story, a tragic heroine, given her death. Magnus had his qualms about murder as entertainment, and about bailing Suzy out after her attempts to keep the knowledge of the hoax to herself. But it was a story that should be told, and Magnus was enjoying his part in telling it.

They had decided to keep Rósa's death out of it. It complicated things, and Eygló and Suzy had no desire to pile more pressure on Einar.

Rósa's death had broken him. He didn't care about the discovery of the hoax; he didn't care about his academic reputation or even his post at the university, who had given him a term's sabbatical. Eygló made sure she saw him every day, and did her best to convince Einar he had always done his best for Rósa.

'That was very good, Magnus,' said Suzy. 'You and Eygló seem to have some real chemistry going, don't you think, Halla?'

Halla was in charge of press relations for the Metropolitan Police, and was keeping an eye on proceedings. 'Absolutely,' she said, grinning at Magnus. For a press officer, she was not known for her discretion.

'Magnus is a true professional,' said Eygló neutrally.

'Of course,' said Suzy. 'You're sure you can give us a lift to Glaumbaer tomorrow, Magnus?'

'No problem.'

Production costs had been cut right down to the bone. Tom had been sent back to England, never to work with Suzy again. Eygló had begged a friend of her sister's to do the camera work for no payment up front and the risk of no payment at all. Ajay was still providing his labour free. Suzy was staying on Eygló's sofa, and Ajay with one of her sisters. There would be post-production costs, but Suzy was doing this on a shoestring. Half a shoestring.

'Have you got time for a walk?' Eygló asked.

'Sure,' said Magnus. He was still working his way through the paperwork, or computerwork, brought about by three murders in two jurisdictions committed by a dual citizen of a third and a fourth. The paperwork wasn't going anywhere.

The sun was out, at least temporarily, and a fresh breeze skipped in from the bay. On one side of them, manic Icelandic drivers misguided tons of metal in unpredictable directions along the Saebraut. On the other, a crowd of ducks, cormorants and swans went about their city business. On the far shore, Mount Esja overlooked it all, its rocky flanks glowing a soft, splendid gold.

'You know this would all be so much more difficult if Professor Beccari had survived,' said Magnus. 'The investigation would have taken months; we would have had to stop you broadcasting anything that might have been prejudicial to his defence.'

It turned out that Beccari had suffered a fatal heart attack after leaping into the sea at Qaqortoq. The shock of the cold that had set Magnus's heart racing had been too much for him. What wasn't clear, and would never become clear, was whether his decision to jump in had been an ultimately successful suicide attempt, or a desperate bid to reach the motorboat and escape.

If the latter, it was never going to work. The boat's engine needed a key, which was not on board.

'He deserved it,' said Eygló. 'I'm just glad that you didn't die too. That was a stupid thing to do, Magnús.'

'I can't argue with that.'

307

They were strolling past the elegant white Höfdi House, standing alone in a patch of green lawn, the former British Embassy where Reagan and Gorbachev had taken the first steps towards agreeing they had better things to do than blow up the world.

'How was lunch with Ingileif?' Eygló asked, as if reading Magnus's mind. Outside the Höfdi House was where Magnus had had one of his first conversations with her, and since then the building had always been associated with her in his mind.

'Polite. Civilized. Awkward.'

'Did you ask her about Ási?'

'I did.'

'And?'

Magnus glanced across the ruffled bay at the broad shoulders of Esja. 'I asked whether he was mine. She tried to laugh it off and asked me where I got that idea. I said Vigdís. She went quiet: she knows as well as I do how Vigdís is observant at that kind of thing. She wouldn't actually say he was mine, but she didn't deny it.

'I asked if I could see him. She said no. I pushed it. She looked like she was going to cry, but she didn't – she's tough, Ingileif. She said her husband was leaving her. He's gone off with a third-rate model, not much more than a schoolgirl really. She said she understood the irony.'

She had actually said more than that. During their constantly shifting relationship, Ingileif had had difficulty remaining monogamous. She had chided Magnus for caring about her occasional lapses. Now, she said, she knew what it felt like to be on the other end of it. She knew it felt bad.

There had been a long silence at the lunch table: they were in a quiet café in Thingholt. Ingileif had looked up at him, her face tight, her eyes tough yet pleading. Pleading for him to come back to her.

Magnus had paid the bill and left. Ingileif's last words were: 'I'll think about Ási.'

Magnus and Eygló turned inland towards Borgartún and the route back to police headquarters.

They were approaching a café, a Kaffitár. Magnus was about to suggest they nip in for a quick coffee when he saw two figures emerge. They were still about fifty metres away. One, the woman, turned away from Magnus and Eygló to her car parked a little further down Borgartún. She had the rolling gate of a woman with a false leg. Thelma.

The other, an older man, headed towards Magnus and Eygló, frowning. He only recognized Magnus when he was ten metres away.

He hesitated, and then growled as he passed: 'Move along now. Nothing to see here.'

But there was. Magnus was damned sure there was.

'Magnús?' said Eygló. 'That was Tryggvi Thór, wasn't it? What did he mean?'

'I don't know.'

Eygló slipped her fingers into his.

Magnus squeezed gently. Then he relaxed. He smiled. He forgot about Tryggvi Thór.

For the first time in a long time, he felt ... good.

AUTHOR'S NOTE

N ORSE EXPLORERS FROM Iceland really did discover Greenland and North America around the year AD 1000. It is all outlined in *The Saga of the Greenlanders* and *The Saga of Erik the Red*, although the descriptions of where the adventurers, including Gudrid and her husband, actually landed are tantalizingly obscure. Until the 1960s some historians believed these sagas were just myths, but then the Norwegian archaeologists Helge and Anne Stine Ingstad discovered the Viking settlement at L'Anse aux Meadows in Newfoundland. Greenland is littered with Norse archaeological sites, including Erik's farm at Brattahlíd.

A history of the discovery of America by Bartolomé de Las Casas written in the sixteenth century quotes a letter from Columbus to his patrons Ferdinand and Isabella describing in enigmatic terms a visit to Iceland in 1477. There is an oral tradition that an Italian nobleman stayed on Snaefellsnes near Ólafsvík, which had been a major port for trade with Greenland. At the time, the sagas, including the two Vinland sagas, were popular in Iceland – many of the greatest saga manuscripts were transcribed in the fifteenth century. If Columbus did spend any length of time in Iceland, and asked the locals about the western ocean, he would have learned all about Greenland and Vinland. Which I find interesting. But there is no evidence that he wrote a detailed letter to his younger brother about it; Emilio made that up.

I have used the traditional English versions of the names in the sagas rather than the modern Icelandic or Old Norse. So Gudrid is Gudrid, not Gudrídur (Icelandic) or Gudrídr (Old Norse).

There are many ways of spelling Erik the Red in English; I picked the most prevalent. Many places in Greenland have two or even three names: modern Greenlandic, slightly older Danish and very old Norse. So Qaqortoq used to be called Julianehåb. I have gone for clarity rather than consistency here, so I use the Greenlandic Qaqortoq and Narsarsuaq and the Old Norse Brattahlíd (modern name Qassiarsuk) and Erik's Fjord (Tunulliarfik Fjord). Inspector Paulsen would probably refer to Brattahlíd as Qassiarsuk, but she doesn't because I don't want to confuse the reader.

I should like to thank some kind and patient helpers: Humphrey Hawksley, Mary Will, Lilja Sigurdardóttir, Christoffer Petersen, Hilary Hale, Josepha, Ellen Sowerbutts, Edwin Thomas, Chief Superintendent Stefán Vagn, Quentin Bates, Richenda Todd, my agent Oli Munson, Florence Rees and my editors Sara O'Keeffe and Susannah Hamilton at Atlantic Books. And, as always, Barbara.

A MESSAGE FROM MICHAEL RIDPATH

Get a FREE 60-page story

I hope you enjoyed reading this book as much as I enjoyed writing it. Thank you for buying it.

I love writing about Iceland. It is an extraordinary country. The overwhelming theme in Iceland is the clash of the old and the new. In 1940 Iceland was probably the poorest country in Europe, by 2007 it was one of the most advanced. Every Icelander seems to have a Facebook page; every Icelander's grandmother believed in elves. The people are a hard-working, manic lot with a highly developed sense of humour, big on irony.

The conflict between the old and the new applies to the landscape as well. Bleak mountains, beautiful white glaciers, fjords, lava fields with mosses nibbling into the rock. It looks ancient, but actually it is very new geologically speaking, work in progress.

It's a great country in which to set a detective series – the perfect place for Magnus to solve all manner of extraordinary crimes.

To write a book is to communicate directly with the person who reads it. I like to build as direct a relationship as I can with my readers and so I send occasional newsletters with information about my books and any special offers.

If you sign up to my mailing list I will send you a FREE copy of a 60-page story set in North East Iceland featuring Magnus, called THE POLAR BEAR KILLING:

A starving polar bear swims ashore in a remote Icelandic village and is shot by the local policeman. Two days later, the policeman is found dead on a hill above the village. A polar bear justice novella with an Icelandic twist.

To sign up to the mailing list and get your FREE copy of THE POLAR BEAR KILLING, please visit my website: www.michaelridpath.com

For more information on my other books, please read on...

From the million-copy bestselling author comes the full Magnus Iceland Mystery series, perfect for fans of Stieg Larsson, Anne Holt, Henning Mankell and The Killing.

"Michael Ridpath is on the war path, trouncing the Scandinavians on their home turf. This is international thriller writing at its best, fine characters, page turning suspense and a great, fresh location."

Peter James

WHERE THE SHADOWS LIE

One thousand years ago: An Icelandic warrior returns from battle, bearing a ring cut from the right hand of his foe.

Seventy years ago: An Oxford professor, working from a secret source, creates the twentieth century's most pervasive legend. The professor's name? John Ronald Reuel Tolkien.

Six hours ago: An expert on Old Iceland literature, Agnar Haraldsson, is murdered.

Everything is connected, but to discover how, Detective Magnus Jonson must venture where the shadows lie...

66° NORTH (FAR NORTH IN THE US)

Iceland 1934: Two boys playing in the lava fields that surround their isolated farmsteads see something they shouldn't have. The consequences will haunt them and their families for generations.

Iceland 2009: the credit crunch bites. The currency has been devalued, savings annihilated, lives ruined. Revolution is in the air, as is the feeling that someone ought to pay the blood price... And in a country with a population of just 300,000 souls, where everyone knows everybody, it isn't hard to draw up a list of those responsible. And then, one-by-one, to cross them off.

Iceland 2010: As bankers and politicians start to die, at home and abroad, it is up to Magnus Jonson to unravel the web of conspirators before they strike again.

But while Magnus investigates the crimes of the present, the crimes of the past are catching up with him.

MELTWATER

Iceland, 2010: A group of internet activists have found evidence of a military atrocity in the Middle East. As they prepare to unleash the damning video to the world's media, to the backdrop of the erupting volcano Eyjafjallajökull, one is brutally murdered.

As Magnus Jonson begins to investigate, the list of suspects grows ever longer. From the Chinese government, Israeli military, Italian politicians, even to American College Fraternities, the group has made many enemies. And more are coming to the surface every day...

And with the return of Magnus's brother Ollie to Iceland, the feud that has haunted their family for three generations is about to reignite.

SEA OF STONE

Iceland, 2010: Called to investigate a suspected homicide in a remote farmstead, Constable Páll is surprised to find that Sergeant Magnus Jonson is already at the scene. The victim? Magnus's estranged grandfather.

But it quickly becomes apparent that the crime scene has been tampered with, and that Magnus's version of events doesn't add up. Before long, Magnus is arrested for the murder of his grandfather. When it emerges that his younger brother, Ollie, is in Iceland after two decades in America, Páll begins to think that Magnus may not be the only family member in the frame for murder...

THE WANDERER

Iceland, 2017: When a young Italian tourist is found brutally murdered at a sacred church in northern Iceland, Magnus Jonson, newly returned to the Reykjavík police force, is called in to investigate. At the scene, he finds a stunned TV crew, there to film a documentary on the life of the legendary Viking, Gudrid the Wanderer. The documentary experts have unearthed controversial evidence that Christopher Columbus knew more about the existence of America than has ever been previously realised.

Magnus begins to suspect that there may be more links to the murdered woman than anyone in the film crew will acknowledge. As jealousies come to the surface, new tensions replace old friendships, and history begins to rewrite itself, a shocking second murder leads Magnus to question everything he thought he knew...

ABOUT THE AUTHOR

Michael Ridpath is the author of eight financial thrillers, a series of crime novels featuring the Icelandic-American detective Magnus Jonson, two spy novels and a stand-alone psychological thriller, *Amnesia*.

You can find out more about him and his books on his website www.michaelridpath.com or on Facebook.

REVIEW THIS BOOK

I would be really grateful if you could take a moment to review this book. Reviews, even of only a few words, are really important for the success of a book these days.

Thank you.